HFCA Publishing House

Ireland

ISBN: 978-1-918152-03-6

www.lexibuchanan.com

First Published 2023

This Edition 2025

Editor: Nadine Winningham

To my family

PROLOGUE
ROGAN - NINE YEARS OLD

A TWIG SNAPPED BEHIND US AND I SLOWLY DROPPED back, allowing Leon and Chase to continue ahead to the river. I didn't want to draw attention to the fact Fallon had followed us. They'd just call my sister names—and me—even though they knew she liked hanging around with us. I always acted as though I didn't care one way or the other, but in truth, I did care. Fallon was my sister and my best friend. Not that I'd admit that little fact to the guys any time soon. They would never understand why I wanted to spend time with her—sometimes I didn't either.

Fallon was thirteen months younger than me, but she was also a lot smaller. She reminded me of a fairy with the freckles across her cheeks and nose. She used to hate them until I told her they weren't freckles but cinnamon sugar, her favorite pancake topping next to sprinkles.

Tall grass rustled as she got closer, but I knew Fallon, and she wouldn't be watching where she was going. She'd be watching us. My heart thumped hard in my chest while I quickly wondered what I could do to make sure Fallon wouldn't get hurt without alerting the guys she was behind us.

The decision was taken away from me when she let out a piercing scream. The hair on the back of my neck stood up as though I'd been electrocuted. Leon and Chase turned toward the sound, seconds before I turned and raced toward my sister; their footsteps pounded behind me.

I almost stumbled into Fallon when I found her dancing around in the tall grass. Her face was stained red and her eyes were puffy from the falling tears. She released her breath in big gulps and hiccups.

"Her legs." Chase gasped, pointing at the angry red blotches on her white legs.

"Poison Ivy," I mumbled, cursing. "Help her onto my back." I turned and waited for Chase to lift her up. "I'll get you home, Fallon."

I fastened my hands under her, taking her weight. "I'll catch up to you both," I told my friends.

They looked betwween themselves, and then Chase

offered a wry smile. "Of course you will." He shook his head.

"It hurts so bad, Rogan," Fallon cried out. She tightened her arms around my neck, nearly cutting off my air supply.

I ignored my two friends as I gave my sister a ride back to the house. For an eight-year-old, she was strong, as were her lungs, the sound ringing in my ears. I glanced down and winced at the red marks and white dots all over her legs. The sight spurred me on and I sprinted through the back gate and up the garden path, running straight into the house.

Both Mom and Dad appeared from different directions when they heard the ruckus.

"Poison Ivy!" I gasped, my breathing heavy. It had been far too long since I'd run so fast, and add Fallon's weight and my panic, and I was sweating like a pig.

Dad lifted Fallon from me and sat her on the kitchen table trying to calm her down. Mom grabbed the medical box for the magic cream she had in there. It worked on burns and stings.

Eventually, Fallon calmed down, and holding a hand out toward me, asked, "Watch a movie with me?"

I offered her a half smile and turned my back. "Climb on."

Dad chuckled and helped her up.

I carried her to her bedroom and placed her gently on the bed, then I spent five minutes fiddling to get the *Goonies* to play. It was about one of the only movies we watched together—we'd seen it too many times to count. I didn't care because she was my sister.

Mine to protect.

My best friend Chase knew how close I was to Fallon, even if he couldn't understand why I would want to spend time with her. The thing was, Fallon and me, we'd always been close, especially with Mom and Dad working full-time, all the time. It had been the two of us since our parents had met and fell in love. I'd been three and Fallon two. Dad said he would love Fallon as his own daughter the day he married her mom. He even gave Fallon our last name —Scott. We were growing up the best of friends, and I wouldn't want it any other way.

Leon, my other best friend, teased me often about Fallon, which got my temper going. Chase had to get between us recently so I wouldn't punch Leon in the nose. It would have made me feel better for a short time, then, of course, I'd have felt bad.

At the end of the day, family was family, and I'd always have Fallon beside me. I hoped to always have Chase and Leon as friends, but that could change. My sister was different and always would be.

Turning, I found Fallon cuddled into the pillow with a picture of a beagle puppy on it. I chuckled and joined her on the opposite side of the bed. We stayed that way until the credits for the movie started to roll, and then I felt her hand slip into mine.

"Rogan," Fallon whispered, drawing my gaze to hers, "will you always be mine?"

Our foreheads touched together. "You'll always be mine, Fallon," I replied, hoping nothing would ever change between us.

PROLOGUE
FALLON - THIRTEEN YEARS OLD

As my social studies teacher droned on about English colonization, I got lost in my thoughts wondering whether or not I could get away with following my brother, Leon, and Chase to the diner after school.

The center of Augusta, Maine wasn't far from school, but Mom and Dad told us we had to go straight home today. *Together.* I was slightly confused by that because Rogan always made sure I never walked home alone. He felt strongly about it. So it made me wonder what he was up to.

Ever since he and his friends turned fourteen they'd been into girls. Leon started to have problems with me hanging with them, but I didn't get why. They hung out with other girls, so why not me as well? I think it was Leon who put Rogan up to leaving me out. Rogan felt bad, I could tell by the way he looked at me with an apology in his gaze. It wouldn't have been Chase because he never really bothered one way or another.

Woolgathering, as my mom would say, took up most of my class time, but that left me with no clue of what I was supposed to do for homework.

And then I was saved.

"Here." Julia Quinn passed me a slip of paper. "I noticed you weren't really in class." She smirked.

Surprised, I took the paper and looked down to see the homework assignment written on it.

"Do you want to grab a coke after school?"

Her eyes shot up at my spur-of-the-moment question. "Really?"

I smiled. "Yes, really." I'd known Julia since first grade, and we sat together during second, but hadn't really become friends.

Rogan said I needed to make some friends with girls. He'd stressed the word *girls*, which I found amusing.

"Okay, let's go." Julia shouldered her backpack.

Rogan wasn't going to like me showing up.

"Let me just tell my brother."

Julia stayed silent as she followed me outside and

into the bright day. I started to sweat before we reached where Rogan, Leon, and Chase waited.

"I'll walk you home first," Rogan said.

"I'm getting a coke with Julia."

Rogan eyed my new friend and shook his head, a half smile on his lips. "Clever. Very clever."

"I thought so too."

"Let's go." Rogan turned and expected us to follow.

Julia moved in beside me. "Are we really getting a coke with them?" she whispered, and I didn't miss the excitement in her voice.

"Probably not," I admitted. "They'll go off and do whatever they had planned. They don't want Rogan's little sister tagging along."

I was right too, except I didn't understand why I was upset with Rogan for hanging out with a bunch of girls without me—but I now had a girlfriend.

PART I

Rogan, 17 / Fallon, 16

1

ROGAN

"Why does she have to come?" Leon grumbled and pointed at Fallon, his face going an ugly shade of red. "For once I'd like to do guy stuff and not have your sister tag along."

I got in Leon's face. "Why can't she hang around with us? She's been with us for years."

"I don't like it now that we're older. What if we want to talk about girls or something? She's going to run off and tell them what we said."

I blinked a few times before I let out a long-suffering sigh. I got what Leon was saying, but I considered Fallon part of the group, or at least I thought she was part of the group. Maybe to me she was but to them she wasn't.

I turned to Chase. "Do you feel the same way

about Fallon?" I tried to calm down and didn't, the flex of my hands as they tightened into fists was a giveaway.

"It's okay," Fallon whispered as she moved to my side and put her hand on my wrist. "I'll go."

I moved to hold Fallon with me, but she backed up, her eyes swimming with hurt.

"It really is okay. I'll go and hang out with Julia." Fallon insisted, before turning and walking away. Her shoulders drooped, which worked me up even more.

"I'm sorry," Leon said, and he loudly exhaled. "You have to admit we can't talk like we would if she wasn't with us. And I really need to talk about something."

Chase laughed. "What is wrong with you? We've talked about all kinds of stuff in front of Fallon before. Why is now any different?"

"Because," Leon drawled, "I want to talk about her"—he pointed lower on his body and his cheeks went a bright shade of red—"um, you know?"

My heart stopped and I stared at Leon wondering if I'd actually heard him correctly. The silence was loud but that was probably the blood pounding through my head. Chase shoved Leon. Leon blinked and cursed under his breath.

"I didn't mean *hers*." Leon's eyes popped wide. "I

don't know why I said it like that." He quickly amended. "I want to talk about a particular girl's…um —" He held his hands out and backed away from me. "I promise I don't mean Fallon's…um… Don't punch me in the face. I have a date."

"Date?" I frowned, his last words stopping me from moving closer.

"Yes…I have a date, which is what I want to talk about without Fallon listening." Leon walked away and I glanced at Chase, who shrugged.

"I don't know anything more than you do." Chase smirked. "I thought you were going to kill him for a minute there." He grinned and wandered off.

Chase wasn't wrong. When Leon had mentioned Fallon and her…*um*…I wanted to knock Leon's head off. No one thought about my sister in that way, let alone talked about her in that way.

Ignoring my friends—if one of them was still my friend—I headed home. Fallon wouldn't have gone to Julia's house, not when she was upset. She'd have gone home and locked herself in her bedroom. I knew her well, and it hurt that one of my friends had hurt her. Leon had needed to talk, maybe ask questions knowing Leon, but he could have said something on the side without Fallon having heard.

Pushing through the gate at the back of the

garden, I spotted Uncle Frank helping Dad weed the garden. More accurately, Dad was weeding while Uncle Frank held a beer in one hand and the garden rake in the other. Sometimes I got the feeling Uncle Frank only came around for the free food and beer. My parents weren't what you'd call well-off, but they worked hard, even though it still meant living paycheck to paycheck. Uncle Frank was jealous of what Dad had with Mom. I didn't know why.

Uncle Frank's wife always seemed to do what he asked. And they had two kids who were five and seven years older than me. Fallon didn't really get on with either of them.

Shaking my head, I ignored Dad and Uncle Frank and rushed into the house. Mom was in the kitchen and gave me a look before nodding her head toward the stairs.

Fallon had locked her bedroom door and, unless she opened it, I wasn't getting inside.

"Fallon," I hissed, "let me in."

"No. I hate you."

Those last three words wounded me, and even knowing she didn't mean them, it still hurt deeply. I dropped my forehead to the door. "That's not fair, Fallon. You know I love you. I was standing up for you, but you were the one to leave." I pressed against the door with the palm of my hands. "Please let me in. You're all I have."

There was silence and then I heard the key turning in her door. I nearly fell inside when she opened it suddenly.

I pulled myself up short and snapped my eyes shut when I saw Fallon standing before me in a hot pink bra and panties. "Fallon!" I hissed in shock.

"What? You wanted me to open the door. So I did."

My eyes narrowed into slits as I glared at Fallon standing there without a care in the world, hands on her hips, glaring back. I knew she was hiding the hurt behind a devil-may-care attitude, but it was too much for me to see her in her underwear. It was probably more than girls wore to the beach, but *she was my sister!*

To keep my eyes from straying over her curves, I made myself busy and closed her bedroom door. "I'm locking it again so Uncle Frank doesn't walk in." Uncle Frank had done that on one or two occasions. He never respected a closed door.

"I'm sorry I was angry with you," Fallon whispered, blinking back tears. "I'm not really. I know you were on my side."

Not letting her state of undress bother me, I tugged Fallon against me and hugged her hard and tight. "I'll always be on your side. Leon was just being an idiot because he has a date and wanted to talk about…*things*."

Fallon tilted her face up to mine and frowned, then a slow smile appeared on her face. "He wanted to talk about the birds and the bees, huh?" Now her face split into a huge grin.

Embarrassment crawled up my neck. "Don't even say that." I covered her mouth with my hand while her eyes danced with amusement. "I mean it, Fallon. You are *never* dating."

Fallon rolled her eyes as she wiggled out of my arms and took a step back. "I'm sixteen, Rogan." She giggled and looked flushed. "Mom has already had *that* talk with me, so I know all about it."

Uncomfortable with the way our conversation had gone, I reached up and rubbed my neck. "Put some clothes on," I snapped, afraid of the way my heart raced when my eyes ran over her.

"Honestly?" She huffed, and shoved her arms into a pink robe. "Better?" She glared at me.

The robe did nothing to hide how beautiful she was. She was going to have to wear a sack to hide from all the boys who would get it into their heads to touch her. But I was the only one who knew how beautiful she was on the inside, and I hated that one day she would be with someone who'd know her better than I did. It bothered me more than it should, and I didn't know what to make of it.

Fallon wasn't only my sister, she was my best friend and the person I relied on the most, and I knew she relied on me just as much. She made me smile. She made me so damn mad I could spit fire. But heck if I knew how to separate those two emotions.

One day that was going to happen, maybe when I went off to college. Fallon was still going to be in high school for another year. Who would she have when I left? I knew she talked to Julia. Julia was her only female friend, although I was sure Julia only initially became friends with Fallon because of my friends and me. Julia pretended to be into me to get at Leon. It was so obvious it was embarrassing.

Fallon cleared her throat and smirked. "You went off into Rogan's world." Shaking her head, she stepped away. "I'm going to take a shower." She raised a brow when I didn't move, and then a teasing light entered her sparkling emerald green eyes.

She dropped the robe, and gave me her back. Reaching behind, Fallon unclipped her bra, letting it drop to the floor to my stunned disbelief.

It took a moment to get my brain working and

realize I gawked at my *sister,* who grinned at me over her shoulder. I narrowed my eyes, and cursed under my breath when I felt a reaction below the waist.

I panicked and got the hell out of her bedroom.

The little tease!

Fallon had known I would run the moment she'd started stripping, but heck, she really had to stop doing that in front of me now that we were older. Plus I had to admit I was a regular horny seventeen-year-old boy.

No way in hell should I react to my sister like I had.

My sister!

I'm going to hell.

My thoughts had certainly not been brotherly when she stood before me, all that sun-kissed skin on display for my eyes, and I had looked—more than I ever should have.

2

———————

FALLEN

My heart pounded against my breastbone as I closed the bathroom door. What was I thinking? I couldn't forget the look on Rogan's face when I took my bra off. He'd looked at me in a way that wasn't allowed—in a way that made my body tingle and caused blood to rush around and into places I had no idea could feel hot and swollen.

I stepped into the shower and let the warm spray pound down against me. I hoped the images on replay in my mind would disappear and I could go back to Rogan being just Rogan, my *brother*. My thoughts about him weren't sisterly, and hadn't been for a while.

The palm of my hands rested against the shower wall while the water continued to pound down, plastering my hair from the top of my head, and down my back.

Maybe there was something wrong with me—there had to be. Nothing made sense when I imagined myself with anyone else. The only time anything made sense was when I was with Rogan. We'd always been together and now that we were getting older, I was scared things would change beyond my control. Things had already started to change—the way Leon hadn't wanted me around, the way Rogan looked at me, the way I reacted when his gaze was on me.

I understood why Leon had reacted the way he had. It didn't mean it hurt any less.

With a flick of my wrist, I turned the water off and, wrapping a bath sheet around my shivering body, stepped out of the shower. In my bedroom, I quickly dressed in jeans and a T-shirt, my feet bare, then spread out on top of my bed with an old photo album I kept in my nightstand. It was filled with pictures of Rogan and me, taken over the years. I often got it out to look through, especially when I felt down or lost. Or when I needed a reminder of the history we shared and the reason why I should never think of Rogan in any way but sisterly.

One picture stood out in the book. It was taken three years ago at the beach. We had our arms around each other and Dad had made some funny comment that made us laugh. Rogan's smile lit up the picture, his eyes sparkling with amusement, his dark hair falling into his left eye, and his smile so wide that I traced his full lips with a finger.

A throat cleared. "I love that picture." Rogan took a hesitant step forward, and then with more confidence, crawled onto the bed. He settled alongside me, his eyes focused on the book in front of me.

I swallowed around the lump in my throat, unable to bring myself to meet his eyes. "It was a good vacation." I played with the corner of the book, and closing my eyes, I whispered, "I'm sorry about before. I never should have done that." My cheeks flushed with embarrassment.

"No, you shouldn't have," Rogan said in a voice so quiet I couldn't decide whether he was angry with me or not. "I think it might be for the best if we forget about it."

I quickly blinked back the unexpected tears to get rid of them, and nodded. "I need to pack."

I knew Rogan watched me from beneath his lowered lids as I moved from the bed and over to the closet. We should talk more about what happened; I really didn't like Rogan's suggestion of forgetting about it. But if we talked, I would end up in tears and that wouldn't do.

"I won't mention it again." I swallowed hard and hoped Rogan accepted my word.

"I guess I better go pack too." I heard, rather than saw, Rogan crawl off my bed and cross the room. As he jostled the doorknob, he said, "Just remember we're camping, not staying at a five-star hotel."

I gasped and quickly turned. Rogan ducked out of the way just as I sent a book sailing across the room. He laughed and so did I, and I felt like a weight had lifted from my chest.

"I happen to love camping," I shouted as Rogan smirked and closed the door.

3

FALLEN

I HATED CAMPING.

My parents had a thing about the great outdoors, and when I was younger I thought it was cool—now, not so much. The slightest sounds spooked me, which was why I stood outside of my tent wondering how much of a baby I'd be if I suggested sharing.

While I debated actually asking, giggles from my parents' tent traveled toward me. I glanced over and sighed at them still acting like newlyweds, which was great, but I really wanted to share a tent with Mom.

A loud sigh came from behind me, so I turned and grinned at Rogan. He was relaxing in a camping chair watching the show. I grabbed my chair and dropped it beside his, and got comfortable.

"Are you really going to ask to share with Mom?" Rogan asked.

I quickly faced him, my brows raised.

Rogan laughed. "It was written all over your face when you stared at your tent then theirs."

I groaned, but then a wonderful idea popped into my head, even though I knew it really wasn't wise.

"I'll share with you."

He rapidly blinked in surprise and sat forward. "Heck no."

"Seriously, Rogan. Mom and Dad want to be alone in their tent. I'll be awake all night waiting for a bear to eat me. We could put all our clothes and stuff in my tent and sleep in yours." I smiled. "Problem solved."

"Fallon," Rogan hissed in frustration. "We're not little kids anymore. You can't share with me."

"I promise not to flash you like I did yesterday."

"It's not that dammit."

"What are you two arguing about?" Mom asked as she poked her head out the tent.

Rogan groaned and I grinned, turning to Mom. "I'm not sleeping in there alone. So either you sleep with me, or you make Rogan let me share his tent."

Mom frowned, so I quickly continued, "You know I get spooked. We'll have our own sleeping bags, and there is room if we put all our clothes and things in my tent."

"Um, well, I guess it will be okay." Mom smiled. "I'll tell your Dad." She pulled her head inside the tent while I turned a smug look on Rogan.

"I can't believe you did that."

"She wants to share with Dad, so it's obvious she'd agree." I headed toward my tent. "I'm going to get changed for bed, and I'll bring my sleeping bag over."

I didn't hear exactly what Rogan mumbled but figured it was about me. I did catch his muttering about being seventeen and not even allowed his own space.

He'd get over it.

Nights in the forest could get cold, but if I remembered correctly from last year, I'd gotten really hot during the night. With that in mind, I quickly changed into shorts and a T-shirt, and left my sweatshirt in my backpack. I grabbed my sleeping bag up and hauled it to Rogan's tent. It bothered me that he really hadn't wanted to share with me. We'd always shared everything and it hurt when he rejected me. My little performance from the evening before popped into my head, but I dismissed it quickly as I opened the zipper on Rogan's tent.

I tossed my sleeping bag inside, and followed,

crawling over it once Rogan spread it out on the double airbed he always used. His white T-shirt stretched over his shoulders and chest, showing some muscle definition, which surprised me.

"You've been working out, huh?"

He glanced down at himself and then slowly nodded. "Yeah, some."

After a pause, Rogan patted the sleeping bag and I slipped inside. We stayed silent, staring at each other until it became dark, and our eyes took a few minutes adjusting to the darkness.

"Rogan," I whispered, "why didn't you want me sharing?" Even I heard the hurt in my voice as I asked.

"We're getting too old to share, Fallon. You gotta know that."

"I don't like getting older if it means I'm going to lose you."

"You won't ever lose me."

"Then please don't hurt me by saying no." I winced when I realized how my words sounded. "I don't mean you should always say yes, or that I'm spoiled, because I'm not. I just hate how it feels when I'm not sure you want me anymore."

Silence followed and just when I thought Rogan fell asleep, he admitted, "I'll always want you, Fallon, but sharing a tent is a *lot* different than sharing an ice pop or a movie." He groaned. "Or even how we shared as kids."

I opened my mouth to reply and then thought about what he *hadn't* said. "Does this have anything to do with last night? Did I do this to us?" Tears hovered on my lashes but I didn't let them fall. "I didn't mean anything by it. I just wanted to…sass you, I guess."

"Last night, I saw you in a way I should never see you. Do you understand me? My body reacts in a way it shouldn't when I'm with you." Rogan hissed and then cursed. "Get some sleep."

He rolled to his back while my eyes searched him out in the darkness. "I'm sorry," I whispered. "I did what I did to make you feel awkward. I promise not to do anything like that again. Please forget you saw me in that way and I'll try to forget how you reacted, okay?"

"What do you mean, you'll try?" Rogan struggled to keep the shock out of his voice. "You have to forget how I reacted. Dammit, Fallon."

Sighing, I rolled the opposite direction and faced the tent, hoping Rogan ignored the conversation and went to sleep.

No such luck.

"Fallon? I know you're awake."

"Go to sleep, Rogan."

He huffed out an angry breath and mumbled something I didn't quiet catch, and then he said, "Last night never happened. You're my sister. You're mine to protect. Let's sleep."

Even though I felt close to tears, I smiled to myself because Rogan hadn't sounded convinced. He wouldn't forget, just like I wouldn't. We should, though. I knew that.

"Rogan?" I rolled back to face him and searched for his eyes in the dark. When I found them, I asked, "Will it be as exciting when I'm in my underwear for a boy who isn't you?"

Rogan blinked a few times before he wrapped his arms around me and tugged me—sleeping bag and all—into his arms. "I want to say I hope not," he admitted, his arms tightening around me, "but the right thing to say is yes. Yes, you will feel excitement when you're standing in front of a boy in your underwear." His voice quivered and because of how close I was to him, I felt the heavy rise and fall of his chest.

"I think I only will for you," I whispered back, wanting to have the last word because I knew it hurt him to say what he had.

I settled with my head on his shoulder, the heaviness in my heart only lifted slightly. I wanted to feel secure in his arms, against his chest. To know that what I did, and how I made him feel, could be over-come, and that we were still the best of best friends. My mind was full, wondering where the path we were on would lead, because I knew in my heart I felt so much more than sibling love for him, just like I knew he did me.

A large warm hand moved from around my waist and cupped my chin. Rogan lifted my gaze to his. "We have to promise to never speak about this night to anyone." His eyes bore into mine. "I mean no one, Fallon. Not even each other. We never mention it again." He dropped his forehead to mine. "We've spoken about things we never should have even thought about." His hand on my jaw trembled as his eyes deeply searched mine.

I didn't want to give him the answer I was about to, but I didn't have a choice, the decision had really been made the night our parents had met and fell in love.

"I promise, Rogan."

4

———

ROGAN

EATING BREAKFAST IN THE FOREST WITH A FANTASTIC view of the lake was what I had done every summer with my family since I was a kid. But this year, it felt different.

The gravelly patch of bare ground ringed by trees and bushes was familiar to me, just like the man-made fire pit was. Dad and I had made it over five years ago. We hadn't had a chance to use it on this trip yet, but I was sure Mom would have the puffy white marshmallows, chocolate, and graham crackers at the ready for s'mores—a favorite of Fallon's and mine.

Tree branches snapped behind me as Dad wandered around in the brush, and the creak of tall trees and leaves rustling in the wind made me smile.

It was peaceful. The fresh smell of pine needles, along with the morning dew in the grass stirred a longing in me to stay.

"I'm going to build a cabin right in this spot," I blurted, my eyes dancing as I faced Mom and Fallon. They stared at me and my neck heated from embarrassment, which I shoved down. "I mean once I'm done with school and have a job." I smiled, liking the idea the more I talked about it, and the more my confidence grew. "I'm going to have two bedrooms and a bathroom, but then everything else is going to be open plan with large windows to take in the view. Oh, and a deck going completely around the cabin."

"Well," Mom mumbled, "I look forward to the day I get to sit out on your deck with your dad." She turned away; shoving things into her backpack once she'd checked everything was in there before the hike.

"What about me?" Fallon asked under her breath. "Do I get to visit you in your cabin?" Her eyes lifted to mine in challenge, and the pain I saw swimming beneath the surface of her vivid green eyes confused me. Did she want to live in it with me? Was she upset because I hadn't mentioned her?

I held her gaze and moved from the deckchair. I leaned in close to pick up a bottle of water, and whispered, "I'm building it for us." The shock registered in her eyes and I quickly crossed to Mom.

It was perfectly normal to want to build a cabin in the woods to live in with your sister. It really was. Nothing wrong with it. I tried and failed to convince myself.

There was everything wrong with it.

At least I hadn't voiced the idea in front of Mom— not sure it would have gone down too well. I took the heavy backpack from her and added my own bottle of water, knowing that I was going to be the one carrying the pack. Usually Dad carried it, but I noticed him pressing on his lower back this morning —probably a kink in it from sleeping on the airbed.

As for me, I had one of the best night's sleeps I've had in forever, and I knew good and well it had everything to do with the girl who'd slept in my arms. Her soft breath had brushed against my neck and it eventually lulled me into a deep sleep. Luckily, I'd been able to hide my body's morning reaction, which had been stronger than usual with Fallon sprawled out on top of me—her curves pressed against me.

"Everyone ready to go?" Dad hollered.

I jerked and dropped the pack, having been lost in thought.

"Yeah," I hissed.

Ten minutes later, we were well along the trail and the bulky pack strapped to my back caused sweat to dampen my skin. My feet treaded across the uneven ground as we moved up a slight incline. Tree roots crisscrossed the trail with branches hanging out. Swatting away insects from in front of my face, I heard the waterfall, which flowed into a small creek up ahead.

As I listened to the birds chirping overhead in the tall trees, I realized Fallon had fallen behind. Softly smiling, I suggested to Dad, "I'll walk with Fallon."

"Good idea." Dad patted me on the shoulder as he moved on. "I don't want to be out on the trail in the dark."

Me either!

Fallon was so lost in a world of her own that she hadn't noticed me waiting for her. While I did, my eyes caressed over her long legs and the shape of her hips. My breathing quickened as I dared to move my gaze higher, where I appreciated the fitted, long-sleeved fitness top clinging to her every curve. I tried to move my gaze away. I truly did, but I found it impossible. The sight before me hardened my body.

She was beautiful and unaware.

My gaze was still on Fallon when she spotted me.

"Why are you looking at me like that?"

Her question snapped me into the present. "Admiring the view," I replied with the truth. "Come on, we'll be here all night if we don't pick up the pace."

Fallon grumbled, but moved forward. "I'm trying to forget about the footbridge up ahead." She shrugged. "I'm actually hoping it's gone so we have to turn back."

I laughed. "You wish, but it's still there."

Her face fell. I took her hand and pulled her along behind me. "It's best to get it over with."

Fallon continued grumbling, as I shook my head and pushed her in front of me. It was only when I met Dad's gaze that I realized there might be a problem— or I thought there was.

"The bridge is okay to cross."

"So, why the frown? You had me worried."

Dad's eyes quickly glanced between Fallon and me, before he answered, "No reason." Dad smiled and crossed to Mom. "Rogan, will you be okay staying with Fallon, and I'll stay with your mom?"

"Yeah, sure."

Fallon turned and I met her worried expression. "That was odd," she commented. "Dad never asks us to pair up."

"Hmm." I stepped to the edge and looked across

the bridge. Nothing jumped out at me, so we were good to go.

Dad moved across slowly with Mom in front of him, so I got into the same position with Fallon. "We'll go slow, and remember, don't look down at the creek," I advised softly, and then added, "Although the view is awesome."

She made a weird sound as my hands gripped her hips. Her chest expanded with the deep inhale she took. "I can do this." She let out a shaky laugh. "Just don't let go, okay?"

She wasn't looking at me, but my eyes were glued to the top of her head. I smiled, grateful I was over a foot taller than she was. I put my mouth to her ear. "I'll never let you go, Fallon. You can trust me."

She stilled and turned her face to search my gaze.

"Trust me," I whispered.

"I do." She nuzzled her face into my neck before inhaling, then she turned back around and slowly moved forward.

It took longer than usual but we crossed and I felt the tension drain from my body.

Mom unpacked sandwiches and juice. I grabbed two of each in one hand and Fallon's hand in the other, and urged her up on the large boulder.

We settled side by side with our lunch on our laps

and quietly ate while taking in the breathtaking view. Sunlight gleamed on the lake and the trees surrounding the area were so many different shades of green that I retrieved my phone and snapped a picture. It didn't do it justice, though.

"The view from here is worth my fear."

Out of the corner of my eye, I checked where Mom and Dad were, and then I took Fallon's hand, holding it against the rock so no one could see. The way she intertwined her fingers with mine made my heart pound hard, and it took me a moment to find my voice.

"I'm proud of you, Fallon, but I knew you could do it. You can do anything you put your mind to."

She sighed and rested her head on my shoulder. "I wish I had your confidence."

"You will." I kissed the top of her head before lowering my face into her hair and breathing her in. I closed my eyes wishing our situation were different. Wishing I could always look at Fallon the way I really wanted to.

When I opened my eyes I ended up looking straight into Dad's. The deep frown marring his brow told me my father had seen everything I felt for Fallon—it had been written all over my face.

Dad shook his head and, after another glance up

at us on the rock, turned back to Mom. By his expression, I knew he wouldn't let it go, which meant I was going to have to come up with an explanation as to what was going on. It was something I didn't want to think about as deeply as I'd started to think about Fallon.

5

FALLEN

Sweaty and exhausted from our day of walking, I dropped my clothing on the bank of the lake and waded into the cool water beside Mom. It felt so good on my heated skin, I dipped beneath the surface and swam further out.

The water was like a caress against me—I felt totally amazing as I finally breached the surface. My eyes widened and a shard of panic went down my spine when I noticed just how far out I swam from the shore. I've never gone so far before and it was terrifying.

My heart pounded and sweat trickled down my forehead. My panic worsened as I noticed bubbles slowly moving closer and closer to where I treaded water, and then a head appeared.

"You're an idiot," Rogan snapped, anger flashing in his eyes. He wrapped his arms around my waist and hauled me to him while he tried to catch a breath. His chest rose and fell in a heavy rhythm until he finally calmed down. "You know better than to swim out this far."

"I didn't realize how far I swam." I gripped him around his shoulders, allowing my legs to wrap around his waist.

His fierce gaze softened to concern as he dropped his forehead against mine.

"I'm sorry. I was hot and sweaty and just wanted to feel the cool water on my skin," I admitted.

"Next time, you wait for me." He coughed to clear his throat, and put a bit of distance between our bodies—but not before I felt something hard and thick against my thigh. "I'd feel better if we were closer to shore."

With reluctance, I unwound myself from Rogan, feeling heat rise through my body at the way he looked at me. It was the same way I'd felt on the trail. It made me nervous in a feel good kind of way. I didn't know how I was supposed to react, or what it meant.

Embarrassed, I challenged him. "I'll race you." I dived under the water once more.

Rogan kept pace beside me, his usual smile back on his face. He was my brother, but the way he'd started looking at me wasn't brotherly at all. And the way my heart pitter-pattered in my chest when I looked at him, or when he was close to me, was not sisterly.

Sometimes I thought there was something wrong with me. I shouldn't be reacting to him like I was. It had become worse since I teased him in my underwear. I wasn't even sure why I did it. *No!* That wasn't quite true. I was annoyed at how *his* friends had treated me and I wanted more of a reaction out of Rogan. I'd gotten one, but now I wondered what exactly had I done.

I was suddenly splashed in the face. I turned my narrowed eyes on my brother, who grinned like an idiot, just as I was splashed from behind.

I whipped around and found Dad laughing, but it was Mom who got the next laugh as she jumped on Dad's back, making him duck under the water.

"Water fight!" Rogan shouted, seconds before he tackled me under the water.

I got him back when I tickled him in the sides. He wiggled and laughed trying to get away from my fingers, but I followed...until Dad snagged me around the waist and tossed me away with a splash. Dad had done that for as long as I could remember, and I loved water play with my family.

Mom swam closer and smiled before we both turned and watched Dad and Rogan goofing around. Rogan saw us, and with his eyes on me, he started to swim closer. Dad noticed where he was headed, and snagged him around the ankle, pulling him back. Rogan went under and came up spitting water.

"So not fair," he grumbled, eyeing Dad.

They exchanged a few words, then Rogan's eyes found mine before he dropped his gaze.

I frowned and turned to Mom, who shrugged. Minutes later, Rogan swam toward shore, waded out and headed to where we'd left the towels. Dad swam toward us with a serious expression on his face as he held Mom's gaze.

"Why did Rogan leave?" I asked, making a move to follow him, but Dad shook his head.

"I'm going to have a talk with him." Dad kissed Mom and me on our cheeks before following Rogan.

"Mom?"

"It will be okay, honey." She smiled.

"Why won't you tell me what's going on? He's my brother. I'm going to him if you won't tell me."

Mom sighed, and glanced at the pebbled bank before she nodded, indicating for me to head back to our towels and clothing. My mind wouldn't stop buzzing with worry for Rogan. Something was wrong. I felt it in my blood.

We quickly dried in silence, then Mom led me over to some larger rocks.

"Now, I'm seriously worried." I struggled to keep the nerves from my voice. "Is Rogan sick or something? You'd tell me, right?"

"Oh, honey, he isn't sick." Mom inhaled and slowly exhaled. "You've always been close to Rogan," she started and I found her frown deepening. "I'm just going to ask, okay?"

I nodded, fear clawing at my throat as I wondered what was going on.

"How close have you and Rogan become?"

"What?" I turned to look out over the lake while panic welled inside of my chest. There was no way they could know about my little teasing display, or that we'd slept in each other's arms the night before. I certainly hadn't wanted to admit of my preoccupation with my older brother.

Swallowing back all the emotions swirling inside me, I replied, "We've always been close. I'm not sure what you want me to say."

"Dad has seen you both together." Mom smiled. "I have too." Mom gripped my hand tighter. "We're worried you're both getting *too* close, which I guess is our fault."

"No!" I panicked. "He's my best friend, Mom." I felt close to tears as I reached up and brushed a wet piece of hair back. "There's no such thing as being too close to him."

"You should be spending your time with Julia. Let Rogan be with his friends." Mom's eyes filled with tears. "That's what normal is."

Shooting to my feet, I let the tears fall. "Who says that's normal? He's my best friend," I cried. "When we were little, you always used to make a fuss about how well we got along to all your friends, and now, you have a problem with it?" I shouted.

"Calm down."

"What are you telling me? That you don't want us to spend time alone together anymore?"

"That's what she's saying." Dad interrupted. "That's what we're both asking you to do, and we'll see how it goes."

I shook my head, not prepared to accept anything that didn't include Rogan.

"Fallon, you are a beautiful sixteen-year-old, and while we have been accepting of your friendship, neither of us thought ahead to when you both started to grow up." He ran his hands through his hair. "You are both at the age of curiosity. Girls and boys. I guess what I'm trying to say is…we don't want you being curious together." He blew out a breath.

I honestly didn't know what to say to that. At least, I didn't know what I could say out loud.

My feelings for Rogan were as complicated as his were for me, but I was old enough to be aware of right and wrong. What I felt might be wrong and scary, but nothing had ever felt so right in my sixteen years.

"Where's Rogan?" I looked around, drying my tears when I realized he hadn't appeared. "What did you make him do?"

"Fallon," Mom snapped. "Grow up. You need to accept how things are going to be and move on. You are not a child anymore. You are a beautiful, young girl with the figure of a woman, and Rogan is at an age where boys can't control the way their bodies react. Do you understand what I'm trying to say?"

Ignoring my parents, I turned and ran back to the campsite. Rogan was pacing when I arrived, and the disheartened look on his face said everything; he was angry and upset, but I sensed he agreed with Dad.

I turned away from him and hid in my own tent.

6

ROGAN

I DIDN'T THINK I'D EVER FORGET THE LOOK ON Fallon's face after our parents had talked to her. It was nearly three weeks ago and my heart still ached for what we had, or even started to have. I missed her smile, her voice, and most of all, I missed having her close.

That day on our camping trip, she looked as heartbroken as I felt, and when I finally had the courage to meet her gaze, she was surprised and upset. A large hole opened in my heart as her expression turned to one of anger.

I didn't know what to do or say when Dad told me he saw exactly how I felt for Fallon. I tried to laugh it off, but it didn't work because Dad had seen me at a weak moment with her.

Dad lectured me on the rights and wrongs of loving Fallon Scott. He convinced himself I only wanted Fallon because I'd never had the chance to find someone else. That wasn't true. Neither was Dad's opinion that my feelings for Fallon would change when I got older and grew from a hormonal teenage boy into a man. My father was delusional.

As for Fallon, well, she hadn't spoken to me since "the talk" and she was breaking my heart. I wished I knew how to make it right, knew how to stop hurting all the time.

I could hardly tell Fallon I was in love with her when it was an impossible love. What good would it do either of us? At the same time, I couldn't go on with the silence because it was killing me.

She was my sister first. Had been for longer than I'd been in love with her. I wanted that girl back. I needed Fallon back. Maybe what I felt would disappear. Even as I thought it, I knew it was a lie. Maybe if I told myself enough times I didn't *really* love her, my feelings would change. I just didn't know anymore.

One thing I did know was that Fallon and I were about to have a long overdue conversation, whether she liked it or not.

She was one stubborn girl, so, being sneaky, I

slowly moved along the hallway in my bare feet to her room.

Not giving her the satisfaction of knocking, I shoved my way inside to find Fallon crying on the bed. Seeing her face ravaged from tears I presumed to have been falling for a while, made pain clutch at my chest. I shook my head when she opened her mouth to speak.

"Don't." I climbed on the bed and pulled her into my arms. And I couldn't help but feel how right it was as we wrapped around each other, our arms holding each other close, our legs intertwined. Fallon burrowed her face into my neck, her sobs slowly subsiding.

"I'm sorry." She hiccupped the words against my skin. "I hate ignoring you. I just didn't know how I should act."

Gently brushing the hair back from her eyes, I caught a stray tear with my thumb. "We're both hurting. I see that now."

I guided her face back into my neck so she couldn't see me. "I came in here mad at you for ignoring me, but I'm not mad at you anymore." I sighed. "Dad's talk threw me and I was confused about what to do. He pointed out that not only are you my sister, but we're both underage."

I kissed the top of her head. "I never lied when I said you'd always be mine, Fallon," I admitted. "Can we please be friends again? You have no idea how much I've missed you."

Her grip around my waist tightened. "I want to go back to being friends. We can pretend everything else isn't there, right?"

No! My breath was trapped in my lungs as I screamed inside my head. It took me a few minutes, but eventually I calmed enough to agree. "Yeah."

She lifted her gaze and held mine; her eyes searched and probably found more than I wanted her to see. Inhaling deeply, I smiled. "We can do this, Fallon. We love each other, which means we can do anything to stay together. Whether we're brother and sister, friends, much more. Anything."

Fallon agreed and with what appeared to be reluctance, pulled away, rolling from the bed. "I'm going to wash up and then maybe we can meet up with Julia, Chase, and Leon." She grinned. "Let's show Mom and Dad we can hang out together as normal siblings."

I laughed and sat on the edge of the bed. "I doubt normal siblings hang out."

Fallon rolled her eyes when she came out of the bathroom, a small towel in her hands as she dried her cheeks.

Her beauty took my breath away, but I swallowed around it. "Friends." I held my fist out, which she bumped with hers.

"Friends."

Heading downstairs and entering the living room, we received a raised brow from Dad but he kept silent.

"We're going to find our friends, and maybe head into town for ice cream."

"Okay." Dad smiled. For the first time in weeks, it was without suspicion clouding his face, which was good, but it made me angry.

Even though it was my own fault for making Dad suspicious, I'd been angry these past few weeks. At the end of the day, he was my dad and I needed his trust. I'd promised to love Fallon, but to only show it as a sibling love—not the love of a man who'd found his soul mate.

"Have fun," Mom shouted from the kitchen. "In fact, why don't you all come back here and Dad can grill burgers?"

Fallon grinned up at me before rushing to Mom. I glanced back at Dad and let my anger go when I saw his face filled with love for me.

"We're good," Dad commented, his attention returning to the game.

Shoving my hands into my pockets, I followed Fallon out the back door.

"Mom's watching," Fallon whispered. "But you know what? I don't care. You're my best friend and we're doing what we've always done—hang out—until I listened to Mom and Dad."

"We're good, but let's not push it," I muttered.

A smile curved her lips as we disappeared through the back gate. "I messaged Julia," Fallon said. "We're meeting everyone at the diner."

"That's good."

"Do you think Chase will like my new top?"

"I like your new top." A pang of jealousy hit me in the gut. "Chase?"

Fallon paused and gave me a mischievous smirk. "Are you telling me you haven't seen the way Chase looks at me?" She laughed. "He actually looks at you the same way, although I haven't been able to pinpoint why." Her long legs ate up the distance as she continued ahead of me, my frown going unnoticed by her.

"Chase stares at everyone," I said, the frown refusing to move from my face.

Offering up a dirty laugh, Fallon turned and started walking backwards. "You don't like the idea of Chase, huh?"

"Stop teasing me." I pushed on ahead, smacking her on the bottom as I did. "I only have so much control, Fallon," I admitted over my shoulder as I left her to follow.

7

FALLEN

The sun shone brightly and reflected on the river, causing it to look so blue that I wanted to get lost in it. Anything would be better than spying on my brother and his friends. It didn't help that my best friend, Julia, had a crush on Leon, but pretended she was crushing on Rogan to avoid embarrassment. Rogan, of course, knew Julia had a thing for Leon and was just using him as a cover, but he ignored her as often as he could. As for Leon, I wasn't sure what was going on with him.

The whole outing to the river was my fault. I made the mistake of mentioning to Julia where Rogan and his friends had gone. It took all of thirty seconds for Julia to drag me outside and down the path at the back of the house.

Julia had us crouched low in the middle of the tall grass so we couldn't be seen, but we could certainly see the boys as they started taking off their clothes.

The minute I saw Chase go for his zipper, I slammed my eyes shut and dropped to my butt. No way was I about to see what Chase had in his pants.

"Fallon, stop sitting there and watch," Julia hissed. "*Oh my God! Oh my God!*" she muttered, and started fanning her face with her fingers as though it would make a difference in this heat.

I was more interested than I cared to admit to Julia, except the boy I was curious about was still fully clothed. I got back on my knees and squinted through the grass just as Chase bent and removed his shorts, flashing us his firm butt. I closed mine again while a blush tinted my cheeks.

Julia panted beside me and grabbed hold of my arm. "Rogan is taking his off now." Her hands tightened on my wrist and I opened my eyes and let them drift toward Rogan when Julia continued, "I think I'm about to hyperventilate."

I didn't get a glimpse of Rogan until he kicked off his shorts from his ankles, and then I really did snap my eyes closed.

"He's really big," Julia gasped, ogling him.

"I've just seen more of my brother than any sister

should," I grumbled, my heart quickened. "And it's all your fault." I didn't add that I'd wanted to see Rogan naked for a while and that I'd wondered about his body.

"But what a sight." Julia had a stupid smile on her face when I tugged her down with me.

"Stop looking," I snapped, feeling angry that Julia was seeing Rogan naked. He was mine and no one else was supposed to look at him the way Julia did.

Julia giggled. "I want another look so I can dream." She sighed softly.

"While you're dreaming about *Leon*"—I put great emphasis on his name—"how am I going to look Rogan in the eye after what I just saw?" Julia stayed silent, so I added, "I'm not supposed to see his junk."

I'm the only one who should get to see his junk.

"Stop being a prude. You got a load of Chase's junk, so it was worth it, right? We both got to see what we shouldn't." Julia grinned. "I hate that we're sixteen. I want to be eighteen."

"We'll be eighteen in just over a year," I told her. Our seventeenth birthdays were quickly coming up.

My heart pounded at what I'd seen. I'd never seen a naked boy in the flesh before—my cheeks were hot with embarrassment. It didn't help that Julia wouldn't stop peeking at Rogan. I really didn't want to hear about what he had or how *hugely* hung he was. Julia saved herself when she added that Chase was a very close second while licking her lips.

"Next time we're staying home, because that can't be unseen."

"I certainly don't want to forget what I've seen this afternoon." Julia smirked. "There is nothing wrong with looking at a hot guy."

I rolled my eyes. "We weren't *only* looking at a hot guy, Julia. We spied on them while they got naked."

"Mm-hmm, I know." Julia fanned herself. "I bet they wouldn't have a problem spying on us girls if the opportunity arose." Julia cocked a brow.

"We need to leave before they get out," I suggested. "And Rogan would kill anyone who spied on me skinny dipping."

"No way. I want to get a look at Leon," Julia said, ignoring my comment about Rogan. "Being on the football team, he's built like Rogan and Chase. I bet he's just as big."

My face felt as though it was on fire.

Hearing Julia sigh, I complained, "I want to go."

"Don't ruin my fun." Julia gasped. "Oh...you have to look."

She grabbed my wrist and tried to haul me up off

my butt, which she eventually did. It was either that or have bruises along my arm.

"What?" I mumbled and my eyes popped wide. "*Oh...*"

"That's Leon."

"I recognize him."

Julia snickered. "Is that so?"

"You know what I mean," I snapped but found I couldn't take my eyes off of him. Leon was all muscle, just like Rogan and Chase, but what held our attention was his right hand, and what he was doing with that hand.

Encouraging shouts erupted from the river, drawing my gaze away from Leon. I wished I hadn't looked because when I did, I met Rogan's gaze. With the distance between us, I wasn't sure he actually saw me, but he was certainly looking directly at where I watched from.

Rogan went quiet in the water and slowly started moving toward the bank. When he rose out of the water, it glistened on his skin. I did the first thing that entered my head; I grabbed Julia by the arm and tugged her up and ran back toward the house—totally busted.

By the time we reached the house and locked

ourselves in my bedroom, I thought I was having a full-blown panic attack.

"He saw me watching, Julia."

Julia was no help as she had curled up on my bed and laughed. Tears ran from her eyes while she offered me an amused grin, wiggling her brows. "You have to admit that it was so much better than spending the afternoon studying."

I flopped down beside Julia. "What am I going to say to him?"

"The truth." Julia turned onto her stomach and held my gaze. "That I wanted to spy and you went along with me to get a load of—"

I slapped my hand over Julia's mouth and nudged into her. I groaned as I stared at my best friend with her blond hair and china doll white skin beside my dark hair and tanned skin.

"I think Rogan would go nuts if he knew I'd caught sight of his friends naked and horsing around. You know how protective he is."

Julia gave me an odd look before she rolled to her back.

In truth, I hated that Julia watched Rogan all the time, and I was sure Julia liked him a lot more than just to make Leon jealous.

Rogan appeared amused when Julia really tried to

get his attention, but that was all I had ever seen on his face. Chase was another matter altogether. The way he stared at me when Rogan wasn't around made me uncomfortable and embarrassed. Sometimes I even wondered if Chase knew about Rogan and me— our feelings, our love.

Rogan had his pick of girls, but he never took them up on the offers I would see in their eyes. I may not be experienced, but I was old enough to know what *the look* meant. If I weren't so embarrassed about anything to do with sex, I'd ask Rogan about it. But I'd decided I didn't want to know how experienced he was. It would hurt too much.

No matter what, Rogan was my best friend, even before Julia, not that I'd admit that to Julia.

Rogan was my brother, something I struggled with calling him these days, but he was someone I could always count on to be there for me. Except, I wasn't sure how I was going to face him knowing he'd seen me at the river. If I knew Rogan, he'd already know it was Julia who'd dragged me after them. It didn't make it any easier because I'd seen him. Naked! That was something I was never supposed to see. What a sight though —all that beautiful, bronzed, masculinity on display.

I was no longer clueless about how the male species looked in the flesh.

8

———————

FALLEN

IT WAS DARK OUTSIDE AND JULIA HAD FINALLY GONE home, but only after her mom had called. She hadn't wanted to leave but, to my relief, Julia's mom hadn't given her any other choice.

After the embarrassment of the afternoon, I had thought it best to stay hidden in my bedroom. Unfortunately, my stomach had other plans as it rumbled unhappily. The protein bar I found in my school bag didn't quite cut it. I tried to study for the test I had in the morning, but even that couldn't distract me. I should have eaten dinner, then maybe I wouldn't be so hungry.

Glancing at the alarm clock, it read twenty past ten. With luck, Rogan would already be passed out. I heard him come up to his room over an hour ago.

Our parents were out with Dad's brother, Uncle Frank, so they wouldn't be back until late. Maybe I could sneak downstairs and make a sandwich. I'd made plenty of midnight snacks in the dark over the years, so avoiding Rogan shouldn't be a problem.

Slowly unlocking my door, I snuck downstairs and sighed when I made it without disturbing him. There was enough moonlight filtering in through the window that I left the light off and moved to the fridge. I quickly grabbed some leftover chicken and the jar of mayonnaise to make a sandwich. Turning, I let out a piercing scream as I shoved the door closed with my hip.

How Rogan managed to catch both the dish of chicken and the jar of mayonnaise, I didn't know, but he had. He put them on the kitchen table and then turned to face me. I was frozen in place. My eyes looked anywhere but at him as I remembered watching him and his friends that afternoon—all that naked skin.

"Look at me, Fallon," Rogan demanded.

"I can't."

He chuckled. "Serves you right for spying on me this afternoon."

Annoyed, I snapped my eyes open and met his

gaze. "I wasn't spying on you. Julia was. My eyes went in a different direction."

Liar.

I moved toward the breadbasket and took out four slices of white bread. I grabbed two plates and started making us both a sandwich while Rogan silently watched me.

"Who?" he growled, moving closer, breathing down my neck.

"Who what?" I asked, playing dumb.

"Chase or Leon?"

Turning, I shoved against his chest so that he backed away. "What difference does it make? You've made it clear that we have to carry on as normal. So I can look at whoever I want!"

His features changed and he looked *sad.*

Briefly closing my eyes, I sighed heavily and admitted, "I'm embarrassed okay. Seeing you like that was never supposed to happen, no matter how much I wanted to." My face heated. "I never wanted to see Chase or Leon like that if you must know."

I shoved a plate with the sandwich over to him and sat opposite, staying silent, embarrassed.

"I ache for you, Fallon." He dropped his face to stare at the table. "But it can never happen."

"Knowing the reason why we can't be together doesn't make it any easier," I admitted softly.

We ate silently until Rogan cleared his throat. He offered me a soft smile. "It's weird," Rogan admitted. "You're sixteen and shouldn't be seeing anything like that."

I choked on a piece of my sandwich as my eyes widened, and then narrowed. "I'm not naïve, Rogan. Jeez, we have the Internet, plus you saw me half-naked once."

"Internet! What does that mean?" he growled, ignoring my naked comment.

"Um, nothing."

His eyes narrowed. "I'll find out what you mean. You know I will."

"Stop threatening me." I munched on the sandwich and was disappointed when it was all gone.

"I'm not threatening you, but I bet all I would have to do is give Julia some attention and she'd tell me what you've both been looking at online." He raised a brow.

"Don't you dare!" I went quiet. "It would crush me to watch you flirt with her." I tilted my head. "She's really after Leon."

"I'm aware. So is Leon." He shrugged. "If she'd stop trying to get into my pants to make Leon jealous, we could all hang out together sometime, but no way am I encouraging her. I won't be used for any reason."

"So, if I get her to stop and convince her you're not interested, we can forget about today and hang out?"

"Yeah," he immediately agreed. "I really miss hanging out with you. It's been a while."

"I miss that too." More than I'd ever let him know.

Leaning forward, amusement clouded his gaze. "Did you watch what Leon was doing?"

My embarrassment was now complete.

"I know you did," he continued. "I do that too, but in the privacy of my bathroom. So when you're remembering what you saw, I want you to picture me."

My heart was ready to jump out of my chest as I held his gaze. "Don't." I averted my eyes and begged, "Please tell me Leon and Chase don't know we were there?"

Rogan stayed silent.

"They know?" I whispered.

Nothing from Rogan. I wanted to shake him, or kiss him, and then his face split into a grin.

"No, they don't know. I had you for a minute." He laughed.

"Ugh!" I stood and shoved him with my hand. "That was unfair."

"You deserved it after watching *me* skinny dip."

"I told you," I groaned, as we headed upstairs, "I wasn't watching you." I stopped for a second, heat already on my face before I teased, "But I'm going to be imagining you from now on." I managed to smirk before I rushed into my room and locked the door.

I slid down the door amused that, for once, I'd gotten the last word. The look on his face was certainly worth my embarrassment. He hadn't been expecting the teasing. I was the one who blushed and stayed silent. Smiling, I put my ear to the door. Five minutes later, I heard Rogan's bedroom door close.

Knowing I was going to have to face him in the morning over breakfast, I questioned the wisdom of my parting words, especially since he knew I'd meant them.

9

ROGAN

I GRINNED AS I ENTERED MY BEDROOM, ACHING WITH want after Fallon's parting shot about thinking about me. My smile slipped as I remembered my reaction to Fallon as she watched me naked in the river. I'd climbed out and stood on the bank with my body tight, a desperate need to be with her rocking me to my very core. She ran and I dived back into the water to hide the throbbing between my legs before Leon and Chase caught sight of me. It took me a while to calm down enough to climb out and dress. We went back to Leon's house until it got dark, and I decided I could no longer hide out at my friend's house.

I dropped on to the end of my bed knowing I had to be the one to keep Fallon away from me. After today, it had to happen. It was the last thing I wanted, but it was the right thing to do. I wasn't sure I could handle seeing the spark go out of her beautiful eyes, and it would go out if I crushed her.

I swallowed hard and fell backward to my bed as tears burned my eyes. They slipped free and trailed down into my hair. I'd never been so mixed up before. My heart told me to stay with Fallon, but I knew deep in my mind that nothing but trouble would come of my love for her.

Confused and unsure if I could go through with hurting her, more tears fell. My heart knew with every breath I took that Fallon was mine and always would be.

10

FALLEN

MOM, DAD, AND ROGAN TALKED OVER THEIR breakfast while I poured some juice into a glass and Lucky Charms into a bowl. Milk sloshed over the rim and ran along the counter before I captured it with a paper towel. I hated that. I always spilled milk when pouring from a full carton.

From the corner of my eye, I caught Rogan watching me with a smirk on his lips. Sighing heavily, I forced my embarrassment from the day before back down where it belonged and took my seat opposite him at the table. He knew I was embarrassed and he was trying to get me to lift my face and meet his gaze. That was so not happening. Then he nudged his foot against mine under the table.

I snapped my head up in his direction and

narrowed my eyes. Rogan grinned and laughed in response.

Mom stopped in the middle of conversation with Dad and looked between the two of us. "Is there something going on between you two?"

"No," I answered quickly.

"Yes," Rogan answered.

"Which is it?" Dad asked, frowning.

"Fallon and Julia followed us to the river yesterday," Rogan blurted and my eyes widened in surprise and panic. "I think Julia saw more than she should have."

I gasped and kicked him under the table.

"Ouch! No need to get violent," he muttered, trying his hardest to keep his laughter inside. "I'm heading to school," he announced. "Want a ride?"

Mom stared with a smile on her face, but Dad continued to frown. The only answer to Rogan's question was, "Yes."

Before I could change my mind, I quickly grabbed my backpack and followed Rogan out the front door to his car.

"You do realize that no matter how hard you shoot daggers into my back, nothing is going to happen?" Rogan drawled, getting into the blue Mustang he loved.

"I can't believe you told Mom and Dad," I complained, dropping into the seat beside him. "They know you guys skinny dip out there...and after *the talk*, I think you should have stayed silent."

"I admit I shouldn't have said anything, but I'm sick of watching what I say in front of them." He shook his head. "I'm sorry, but it was worth the look on your face."

I narrowed my gaze. "I probably wore the same look you did when I told you I imagined you the way Leon was." Smirking, I turned and watched the houses as we passed them by on the way to school.

Rogan simmered all the way to school, his knuckles white, clenching the steering wheel. He didn't speak or acknowledge me until he pulled into his usual parking space. Exhaling heavily, and with a blank stare out of the front window, he said, "Yesterday, at the river, never happened."

I blinked as I watched him get out of the car and run over to greet Leon and Chase with only a glance back at me before he headed inside.

There was a lot of "never happened" adding up.

I was still sitting in the car five minutes later when Julia appeared.

"Why do you look like you've seen a ghost?"

"Um, what?" Grabbing my backpack, I got out of

the car and slammed the door closed. "Rogan is being an asshole."

Inwardly, I cringed at the word I used to describe him, but it was the only one that came to mind. After our conversation last night, I wasn't sure how to take him. He wasn't usually so moody and forward.

"Does it have anything to do with yesterday?" Julia whispered, a dreamy look on her face.

Nudging into her, I admitted, "It has everything to do with it, and I really would rather forget all about it."

"Are you serious?" Julia tugged me to a stop. "How can you ever forget seeing what we did?" She smirked. "Your brother is...*big*."

I groaned and sagged against my locker. "That's it. He's my *brother* and I interact with him all the time. It's embarrassing knowing that he knows I saw his junk." I turned to my locker. "It's awkward and I hate it."

Julia watched me closely and agreed. "Okay. I'll stop mentioning it."

"I'd appreciate that." I sighed. "Rogan said if you stop trying to get into his pants to make Leon jealous, we can hang with them again." I watched Julia from the corner of my eye. "I miss being part of their group. I also miss making Corinne and Amber—to name two members of Rogan's fan club—jealous."

Julia closed her locker and slouched against it. "I really have to stop going after Rogan to get at Leon, huh?"

"Yeah, you do."

"Does that mean you have to stop making goo-goo eyes at Chase?"

I rolled my eyes. "I do no such thing."

"Whatever," Julia uttered as though she didn't believe me, but when Julia stilled and watched over my shoulder, I knew it was either *Corinne* or Rogan approaching.

"Out of favor with your brother, I see," Corinne let the words drip off of her tongue with relish.

One day, I was going to put Corinne in her place, and I'd take great pleasure in doing so. "There is nothing wrong with my brother and me." I turned and faced Corinne. "He's always grumpy in the morning."

She sniggered. "He wouldn't be grumpy in the morning if he'd spent the night with me."

Feeling the anger and, dare I admit it, jealousy rising inside of me, I snapped, "That's my brother you're talking about. Stop it!"

Corinne's eyes widened and Julia grabbed my wrist. "Let's go," Julia whispered.

I held Corinne's gaze and watched as the girl's face reddened. I was pretty sure it was with anger and not embarrassment. But I wasn't going to stand there and take whatever Corinne wanted to say about Rogan. He might be confused and maybe a bit annoyed with me, but he'd always be my brother.

The bell rang to announce start of class, so I allowed Julia to drag me away while an arrow pierced my heart.

We took our seats and Julia whispered, "I thought you were going to punch her."

I raised a brow.

"Seriously. I never knew you had that in you," Julia added.

"Me either."

11

FALLEN

THE COLD METAL LOCKER UNDER MY HAND MADE ME shiver, and the grumble from my stomach reminded me it was lunchtime. My fingers fiddled with the lock until I finally got the numbers aligned and it snapped open. I quickly shoved my backpack inside, once I'd retrieved my wallet.

Julia nudged into me as I locked my belongings away. "Why are you taking so long?" Julia grabbed my arm in excitement, the gum in her mouth loud as she chewed. "Leon has been giving me the eyes. We *have* to go and sit with them, but it will be less obvious if you're there too."

"We always eat lunch together." I pushed away from the lockers and smirked when Julia caught up to me. "And everyone knows that, so it wouldn't look obvious at all."

Groaning, Julia admitted, "I'm nervous, okay? Leon is looking back at *ME*," she hissed loudly in my ear while bruising my wrist in the tight grip she had on me.

Prying Julia's fingers from my wrist, I rubbed at the bruise already forming there before I grabbed a tray. The cafeteria had been redone over the summer and was nice and modern with bright yellow walls. It was certainly better than the prison gray they had before. The menu was much improved with healthier options available, but I still leaned toward the pasta when it was available. I told myself it was healthy because it was served with salad.

Sliding into seats opposite Rogan, Chase, and Leon, I felt Julia's leg start to shake. It soon stopped when I nudged into her under the table.

Noticing the fork being waved in front of my face, I lifted my eyes and saw Rogan grinning back. "One of these days, you'll remember," he said.

"Maybe." I always remembered the food but rarely the utensils.

"So..." Leon grinned as though he knew something we didn't. "Rogan has a *date*."

The food in my stomach turned to sawdust as my

eyes found Rogan's. Behind the betrayal I felt, I noticed his embarrassment, and anger. "We'll talk at home," he hissed under his breath.

I wasn't an idiot and knew our attraction to each other couldn't go anywhere, but I couldn't believe he'd date without even mentioning it to me. A warning would have been nice. I tried to continue with lunch, no longer paying attention to anyone or what I shoved into my mouth.

I sensed Rogan staring, but, in the end, I cleared my dishes and headed back to my locker.

All the way through history, I sat in a world of my own, my head conjuring up all kinds of scenarios for Rogan and his date. I hoped whoever *she* was got covered in poison ivy so she couldn't make it. I suddenly pulled myself back. What was wrong with me? I'd never wished bad things to happen to anyone before.

You're jealous that your brother is going out with someone other than you!

Swallowing hard around the tears in my throat, I tuned in briefly to Mr. Schwartz and his lecture on the American Civil War. Concentrating hard on what he was saying about the Confederates, my teacher lost me again to thoughts I shouldn't be having.

Thoughts about teasing Rogan again, like I had

once before. He'd had a reaction to me. In fact, he'd had more than one reaction to me on the summer camping trip.

"Fallon?" Julia called.

"Huh?" I glanced around and saw everyone grabbing their belongings and leaving. "Oh!"

Julia gave me an odd look but didn't voice her opinion, although she wouldn't stay silent for long.

"Miss Scott," Mr. Schwartz called as I was on my way out of his class. "A word, please." He added, "Alone," when Julia stayed beside me.

Once the door closed behind Julia, Mr. Schwartz gave me his famous narrowed-eyed stare. "You are usually my brightest student. You always take part in my class. Today I'm not sure you actually heard a word I said. Why?" He steeped his fingers as his elbows rested on his desk.

"I, um…" I sighed heavily and admitted, "I'm upset about something at home. I'm sorry. I won't daydream in class again."

His beady eyes searched mine but I kept my thoughts to myself.

"Very well."

I moved to leave.

"Miss Scott…Fallon, if you ever need to talk, I'm here for you, as I'm sure are other teachers."

He became flushed, which made his offer all the sweeter. "I appreciate that." I smiled. "Thank you."

I quickly left, and the moment I did, Julia grabbed my arm and hurried me down the hallway and straight out of the building.

"What is going on with you? You've been acting weird since lunch," I asked, not mentioning my own woolgathering. "I guess you've been preoccupied with Leon?"

"I can't decide if he likes me or not. One minute he's staring at me, or rather my chest, and the next he's frowning as though he's angry. I'm not sure what to do."

"I'm not one for advice, but I'd say don't do anything. Knowing Leon, he can't decide why he can't stop staring at you. He'll get there in the end. Just might take a while."

Stopping at Rogan's car, sweat was pooling under my long thick hair, making me uncomfortable. The tie that was holding the mass of hair from my face and back had snapped in second period and I hadn't been able to find a spare.

"The guys are coming." Julia smiled. "I'm going to continue flirting with Rogan. Might get Leon to make a move."

I refrained from telling Julia that nothing would

get Leon to make his move until he was good and ready. Out of our three friends, Leon was the most stubborn.

The drive home was quiet and as we parked at the house, Leon was the last friend to part. He lived next door.

Rogan gave me a sidelong glance before heavily sighing. "I have no interest in dating, Fallon. I was put on the spot and didn't want to embarrass her or me, so I agreed. We'll just go the movies."

"Who?"

"Corinne Roberts."

My eyes widened. "You're taking *her* on a date? Do you have a death wish?" I slammed out of the car. "Whatever you do is fine." I snarled, jealousy eating away at me. "We need to carry on as normal." I started heading around to the back of the house. "So if you're dating, then there is no reason why I can't."

I heard a weird noise come out of Rogan before my backpack was on the ground and he had me pinned between his body and the house, his face furious.

His chest heaved as he tried to pull his anger back, but some seeped out when he growled, "You will not date anyone. I told you that you would always be mine." He pressed against me, leaving nothing of his body to my imagination.

I held his gaze and my anger at his anger subsided when I realized he was slowly losing it. "I'm not going to date, Rogan. I have no interest in anyone else." I swallowed back tears but they fell anyway. "It hurts so much knowing you are."

Rogan cursed and crushed me in his arms. "I'm doing this because I have to." He pulled back and stared into my eyes, and I could see that he wanted me to understand everything behind those words. Then, with a hard kiss to my forehead, Rogan quickly disappeared inside the house.

Instead of following him, I detoured to the gazebo in the back corner of the garden. Dad had built it as a surprise for Mom a few years back. I slumped down on a sun lounger and wondered what I was doing with my life. What Rogan was doing with his?

I was sixteen years old; too young to know what I wanted when I was older, even if my heart was crying out for Rogan.

Neither of us knew what life would throw at us, or the people we would meet along the way. One thing I did know was that I had to get on with my life, and no matter how much I loved Rogan, I needed to pretend otherwise.

It wouldn't be easy but, as Mom once said, the best things in life were worth waiting for.

I had to concentrate on a sibling relationship, even though I knew my anger and jealousy would eat away at me. It would hurt because my young heart was falling more and more in love with my *brother*.

I couldn't help the joy that shined on my face when he looked at me in the special way he reserved just for me. It was deep and dark, his eyes hooded. Intense.

I had a feeling I would always want Rogan Scott.

12

ROGAN

As the days passed I considered myself a saint.

Most days I could convince myself that nothing good would ever come out of loving Fallon in the way I did. I'd given her my heart when I was too young to understand what that truly meant. At least, that's what I told myself. It was the only way to carry on as her brother and nothing more.

I noticed the way her face would light up when we were alone. I noticed how her body reacted when I was close. I noticed the way we refused to acknowledge the way we reacted to each other. It was for the best, considering our actual relationship to each other. It didn't change my love for her. I was afraid it never would.

Fallon, oblivious to the thoughts running through

my mind, chatted animatedly to Julia across from me. Leon and Chase both wore shades, and Leon couldn't be more obvious as he stared at Julia.

The smell of hamburgers cooking on the grill made my belly grumble. A smile split my face as I watched Dad flip them over as he ignored Uncle Frank. Our uncle had been around at the house more often than usual. Dad said he was escaping the wedding madness at his house.

Uncle Frank's daughter, Leticia, was getting married soon and both Fallon and I were part of the wedding party. We hadn't wanted anything to do with it, but Dad took the choice away from us.

Focusing back on Fallon, I noticed a blush on her face while she continued to whisper with Julia. They were up to something, or maybe talking about us. Their eyes kept drifting toward us before they whispered some more.

Leon hissed under his breath and, being *Leon*, stuck his tongue out.

Fallon's eyes widened in surprise and Julia giggled. Before Julia could comment, Fallon slapped a hand over her mouth, shaking her head. Fallon's eyes darted toward Dad before going back to Julia, who rolled her eyes.

Julia tugged on Fallon's wrist. "I'll be good."

"I bet," Leon muttered.

Chase sniggered.

My eyes stayed on Leon until he finally gave me his attention. "What are you doing?"

"I want to know what they're whispering about."

"Whispering is rude, girls," Dad shouted, having overheard.

Fallon giggled and her gaze landed on me. I noticed how her breath caught in the back of her throat before she inhaled sharply. Her eyes dropped to her hands just as Dad piled a plate high with burgers.

"Come get them before Uncle Frank eats them all."

Lazily, we clambered to our feet, but, as usual, Leon and Uncle Frank beat everyone to the food.

I found myself behind Fallon as we reached for hamburger buns. Her flowery scent washed over me, and I briefly grabbed hold of her hips before moving away. The touch happened in the blink of an eye, even though I felt it in every beat of my heart.

I cast a sly glance Fallon's way and noticed she was pulling on my sweatshirt, her cheeks coated in a pale pink blush. It always thrilled me to see her wearing my clothes, and as the sweatshirt drowned her, my heart thudded wildly.

"Fallon, are you cold?" Mom questioned, bringing out the potato salad.

"Too much sun," she mumbled, her gaze briefly touched on mine before she concentrated on her food.

Making good work of the two burgers on my plate, I wondered why I was driving myself crazy.

Perhaps it was my age as I became more mature. I'd had a few years to grow up from the love I'd first felt for Fallon. We'd both changed—Fallon with her more feminine curves and me with the bulk I'd added through regular exercise.

My attitude about my future had changed too. One time I hadn't thought about what I wanted out of life, now, it was all I could think about.

I tried so hard to not dream about Fallon and our future, but the harder I tried, the harder it became. I knew in my heart my plans would always include her, unless I did something to keep her away from me for good. I just didn't have the willpower to stay away from her.

I told myself it was just a few more years. To hold on until we were old enough to live away from home together. I loved my parents and the last thing I ever wanted to do was hurt them. I never wanted to see disappointment in their eyes like I saw in Dad's eyes during the camping trip when he had "a word" with me. That had hurt, but I knew everything he said was true. Except the point he made about falling for Fallon because there was no other girl around—that hadn't been true. I let him think that was the case, though.

They'd seen Fallon and me together often, and had finally relaxed about us both, although on occasions, I noticed Dad watching us closely, a weary expression on his face.

Fallon was always going to be number one in my heart, but I thought it was time to finally let our parents *think* I'd moved on.

I just hoped Fallon would forgive me.

13

FALLEN

The bridesmaid dress was beautiful in rose gold with a strapless bodice and a straight skirt to the floor. Mom had told me that I looked beautiful and that made me nervous.

The looks Rogan had been giving me recently were hotter, darker, and more intense than before. I welcomed his gaze and hoped it would be on me during the day, even though it was wrong of me to want that.

Each day was becoming more of a struggle to stay only friends. I saw the longing on his face when he thought no one else was looking, just like he saw on mine. Sometimes when I was feeling down, I wore my heart on my sleeve and the struggle Rogan had when he saw that wasn't easy.

In fact, it wasn't going to be easy for either of us during the wedding. I was sure Rogan and me being part of the wedding party was only because Uncle Frank and Dad insisted on it. Uncle Frank's son and daughter had never been easy to get along with. Not that I was bothered. It just felt strange, but at least the groomsman to walk me up the aisle was going to be Rogan.

I was excited to see him in his tux, but nervous for him to see me. Our parents were guests, of course, being a family wedding and all, so we'd be on our best behavior, even if we were both sick of being good. Just once I'd like to be bad—with Rogan.

Sighing heavily, I followed the others out of the room and felt my throat go bone dry when I glanced at Rogan. He was just as frozen in place as me, except I found my feet moving toward the boy I loved. He was so handsome in the tux, which I'd known he would be.

He stood taller than me, even with the high heels on my feet. Mom had nagged him to get his dark hair trimmed so that he didn't look like a laid back bum—Mom's words and she'd been right.

I thought I preferred the overlong hair, except now that I saw him; the short crop was working for me. His eyes were more vivid and currently shining with heat and amusement as he held my gaze.

"You look"—he swallowed hard—"beautiful." He started to reach out for a lock of my hair, then hesitated. He dropped his hand back to his side, a sad smile on his lips.

Not today!

Today we were going to have a good time together, even if it had to stay innocent.

The music started up outside and Uncle Frank glared at us before turning to his daughter.

Rogan reached for my hand and threaded my arm through his. When I looked up, he winked. "At least I get to walk you down the aisle."

His words held a teasing light, but they affected me in a different way than he'd intended. His face dropped when he realized what he'd said.

"Fallon…I didn't think." He frowned. "And now that I have, I feel like crap," he whispered.

"It's our turn." I forced a smile, as did Rogan, and we walked up the aisle, something I wouldn't ever be able to do and have Rogan waiting for me at the top.

The actual wedding became a blur, something I switched off from, until I was next to Rogan in the limo on the way to the country club on the outskirts of town.

I was passed a tall glass filled with a bubbly liquid by another bridesmaid. Rogan reached for it, but I was quicker and moved it out of his reach.

"No way," I told him. "If this is champagne, then I'm going to drink it and no one will know." I grinned. "Unless you tell them, of course." I raised a brow, daring him.

Rogan rolled his eyes and reached for a glass. "We're both underage to drink." We clinked glasses. "As the British would say, bottoms up." He guzzled the sparkly in one gulp.

I wasn't one for being outdone, so I followed with, "Down the hatch."

The moment my glass was empty and I pulled it away from my mouth, I hiccupped—loudly. Beside me, Rogan chuckled and refused to let me have another glass of bubbly.

"You're already tipsy after only one glass." He groaned. "Mom and Dad will kill me."

Giggling, I placed my head on his shoulder and watched his face flush, his eyes filled with love for me. It was a look I'd always want and cherish, because I knew it was only reserved for me.

"I thought you two were related?" a groomsman asked, looking between us.

Rogan's body tensed under mine and I decided to

play the situation up so as to throw off the suspicion I felt from the others. "He's my brother." I grinned at the man and forced the smile into my eyes. "He's also my guardian and supposed to prevent me from drinking alcohol." I smirked. "That didn't work out too well because I think I'm drunk." I burped, very unladylike.

I nuzzled into Rogan's neck and announced to everyone in the limo, "I need a nap, Rogan. Please don't tell Mom and Dad I'm drunk." I closed my eyes and pretended to sleep. Instead, I enjoyed the heady scent coming from Rogan's neck, where my nose was buried.

His cologne was perfect for the boy wearing it, and I really didn't want to give him up when we arrived at the club.

I heard others exiting the car, and then Rogan whispered, "You can wake up now, we're alone."

My eyes fluttered open and with a gentle tease, I brushed a soft kiss on his neck. I felt the tremble in Rogan's body at my touch.

"Do we really have to go inside?" I moaned.

"Yeah, we do." He tugged me up with him. "Let's go and eat. Sober you up." His hand rode low on my back as he guided me inside the country club with the fancy white entrance of pillars and carvings.

The meal continued into the evening and then the dancing began. Half the guests were drunk and the other half were well on their way to joining them. As for me, I was stone cold sober with sore feet.

I'd danced so many times and had to watch as Rogan did too. Seeing him heading outside with his last dancing partner, I was angry—*and jealous*. So I followed, intending to give him a piece of my mind. However, I paused when I saw him backing away from the girl, only to have her advance on him. The girl reached her hands up to his handsome face. Rogan turned at the last minute and she kissed his cheek instead.

That was my cue.

"Rogan," I snapped and narrowed my eyes at the look on his face. "I need to talk to you."

The blonde slammed her hands on her hips. "He's busy, *slut*."

My eyes widened at what the blonde had called me. Rogan grabbed the girl's arm and spun her to face him. "The only *slut* here is you." He released her and moved to me, then took my arm, and led me into the gardens.

"I was pissed at all the guys you were dancing with," Rogan admitted before I could even ask anything. "So I danced. I hate dancing." He shoved his hands into his hair only to find it short and giving up, clenched his fists at his side. "I only wanted to dance with you," he drawled, angry.

"I'm standing right here, Rogan." I opened my arms wide. "I want to dance with you more than anyone." I offered him a wry smile. "You never asked me."

Rogan watched me for a moment, and then I found myself caught up in his big strong arms, our bodies pressed together. My arms held him tightly and when I caressed the hair at the nape of his neck, he shuddered, squeezing me tightly.

Seconds later, the heavens opened and the rain fell, soaking us both to the skin. I tugged Rogan's head toward mine until our foreheads pressed together.

The fresh rain pounded down and all I saw was the boy in front of me. "Kiss me, Rogan," I pleaded. "Just once, pretend I really can be yours." My heart pounded in time to the rain while I waited for him to reach for me with his lips.

His eyes closed as though he was in pain, and when he opened them, they blazed with a heat I hadn't seen before. "If I kiss you, Fallon, I won't ever be able to stop." His lips pressed hard against my forehead before he took my hand and pulled me with him back to the club and shelter from the summer storm.

Rogan quickly disappeared as Mom rushed to me, my tears not going unnoticed by Rogan, or Mom.

14

ROGAN

I PANTED HARD, TRYING TO GET OUT OF SIGHT OF MY family as I quickly moved around the side of the country club and collapsed against a pillar. The rain pounded down hard and I was soaked to the skin, but I didn't care. My heart threatened to explode out of my chest at the overwhelming need I had to go back to Fallon and take what she'd offered me.

Kiss me, she'd whispered. *Pretend I really can be yours*. Her words had nearly broken me. From somewhere deep I'd managed to push her away and run. I shouldn't have run, but it was the only way to stop myself from taking what was mine.

I gasped for breath and pushed myself away from the concrete slab I clung to. On unsteady legs, I started to walk down the driveway that led to the main road. Water splashed up over my legs from speeding cars as I hunkered down into the collar of my tux, which didn't do anything to protect me from the storm. With any luck, Leon and Chase would still be hanging out at the diner in town, and I'd be able to hitch a ride home with them.

By the time I arrived at the diner, I looked as though I'd been for a swim in the river before heading into town. Soaked to the bone and feeling chilled, I opened the door to the diner and stopped at the sharp gasp. I turned my head and found Leon and Chase sitting at a table with Corinne.

That's all I needed.

"Rogan Scott, what on earth happened to you?" Gladys asked from behind the register, and in the next breath she was toward me with a towel.

I had to laugh when she tossed it to me. My reflexes were quick and I caught it mid-throw, otherwise it would have smacked me in the face if I'd been any slower.

"Thanks." I smirked. "You have noticed the rain bouncing off the sidewalk, right?"

Gladys rolled her eyes. "Don't sass me." Her finger shook in my direction.

"I wouldn't dream of it, Miss Gladys." I smiled and

kissed her on the cheek as I walked past. "I'd love some coffee to warm me up."

"I'll warm you up."

The moment I caught Corinne's words, my eyes briefly met Gladys', and she whispered, "Mind that one."

"Yes, ma'am." I winked at the woman who I'd known since moving to town so many years before.

Dropping the towel in the space beside Corinne, I sat and winced as my wet clothing stuck to my skin, causing goose bumps to spread across my flesh.

"I'm not sure it was wise coming inside."

"Thought you were at a wedding," Leon commented.

"I was. Needed to get away." I could see Corinne out of the corner of my eye watching me closely.

Tired and heartsick, I sighed and leaned against the back of the seat. I closed my eyes and immediately thought of Fallon. What was she doing? Had she stopped crying?

Someone kicked me beneath the table and my eyes snapped open and zoomed in on Leon, who glared at me.

"What?"

"You're acting weird." Leon tilted his head and continued staring.

"Don't be silly." Corinne paused. "Rogan always has the brooding look going on. Why do you think all the girls like him?"

I silently groaned, and turned my head to look at Corinne. She was a pretty girl, but she sometimes got lost in her looks, which wasn't attractive. She worked hard in school, and that was a point in her favor, but her eyes were always on me, and mine were always on Fallon.

Maybe Corinne was what I needed to get my mind off my sister. Could I actually date her, though, and continue to do so, without confusion and frustration with Fallon clouding my judgment? It was something to think about, but for now I was too exhausted to even move.

Gladys placed a steaming cup of dark coffee in front of me. "Enjoy, Rogan." She patted my shoulder and winced, then grabbed the towel tucked into her apron and dried her hand.

"Thank you, Gladys." I took a sip. "I mean it. Thank you."

"You're always welcome, Rogan."

"What was that about?" Corinne asked, sounding jealous, which made me laugh.

"It's private."

Gladys had always looked out for us. She was a

friend, or like a grandma. She was always ready with the advice, whether we wanted it or not.

Corinne pouted, then quickly smiled. "So, when are we going on our date? I'm still waiting, Rogan."

My stomach rolled. I couldn't think about that now, not when Fallon's words and the feeling of holding her in my arms were still fresh in my mind.

"We'll do something soon."

Chase glared at me before he turned to Corinne. My friend had been the silent and brooding one, which had me concerned.

I frowned. "Everything okay?"

Leon turned to look at Chase, and with all eyes on him, Chase blushed. He'd always hated to be the center of attention, even with Leon and me, who were his best friends.

"Didn't sleep last night," Chase admitted. "In fact, I think I'm going to head home if you're both finished."

"Yes. I'm in need of a warm shower and dry clothes."

"Let's go." Leon slipped from the booth and Chase followed. "Corinne, we'll walk you to your car first."

"I guess. It's early, though."

Chase tugged me from the booth and Corinne followed at a slower pace.

"We're all tired, Corinne." I guided her toward the

door. "We'll see you at school." I didn't leave her any option but to follow us outside into the storm after I'd said my goodbye to Gladys.

"I'm not sure I want you in my car," Leon said, looking between his car and me.

I smirked and ignored my friend, and climbed into the back seat. As soon as Leon started the engine, heat from the vents started to fill the car. By the time Leon pulled into his driveway, I didn't want to move. I was exhausted, but I knew I'd be sick if I didn't get my butt out of the car and into my own house, where a really hot shower waited.

"Thanks," I said to Leon over the hood of the car.

The rain had stopped and we hovered outside.

"What do you think of Corinne?" I asked.

"She's okay." Leon paused and searched my gaze for something. "You're not really into her, and we both know once you get the date out of the way it won't be happening again, so why are you asking?"

I rubbed at my brow. "Just thinking." I pushed myself away from the car and slowly started to make my way to my house. "I'll see you tomorrow."

I entered my dark house and went directly to my bedroom. I tossed the wet clothes into the hamper and climbed into the shower, enjoying the feel of the steaming water on my aching body. My hands pressed against the shower wall and I dropped my head, and stared at my feet. I really was bone-tired, but obviously not tired enough to keep Fallon out of my head, because there she was. Front and center. My eyes quickly snapped shut, which did not help any. All I saw was the girl who sassed me in nothing but her underwear.

My breathing became heavy with the image I had of Fallon and her body. Thinking of Fallon gave me another ache. One deep in my groin. My hand reached for my throbbing dick and as I slowly started to rub, I wondered if I'd ever be free of her.

15

ROGAN

After I'd left Fallon in tears at our cousin's wedding, and with my confusion over what to do about Corinne, I found it difficult to be around Fallon. I wished things between us weren't awkward because I really missed her.

For so long, she had always been by my side, one of the guys. She was the one person I knew would always be there for me, like I would her. But our relationship changed during the summer. It was my entire fault for not keeping my mouth shut and my hands to myself. I had no wish to go back to how things were before though, because I really did love her. I wished it were as simple as that instead of complicated.

Fallon had developed into a beautiful young woman with the body of someone older.

Leon had made the mistake once of commenting on Fallon's chest, and before I could blink, I had him pinned to the ground, as Chase scrambled to pull me off of Leon. They quickly got that she was out of bounds, but it was the other guys our age and older who drooled over her that got me angry. Fallon was oblivious to the attention she received and that made me smile, but it also drove me crazy. Her attention was always on me, which was why she had no clue. That filled me with a warm kind of excitement.

Moving to my bedroom window when I heard a noise, I watched Fallon settle on her belly on a lounge chair. Her bikini panties were small and showed far more than she should flash in public. The sun blazed down on her, and her long, bronzed legs spread out as she got comfortable.

Before I realized what I was doing, I was outside and crashing onto the chair next to Fallon's. I grinned when she turned her head, a light blush coating her cheeks as her eyes trailed over my chest. My blood thickened and caused a rapid swelling in my shorts.

Silently groaning, I laid on my front, trying to get comfortable, hoping she hadn't noticed my reaction to her. I did try to ignore her body, but my eyes had other ideas as they strayed to her chest when she sat up.

I quickly turned my gaze away and tried to think about something else, like college. College was good. I needed to consider a major, and it wouldn't be anatomy.

"Are you not going to talk to me?" she asked.

"Just ignore me," I mumbled.

"That's not easy to do," she muttered while I kept my eyes tightly shut.

A few minutes later, I heard rustling beside me and opened my eyes to see what she was doing. I found her sitting on the side of her lounger looking at my thighs, her gaze moving upward.

"What's wrong?" I asked, my voice husky.

"You don't have any sunscreen on," she commented. "You'll burn."

"I don't need any."

She smacked me on the butt, causing more of a reaction in me than she probably expected. Breathing heavily, I dropped my face into the towel beneath me and wondered what the heck I was thinking coming out here with her. My body was hot and tight and ached so badly that I was afraid to move.

"Don't be a jerk. I'll put it on you."

My brain shut down completely, but the moment I felt cool liquid hit my back, followed by her hands, my body shut down and all the blood rushed south. I throbbed unbelievably hard and fast from her touch. I couldn't move away. I wasn't sure I would if I could. Her touch felt so good I struggled to breathe.

I really wished I could see her face right then, see whether or not she was reacting to me, whether her body was suffering the same as mine was.

"Legs," she mumbled, her voice husky. She cleared her throat. "It's going to be one of the hottest days so far this month, so you need plenty of lotion on. You can do me next."

I slammed my eyes closed and clenched my jaw. I was sure she hadn't meant her words the way I'd heard them, but I was in so much trouble. No way could I turn back over with the hard problem in my shorts.

She dribbled lotion over my legs and then her hands were all over my thighs, dipping in between, making sure the lotion got to every part of bare skin. My breath got trapped in my lungs as her fingers slipped under the hem of my shorts, the tips grazing my butt. At that point I lost it and buried my face in the towel beneath me as my body became strung tight.

Concentrating hard, I fought not to thrust my hips, and, especially, not to moan out loud. Goose bumps covered my skin as I came in my shorts from her sensitive touch. Her hands not stopping told me she had no idea about the pleasure I'd just experienced. But as I concentrated on breathing again, I realized I was never going to survive spreading the lotion over her skin—over her curves, up her long legs to the curve of her butt.

I needed to leave.

Inhaling, I grabbed the towel and kept it in front of me as I quickly jumped to my feet. "I just remembered I have to do something."

Fallon frowned as I quickly turned and ran into the house and upstairs to my room.

I tossed the towel, kicked off my shorts, wincing at the sticky mess I'd made, and headed into the shower.

Her hands had felt amazing on my heated skin. I'd desperately wanted to return the favor, but no way would I have been able to control myself. I'd already lost it with her hands on me.

Her voice had been husky, which made me wonder if touching me had affected her just as badly.

One thing I did know was that somehow, some-
way, the madness had to end before we destroyed our
family.

Fallon did and always would mean the world to
me...*as a sister.*

It could never be more.

So you keep saying!

16

FALLEN

JULIA AND I WALKED TOWARD GREG'S HOUSE PARTY AND I was so tempted to tell my friend about Rogan's reaction that afternoon. I'd always told her everything, well…almost everything. I couldn't tell Julia how I really felt about Rogan. I couldn't tell her what touching him had made me feel. I suspected he'd enjoyed it more than he should have, especially when he escaped into the house before anything could be said.

I'd been tempted to follow him, but Julia had chosen right then to call about Greg's party.

The lawn in front of Greg's house was already littered with empty cups, and bodies. Rogan came striding toward us from the direction of the front door. He was in black jeans and a white T-shirt, his dark hair stuck up in spikes.

"What are you doing here?" Rogan hissed with Chase and Leon on his heels.

Rogan quickly moved his hooded gaze up and down my body, causing heat to rise to my cheeks. The tinge of red on his own face probably had something to do with the low hung jeans and the fitted pink T-shirt I wore. My choice of clothing certainly did nothing to cool his temper as his jaw hardened.

"You shouldn't be at this party."

"Why?" I stepped nose-to-nose with him. "Why can you be here and I can't? I was invited."

Rogan clenched his jaw while Leon and Chase watched him, a frown on their faces.

Chase stepped forward and slung an arm around Rogan's neck. "We can keep an eye on them," he suggested. "Loosen up, man."

I was tempted to glance at Chase and thank him, but I refrained. My eyes stayed on Rogan, wondering what was going through his head. He was always protective of me, but tonight he seemed to be going a bit over the top, even for him. We were at the same place, so he would be able to keep the boys away, as always. I wasn't worried and neither should he.

"Rogan." I reached out and intertwined my fingers

with his, trying to calm him. "I promise not to misbe-have. I just want to have some fun with my friends, and you." I offered him a small smile. "I knew you'd be here." I made sure he knew what I meant.

He slowly inhaled and exhaled. "I'm being over-protective, huh?" He squeezed my hand.

"Just a bit." Then I suggested, "We could hang out together…unless you think we'll cramp your style."

"Hell yeah, of course you can hang with us," Leon said. "Who wouldn't want to be seen with two hot chicks?"

"What?" Rogan turned on his friend, his eyes shooting fire while his hand tightened around mine.

I tugged him back around to face me while Leon took a step away. "Breathe, Rogan. Chill out, okay?"

He turned to his friends, still keeping hold of my hand. "No one touches her." He glanced at Julia and sighed quietly. "Or Julia."

"Hey!" Julia took exception. "You're not my brother, so no protection thingy is going to work on me." She stood with her hands on her hips and I smirked at my sassy friend.

"Let's go inside before everyone sees us arguing like a bunch of old women," Chase said, heading toward the front door.

Leon smirked and the others disappeared while

Rogan held me back a moment longer. "I'm sorry I ran off this afternoon." He blushed.

"Oh."

He cleared his throat and let go of my hand and I immediately missed his warmth. He shoved me inside of the house in front of him, the warmth of his body against my back.

When my eyes focused, I was shocked to see Corinne across the room on her back while another girl licked something from her stomach. An audience cheered them on. I glanced at Rogan to see if he'd noticed, and he had, but he turned to me and rolled his eyes. He grabbed my hand and pulled me past sweaty bodies and into the kitchen. He snagged a beer from the large cooler before we headed out back.

Julia ran up to us, appearing half drunk already. "Isn't this fun." She giggled and burped. "Oops." She covered her mouth and rushed off toward the shed at the end of the garden.

Someone had gone to the trouble of stringing up colored fairy lights to anything unmoving in the garden. It cast a soft glow in the dark. Couples made out in the shadows and I wondered if Julia would be okay.

I was nervous and chewed on my bottom lip,

feeling out of depth, which Rogan would be aware of and would be the reason as to why he was keeping me close. I felt guilty letting Julia go off by herself because my friend never thought first—that was always me.

"Let me go check on her." I moved forward but found my wrist captured in Rogan's much larger hand.

"Be careful," he warned when I met his gaze, a hint of something crossed his features.

"Let her go," Chase grunted. "What's gotten into you?" He punched Rogan in the arm and I found myself free to go after Julia, even though I felt the heat of Rogan's gaze on my back.

I quickly followed the sound of Julia's high-pitched giggle from behind the shed until silence descended.

Almost afraid to walk around the back, my mouth dropped open in surprise when I did. Julia was strad-dling a stranger on the ground while she kissed the hell out of him. The poor guy actually looked like he was in a daze. His hands were under Julia's dress, clenching her butt, which was barely covered in flaming red panties.

"What are you doing?" I stumbled over my words. "Julia?" I hissed.

Julia looked up and gave me a drunken smile, then dived back in.

I opened and closed my mouth like a fish out of water, and then I noticed another boy in the shadows, watching what was going on. His white teeth flashed as he smiled and moved toward me. "Want to join the party?"

"Hell no!" The words slipped out before I could stop them.

Mr. Voyeur wasn't impressed and took a step closer as I took a step back.

"Where are you going?" he asked, reaching toward me with a meaty paw.

His fingers skimmed my arm but didn't get a grip. *Thank God.*

My breath jammed in my lungs and I panicked because I didn't know what to do. I needed to get help, but at the same time, I didn't want to leave Julia. I glanced at my friend and thought she'd be okay for now, so I made the choice to find Rogan or one of their friends.

I turned tail and ran back up the garden, only to hear the beast gaining on me. Just as I came into the light from the patio, he grabbed me from behind, my feet leaving the ground. I screeched and tried to kick him. He was too strong for me, but my scream had drawn everyone's eyes to the baboon that had me clenched in his arms.

To my relief, I heard, "Get your hands off my sister."

Rogan.

I spotted Leon in the crowd of spectators and shouted, "Go help Julia behind the shed."

Leon blinked and seconds later took off with two others from the football team while Chase stood side by side with Rogan.

"Let her go." Rogan dropped his beer on the deck and moved closer, his hands flexing at his sides. "Now."

The baboon did and I dropped to the ground—my butt taking the brunt of the fall. The baboon took off running.

Someone shouted, "We'll get him," as others took off after him.

Rogan didn't. He was quickly by my side, pulling me to my feet.

"You okay?" he asked, tugging me against his chest when he noticed how much my hands trembled. "What did that asshole do to you?"

I clenched his T-shirt in my fist and buried my face against his neck. "Nothing," I whispered. "He took off after me. Scared me." My other arm slipped around his back, my fingers clung to his belt.

"You want me to take you home?"

I nodded. "I need to make sure Julia is okay first."

I inhaled Rogan's familiar scent, which helped in calming my nerves. My heart slowed, and then I released the death grip I had on his shirt and belt before I finally lifted my gaze to his.

His hands gripped my forearms and he offered me a soft smile. "We'll take Julia home first, okay?"

Tears hovered on my lashes and, although I tried to hide them from Rogan, he was too observant. He caught my jaw in his warm hand and turned me so he could look more closely. His lips were so close.

"Don't hide from me. I'm your home, Fallon. Your safety. Always." He kissed me on the forehead and wrapped an arm around my shoulders as we waited for Leon to reach us with an unconscious Julia in his arms.

"She's okay," Leon stated. "Too much to drink."

I frowned. "How? We haven't been here long enough."

"That's true. I haven't even finished one." Rogan frowned and shook his head.

"She had a couple of shots," Leon admitted.

"Let's just get her home. I've had enough of this party."

I didn't say anything as I hid my face in Rogan's shoulder and let him lead me out of the place.

Rogan was right.

He was my home. He was my safety.

I CURLED UP IN BED AND COULD FEEL THE GLARE coming from Rogan, who was spread out on the sofa in my bedroom. It was actually a sofa bed when it was pulled out, but, for now, he was lounging on it with a cushion hugged against his chest while we watched a movie—*Pretty in Pink.*

I grinned when I thought about how many times over the years I'd made him watch the old eighties movie. There was just something about it that had a hold on me; it was one of my favorite movies. I was surprised Rogan hadn't already fallen asleep because he could probably recite it word for word at this point, just like the *Goonies* when we were kids.

I let my eyes travel over Rogan as I remembered how Julia had once described him—tall, dark and sexy. I had to admit, he was. His dark hair had been cut for the wedding and although I liked it short, I missed the longer strands. Rogan didn't look seventeen with his height and physique; he looked like he was in his early twenties. Julia said he always looked like he'd just had hot sex.

My eyes landed on his bare legs, his thighs were strong, and covered by dark hair. I remembered the feel of them under my hands when I'd rubbed sunscreen onto his skin. From the way he reacted, I knew he'd enjoyed my touch. I'd felt him shiver when my hands had been on his thighs, which was why I'd slipped the tips of my fingers beneath the hem of his shorts. The feel of him had made my body feel hot and swollen.

Rogan cleared his throat and my eyes snapped into focus. He watched me closely with a raised brow. "The movie finished five minutes ago."

"Oh." I grabbed the remote and switched it off before I switched the lamp off at the side of the bed. It was so much easier to hide, not only my embarrassment, but also my longing.

The silence made me nervous, and then I felt the bed dip.

"Talk to me," he said. "Something is going on. It's annoying as hell not knowing everything that's going on in your life, so you need to talk to me."

I forgot about everything else and turned toward

my brother, knowing he'd always be there for me regardless of our forbidden attraction.

"Fallon," he mumbled. "Why do I get the feeling you're not going to say anything?"

"Because I'm not." I sighed. "I don't really know what's going on." *Liar!* "Maybe it's hormones or something. I just feel changes taking place in my body and I don't know how to handle them." I teased without thinking about it. "Even my boobs have grown and I'm bursting out of my bras." I sulked. "I hate having big boobs."

"Jesus!" he cursed. "You need to discuss that shit with Mom."

I giggled at my big strong brother sounding hot and bothered. "You're supposed to be my older brother. Someone to show me the ways of growing up." I poked him in the chest. "You know? Teach me about boys and sex."

He made a weird noise, and it was all I could do not to laugh. Make no mistake, if it weren't so dark in my room, I wouldn't have said anything. But in the dark, I felt brave and didn't care about what came out of my mouth.

"I think..." He paused and cleared his throat. "I think this conversation really does need to happen with Mom...while you're getting new...um... underthings."

I rolled my eyes. "Underthings? Really? Since when have you been shy, Rogan Scott."

"Since my sister, Fallon Scott, started talking about boys and sex. I don't even want to think of you and that shit." His voice darkened and he became serious. "I can't ever think about you and a boy, Fallon. It will kill me."

"You're a boy." I knew what he'd meant but I tried to lighten the sudden rise in temperature.

"Oh, I hadn't noticed." He teased.

"Wiseass." I poked him again. "What I mean is that you're a boy and know all about sex. So why can't you tell me?"

The silence grew between us and, as I searched his face in the dark, I realized he had his eyes closed tightly. "You are too young to know about boys and sex...and because you have no idea how much I want to *show* you."

My heart pounded. "After what I witnessed by the river, I don't think I'm too young. Besides, watching Leon do what he was doing was...um... enlightening."

He cursed. "You seriously did not go there? That wasn't meant for you to see."

"Well, I did. So did Julia." I smirked. "He's really big."

"I'm going to bed," he grumbled, sounding annoyed. "Forget about Leon."

If it wasn't so late I was sure he would've banged the door closed when he left my room, but before the door completely closed, I whispered, "I can't forget what you looked like."

His back tensed, but he didn't face me or come back inside. Instead, he made sure the door was closed properly, and then I heard his own bedroom door closing.

Why didn't I keep my mouth shut? I didn't want to be alone tonight; I wanted him to stay with me. But, of course, I became brave and teased and pushed him until he left.

Nice going, Fallon.

What I said was true, though. In the back of my mind was the image of Rogan as he'd turned in my direction, fully nude. The sun had kissed his skin, leading down to the most private part of him and the patch of dark hair surrounding it. I'd tried my best not to think about him like that. I shouldn't think about him like that, but how could I not? He was beautiful and shone brighter than his two friends.

Even thinking about Rogan in that way made my

skin feel hot and tight, and my body reacted in a way that was new to me. I knew it wasn't normal. But when I thought about it, nothing had been normal about my relationship with him. We'd always been close and done stuff together. He had never once told me to get lost and leave him alone. He'd always been there.

Was that why he'd started looking like my favorite dessert and I'd fallen in love with him? We never talked about our last camping trip, or the wedding where I begged him to kiss me. His words had sent my heart soaring seconds before he crushed it as he dragged me back inside the country club.

I did understand why things between us had to be different but, at the same time, the same as usual. I just didn't like it.

As I drifted off to sleep, I dreamed of Rogan as I saw him by the river.

17

FALLEN

JULIA AND I WERE AT THE RIVER WITH THE BOYS AFTER Rogan had made a big deal about the last time he'd gone swimming with his friends. We all had swimsuits on this time, but, unfortunately, one of the guys had invited Corinne and her friends along. I suspected Corinne had been the one to wrangle the invitation out of them. Corinne, Mandy, and SuAnne got comfortable on towels opposite me and Julia.

Rogan still hadn't gone on his *date* with Corinne and she wasn't happy about it. I couldn't understand why he didn't just cancel instead of keeping her hanging. The girl could barely hide her anger when the guys had dropped their things beside me. It was how it had always been, especially for Rogan. He knew I wouldn't let anyone do shit to his clothes while he was swimming or just messing around.

I didn't miss the look Corinne kept giving Rogan, and not only was it annoying me, it was bugging the shit out of Julia too. I was still annoyed at Rogan for agreeing they could join us. Surely he could have disagreed, but he didn't. We'd never hung out with the other three before, and I was jealous. I shouldn't be, but it was there, eating away at me.

"Ignore them," Julia whispered.

"It's not that easy," I hissed.

I got an uneasy feeling as I moved my gaze toward my best friend before I focused on the guys. Today they wore shorts while I wore a bikini, along with Julia. I was sure Rogan would go nuts when I removed my shorts and T-shirt. He hated his friends looking at me, and they would be looking once I revealed the skimpy bikini.

I glanced out of the corner of my eye and watched Julia strip down to her blue bikini while Leon tried his best not to be too obvious about staring at her. Chase thumped him on the arm, and Leon lost his balance and fell into the river. While Chase was bent double laughing at the idiot, Rogan gave Chase a shove and he fell in too.

They both came up spluttering water.

While Rogan was distracted with the two idiots, I tossed my clothing to the side and sneaked up on him. Rogan turned just as I reached out and shoved him. His eyes widened as he lost his balance. I wasn't quick enough and he grabbed my wrist, pulling me in with him.

I screamed and then I was choking as I went under the cold water. An arm went around my middle seconds before a large body pulled me to the surface, where I spluttered and cursed.

"Watch your mouth," Rogan hissed in my ear, although he was laughing, splashing me with droplets of water as he shook his head just like a dog would do.

Julia joined us and jumped in close to Leon, and the boy didn't disappoint. He tugged her up to the surface and laughed when she attached herself to him. His grin became wider when he swam off with her without anyone complaining.

"At least she's no longer using me." Rogan kept us afloat, and I let him, enjoying the feel of being pressed against his hard body.

"She saw Leon the other week, so I think she has ideas...being obsessed with sex and everything."

Rogan tightened his grip on my waist and pulled me in close until his reaction to my closeness pressed against my thigh. He cursed under his breath and put me slightly away from him.

"I thought I told you to forget about that." He glared, and his chest heaved. "Fallon, answer me."

"You didn't ask me a question." I rolled my eyes and tried to move away but he wouldn't let go.

"You're a pain in my butt," he growled, climbing out of the river. He held his hand out for me and, with a tug, we were both standing on the bank dripping wet with Corinne and her friends glaring at us, or rather me. The look Corinne gave Rogan was meant to entice, but he ignored her.

Inside I was laughing my head off, but thought better of doing it to the girl's face, even with Rogan standing next to her.

I bent over and grabbed a towel, tossing an extra one to Rogan. His eyes widened and his jaw visibly tensed when he looked me over. I knew he would be annoyed at my bikini, but I thought he'd let it go since we weren't alone. He usually did, but I didn't think I was going to get away with it this time.

In one stride, Rogan moved in front of me with his back toward Corinne and friends, and hissed between clenched teeth, "What are you wearing?"

"What does it look like?" I held his gaze, anger flashing in my eyes. "There is nothing wrong with it."

"You're showing too much skin." Rogan turned and headed toward the water, but then stormed back. "Chase can't take his eyes off of you in that. I really don't want to kill him for having dirty thoughts about you." He stormed off and hurled himself into the water, but not before I heard him curse loudly.

"Seems like there's trouble with the Scott siblings," Corinne said, gloating. "Love dies." She sighed. "I can't wait for that to happen between you two. Maybe he'll concentrate on what's around him, instead of trying to keep you safe from his friends." She rolled her eyes. "Chase only wants you because you're forbidden fruit. As soon as he's had you, he'll throw you away."

I hid my reaction, instead of letting the *bitch* see how much she'd gotten to me. "Yeah well, that's the thing about siblings. One minute we're arguing and the next we're best friends again." I grabbed my things together and turned to face Corinne. "I love my brother and I'm not embarrassed to admit it. That won't ever change."

"Corinne," Rogan shouted, moving closer to me, water dripping down his body with Chase beside him.

I couldn't think with the beautiful sight in front of

me, but Rogan's angry glare at Corinne certainly brought me back to the present.

"What is your problem? Fallon is my sister and we'll always stick together, so leave her alone." He stared at Corinne for a few tense moments before he slung his arm around my shoulder, and turned me toward home. "Go change," he whispered.

I was about to say something back, but the look Rogan gave me was serious, so I decided to keep quiet and headed toward the house instead. I wasn't going to do what he wanted, though. We were supposed to be going to the movies soon, so if he thought I was going to put jeans and a sweater on in this heat, he was mistaken. Rogan hadn't been specific, but he'd meant for me to be completely covered so his friends wouldn't look at me. His best friends were off limits. I wasn't even sure I'd date them if I could. I liked Chase, but I'd known him since I was five, which made no sense considering how obsessed with Rogan I'd become. I'd known him since I was two.

"Stop talking to yourself." Rogan ran up beside me. "Julia was complaining you were alone, so I came to rescue you since Corinne volunteered."

My head snapped around. "You better keep her away from me. That girl is trouble."

"That's exactly what you are in that scrap of material." He glanced over me again before averting his eyes.

"God," I grumbled, "you sound just like Dad."

"That's because Dad knows exactly what teenage boys want," Rogan said.

I stopped and forced him to look at me. "You're only thirteen months older than me. Still a teenager. Just like Chase is." I smirked. "He's hot." I ignored Rogan when his jaw dropped open and I quickly entered the house and ran upstairs to my bedroom.

A few minutes later, as I tugged a maxi dress over my head, Rogan pushed his way into my room and slammed the door closed. He leaned against it with his ankles crossed.

"You can't be encouraging my friends, Fallon."

"I could have been naked in here," I commented, dismissing his.

His eyes heated. "You're not."

"I could have been." I snapped my mouth closed and pulled a pair of socks on before sitting on the bed to put my Converse on. "Not that you'd notice," I muttered.

Rogan rubbed at his forehead. "I'd notice…What is going on with you?"

"You keep asking me that."

"Because you haven't answered."

"I can't answer if I don't know the answer." I shrugged and laid back so I could stare at the ceiling. "Do you ever get tired of having people watching you all the time? Like they're waiting for you to put a foot down wrong before they pounce and point out what an idiot you are."

"Let me grab a towel." He headed toward the bathroom. "Don't go anywhere."

I stared and wondered what was going through Corinne's head if she was waiting for me to have a big falling out with Rogan. That wasn't all, what did Corinne mean by looking around him? Rogan saw just fine. He had his head screwed on better than anyone I knew.

Rogan came back into the room and my eyes widened when I saw a blue bath towel wrapped around his waist.

"My shorts were wet," he said in explanation. "Don't want to soak the couch." He shrugged, dropping onto it. "The answer to your question is yes, I get fed up with it all. Always having to be on top in order to perform on the field. Everyone expects something from me...except you." He smiled softly. "You never expect anything from me, and yet, you're always there cheering me on, defending me."

"You do the same for me."

"I'm supposed to. I'm your older brother." He smirked, knowing how much him saying that annoyed me.

"By thirteen months." I grinned. "Remember that."

He rolled his eyes and laughed. "As though you'd let me forget."

"Right, buster." I rolled to my stomach. "Does Leon really like Julia?"

Rogan laid on his stomach and frowned. "He doesn't really say much, but, after today, I'm guessing he does. He likes to jerk around, but he only does it with the girls he really likes."

"I've seen firsthand how Leon likes to *jerk* around."

Rogan narrowed his eyes and I grinned as I rolled over to stare at the ceiling again.

"If you keep bringing that up, I'm going to tell Leon that Julia and you watched him," he growled.

I turned my head and met his gaze, swallowing hard. "I bet you don't tell him that it's you I dream about doing that."

Rogan dropped his face into the sofa, his fists tightly clenched. When he finally lifted his face, he said, "You can't talk like that."

"Can you look me in the eye and tell me you don't imagine me naked? Touching me? Imagine what it would feel like to have my hands touching you?" My breathing was as heavy as Rogan's. "Because I imagine what it would feel like to touch you. How it would have felt if you'd been lying on the lounger on your back and my hands had slipped into the front of your shorts instead of the back. I dream, Rogan."

"You shouldn't be saying shit like that to me." He closed his eyes. "I'll never get what you said out of my head." His gaze met mine.

"I'm sixteen and in love with my brother. I've never been kissed. I bet you had by the time you were my age."

"Jeez, make me feel old, why don't you."

Silence followed and I was sure Rogan was asleep, but then he mumbled, "Don't rush into anything, Fallon… Please."

Meeting our friends for a movie was forgotten.

18

FALLEN

I HEARD A CAR OUTSIDE, AND TOSSED THE COVERS OFF the top of the bed to pad to the window. I looked out through my curtains and saw Mom and Dad drive off, and then noticed the time on the alarm clock. Just past ten. At least they'd left me in bed instead of trying to get me up and dressed for church. I didn't mind going, truth be told, but the weekends were my only time to sleep in during the school year.

I was still half asleep when I glanced toward the sofa where Rogan had fallen asleep. I'd settled down not long after, so I wasn't sure when he'd left my room, or even what happened to Julia and the others. That made me feel like the worst friend on Earth. I shouldn't have left the river without Julia, although I did trust Leon and Chase to get her home.

My clothes from the day before were wrinkled, I'd been too exhausted to wake and change. I shook my head and headed out of my room but stopped when I noticed Rogan's door slightly open.

He never left it open.

I peered through the gap and didn't see him, so I slipped inside while my heart pounded. I wasn't supposed to be in his room without him, but it was too tempting. I moved toward his bathroom and just as I poked my head around the corner, the shower came on.

Sweat broke out on my forehead and my hands clenched together against my chest as if I could keep my heart from beating right out of it. Water ran over Rogan's head, pounding down his strong back to slide over the firm globes of his butt. I gulped, unable to move. My eyes traveled down his strong thighs to his feet and then slowly moved back up the body I couldn't stop dreaming about, let alone looking at. He turned slightly, and I got a whole new look at him.

It took me a moment to realize my body throbbed in reaction to the sight before me. My eyes moved to Rogan's face but his eyes were closed, which I was glad about because my eyes wandered back to the part of him that really did make him a man. He certainly didn't look like a boy.

He was thick and swollen, larger than I thought possible. One hand gripped his penis in a tight hold as he threw his head back. The other landed on the glass shower door while the one gripping his flesh sped up. I found my breath was in time with his, and as Rogan started to groan and curse, my eyes wouldn't leave what he was doing. I watched, wanting to know what happened next. I knew what happened at the end because Julia and I had watched something on the Internet once. But I wanted to finish watching Rogan. It was so much hotter and exciting than the video we'd seen. My young body craved something unknown and I felt hot and flushed. A loud grunt and hiss from Rogan ended my musings as I watched him in the height of pleasure.

"Oh," I mumbled, and panicking, I quickly turned and ran back to my bedroom, making sure my bedroom door was locked.

I'm going to hell!

I moved quickly, and tossed my clothes off. I headed into the shower, thinking that maybe I could wash away what I'd just witnessed. Why couldn't Rogan have locked his bedroom door? I always locked mine when I was about to take a shower. Did he do it on purpose knowing we were the only two in the house? I shouldn't think like that. I couldn't.

The hot water didn't do anything for me as my heart continued to pound. My hands clenched into fists while I let the water pour down, soaking me. I had to force my hands up to my hair, which I quickly washed. I then stood on the mat, drying myself, gasping at the feel of the rough towel against my sensitive body. Just the slight touch was enough to make me blush. I was so grateful Rogan had kept his eyes tightly closed and had no clue I was there. I wasn't sure how I was going to keep the knowledge from my face. I blushed so easily, and the moment I did, Rogan would know something was up and that I was embarrassed. With my luck he'd know exactly why I was as red as a tomato.

I pulled shorts on, along with a white T-shirt and white Converse, the damp strands of my long hair haphazardly pinned to the top of my head. I coated my lips in a pale pink lip-gloss, smacking them together to make sure it was even. The full-length mirror on the closet door told me I looked good. The tee I wore used to be baggy in the chest area, but was tight after the growing up I'd done over the summer.

Not being able to put off leaving my bedroom a moment longer, I headed downstairs. Nerves fluttered in my belly after what I saw in the bathroom. I kept telling myself that I could do it. I could face

Rogan without one bit of embarrassment, or at least not where he could see it.

As luck would have it, Rogan hadn't appeared, so I popped some bread into the toaster oven and got the Keurig going. I didn't drink a lot of coffee and tended to save it for Sunday mornings. That way it was a treat. Something to savor.

"Make me one, will you," Rogan said, appearing in the kitchen. "Please," he added.

I made him a cup of coffee along with two slices of toast and jam. We ate it in silence at the kitchen table.

It was weird because I kept feeling Rogan's eyes on me and didn't really know what to make of it. I hoped he hadn't spotted me leaving his room, and that he wasn't trying to figure out what to say to me. So I waited for him to meet my gaze and then raised a brow in question, trying to forget what I saw while I sat with him over breakfast.

"Your tee shrunk in the wash." Rogan went back to his breakfast and avoided eye contact.

I smirked. "It hasn't shrunk, my boobs have grown."

The sound of a plate breaking on the tiled kitchen floor pulled my eyes toward him just in time to see him reaching for a jagged piece.

"Don't touch it." I jumped up. "I'll get the broom."

He sighed and let me clean the mess up while he did the few dishes we'd used.

"Are you meeting Leon and Chase?" I asked, looking for something to say.

"I am," he mumbled, avoiding my gaze, which ate at my curiosity.

"Am I missing something?" I asked, frowning while watching him closely. There was something he was trying to avoid telling me because it looked like he was squirming at my questions.

I was sure of it.

"No," he lied.

I narrowed my eyes at my *brother*, and announced, "In that case, I'll come with you."

His head snapped up and panic crossed his face.

"I have nothing else to do." I shrugged.

Rogan stayed quiet as I moved to stand in front of him. "Unless, you really don't want me to hang out with you?"

He inhaled and slowly exhaled. "That isn't it."

"Good. Should I ask Julia?"

He looked sick as he rubbed at his brows. "Leon already asked her." He winced.

I didn't want him to see the hurt on my face, so I gave him my back.

"Fallon," he called, an apology in his tone.

I ignored him. "I'll grab a jacket."

It hurt that he obviously hadn't wanted me to go with them—more so because Julia would be there, and Julia had been invited.

———

FROM WHERE I SAT IN THE BACK OF ROGAN'S CAR, I could see the way his thighs moved when he changed gears. I wished I were in the front instead of being squished into the back. Julia was in the middle with Leon next to her. Chase of course was in the front messing with the radio while Rogan got pissed at having the channel changed.

I hadn't had a chance to talk to Julia about what happened yesterday, and from the way she kept looking at me, I thought Julia had something to say. Not about me, but about what she had gotten up to with Leon. Which brought the image of Rogan in the shower to the forefront of my mind.

"I think I need to wash my eyes with holy water," I blurted, causing Rogan to suddenly break.

"What! Why would you make a comment like that?" Rogan looked over his shoulder and narrowed his gaze.

Sometimes I wished I could keep my thoughts to

myself because there wasn't always a filter between my brain and mouth.

Heat spread from my chest to my face and it was only Chase's laughter that got the heat off of me.

"What?"

"Ease up, man." Chase shook his head. "You probably don't want to know what she's seen."

Julia snorted.

I finally found the funny side and giggled.

Rogan threw another glare over his shoulder and I shrugged. "It's nothing to worry about."

I wondered if he could hear the nervousness in my voice. He would worry if he ever discovered what I'd seen. I didn't even want to think about what I'd seen anymore. Perhaps I needed something more than holy water.

Julia nudged me. "Holy water?" she whispered, and chuckled. "I think we need to talk."

"*We* do need to talk," I mumbled, hoping only Julia heard me.

"Good." Julia clapped her hands together. "We're here." She shoved me out of the car and laughed before slipping her arm through mine. "Restroom," Julia announced and dragged me off before another word was said.

I glanced back at Rogan from over my shoulder

and caught his gaze on me. He looked worried, which sent a bolt of unease through me. He hadn't wanted me to come with them. Why?

Shaking my head, I entered the diner with Julia. It wasn't busy, but it would be within the hour as church came to a close and families came to eat Sunday brunch. Luckily, the restrooms were empty.

"Oh my God, your face went bright red," Julia said the minute the door shut.

I turned away. "It did not go bright red."

"I'm not color blind. You were red!" Julia bumped my hip with her own while watching me through the mirror. "I'm still waiting for an explanation about the holy water."

"It just popped out of my mouth."

Julia narrowed her gaze, but let me off the hook. "So, I went swimming with Leon, and to my surprise, my best friend had disappeared with her brother. Corinne was pissed. Want to explain what happened?"

"Nothing happened." I sighed. "Rogan wasn't impressed with what I was wearing. We argued." I glanced at her. "What happened with you and Leon?"

Julia blushed and I laughed at the sight. I had no idea Julia could blush so *brightly.*

"He kissed me," Julia said so softly, and there was a

look on her face I hadn't seen before. "More than once." She clutched my arm. "He touched me and… and he gently rubbed my…you know." Julia glanced downward.

I frowned. "Boobs?"

Julia blushed even more. "Further down," she barely whispered.

My eyes widened. "What did it feel like?"

"Oh!" Julia's hands covered her cheeks as she turned the cold water on. "So good. I lost my mind." She splashed her *very* heated face. "It made me feel so good, and when he pulled my panties to the side and then touched me, I couldn't have told you my name. My body lost control."

"I feel really warm."

I splashed cold water on my face while I imagined having Rogan touch me there. Then I snapped my eyes shut tightly when the image in my head became vivid. I didn't even want to think about that. But the image wouldn't disappear. I saw his large hands moving closer and closer to my panties…

"I want to get him alone to do it again," Julia admitted, breaking into my fantasy.

Thankfully.

"Did Leon, um, you know?" I glanced down and wiggled a brow.

Julia giggled. "I'm not sure, but he felt thick when he rubbed against me." She got a sappy look on her face. "I think next time I want him to do the same but without any clothing between us."

My eyes widened and I opened my mouth to speak, but Julia quickly slapped her hand over it. "Don't say anything. I don't mean have sex. Just mess around. I want to learn everything there is to know about the opposite sex."

I nodded. When Julia removed her hand, I asked, "You do like Leon, though, right? I mean, you're not just using him?" Julia looked hurt by my question, so I added, "I'm sorry, it's just all so new to me. I don't want either of you to get hurt."

"It's okay. I laid in bed last night wondering the same thing, and you know what conclusion I came to?"

"What?"

"I really do like him. He's handsome. Looks older than he is just like Rogan and Chase do. He looks after his body. He can do calculus in his sleep—probably. He likes talking to me, and well, the way he looks at me is so sweet. I want to spend time with him."

Julia meant every word she said, and for Julia that was a lot of words in one sentence.

"Now," Julia said, "tell me the truth about the holy water. What do you need washing from your eyes?" She raised a brow and leaned her hip on the sink. "I'm your best friend and told you what happened with me, so spill."

Silence followed until I huffed out a breath, knowing I had to tell Julia something she'd believe. "I accidentally walked in on Rogan taking a shower," I admitted.

Julia gawked, and I quickly continued, "He has no idea and I'm begging you not to tell him, or anyone else for that matter. I got out of there quickly. I'm just really embarrassed."

"Why didn't he lock the door?"

"I have no idea."

"So…" Julia smirked. "Is he as big as we saw the other week at the river?"

My embarrassment was complete.

"In order to answer that question, I'd have to think about it, and I really don't want to think about it. I shouldn't have ever seen him like that once, let alone twice."

"Chase likes you," Julia said out of the blue. "Leon told me."

"I like Chase."

But it's another who I can't stop thinking about.

"We better go before they come in here looking for us." I led the way outside and nearly stumbled when Julia said, "We should double date."

"Who's double dating?" Rogan asked, having overheard Julia.

"No one," I replied at the same time as Julia said, "Leon and me, and Chase and Fallon." Julia grinned. "And you and Corinne."

Scowling, I whipped my head around to stare at Rogan. "Corinne," I mumbled, and then saw red. "You're dating Corinne? How could you do that when she's horrid to me? I thought you cancelled the *date* because you haven't been out with her."

"Jesus," he cursed. "Thanks for that Julia."

"She had to find out sooner or later," Julia added, and sauntered over to where Leon was sitting on the hood of the car, and eased her way between his legs.

I turned back to Rogan and noticed the guilt on his face.

"You really are dating her? That's why you didn't want me here today, isn't it? Are you meeting her?"

He ran a hand through his hair, refusing to look me in the eye. "We're going on one date. One. It's no big deal. I already told you this."

"Then why didn't you tell me it was happening today?"

His shoulders drooped and he said quietly, "I didn't want to hurt you."

I had difficulty breathing and wanted to hurt Rogan as much as he was hurting me. I walked toward Chase, who suddenly looked good enough to eat. I'd always liked him, but all of a sudden jealousy was eating away at me because of my insensitive *brother.*

To Chase's surprise, I moved in close and wrapped my arms around his waist, and nuzzled my face into his neck. He stilled and, seconds later, his arms wrapped around me.

"Julia said we're going to double date," I teased, and saw his eyes light up.

"I'm game, providing Rogan doesn't kill me first." Chase looked over my head.

I followed his gaze, and realized Rogan hadn't been watching us, but instead looked off toward the entrance of the diner. My heart sank when I saw Corinne walking toward us, or rather, Rogan.

Rogan dipped his head and glanced at me from beneath his brows, resignation on his face. Then I watched as he walked toward Corinne.

Chase held me around the waist and whispered, "She's the reason we're here. He invited her."

"Oh." What else could I say? Rogan brought us all on a date with *her*. "I hate her."

"We know," Chase whispered. "I think that's why he agreed to this."

I frowned and glanced up at Chase. "What do you mean?"

He opened his mouth to reply, then shook his head. "I'm probably wrong." He slung an arm around my shoulders, not letting me go.

Was Rogan doing this to hurt me on purpose? Did he want my eyes and heart focused elsewhere because of how wrong our feelings for each other were? He certainly had gotten something right and hurt me.

I looked at the ground, wishing to be anywhere but here, wondering how I was going to get myself out of it. I really did like Chase and thought he was a great guy, but I didn't *like* him in that way. Now that I'd thrown myself at him, I was stuck, unless I wanted to appear as a bitch or a tease.

One of these days I'd think first.

Rogan didn't touch Corinne in any way, regardless of her attempt to get him to hold her hand. It made me smile and my heart lighter knowing he wasn't into Corinne as much as I thought he'd like me to believe. But I frowned when I really thought about it. I didn't want him to be lonely, but at the same time, I didn't want him getting close to Corinne. The one person at school that I despised the most and he had to ask *her* to go out with him, or in this case, to hang with us.

Chase fidgeted beside me as we sat in the movie theatre. He had Leon and Julia on his other side while I had Rogan beside me. Of course, Corinne was on Rogan's right. He made it clear to Chase that he had to keep his hands off of me in the theatre. I was annoyed with him because of that comment. Rogan growled and proceeded to make sure he sat beside me.

I tilted my head to the side and watched Corinne. To her credit, Corinne appeared nervous, although I thought the girl wanted to hide the fact. Corinne came across as the most confident girl at school, and always had, but was that who she really was? Who knew? Corinne looked up and caught me staring, and she sneered in response.

I leaned in to Rogan and rolled my eyes. "I know

why you asked her out and it hurts like hell, Rogan. You had to ask the one person I don't like. Why?"

He gave me a sidelong glance. "You know why," he mumbled behind his hand. "Chase?" He held my gaze. "You know I don't like it," he growled.

"Yeah, well, I don't like who you have with you."

I sat back in the seat and tried not to make my sulking obvious. I was really annoyed with him and if I was truthful, I hated that he had someone else to give his attention to. Not that he was doing much of that. But still. I was used to being his focus, and I wasn't sure I liked anyone else getting that attention instead of me.

Huffing out a breath, I kicked my feet out to rest on the chair in front of me, and slumped down as the theatre went dark and the screen lit up.

I could still feel Rogan stewing in his seat beside me while poor Chase was right in the middle, figuratively.

Twenty minutes of adverts and trailers and I smiled when Rogan cursed close to my ear, then his arm went around my shoulders. He tugged me so that my head was on his shoulder.

"You love me. Can't be giving me the silent treatment," he whispered into my ear. "I love you too,

Fallon." He kissed my cheek and his lips lingered against my skin like a caress.

I smiled, staring at the screen while my heart thumped wildly.

"HE'S YOUR BROTHER, I GET IT," CORINNE SAID THE moment she entered the restroom and spotted me at the sink. "But why can't you *butt* out when he's on a date?"

I wasn't going to have this conversation with her because I knew it would become more of an argument. Ignoring her, I left the restroom and found the others waiting. Chase glanced between Rogan and me while Rogan concentrated on the restroom door until Corinne came out spitting fire. His eyes widened as she approached.

"I don't like being ignored," she hissed, pointedly staring at me.

"Answering won't get us anywhere, so what is the point." I sighed.

"What's going on?" Julia asked, holding Leon's hand.

"Rogan invited me out with you all, but he spent the whole movie with his arm around his *sister*."

Corinne crossed her arms in front of her. "It should have been me."

Chase nudged into Rogan when no one said anything. Rogan breathed heavily and ran his hands through his hair and down his face. He glanced at me and I noticed a small wince cross his features.

"I'm sorry. My arm should have been around you." Rogan moved into Corinne's space and tipped her face up to his.

Chase moved closer to me and slipped his arm around my waist. I needed support and, as usual, Chase didn't let me down.

Rogan continued, "Fallon is my sister and we're close. I didn't like having a disagreement hanging over our heads. We're good now. So why don't I come with you, and let the guys drive my car home."

It was on the tip of my tongue to tell him that wasn't going to work, but with one glare from Julia, I stayed quiet. I wanted to throttle Rogan. I also needed my head examined. I shouldn't be jealous of Rogan going off with another girl. He wasn't mine. Well, he was, but not in the way a man and woman were supposed to belong to each other. He needed that from someone else. Someone who he could be with where the relationship wasn't forbidden. It depressed me to think of him with anyone but me. It also caused a sharp pain in my chest.

He needed me, damn it!

I was more annoyed because of whom it was he was with, at least, that's what I convinced myself of because any other kind of jealousy was wrong.

At least we weren't as squashed together on the ride home with Rogan abandoning us. I sat in the front passenger seat while Chase drove back to the house. Instead of being annoyed, I decided I was going to enjoy my time with him. He deserved my time for sticking in there and for having my back while Rogan was being a pussy with Corinne. Begging my forgiveness.

"Who's up for a water fight?" Leon asked into the silence.

"I'm not playing in this outfit," Julia drawled. "Although, I wouldn't mind playing in another way."

I turned and smirked when Leon blushed, even though he was wearing a goofy grin. Chuckling, I glanced at Chase, whose eyes were filled with amusement and something else—worry.

Julia was currently whispering things into Leon's ear, so I gave Chase my attention, and asked, "Is everything okay?"

He smirked. "You stole my line."

"I'm sorry. Everything is okay, really. I'm just annoyed that out of all the girls at school, he had to ask *her*. She hates me."

"She doesn't hate you. She's jealous of you."

"What? No way? Why would she be jealous of me?" I stared at Chase, who conveniently decided to spend more time watching where he was going.

"You don't see it. How Rogan is with you compared to everyone else. Even us. His best friends." Chase briefly turned and smiled before looking back at the road. "He's possessive of you, and you encourage him."

"I do not." I sat back against the seat and thought about what Chase said. Did I encourage him? I probably did when I thought about it. I just didn't like others picking up on it. "He's my brother," I said to no one in particular, and then realized how stupid that sounded. "I mean, it's always been Rogan and me. I can't imagine him not being in my life."

"No one would expect anything different; it's just that the way you are together. It's like you're more than best friends—more than siblings. To someone who doesn't know you both, it looks weird is all I'm trying to say." Chase finished on a mumble.

"Hmm. I guess." I couldn't really say anything else because it was true. I should feel guilty for the way I monopolized Rogan's time, but I didn't. I was used to him being with me all the time and it felt weird when he wasn't. I really didn't want to think about what he was doing with Corinne.

Chase pulled the car into my driveway, and relieved, I stumbled out having to blink back tears.

Chase glanced at me.

"Come on, I'll get us something to drink." I suggested and grabbed his hand. "I'm sorry."

He smiled. "You don't have to apologize. In fact, I figured I'd have some apologizing to do when we got back here if I wanted an invitation inside."

I squeezed his hand. "You only spoke the truth. Nothing to apologize for. I'll get over it."

He muttered something but when I eyed him, he grinned. "I think there's a game on."

"What?"

"Baseball. I can hear the sounds coming from your living room."

"Really?" Laughing, I opened the door and followed the sound. Chase sat right down on the sofa and forgot all about me, much to my amusement.

Dad noticed us. "Honey, can you grab me a beer and some chips." He glanced at Chase. "No beer for him, but chips."

In the kitchen, Mom was making lasagna for

dinner while she listened to an audio book. It wasn't until I heard, "swell of his manhood," that I made my presence known, much to Mom's embarrassment.

She laughed it off. "Sorry. I thought you were out with Rogan."

"Ugh! I was. He dumped me for Corinne, of all people."

"Oh, honey." She patted my hand and turned back to layering the meat and noodles. "Where's Julia? Can't you hang with her, instead of your brother?"

I frowned. "Mom, I usually hang with Julia."

"Did you say where she is?"

"No, I didn't. She's out with Leon."

"Oh," Mom mumbled.

"Chase is in the living room with Dad."

She turned and stood with her hands on her hips, a big smile on her face. "Chase, huh? I always knew that boy liked you."

"Mom, it isn't like that." I wasn't entirely sure what it was like. "Chase is… I don't know." I dropped my arms and faced the table.

Mom came up behind me and stroked my hair. "There's no rush, honey. You'll be seventeen in a week and you have your whole life ahead of you. Just because Rogan is finally getting out there and dating, doesn't mean you have to." Mom sighed. "I want my baby girl to stay mine for a bit longer."

I smiled. "I'll always be your baby girl, Mom, even when I'm married with kids of my own."

She chuckled. "I'll remind you of that when I'm butting into your adult life."

"Butt in all you want. Anything to stop me from making the wrong choices."

"Hmm." Mom sat beside me and asked, "Do you want to tell me what is really bothering you?"

"Not really."

"That wasn't an option."

"Figured," I mumbled and turned my face toward her. "I hate that Rogan has gone out with someone I can't stand. She's always saying bad stuff to me at school, and degrades Rogan." I moaned. "Why is he doing that to me?"

Mom sighed. "Does he know how you feel?"

"Yes."

"Then perhaps he's hoping that if he dates her, you'll accept her and maybe become friends."

I didn't want to become friends with her.

"Maybe," I replied, not really believing it.

A knowing look crossed her face. "Wouldn't you want to be friendly with the girl if she makes your brother happy?"

"I..." I opened my mouth to speak, but paused before I continued. "Yes, I would."

"There you go." Mom got up and placed the lasagna in the oven. "Dinner will be in an hour. Why don't you take that beer to your dad, and the chips and dip into the living room? Maybe watch the game with Chase." She grinned.

I rolled my eyes and took the offerings from Mom and went to join the boys.

19

FALLEN

It was my seventeenth birthday and I was miserable.

For the past week, I'd been putting on a brave face, but it hurt seeing Rogan and Corinne together. When Rogan was with Corinne, she was all smiles and acted shy, but when it was just me, she was a bitch to put it mildly. I didn't know what her game was. I'd been waiting for Rogan to realize what Corinne was really like, which I actually thought he knew already.

I'd spent more time with Chase because of Rogan's defection, and we'd both agreed we did better as friends than anything else. Chase had tried to kiss me and it was awkward to say the least. I hadn't been comfortable and was more shocked than anything. We'd laughed it off and hadn't mentioned it since. He was a great friend, and I thought he realized how upset I was about the whole Corinne thing.

Sighing heavily, I zipped up the side of my dress and stood in front of the mirror in my room. The dress was cream with green leaves. It came to mid-thigh and fluttered around me in soft waves. The back fastened behind my neck with an opening to the waist. I was a bit nervous about not wearing a bra, but my breasts, albeit on the large side, were firm. I was lucky, at least that's what Julia had said. The dress was daring for me as I got used to the new figure I'd acquired over the summer.

I smiled to myself and pinned my hair loosely to the top of my head, and then applied new red lip-gloss. I pouted and thought about what Rogan would say about my choice of dress. I'd done well the past week with my thoughts being on the more *healthy* side of our sibling relationship—the side we should have been on all along. I was still annoyed with him. He knew it too by the way he had stayed away from my room. I wasn't sure what to make of his absence.

We'd always been back and forth between each other's rooms. Not a day usually went by without one of us searching out the other. That had changed and I didn't like it. I missed him.

A gentle knock sounded on my bedroom door. I

frowned and opened it slowly. Rogan stood on the other side, and, for once, looked unsure.

"Are you going to let me come in?"

I stepped back.

Rogan closed the door and slowly looked me over to the point that I twitched, waiting for him to say something. When he did, I hadn't been expecting his words.

"You look beautiful." He cleared his throat. "So grown up." He frowned and glanced away.

That was when I noticed he held a small neatly wrapped present in his trembling hands. "Is that for me?"

He smiled and briefly met my gaze. "You didn't think I'd let your birthday go without buying you a present, did you?" He shook his head. "Shame on you." Passing me the box, Rogan watched me nervously as I opened it, a smile on his face.

I felt giddy as I ripped into the paper and gasped when I found a pair of earrings. The exact same pair I'd had my eye on in the town's jewelry store. The small delicate circle of gold had a lilac stone in the center.

"They're so beautiful." I looked up at Rogan and saw pleasure spread across his face.

"I have something to go with them." He handed

me another package and grinned. "You need a matching set."

Passing Rogan the earrings, I tore into the other package and found a matching necklace and bracelet.

"Rogan," I whispered, looking up into his eyes. "Thank you." I felt tears prickle behind my eyelids as I threw myself into his arms.

He laughed and wrapped his arms around my waist, holding me tightly. "Happy Birthday, Fallon."

The air became thick and I struggled for breath. My heart threatened to thud out of my chest with how close he was. My breasts were pressed into his chest and it wasn't supposed to feel so good to be held in his arms. My body wasn't supposed to come alive in that way. Not with Rogan. Never with him.

I quickly pulled away and gave Rogan my back so he couldn't see the reaction he caused in me. I passed him the box with the jewelry in it. "Will you fasten the necklace for me? I want to wear it to dinner."

Rogan made a funny noise and, after a pause, slowly reached around and brought the necklace to the front of me, fastening it in place. He stayed there and it caused a shiver to ripple down my spine when I felt the light touch of his fingers in the opening down the back of my dress.

"You're showing too much skin," he whispered. "You need a jacket."

"It's too warm for a jacket and I like this dress," I replied, moving out of his reach. "We should go." Slipping my feet into a pair of high-heeled sandals, I sat on the bed to fasten them, my hands shaking so badly that I ended up struggling.

Rogan knocked my hands away and knelt at my feet. "We'll be here all day." He took my ankle and gently fastened one sandal and then the other.

When he straightened, I admitted, "You look good, Rogan."

He was wearing a pale blue, long-sleeved tee with his best blue jeans. Instead of the usual Converse on his feet, he had replaced them tonight with his brown boat shoes.

"Thanks." He offered me his hand, and I felt bad when he asked, "Are we good? I hate falling out with you."

"I hate that too and I miss you…but, I don't want to hang out with Corinne." I sighed. "I'm sorry, but she doesn't like me, and the feeling is mutual. Seeing you with her hurts a lot. You obviously don't mind her; so let's just go out to dinner before we end up arguing. I want my brother by my side tonight." I smiled and slid my arm through his.

"Rogan," Mom shouted. "Corinne is here."

I froze and glared at Rogan. "What? Please tell me she's not coming to dinner with us."

Rogan paled. "I was going to tell you—"

Annoyed and upset, I yanked my arm from his and stepped away. "Tell me now," I demanded, tears threatening to override my commonsense.

"Corinne's parents have arranged something…" He trailed off, and his meaning slowly sank into my brain.

"You're dressed up to go out with her, aren't you? You're not coming with us?"

"I am coming with you, then after, I'm going to her parents' thing. I'm sorry, Fallon. I didn't know what to do." He tilted my face up to his. "I told her I wasn't missing your birthday for anyone." He winced. "She wasn't happy, but you come first."

"I sound like a child complaining when I tell you I don't want her to come with us. I was looking forward to having you to myself. She's always around now and I hate her." My lips trembled while I was on the verge of a full meltdown, my heart breaking.

He hesitated and kissed the side of my head, whispering, "It's for the best…I'll see you downstairs."

The bedroom door closed seconds later.

IT WASN'T AS DIFFICULT AS I THOUGHT IT WOULD BE TO ignore Corinne. Corinne's smile went through me and I wanted to strangle the girl, or punch her in her smug face. Thanks to Mom, I ended up sitting opposite Corinne and Rogan. Corinne was *his* date after all.

Mom wanted me to be friends with Corinne because of Rogan, but I just couldn't bring myself to take that step. Corinne wasn't the nice girl my family thought she was, so I was totally okay with ignoring her.

We all ate in silence and I couldn't bring myself to break it. It was the first year where my birthday dinner had been a total disaster and I couldn't wait to finish eating and leave.

Mom and Dad kept passing glances back and forth while I was sure Rogan felt just as uncomfortable as I did. Corinne on the other hand looked to be enjoying every moment of the awkwardness. I wanted to lean over the table and scratch her eyes out for ruining my birthday. I was actually dreading Rogan's birthday in four weeks' time. Why couldn't he have chosen someone *I'd* like?

Because you wouldn't like anyone he was with. That's why!

Sulking, I winced when my usual birthday dessert was pushed in front of me. I wanted to hurl. I looked up and noticed everyone watching me, and instead of picking up the spoon to dig into the mountain of profiterole, cream, and chocolate sauce, I swallowed around the lump in my throat and pushed the plate away.

"I can't eat it." I looked at my parents and saw the worried look on their faces. "I'm sorry." I got to my feet, and added, "I need a minute."

I didn't wait for a response as I quickly made my way to the back patio, which, luckily for me, was empty. I wrapped my arms around my stomach as I moved into the dark, not wanting to be seen from the windows. Goose bumps prickled my arms when I heard my name whispered.

Tears hovered and fell from my eyes as I fought for control, but I was slowly losing it. I had everything most people wanted: parents who loved each other, a roof over my head, my own nice things, and love. So why was I so unhappy?

"You can't continue to ignore me," Rogan whispered from directly behind me. "I'm sorry, Fallon. I've ruined your birthday by bringing Corinne. I shouldn't have done it."

"Just leave. Take her and go. Maybe if she isn't in my sight, I might be okay." I dipped my head not really believing it.

"I'm not leaving until you've danced with me. We always dance on our birthdays. Ever since we were younger."

I felt the heat from his body against my back as he moved closer, and after a slight hesitation, he slid his arms around my middle and pulled me against his body.

He rested his chin on the top of my head and sighed. "You scare the shit out of me," he admitted, and placed a kiss to my shoulder before he turned me around. One arm went behind my back, keeping me tightly pressed against his big body, and his hand captured one of mine. "We're dancing out here tonight." He slowly started to sway to the music in his own head. "Relax and let me give you this much."

I sank further into him, burying my face in his neck while my tears continued to fall. His hand slipped into the back of my dress and his fingers caressed my skin, causing shivers of pleasure to ripple through me. I pressed my breasts against his chest and he moaned, holding me even tighter. I felt him move against me and my heart pounded. My tears stopped as I concentrated on the feelings coursing through me. Things I shouldn't feel because of the boy who currently held me as though his life depended on it. We'd entered dangerous territory and I didn't think he cared. I didn't. How could I when my heart craved him close, if not closer?

He swallowed hard when my lips brushed his throat. I felt his reaction in the rigid pressure against my belly. His hand slowly moved from my dress and gently pressed against my bottom. Smoothing my dress down, he massaged the round globes of my flesh. My whole body was coming alive just like I'd read in romance novels.

Rogan's hands shook as he moved them to my shoulders and pushed me away from his body. I moaned and tried to get back into his arms, but he held me steady.

When I looked up into his face, he was fighting with himself.

"We can't ever be in this position again," he whispered. "We can't, Fallon. It's wrong. You know it is. So do I."

I felt him slipping away from me, and mumbled, "But you want this as much as I do," not wanting to give him up. "You want me?"

"I'll never have you." He quickly turned and dashed back inside while I was left in the dark with tears running down my face.

Mom found me sitting on the patio steps of the restaurant ten minutes later. She didn't say anything but wrapped an arm around me, allowing me to bury my face into her shoulder.

"I hate her, Mom."

She sighed. "I know honey." She kissed the top of my head. "Everything will work out in the end. You'll see."

I cried until I didn't have any tears left, and then I said, "I want to go to Julia's house."

"We'll drop you off on the way home," Mom suggested.

"Can't I drop you guys off and then I'll have the car to get home afterward?"

Mom hesitated.

"I've taken the car before."

"If your father agrees, then you can take the car."

We both knew Dad would say yes. He always did after he gave me a careful driving lecture.

I smiled and threw my arms around her. I was glad she had agreed because I had no intention of going to Julia's. I just wanted to be alone to think and cry without anyone hearing me.

PART II

Rogan, 18 / Fallon, 17

20

ROGAN

THE GRIEF I FELT HOLDING FALLON'S PALE HAND IN mine was nothing I ever wanted to feel again. Fallon was everything to me, and because of a sense of right and wrong I'd pushed her away and pretended I had feelings for Corinne. That was the worst mistake I could have made. I'd only continued with the annoying girl because I knew how much Fallon hated her, and that kept her away from me. *My* sister. The girl I was in love with. Every time I thought about my feelings for Fallon my stomach rolled.

My eighteenth birthday came and went since she'd been in the hospital. I barely left her side and I pushed everyone away. Including Corinne. I told her it was over the moment I got the call about Fallon being involved in an accident. The bitch Corinne had asked if I could wait another couple of hours for her parents' party to be over before I ran to the hospital. I'd barely controlled the urge to shake her.

The call from Dad on the evening of Fallon's seventeenth birthday had turned my world upside down. She'd been coming back into town from who knows where when a driver in a truck ran a stop sign. The bastard crushed the family car and had very nearly taken Fallon's life. As it was, Fallon had been in a coma for a month, and I knew the doctors were now wondering if she would ever wake up. In order to stop the internal bleeding, they'd had to remove her uterus. She would never have children, the family I knew she wanted one day.

I never got to tell her how much I loved her and that I still considered her my soul mate, even though I told her every day she'd been in the hospital. The one good thing with her being in a coma was that she was mending without having the pain to deal with, and she was breathing on her own. I prayed for her to wake up and talk to me. So I could tell her how sorry I was for being a jerk. For trying to do the right thing. I had done and said what I had because of who we were to each other. Never did I think she'd nearly lose her life so shortly afterward.

I was supposed to protect her from the world, but

I'd failed. I hadn't been there. I wasn't with her to hold her hand when she realized the truck was heading toward her and there was nothing she could do to avoid it. I couldn't get that image out of my mind.

It haunted me when I closed my eyes.

I dropped my forehead to the bed beside our joined hands and jerked at the sound of the door opening. My eyes lifted to the doorway, and I saw Mom and Dad's worried expressions.

"You need to go home, Rogan, and get some proper sleep," Mom said.

I shook my head and said, "I'm not leaving until Fallon does." My voice broke and I had to swallow back tears. "I can't, Mom."

She sighed. "I know." Her shoulders dropped as she moved behind me and placed her arms around my neck. "I had to try. You're my son and I'm worried about you."

"I'm fine." I closed my eyes, not believing my words.

"Let us sit with our daughter for a while," she said softly.

She wanted me to move so she could take my seat, but I wasn't sure I had it in me to move. I was afraid if I did, I wouldn't see Fallon again. It terrified me.

Mom knew this. "I promise to look after her while you're gone." She smiled. "Please go and take a break. They've just started serving dinner in the cafeteria, go eat something proper, and then come back." She kissed me on the cheek. "What happened wasn't your fault, Rogan. Please accept that."

I stood on unsteady legs, knowing I was about to break down if I didn't get out of the room quickly. I let Mom pull me into her arms and kiss my forehead. Dad squeezed my shoulder.

"We love you. Now go and take an hour." Dad smiled.

I quickly made my way outside of the room and then found my feet wouldn't move. I fell against the wall and slowly sank down, ending up on my butt. I drew my knees up and rested my forehead on top of them while I breathed and tried to concentrate.

I was a wreck.

A mess.

Was that normal?

I couldn't stop thinking about what Fallon truly meant to me and, every time, I came to the conclusion that she was more than my sister. She was everything to me. I couldn't survive without her. I had no wish to. Fallon wasn't only my sister; she was the girl I'd given my heart to.

As I felt myself tempted to give in to my desire for her, I'd pushed her away. Something was going to have to change *when* she woke up, because I wasn't letting her go. I realized that. I wasn't even sure I was actually able to let her go. So what did that make me?

Suddenly, alarms went off and I stared at the flashing light above Fallon's door. I couldn't comprehend what was happening as medical staff rushed into her room, and then Dad appeared out of nowhere, tugging me to my feet. He threw his arms around my shoulders and pulled me tightly against him. His face wet against mine.

My head buzzed as I tried not to think the worst, and then Dad cupped my face in his large hands. "She's awake." He sobbed, holding onto me.

I raised my face to his and searched his eyes for any sign of something, I didn't know what. Dad gently shook me, and smiled through his tears. "She's awake." He laughed. "Your mom panicked and hit the wrong button, which is why all hell broke loose just now."

"She's going to be okay," I mumbled and proceeded to break into tears.

Dad looked stunned but then pulled me back into his arms and held me while I cried. It was the first time I'd truly let my tears free since I'd gotten the call about Fallon. I couldn't stop. Sobs racked my body as Dad held me up, and it was only when I felt a soft hand on the back of my head that I calmed enough to lift my face.

"The doctor is assessing her and then he'll remove the tubes," Dad whispered. "You can see her soon." He patted me on the back.

I spent the next forty minutes pacing outside of her room when Mom finally came out. She reached for me and cupped my face. "I promised Fallon I'd go and find you." She smiled through her tears. "Go and have a few minutes alone with her. She wants you."

I nodded, and ignoring the wreck I must look, I pushed into her room.

I swallowed hard as I met Fallon's gaze. She still didn't have a lot of color, but she was slightly propped up on pillows in the overly large bed. Tears fell slowly down her face as she looked at me, and that got my feet moving. Careful of her injuries, even though most were more or less healed, I slipped off my sneakers and climbed onto the bed bedside her.

Fallon tried to cuddle into me as I slipped an arm around her shoulders, but we got a bit tangled with the wires. Smiling, I sorted them out and sighed once she was settled. She was partly on her side as I cradled her against my chest. I had to remind myself not to crush her.

"Mom said you never left me, only when she made you." Her voice was weak, but with each word she spoke, it seemed to gain strength. It assured me that she was going to be okay.

"You're everything to me, Fallon." I kissed the top of her head. "How could I ever leave you?"

"I don't know whether I was dreaming or not, but I heard you talking to me. Telling me how much you loved me. How sorry you were for, and I quote, 'The bitch.' I'm pretty sure you called yourself an asshole once or twice too."

Groaning, I couldn't help the smirk on my lips. "To my embarrassment, you weren't dreaming." Fallon tilted her face to look up at me, so I admitted, "But I'm glad you heard me." I looked away. "I am sorry, Fallon. For everything. For the hurt I caused because of Corinne."

"Look at me Rogan."

I turned and met her beautiful green eyes.

"I know what we feel is wrong, but it's there anyway and we're just going to have to live with it. I don't ever want to feel like I did back at the restaurant again." She sighed and snuggled closer, and then clarified. "I enjoyed dancing with you, and the way being close to you made me feel—made you feel—but I hated that you left to go to her."

"It wasn't by choice," I admitted. "I was scared about how I felt. I was losing control around you." I kissed the top of her head. "We've always been friends and that's what is important. We can't ever lose that between us again. No matter what."

I felt her tears seep through my tee while my own fell down my face and into my hair.

I needed Fallon to breathe.

21

———

FALLEN

It had been three months since I'd left the hospital, and physically I'd made a complete recovery. I had scars I hadn't had before, and I no longer got a period, which had its advantages and disadvantages considering my young age. I was aware that one day the fact I couldn't have children might affect me more than it currently did, but I was handling it okay.

Part of me felt like my family was walking around on eggshells. As though I had deliberately put myself in the path of the truck because of how upset I'd been. That wasn't the truth. I'd do anything to turn back the clock and not be at that particular intersection at that particular time. What happened couldn't be undone and it was something I had to live with, and so did my family.

My relationship with Rogan was stronger than ever, but we made sure never to be alone because of how our feelings had grown beyond anything they ever should have. He was the only one I saw when I should never have seen him in the first place.

In the privacy of my own room, with the only light being from my e-book reader, I read one of my romance novels. My breath caught as the main character started to touch himself in the shower. The image in my mind was of Rogan when I'd watched him shower and witnessed his pleasure. The images were always Rogan and myself, of our bodies entwined together.

I had never even been kissed, which made me sad. I didn't think Rogan would help me out with any of that kind of life experience. He'd probably be mad if I asked him. The truth was he'd be mad as hell if I asked anyone else.

Frustrated, I tossed the e-reader to the bedside table and turned onto my stomach. I couldn't go on in the same way anymore. Desiring someone I was never supposed to think about in that way, let alone crave.

With dreams in my head, I slowly slipped into sleep.

I'M TIRED AS I PULL UP TO THE INTERSECTION.

The light turns green and I continue through.

A loud car horn blares and I turn to look, only to have something smash into the opposite side of the car. Pain rips through me, and I scream for Rogan...and scream...and scream...

"Fallon, wake up."

I was rocked from the side and felt a warm body beside me.

"Fallon," Rogan growled. "You need to wake up now."

"I'm awake," I mumbled, not recognizing my voice. "I think."

"You scared the life out of me when you screamed. I thought you were being murdered." Rogan pulled me against him and I felt his heart thudding wildly in his chest. "You scared me." He wrapped himself around me, so I turned in his arms and wrapped mine around him.

He only wore shorts and his chest was warm as I snuggled against him.

"I'm sorry I woke you," I said, not really meaning it. I was in his arms so how could I be sorry?

"It's okay. I couldn't sleep anyway," he grumbled. "What were you dreaming about?"

I buried my face into the crook of his neck so that he wouldn't see my tears. "The accident. For the split second I had before I lost consciousness, and…and… how I screamed for you."

His arms tightened around me. "It was my fault that you went off on your own. I should never have left you on your birthday, of all days."

I shook my head, no longer worried about him seeing my tears. "You did what you had to do, and although I'd rather not have had to go through that with you on my birthday, I understand it. I don't like it. It hurts too much. But I get it."

Rogan stared at me, his eyes searching my face for something—I didn't know what— while I searched his. He was so handsome with his chiseled jaw, high cheekbones, and overly long sexy hair. The girls at school were all in love with him. Not as much as I was. But he featured in a lot of girls' dreams, yet here he was, in my bed. Holding me from a bad dream about the crash. He was at home every night. Never snuck out to be with anyone else. He was always here, making sure he was close by if I ever needed him.

Our parents had accepted us being close, and I wasn't sure what to make of that. I knew they worried, and were always checking on me. So maybe they considered Rogan my watcher. Rogan certainly didn't think of himself as that.

Then something else registered with me.

"Why didn't Mom or Dad wake and check on me?" My hands fluttered on Rogan's shoulders.

"Dad opened their bedroom door, but I told him I'd go." He shrugged, and glanced away. "He knows I still would have come to check on you if he had, so he went back to bed." He blushed and then winced. "I think you may have interrupted them."

"Interrupted?" I frowned and then blushed bright red. "Eww, I didn't need to know that."

He chuckled. "You little prude."

I pinched his side and he wiggled, his hard penis slipped from his shorts and pressed against my thigh. We both froze. Rogan closed his eyes and his fists tightened on my hips, and as I slowly breathed, he moved his lower half away. "Forget that happened."

Swallowing, I met his gaze. "You want me?"

"You're not helping, Fallon," he growled.

"I've never felt a…a…um…thingy before. I mean a naked thingy on my skin before."

He looked stunned and then burst out laughing. He rolled over to his back and quickly shoved his penis back into his shorts and covered his groin with a hand. I felt his loss when we no longer touched, but perhaps it was for the best. I tried to think of it in that way.

"Thingy?" He turned his head and held my gaze. "You mean my—"

I covered his mouth. "Yes, or anyone else's for that matter."

He frowned. "You better not be touching anyone else's." He stared up at the ceiling and cursed.

"And it is eww, the thought of Mom and Dad doing it."

He blinked as if he was getting his brain back into the previous conversation.

"I mean—"

"Can we not talk about it." Rogan changed the subject. "Did you know Uncle Frank is coming over tomorrow to talk to Mom and Dad about something? I overheard Dad telling Mom, but he has no clue as to what is really going on with his brother."

"Well, that's changing the subject." I rolled to my side. "He sees too much."

Glancing at me, Rogan played with a curl of my hair before he asked, "Are you okay now if I go back to my room?"

I wanted to say no. "Yeah, I'll be fine."

He swallowed and stared at my lips before snapping his eyes up to mine. Within seconds, he was out of my room and behind the closed bedroom door.

Sadness seeped into me as I cuddled the pillow Rogan had used to my chest. I shouldn't be sad about him leaving my bedroom. I should be like any other sister and close my eyes and go to sleep, instead of playing over and over in my mind what it had felt like to feel Rogan's flesh reaching for me, pressing against my bare thigh.

If it was so wrong, why did it feel so right?

22

───────

FALLEN

ROGAN WAS NEXT DOOR HANGING OUT WITH LEON, and I was left alone to listen in on Mom and Dad's conversation with Uncle Frank. It was more information than I wanted to hear, but I found myself too intrigued to shove my ear buds into my ears and listen to music.

Apparently, Aunt Sally, Uncle Frank's wife, had had enough of him and had finally seen wisdom by kicking him out of the house. Dad was currently trying to talk him out of moving in with his "bit on the side," and Uncle Frank didn't have the sense to lower his voice down. I would be surprised if the neighbors couldn't hear every damn thing.

My ears certainly perked up when my parents said he could stay with us while he looked for his own place. The blood pounded through my head when Mom suggested Rogan move in to share my room and Uncle Frank could have Rogan's room. What was Mom doing? Didn't she know how difficult Rogan and I were finding it to keep our hands off of each other? Sharing a room wasn't going to help with that, it would only make temptation harder to resist. I teased Rogan into more, but I wasn't sure what I would do if he actually took me up on the offers…and why wasn't Dad reminding Mom of this past summer, and the conversation that took place then?

Rogan was certainly not going to be happy with the new development. There was also a matter of where he'd sleep? I had a double bed, and there was a pullout sofa bed that was uncomfortable as anything to sleep on.

They just couldn't put us together.

Quietly, I abandoned my listening post at the top of the stairs and made my way back to my room. With panicked eyes, I looked around and tried to imagine Rogan permanently in it. The sad truth was, I could imagine him permanently in the bedroom with me, which was why I knew it could never happen.

I flopped down on top of my bed, spreading my arms and legs wide as though I was making a snow angel, wanting to disappear. I didn't know one girl at school who didn't want to get naked with Rogan, and it made me angry and jealous.

Other than the farce of a relationship with Corinne, I only knew about his *date* with Debra Taylor when he was sixteen. I'd been eaten with jealousy when rumors had spread through school about the girl and Rogan.

Sighing, I suddenly realized the moment Julia found out Rogan was sharing my room I'd never hear the end of it. I'd also get some knowing looks from her, Chase, and Leon because they already thought we spent too much time together.

The door to Rogan's bedroom slammed closed, and I jumped up from my bed, ending my musings. I snuck out of my room and walked along the edge of the red runner because it was the only place where the landing didn't creek.

Usually, I'd knock on Rogan's door but what I'd just discovered meant that I barged in—stealth mode.

Not seeing him in his room meant he was in the bathroom, so I took a running jump and dived onto his bed and laid with my head hanging off. I blinked a few times when I spotted him standing in the doorway to the bathroom with a towel held in front of his groin as though he was about to shower.

"Forget how to knock?" he asked, his free hand holding onto the top of the doorjamb.

I didn't miss his eyes searching over my body, or the way his body was on display for my gaze. The way the hair around his belly button disappeared beneath the towel that was very low, showing more than he realized. I snapped my eyes closed and breathed deeply.

"Mom wants us to share a room so Uncle Frank can stay in here for a while," I gushed out and finally met his gaze.

Rogan narrowed his eyes, and getting dizzy, I flipped over to my stomach and watched my brother, who fidgeted under my gaze.

"No way is that going to happen." He shook his head in denial. "Not after *the talk*."

"That's what you're hoping, but I'm telling you, Rogan, that's what I heard. And Dad agreed." I chewed on my bottom lip.

"There is no way we can share a room," he stated with confidence, just as his towel started to slip.

He made a grab for it while I took my time really looking at him. He'd become a man. A hot one at that, so it was no wonder all the girls drooled after him. I was his sister and I couldn't keep my gaze from him, or my mind from wondering about him. Or my heart from longing for something I wasn't allowed to even think about, let alone have.

He fidgeted again and took a step back into the bathroom. "Fallon," he growled. "You have to stop looking at me like that."

"Like what?"

"Like you want to…to…never mind."

Rapidly blinking, I wondered what the hell I was doing, because he was right.

"I can't help how I look at you. You even look at me with the same hunger on your face. You know you do." I swallowed around the lump in my throat. "My friends are always telling me how hot you are. That's all I hear, so can you imagine what it will be like if word gets out that we're sharing a room." I looked anywhere but at him. "They won't leave me alone because they'll want a glimpse of you like I'm getting right now."

"You need to leave," he snapped, turning his back, which made my eyes pop wide and a smirk spread across my face.

"Um, nice butt." I giggled and had to slam a hand over my mouth when I heard someone walking upstairs.

Rogan secured the towel but not before I caught him watching me from the corner of his eye. I placed a finger over my lips before turning to the door. I should have locked the thing once I entered his room.

"I'm going in the shower," he hissed. "You have to go."

"No way." I shook my head.

Rogan grinned, a devil glare in his eyes. "The door won't stay closed, so unless you want to watch me take a shower, then I suggest you *leave*."

Telling him I'd already watched him shower was on the tip of my tongue, but I knew he wouldn't let that comment go if I blurted it out, so I kept my mouth closed, telling myself I really did need to leave. I just didn't want to face Mom and Dad, or even worse, Uncle Frank, without having a united front with Rogan.

"I'm staying and then we'll go downstairs together."

His gaze narrowed and then he grinned. I got a really bad feeling.

"Suit yourself, then."

He turned his back, dropped the towel, and stepped into the shower.

I stared transfixed at the image he made and when he turned, I got a view of his junk. His hard, thick, and long junk that looked ready to burst from the look of things. He made no attempt to cover himself.

My heart told me to take my clothes off and join him, but my head told me to get out of his room while I still could. I did neither. He shouldn't be teasing me in that way. Why was he? I couldn't catch a proper breath as I watched him stroke himself in the shower. His eyes were fixated on my body. He could probably see everything through my thin white tee. My breasts felt heavy and swollen, tingles shot to the tips. I hadn't planned on going anywhere, which was why I had no bra on.

I desperately wanted to join him, but I didn't. My feet took me back to my bedroom and I slid down the bedroom door and buried my head in my drawn up knees. I desperately tried to get the vision of Rogan in the shower out of my head. Nothing worked. I didn't think I'd ever forget the look on his face as he stroked his penis. It had looked painfully tight with need.

I stayed on the floor until there was a knock on the door.

"Fallon, open the door," Rogan whispered and knocked again. "I know you're in there."

For some reason, my lust turned to anger, so I narrowed my gaze, and quickly scrambled to my feet, and yanked the door open. Rogan stood there in jeans and a white tee, his hair all messy with a bashful smirk on his handsome face. Instead of throwing myself into his arms like I wanted to do, I grabbed him by the arm and yanked him into my room. He lost his balance and caught himself by grabbing onto me. We crashed into the dresser, my hip taking the brunt of the fall.

He straightened us out and, after one look at me, he cursed. "Where are you hurt?"

"Hip," I whined like a five-year-old. "God it hurts."

"Stop being a baby and let me look."

That snapped me out of the pity party of pain. "No way am I dropping my jeans for you."

"Jesus Christ, Fallon. Why don't you shout it out the window?"

"You smashed into me."

"You dragged me in here." He pulled his lips tight and pressed against the bridge of his nose with a finger and thumb, and said, "If I asked you to drop your jeans, let's make no mistake, you would."

"I'm not even going to think about that," I mumbled between bouts of pain.

He grinned and added, "Make sure you check that out."

"I will." I hobbled over to the bed and tried sitting down but shot back up. "My jeans are too tight to sit in now that I've hurt my hip bone. I have some shorts in the bathroom. Give me a minute." I quickly changed and dashed back into the bedroom, only to wince when I sat down in the window seat.

"How bad is it?" Rogan asked from his position lying on the bed.

"I haven't looked."

He raised a brow.

"I'll look later. You were about to tell me why you're here?"

"I forgot." He grinned.

"An apology, maybe?" I suggested.

"Apology for what?" He gave me side-eye, a sexy smirk on his fine lips.

"As if you didn't know—"

"Fallon, Rogan, can you both come downstairs, please?" Mom hollered.

"Oh God, what are we going to do?" I moaned and accepted Rogan's offered hand up from the seat. "We can't share a room, especially after that show you put on earlier. I can't be seeing that on a daily basis. I mean, I want to see that on a daily basis. But I can't. We can't. I mean—"

"Fallon," he growled, slamming his hand over my mouth, "stop waffling." He smirked. "I bet you haven't seen one that big before, huh?" He teased.

"What has gotten into you?" I snapped. "We go out of our way so that we're not alone. So that we don't end up naked together, and then you go and stroke yourself while staring at me!" I poked him in the chest. "You know I've only ever been up close and personal with you. Jerk." I mumbled the last part as I moved away from him.

Rogan frowned and looked as though he was as confused as I was, and I continued, "You can't be doing that again or saying shit to me like that." I swiped at a tear as Rogan watched me. "It hurts me, Rogan. Knowing that you're right in front of me, but I can never be with you. We need to stop teasing each other and try and get on with our lives. We have to."

He wrapped his arms around me and breathed into my ear, sending goose bumps down my spine. "I love you."

He kissed the top of my head and, taking my hand, led me out of the bedroom.

SITTING NEXT TO ROGAN AT THE KITCHEN TABLE, MY heart pounded heavily in my chest. I was supposed to be listening to our parents, but nothing was going in with all the blood rushing around in my head. I wanted to cry for everything going on in my life. Because no matter how much I craved Rogan, I knew deep down I'd never be able to say he was mine. We could never be more.

Glancing at him, I noticed his eyes on me, which made me nervous, and I blinked trying to rid my mind of his attention. My hands began to tremble while I wondered if he knew where my mind was. I wiped a sweaty palm on the leg of my shorts and made sure my arms covered my breasts. I should have put a bra on before coming downstairs, but I hadn't thought that far ahead.

Rogan noticed what I was doing and with a slight grin, he stood and reached for his sweatshirt hanging up beside the kitchen door. He passed it to me and I quickly shoved it over my head and tugged it down, covering my body.

I briefly met his gaze before he looked away and got a glazed look in his eyes. I kicked him under the table and smirked when he jerked his gaze back to mine.

His eyes snapped to our parents and Uncle Frank before returning to me.

He grinned, and asked, "What'd I miss?"

I rolled my eyes and gave him an angry scowl. "Stop daydreaming! Mom and Dad want us to share a room, remember? I've told them it's unfair considering our ages to expect that." I then hissed, "Do something."

"Um," he mumbled and got another glare from me. "She's right for once. You can't honestly expect us to share a room now." He pointedly stared at Dad. "And have you forgotten the talk?"

"What talk?" Uncle Frank asked.

Dad held Rogan's gaze and then sighed, ignoring Uncle Frank. "I haven't forgotten, Rogan, and I also think I may have overreacted." He looked between Rogan and me. "I trust you, okay? It isn't going to be for long. Just until Uncle Frank finds somewhere else."

"He has nowhere else to go," Mom added, very nearly whining.

"What about Leticia's place?" I asked, remembering his recently married daughter.

"They're newly married and don't want their father ruining it for them," Uncle Frank said. "I'm not sure I want to be there either." He glanced at us. "I'm really sorry about this, and I promise it won't be for long."

Part of me filled with a sense of dread, but another part felt elated that I was going to be able to spend more time with Rogan instead of him shutting himself up in his room all the time. Like I did, I guessed. I was just sick, but I couldn't seem to stop myself from wanting to be closer to him.

"The way I'm looking at it"—I grabbed hold of Rogan's hand—"is that this is happening whether we want it to or not. The decision has already been made and Mom and Dad are telling us this is happening." I turned to look across the table. "Want to tell me I'm wrong?"

Dad ran his hands through his hair and slowly shook his head. "You're not wrong. I'm sorry…we're sorry. I can't let my brother go homeless when, with a bit of shuffling around, we have a room for him."

The tears fell down my cheeks while I watched Rogan, who looked like he'd been punched in the stomach. I silently promised him I wouldn't spend our nights teasing him, like he did earlier with me. I was upset enough without adding anything more.

"When?" Rogan asked.

Dad didn't pretend to misunderstand him, and replied, "Now," with a wince.

I gasped and quickly left the room, my feet pounding up the stairs.

Rogan followed me upstairs and stood in the doorway of my bedroom as he watched me gaze out the window.

"We're too old to share a room," I whispered, my

voice laced with tears. "You know I want to more than anything, but this situation is wrong. I can't believe they'd even suggest it after what's been said in the past."

His feet carried him to where I was standing and he rested his hands on my shoulders. "We don't have a choice." He squeezed my shoulders and added, "I'm going to go and start moving my stuff. I don't want Uncle Frank messing with it."

I slowly inhaled and turned, blowing out a loud breath. "Let me make some room in a drawer and the closet for you and then I'll help."

"I thought you'd make me sleep in the bathtub." He joked, and my eyes widened in surprise.

"Where are you going to sleep? That pullout is lumpy."

"We'll work it out later...we've got this, Fallon. I promise." He gave me a one armed hug and then left the room.

"I hope so," I whispered after him, staring at the closet.

Sighing, I opened the door and shoved my clothes over, and then on the shelving unit, I tossed my things onto the top two shelves, leaving the bottom two for Rogan.

I still had no idea what Mom and Dad were thinking having us share a room. It wasn't right, and they were aware of that. Mom even whispered to keep our sharing to ourselves for the time being. We didn't have a problem with that, but how were we going to prevent our friends from finding out? Leon lived next door and never knocked, he just walked into our house, like we did at his. Julia was always around too. She walked in and straight up to my room.

Our parents hadn't thought it out at all. Tears filled my eyes at the problem that had been created because of their decision. As much as I wanted to be with Rogan, this wasn't the way I'd wanted it. I doubted it was the way he wanted it either. We'd pushed the boundary between our sibling relationship on more than one occasion, and now I was afraid of what was going to happen between us. We were going to be alone in the dark together, and I knew Rogan was dreading that as much as I was. It was wrong to crave the other, and we had been doing so well.

"We'll manage," Rogan whispered, watching me from the doorway. He offered a wry smile and tossed his clothes onto the bed before standing in front of me. "We're not like most siblings, Fallon." He swallowed hard. "But we can do this." He tucked a lock of hair behind my ear.

"You really believe that?" I asked, close to tears.

"If we both accept that nothing can ever happen between us in the, um, romantic way, then we can do anything."

My words lodged in the back of my throat so I nodded, and as I searched Rogan's gaze, I realized he was struggling with the situation just as much as I was.

"We can do this."

As he spoke those words, I wasn't sure if he was trying to reassure himself or me; maybe he was trying to reassure us both.

23

———————

FALLEN

Slamming my locker closed, I jumped to find Julia had been standing behind it. The look on her face wasn't one I'd wanted to see and I knew what was coming, so I quickly admitted, "Uncle Frank is staying at our house, and Mom and Dad thought it best if our friends don't come around while he's there."

Julia let out a sigh of relief. "I thought you were avoiding me."

My heart thumped in my chest and I felt a flush working its way up from my neck at the partial lie I'd just told. Mom and Dad had agreed to go along with the excuse. Uncle Frank had a big mouth and found our predicament amusing, until Dad had told him to shut up or find somewhere else to crash.

Last night had been awkward, but we'd managed it, even though I didn't think either of us had gotten any sleep. Rogan looked sexy and rumpled, and I wished he'd had time to straighten himself up a bit because all the girls were giving him the eyes while sticking their chests out.

"You know," Julia drawled, "if you stare hard enough you'll set them all on fire."

I blinked and faced my friend. "What are you talking about?"

Rolling her eyes, Julia laughed. "Your brother is the sexiest man alive and looks like he just rolled out of bed, which is why he has so many eyes on him, and you are looking like you want to burn them all at the stake."

"I don't—" Snapping my mouth closed, I glared at Amber, who was currently running her fingers over Rogan's shoulders. "I'm going to kill her."

"Hmm…" Julia narrowed her eyes. "I think you need to come with me." She slid her arm through one of mine and pulled me along.

"Where are we going?" I hissed, and caught a frown on Rogan's face as he watched me before Julia tugged me out of sight.

"We have five minutes before we have to be anywhere."

"You need to slow down," I panted. "I'm not supposed to move so quickly."

"Shit. Sorry. I forgot with holy hotness in there." She indicated the school behind us with a tilt of her head. "Look"—Julia tugged me to a stop—"I know Rogan and you are really close, especially since your accident." She chewed her lip then continued, "People are not going to be nice if you get all up in their face because they drool over your *brother*."

I ignored the way she said "brother" and swallowed back my guilt. "I can't explain it, but I hate sharing him." Which was the truth. "I know a lot of siblings at school don't get along, but Rogan and I do. I have no wish to change that for anyone."

"Then don't make it so obvious." Julia huffed. "If you weren't siblings, I'd think there was a lot more going on than what there is."

Luckily, the bell rang for the start of the school day, so Julia didn't notice my momentary panic at her observation. But as I dragged my feet back to class, I didn't know what I was panicking over, because nothing had happened.

Rogan had spent the night on the lumpy pullout while I'd slept in my bed—nothing wrong with that. We'd fallen asleep on my bed before now while watching a movie, so it was all innocent.

Keep telling yourself that.

"I don't feel well," I mumbled, and the truth was, I really didn't.

I wondered who else had noticed my jealousy where Rogan was concerned. And who else had noticed it wasn't as innocent as it should be. Julia hadn't said anything, but if I didn't get my feelings under control, Julia would.

Julia knew me and had always been around, even when Rogan and I were younger. We would defend each other against other kids. Now that we were older, I knew it wasn't right, but Rogan was mine to defend, and I was his.

"You look pale," Julia commented, finally glancing over her shoulder at me. Julia slowed and rested her hand against my forehead. "You don't feel warm."

"I just feel off. Dizzy." I offered Julia a small smile. "I'll be fine. Let's just get to class before we get in trouble."

Julia shrugged. "You know I'm only looking out for you, right?" She slid her arm through mine, her favorite thing when she was talking to me.

"I know and I guess it does look weird. I can't help it. He's always there for me, and we spend our free time together around the house. I can't just switch off from that when we're at school. It isn't that easy."

"I get that, but I think you need to try, because today, you looked like you wanted Amber to burn." Julia opened the door into the school building. "What it looked like, to anyone who doesn't know you and Rogan, is that you're a jealous girlfriend."

I made a gargling sound at the back of my throat and felt all color leaching from my face.

"Fallon?" Julia questioned. "Fallon!" Julia grabbed at my arms as I dropped like a brick to the hard floor.

MY HEAD HURT LIKE A BITCH AS ROGAN'S VOICE filtered into my mind. He was arguing with someone and I heard my name, but nothing else made any sense. All the words were jumbled.

Blinking my eyes open, a fierce pain ripped through my skull so I quickly snapped them shut again and groaned. "My head," I gasped, reaching to press against my temples.

"Fallon, thank God," Rogan whispered right next to my ear. "The paramedics are on the way up, but I'm not going to leave you, okay?"

I grabbed blindly for him and relaxed slightly when he clasped my hand with his. "I'm not leaving you alone, Fallon," he stated.

"What happened?" I mumbled.

"You collapsed on top of Julia." I caught amusement in his voice before he said, "You just went and Julia wasn't strong enough to stop you from clonking your head on the floor."

"Is she okay?"

"Worried about you, but yeah, she is."

"All right, back to class," Principal Tanner muttered. "You as well, Rogan. Your sister is in capable hands now that the paramedics have arrived."

"Hell no!" Rogan shouted and then lowered his voice. "I'm not leaving her. Where she goes, I go."

There was silence until the paramedics entered the room and then I heard Rogan telling them what happened, and about what had happened to me over four months ago, while they examined me and put a collar around my neck.

The moment the collar snapped into place, panic set in. I hated being restricted and that was how I felt right at that moment. My breathing turned heavy and my body became warm and hot, too hot.

Then I felt Rogan stroking my face. "Fallon," he whispered. "Breathe for me. I'm not going to leave you. I promise." I felt him brush a kiss to my forehead.

"Is there anything else we need to know?"

I slightly peeled my lids open and caught the tail

end of what the paramedic was asking, but my half-gaze was fixed on Rogan.

He smiled and although he was holding my gaze, he answered, "I told you she was in a serious car accident." He swallowed hard. "She was stuck inside. The collar you just put on her is causing her to panic."

"Ah, I understand now." A paramedic moved into my line of sight. "Hopefully it won't be on for long, but we do need to strap you down to transport you to the hospital. We need to make sure nothing else happens to you."

"I've got this." Without thinking, Rogan picked me up into his arms. "Lead the way."

"You shouldn't be doing that?"

"It's the only way to do it and keep her calm." He held me closer and whispered, "I've got you."

My eyes drifted closed as I settled with my face hidden in Rogan's neck. His scent calmed me and I drifted off to sleep knowing I was safe.

***

"Why does my head hurt?"

I reached up and touched my forehead before I peeled my lids open. The light coming in through the window was bright so I turned my face away. That was when I noticed Rogan spread out on one of the chairs in the room. A frown appeared on my face when everything came rushing back to me.

"I passed out at school?"

"Yeah. You did. Scared the crap out of me when Julia burst into my class announcing the fact."

I groaned. "What did she say?"

"She looked directly at me and shouted over the class that you'd collapsed and weren't waking up." Rogan closed his eyes and ran a hand over his face. "My heart dropped to my feet." He sighed. "Luckily, you have a hard head and everything is fine in there."

"I hope the headache goes away."

"It will. They're keeping you tonight for observation, but you should be good to go home tomorrow."

"Can't I go home today?"

He shook his head. "You had a nasty bang to the head." He leaned forward and took hold of my hand. "I know you don't like hospitals, but please, don't argue about this. They just want to make sure you're in the right place if you have any other problems. I'll worry less."

I opened my mouth to reply before thinking better of it. "You're right, I guess," I admitted grudgingly.

Rogan laughed. "You really need to stop because these hospital chairs are playing hell with my back."

Wincing as I turned onto my side, I smiled. "You're staying with me again, huh?"

"Try and stop me." His eyes held mine. He'd stay for as long as I was in the hospital. I would do the same if our positions were reversed.

"Try and stop you from doing what?" On entering the room, Dad glanced between us and then Mom appeared behind him.

"Oh, honey," Mom whispered, bending closer and kissing me on the cheek. "Are you really okay?" She brushed hair from my sweaty forehead before she moved and held my hand.

"Rogan says I have to stay the night, so he's going to stay with me. It's just a precaution."

"I want to talk to your doctor," Dad said, running a hand through his hair.

"He had an emergency." Rogan informed him. "He said he'll come back and check on Fallon as soon as he can, but to call for a nurse if she needs anything before that."

"Hmm, what happened? You seemed fine this morning?" Mom asked, taking the seat Dad shoved behind her.

I was hardly going to admit that it was my conversation with Julia. No way.

"I didn't eat breakfast." I shrugged. "And yes," I added, knowing how Mom would fuss, "I promise to eat breakfast from now on."

"Yes, you will," Rogan stated.

Dad frowned as he watched Rogan watching me.

"Well!" Mom clapped her hands together while getting to her feet. "I'm going to take Rogan to get some snacks and drinks. Your dad can keep you company." She smiled.

Returning her smile, I laughed with how she was pushing a reluctant Rogan out of the room. Dad shook his head and sat in the seat Mom vacated.

"She has to be doing something when she worries. Stops her from breaking down and crying over one of her babies. It does things to my heart knowing she worries about Rogan the same as you. I'm also glad that you and Rogan are close, and I'm sorry for the things I accused you both of. It's difficult sometimes, being a parent. I want to get it right, and never have you regret me adopting you." He coughed to clear his throat. "I love Rogan, and I also love you, Fallon." He smiled. "I know I don't say it often enough, but I'm so proud to have you as a daughter."

He shrugged, and a reddish tint coated his cheeks. "Just thought I should tell you without an audience."

I tugged on his hand. "I need you closer," I said, holding my arms out. Dad smiled and wrapped me up against his chest. "I love you too, Daddy."

He was just as choked up as I was when he sat back down. He breathed a huge sigh of relief and smiled. "You really do need to stop giving us such a fright you know," he grumbled.

"I'm sorry I caused everyone to worry. I've never passed out before, so it was, um, enlightening. I won't go without breakfast again."

"That's my girl." Dad smiled, which Mom and Rogan walked in on.

Mom wrapped her arm around Dad's shoulders and he wrapped his arm around her hips, keeping her anchored to his side. Rogan smirked behind them and wiggled his brows.

Laughing, I winced when my head thumped, the pain intermittent.

"I think we should leave you to sleep through this," Mom said, a worried frown on her face. "I don't want to leave you, though."

"Mom," Rogan groaned. "I told you I would be here with her. You know she's going to be okay."

"I'm her mom." Mom pushed Dad from the chair and plunked down. "I'm going to stay." She smiled.

Rogan's eyes widened and I met his. I wanted him to stay, and I knew he wanted to be with me, but what could we say? Dad knew this as he frowned, probably debating the wisdom of his apology, but he too wouldn't say anything to Mom.

"Come on." Dad slung his arm around Rogan's shoulders. "Let's leave the ladies with the snacks." He raised a brow. "We'll eat on the way home." He grinned. "Uncle Frank can fend for himself for a change."

After hugs and kisses, Rogan and Dad left me in Mom's care, but I ached to be with Rogan right then. I wished there had been a way to tell Mom she could go and sleep in her own bed instead of in this uncomfortable hospital room.

I only had one mom, and I loved her, but Rogan was an entirely different matter. I loved him with every breath I took and I had a feeling I always would. It hurt being away from him, which made me wonder how I was going to survive him going away to college. We only had a few more weeks until the school year ended and Rogan graduated. I thought I was a selfish person because I really didn't want him to go anywhere unless he took me with him.

"What are you thinking so hard about?" Mom watched me and I didn't know how to reply because I certainly couldn't be honest. "You're disappointed I stayed," Mom added.

My eyes snapped to Mom's and I found it difficult to hide the truth. My reaction said it all. "I do want you here, Mom. I'm sorry. I'm so used to being with Rogan that it feels strange him not being with me."

She frowned. "I'm glad you're close, but"—she tipped her head—"perhaps a bit of distance won't hurt, considering how cooped up you both must be feeling thanks to your dad's brother."

"Yeah," I agreed. It was easier than going round and round in circles with her. "I think I'm going to take a nap."

24

FALLEN

THE BREEZE COMING THROUGH MY BEDROOM WINDOW was nice as I sprawled out on top of my bed. Mom had brought me home from the hospital that morning, and, apart from being tired, I felt okay. I'd hid my disappointment at Rogan not being at home, but it was during the school day, so what exactly did I expect?

The floorboards creaked, drawing my gaze to the open bedroom door. Uncle Frank leaned against the doorjamb. "You're okay?"

I felt uncomfortable with him seeing me wearing only sleep shorts and a thin top. If I'd known he was around, I'd have closed the door.

"I'm fine. Trying to sleep." Hopefully he'd take the

hint but he didn't and stared. "Did you want something?"

He stayed quiet and hearing Mom's feet on the stairs, he said, "I hope you're feeling better soon," as he moved away.

I hadn't been aware of holding my breath until I let it out once he'd gone. Mom looked in my bedroom and then at Uncle Frank's retreating back. She didn't say anything, although a frown appeared on her face. "I'll close your door."

"Thank you."

I rolled to my side and stared out the window, waiting for Rogan to get out of school. He hated going and looked too old to actually be there. I'd even seen the double take one of the substitute teachers had done in the hallway a few weeks ago. The teacher had flirted with him and then been mortified when she'd realized he was a student. Rogan had been embarrassed too.

I'd teased him but not for long because he really had hated the teacher's reaction. He was gorgeous, though, and I wished my eyes would go in a different direction, but they refused.

My ears picked up the sound of a familiar car engine. Peering through my window, I sighed when his blue Mustang appeared on the street, the tires crunching on the gravel of our driveway. He was home and I smiled, feeling happy to see him.

However, that happiness quickly faded to frustration when he didn't immediately come upstairs. The clock ticking away in the room was loud while my heart thudded in my chest.

Finally, I heard his feet as he ran upstairs, then the door flew open and he was standing in the doorway. His eyes roamed over me, a blush heating his cheeks.

"Will you get in here and shut the door. Uncle Frank has been lurking around."

He frowned but quickly did as I asked. "What did he do?" Dropping his school stuff to the floor, he kicked his sneakers off. Before striding over to me, he stopped and went to lock the door.

Rogan climbed on the bed and lay facing me. "You were about to tell me about Uncle Frank."

"He didn't do anything. He just stood staring at me from the doorway until he heard Mom coming upstairs." I shrugged. "It was weird and put me on edge."

"Christ," he cursed and tugged me into his arms. "From now on, we keep the door locked, okay? I never thought he'd do anything like that, but I don't want any chance of him getting you alone."

"Hmm," I mumbled, snuggling deeper into his arms.

One of his hands cupped the back of my head while the other stroked back and forth along my spine. His touch made my body tingle and tighten. My breasts ached as they pressed into his chest, but I didn't know what for.

He made a funny noise and his breathing came in heavy pants as he tried to put distance between us, but I wouldn't go anywhere. "Fallon," he hissed, "I can't handle feeling you against me... Oh God," he groaned. "I feel...digging into my chest...this can't happen."

"They ache," I admitted, rubbing against his hard chest as a pulse now throbbed lower in my body.

Tilting my head, I realized Rogan was losing control over the situation we were in and, right then, while he was making my body feel so hot, tight, and tingly, I wanted more.

"Rogan?" I whispered, moving so there was no space between us.

He trembled and went solid, his body, and the flesh between his legs currently pressing against my groin.

"Hmm." He gasped and moaned when I rubbed against him.

"Will you kiss me?"

"What?" His eyes snapped open and he glared down.

"I've never been kissed and want to know what it feels like."

I slung a leg over his hip and goose bumps covered my body at the feel of him, big and hard, pressing where I felt swollen and ached.

"This is wrong," he panted. "So wrong, Fallon." His hips slowly rocked, rubbing and building the ache while I teased him with the feel of my breasts against his chest.

Feeling daring, as we'd come so far, I tugged his T-shirt free and tossed it to the floor, letting mine follow. My hands slipped to his back and I held him close as our bared chests met. The feel of his hair-roughened chest against my smoother one caused an uncontrollable shudder to work its way through my body, and I felt Rogan pant as his flesh swelled even more.

"What's happening to me?" I writhed in his arms.

Rogan's eyes darkened when he met my gaze. "Your body craves the connection with mine." He clenched his jaw tightly. "We can't do that." He laughed without mirth. "We shouldn't even be doing this."

"It feels too good, feeling you like this."

"*Fallon*, we're going to hell."

"I don't care, just don't stop," I begged. "Teach me how to kiss a boy…how to kiss you."

He flipped me over to my back, fitting himself between my spread legs. His hands grabbed my wrists and held them over my head and then he became serious. "I want to be your first kiss. You don't know how much." His eyes caressed my bared breasts, a flush appearing along his cheekbones. On a shuddering breath, he dipped his head and kissed each hard nipple. My breath caught and I gasped in surprise at the feel of his mouth there. He moved back up my body and his eyes moved to my mouth, his tongue slipped between his lips, licking his own in anticipation.

"I want to touch you," I moaned. "Like you did me."

He growled. "You touch me and this will be going too far. So far that we won't ever be able to come back from it." He glared into my eyes. "Do you understand what I'm saying?"

"Yes," I whispered.

"I'm not sure you do," he muttered before he dipped down and traced the soft fullness of my lips with his tongue. Then his control snapped and his mouth covered mine with a hunger that surprised me at first. But his kiss demanded a response, which he got when I thrust my tongue into his mouth. The taste of his possession burst on my tongue and I moaned while rubbing my aching body against his.

Holding my wrists with one hand, he burned a path down my body with the other, slightly hesitating before he cupped my bottom, tilting me so that I got more friction as he rocked his hips.

My young body felt alive, and all because of Rogan. A pleasure like nothing I'd felt before started to coil in my stomach, and lower. It was all too much and I didn't know what to do with what he was making happen in my body as I pulled my mouth away from his, gasping for air.

His eyes gleamed and a flush coated his cheeks as sensations rippled through my body in a confusing cascade of need. I didn't know what was happening inside me but I didn't want it to stop. A pleasure started building, lower and lower, my back arched and my eyes widened when it snapped, and as I opened my mouth to shout his name, his mouth swallowed my words. My body convulsed and pressed for more until I finally collapsed back against the bed, totally exhausted.

Rogan moved his mouth from my lips, and kissed

my cheek, then nibbled on my earlobe, before hiding his face in my neck. He released my wrists and I immediately wrapped my arms around him, my fingers sliding through his long dark hair.

"I'm not sure what the hell you just did to me, but I want more."

He stilled and then he was jumping from the bed, glaring down at me. My eyes traveled over his fine body while I ignored the daggers shooting from his eyes. I noticed the large damp spot on the front of his jeans. I wasn't sure if it was from me or him—maybe us both.

He snapped his eyes closed when I finally met his gaze. He breathed in and out a few times and then his gaze cleared. "We can't ever do that again."

Feeling tears close to the surface, even though I knew he was right, I asked, "So you're okay with me doing it with someone else?"

He opened his mouth but thought better of it and clenched his teeth together. Turning, he stormed into the bathroom, slamming the door behind him.

Swallowing hard, I reached for my top and pulled it on before I snuggled under the covers and let the tears fall. Exhausted both physically and emotionally, I allowed my sobs to lull me to sleep…finally.

25

———

FALLEN

I STARED AROUND THE BRIGHT ROOM IN CONFUSION when I woke up. I couldn't remember what time I'd fallen asleep and it felt like I'd slept for hours, but it was still light outside.

"You're awake." I heard from behind me. "It's twenty minutes before we have to get up for school."

"I slept all night."

"Yeah."

Rolling over, I smiled when I found Rogan stretched out on top of my bed, and then my eyes widened when I remembered everything from the night before.

He focused on the ceiling and I watched his Adam's apple move when he swallowed hard. "I nearly disappeared before you woke."

"Oh," I mumbled, feeling my nose twitch as tears welled in my eyes.

"I couldn't do it because, as much as what we did should never have happened, I wanted to be like that with you. I want a lot more. More than I should even dream of. So I stayed and watched you sleep."

I smiled. "You watched over me."

"I was afraid you'd wake up and be angry with me after what I did, especially leaving straight after."

I leaned up on an elbow and cupped his cheek in my hand, and turned his face to look at me. "What happened last night wasn't just your fault. It happened because of us both." I crawled into his arms and heard him sigh as he wrapped me close.

"I don't know what to do anymore," he confessed. "I was all set to finish school and go to college, but now I'm not sure how I'm going to manage not seeing you every day. Or how I'm not going to be able to touch you, even if it's just holding your hand."

"I'll always want you with me above anyone else."

"I can't believe I'm jealous of Julia," Rogan mumbled.

Not knowing what else to say because I found his going away too upsetting, I said, "It's not for a few months. We just need to figure out what we're going to do."

"We both want the same thing, Fallon. I'm just not sure it will ever be possible without breaking our family apart."

My heart thumped hard in my chest. I wanted to be with Rogan, but Mom and Dad meant a lot to us both. Rogan knew what I was thinking as he held me closer, his fingers playing with the tangled mess on my head.

"Julia knows there is something going on." I sighed. "That's what we were talking about when I passed out yesterday. I think I just became over-whelmed with fear at hearing her words." I finished telling him what Julia had said and he didn't seem bothered.

"I like that you're jealous." He frowned. "I shouldn't."

"I hate the feeling." I brushed my lips across his.

Just as he was reaching for me, I climbed off of him and felt a smack on my bottom.

"Serves you right for teasing me, and last night"—he swallowed hard—"seeing your fantastic tits, um, breasts, I can't get the image from my head."

It delighted me that he found my body unforget-table. "No one has ever seen me the way you have," I admitted. "No one ever will." I offered him a soft smile as I leaned against the dresser. "You're my best friend, and no matter what happens, I don't ever want to lose that."

"You won't."

"Promise me."

He searched my gaze. "I promise, Fallon."

My head turned at the knock on the door. "Are you two awake for school?"

"Yeah, Mom. We'll be down soon."

"I'll meet you downstairs," Rogan said once Mom moved away from the door. "Lock the door behind me before you shower." He frowned. "I really don't like that Uncle Frank came in here."

"Me either, but he won't again." I smiled and after giving him a hug, I locked the door.

My shower was quick. After it, I felt refreshed and full of energy. I pulled on my white-cropped jeans and pale blue tee, my belly fluttered with nerves. I didn't know why but it became clear when I got to the bottom of the stairs.

"Why did you lock your bedroom door last night?" Uncle Frank was obviously asking Rogan.

I could almost see him narrowing his gaze at our uncle. "It was locked to keep you out," Rogan growled.

"What?" Mom gasped.

Oh, great!

"What the hell," Dad shouted. "Explain. Now, Rogan!"

I hovered, not knowing whether to enter the kitchen or sneak back to my bedroom.

"He stood and watched Fallon rest on her bed yesterday. So, from now on, the door stays locked, and if he doesn't like it, then he can leave."

Smiling at the defensive note in Rogan's voice, I finally entered the kitchen.

Dad shook himself free. "Is what Rogan said true?" The question was directed at me, but he glared at his brother.

"It was creepy, okay. So Rogan locked the door. I felt better then." I shrugged and moved closer to Rogan, freezing when Uncle Frank pushed back.

"Don't you think it's strange how they're always together, and now they're sharing a room?"

Dad got in Uncle Frank's face. "They are sharing a room so you have somewhere to stay because you got caught with your pants down. Our patience is wearing thin."

Uncle Frank snapped his mouth closed, giving his brother an angry glare before he stomped out of the house, slamming the front door behind him.

My relief was only short-lived.

"What is really going on?" Mom asked.

I turned and faced her. "What do you mean? We just told you. He was just staring at me while I laid on my bed. He didn't say anything until I turned around and even then..." My voice trailed off as I thought about how strange his behavior had been. I looked into my mother's eyes, silently imploring her. "I mean, you saw him, that's why you closed my door."

She sighed. "I didn't see exactly. I only saw him walking into Rogan's room. I did get a weird vibe, which is why I closed your door." She looked at Dad. "When he calms down, perhaps you need to talk to him about boundaries, and urge him to look for somewhere else to live. The sooner this house gets back to normal, the better."

With that, everything was solved and Mom started banging around the kitchen as she returned to making pancakes.

Rogan offered me a small smile. "Breakfast, then I'll drive you to school. No more going without." He wiggled his brows while we were unobserved.

I moved closer and poured myself the one cup of coffee I allowed a day, but not before I poked him in the stomach. "No more going without, huh?" I whispered for his ears only.

Chuckling, I poured creamer into the cup and then joined my family at the kitchen table. It felt a lot more relaxing than it had been for a while, and some of that had to do with the easing of the tension that had been building between Rogan and me. Some of that was slacked yesterday afternoon, but I was sure it would be building again real soon. Already, I felt my body leaning toward him. After having him so close and feeling him against me, I wanted that all the time. I wanted him to show me how to touch a boy, even though he had the body of a man. I'd certainly felt his arousal pushing and throbbing against me yesterday. At this point, I would even settle for just sleeping in his arms every night, and waking up like I had this morning with him next to me.

One of my biggest questions was why do people crave what was forbidden to them? Was it because it was more enticing?

Rogan and I had spent all our lives together since the day our parents had met, and, in some way, we'd made a connection that day. We'd never been like other siblings. What was there between us that was so different? Why did we feel what we did for each other regardless of how wrong it was? Our feelings didn't make sense to me, but it was how I felt. I loved him.

"Do you have something to share?" Dad nudged my foot, interrupting the thoughts whirling around in my head.

"Um, no." I glanced at Mom, who frowned, and Rogan, who wouldn't meet my gaze. "I was thinking about school."

Rogan snickered and took our dishes to the sink and rinsed them before putting them in the dishwasher. "Let's go."

Quickly saying goodbye, I found myself in Rogan's car faster than usual. As we headed for school, I kept catching him glancing at me, so I turned in the seat and stared at him.

He grinned. "You were so not thinking about school. Your cheeks were red."

My face flushed and he chuckled.

"Stop teasing me."

"You teased me while you were thinking about me over breakfast."

"I did not."

"Did too." He smirked. "Before you get out of this car I want to know what you were thinking about."

Groaning, I gazed out of the window so he could no longer see my face but the silence eventually got to me. "I was thinking about why *we* want each other." I continued to think, as we got closer to school. "Why us? What's different about us?"

Pulling into his usual parking spot at school, we sat in silence until he whispered, "I don't have answers to those questions, but I do know you were thinking about more than that because you were bright red." He quickly kissed me on the cheek. "Have a good day at school today."

And then he was gone and I watched him bump into his friends. They always got to school before us. Leon could be a jerk but he was pretty anal about being on time. He got bent out of shape if he thought he was going to arrive at school later than fifteen minutes before the bell. And since Leon gave Chase a lift to school, Chase beat us here too.

For some reason I always ended up being the last one out of the car. Probably because Julia wasn't always on time and I'd rather sit by myself instead of having girls trying to be nice to me so Rogan would notice them. He never did, but it didn't stop them from trying.

While woolgathering, I spotted Julia smacking Leon on his butt before she carried on running toward me. I climbed from the car and rolled my eyes. "You are going to be in trouble one of these days. The poor guy can only take so much."

She laughed. "The poor guy hasn't figured out what to do with me yet." Her eyes lit with mischief.

"You've been, um, flirting with him for months

now. Shouldn't he have figured out which parts of his body connect with yours?"

She blinked and bent over laughing to the point that tears ran down her face. I frowned as everyone around us on the front lawn turned to see what was so funny. Grabbing Julia's arm, I pulled her inside the building.

"Shush! Jeez, Julia. I didn't think it was that funny."

Leaning against our lockers, Julia winked and her face split into a wide grin. "Leon is built, if you know what I mean." She glanced down and back up to my face. "And he knows *exactly* how to connect our parts."

"You didn't tell me?"

Julia sighed and looked upset. "I didn't tell you because I don't know what to tell you. We haven't done *it*, but touched—for months. I want him, Fallon. I'm just not sure he wants me anymore."

"Trust me. I saw the look on his face when you smacked him. He wants you hot and sweaty under him."

"We'll see," Julia mumbled. "Anyway, how are you feeling? I talked to your mom last night and she said you were in bed asleep."

"Yeah, I crashed pretty hard." I unfastened the

padlock and opened my locker to hide the flush I knew coated my cheeks.

Of course Julia narrowed her eyes at the sight of my embarrassment. Instead of letting Julia form her own suspicions, I let her think it was anger as I told her about Uncle Frank. Looking back, I wondered whether he was only there because he was wondering about Rogan and me, especially after the questions I'd overheard this morning. Perhaps I'd completely misunderstood the situation—something to think about.

"Ugh." Julia nudged into me. "Amber alert."

"What?" I glanced at my phone thinking an Amber Alert had been issued, but then I spotted *Amber* quickly walking toward us.

I glanced at Julia and noticed the smirk on my friend's face. I fell for Julia's "Amber alert" every damn time.

"Why is she gloating?" I hissed under my breath.

"I don't know. First time I've seen her today."

"Morning, Fallon...and *Julia*." Amber had been a thorn in my side since preschool and it was still stuck in there, more so after Corinne had switched schools not long after my accident.

"Why are you so chirpy this morning?" Julia, of course, couldn't resist asking.

"I was just asked to the prom," she babbled. "Can you believe it? I'm going to with Rogan."

Everything inside of me froze as I heard Amber's reply, the buzzing in my ears getting louder until Julia pinched me in the side.

"No way did Rogan Scott ask you to prom."

Amber scowled at Julia. "He's on his way in with Chase and Leon. Why don't you ask him?"

"You know she's joking, right?" Julia huffed.

Amber stood gloating with her arms crossed and a delighted smile on her face. I wanted to smack it off as I clenched my fists at my sides.

My breath felt as though it was choking me, but I said, "I don't think she is." While I was upset, I was also confused. Why would he do that without considering taking me with him? And most importantly, why wouldn't he talk to me about it first instead of letting me find out in this way? After what had happened between us the day before, my mind struggled to accept that Rogan would hurt me in this way.

As the bell rang to signal the start of day, my eyes froze on Rogan across the hallway. He turned his head toward me, and when his eyes spotted Amber standing in front of me, I saw realization sink in, and he paled.

"I have class," I mumbled, ignoring everyone as I

headed to the back of the building and the dark basement. I needed some time to collect my thoughts, and unless there was a tornado warning, no one but the maintenance guy ever went down there.

It was only when I slowed my footsteps that I knew Rogan had followed me.

"What changed between yesterday, our teasing in the car, and you asking Amber to prom?"

Resting my forehead against the wall, I heard his books thud on the concrete steps and then I felt him behind me. His hands slipped around to my belly as he wrapped himself around me.

"I didn't ask. She asked and Chase answered for me. Then she ran off while I went to hit Chase."

I slowly turned in his arms and tilted my face up to his. "You hit Chase?"

His jaw clenched. "No. Mr. Malcolm was walking past and gave me the look. I sure as hell don't want detention."

"The whole school probably knows you're taking her by now." I blinked tears of frustration away, but they fell and Rogan caught them with his fingers.

"Please don't cry." He leaned in and kissed my tears away. "I don't know how I'm going to get out of it, but I will. The last thing I want is you hurting, or a date with someone who isn't you."

"Wait! What if you do go with her to prom?"

"What? You're not serious?"

"As long as you're aware that I'll hurt her if she kisses you, then I am serious. We can't go together when I think about it. So this way you go and show your face, you don't appear like an asshole for cancelling on her, and"—I grinned—"I'll get Chase to take me so I can watch her every move. He already said he wasn't asking anyone."

"Chase likes you." He frowned.

"He doesn't *like* me in that way. I promise you that." I reached up and quickly kissed his lips. "You better keep her away from you and the house, or I won't be responsible for what I do." I narrowed my lids. "I'm serious, Rogan."

"God help me, I'm in love with a femme fatale," he mumbled. "This isn't going to be a fatal kind of attraction, is it?"

I grabbed his tee in a tight fist and brought him so close that I breathed the next words against his mouth. "I love you. That's all you need to know."

His whole face lit up and then he looked bashful. "So, I'm forgiven?"

I moved away and said over my shoulder, "Her lips touch you, then no, you're not."

"Fair enough," he agreed quickly. "Just remember

the same goes for you." He grabbed me around the waist and pinned me against the wall, leaving me breathless.

His hips held me up while he held my arms above my head in one of his large hands. I wrapped my legs around his waist, our fingers intertwining.

"This position feels really good," I mumbled, not all that sure what I was saying.

His free hand grabbed my bottom and massaged, pushing me on him. "This is only for you. God help us, but I want to spend the rest of my life doing dirty things to you."

I hissed into his ear and felt him jerk against my lower body. "Make me yours, Rogan."

His heart pounded against my chest while he dropped his face into the curve of my neck. "Not here." He panted. "I need you to go to class and leave me here."

"Why?" I frowned because he felt too good to leave right now.

He lifted his head and glared down at me. Between clenched teeth, he hissed, "Because"—he groaned and helped me get my feet under me—"I ache for you."

I couldn't help it if my eyes drifted to where his ache was to check out just how bad the situation were. I also couldn't help it if my hand, without thinking, reached out and pressed against the ache.

Rogan cursed and grabbed my wrist, and his eyes shot daggers at me. "I don't want to come in my jeans, Fallon." He let me go and started pacing. He was breathing like a bull about to charge.

"I better, um, go."

He nodded and kept his head turned away.

I quickly ran to class, apologizing to the teacher as I took my seat beside Julia, who nudged into me.

"Where did you both go?"

"Basement. Rogan followed me."

"He didn't ask her," Julia said. "Leon told me she asked him, and Chase accepted for Rogan."

"I know, he told me." Ms. Procter gave us a dark glare so we zipped our mouths, at least for now.

Julia wouldn't leave it, though. Not anymore.

My whole world was changing and everything currently evolved around Rogan.

That needed to change, but I didn't know how to separate Rogan and everything else.

On a heavy sigh, I wondered if this was how Mom had felt when she fell in love with Dad. If I was in love with anyone but Rogan, then maybe I could have asked her.

WITH A PROMISE TO MEET UP WITH JULIA, LEON, AND Chase in an hour to head over to watch the new Spiderman movie at the theatre, I hurried inside with Rogan hot on my heels.

Something had changed between us and it was as though a dark cloud had lifted. For months we'd tried to avoid each other because of how our feelings had changed, but today, by silent agreement, we'd both finally accepted that we loved each other, and that wasn't about to change.

Yesterday afternoon happened and the only way to go was forward. I certainly had no wish to go back to how we had been—afraid to be alone together. Now I wanted to spend every single moment alone with Rogan.

"We need to get homework done before we go out," Rogan said, watching my every move through half-lidded eyes, his foot paused on the first step of the stairs.

"Okay." Agreeing wasn't what he'd expected, but I had a plan, which he would hopefully fall in with the moment I took off my clothes.

Racing upstairs, I heard him following, and once he was inside our bedroom, I closed and locked the door with a teasing smile on my face.

Rogan backed away from me and ended up dropping his butt on the bed. "What are you up to?"

"We need a shower"—I tossed my shirt and bra into the laundry hamper, my hand on the button of my jeans—"before doing our homework." I slid my jeans and panties down and then stood before him naked, wanting his eyes on me.

His eyes caressed over my body causing a reaction I hadn't expected. Rogan let out a loud groan. "You are beautiful." His eyes strayed between my breasts and lower while I watched his chest heave and his body react to his first sight of all of me bared to him.

"I ache to be touched." My eyes searched his when he finally lifted his gaze from my lower body. "Show me how to touch a boy."

Swallowing hard, Rogan slipped off his sneakers and threw his tee to the floor. His hand slipped to the bulge he couldn't hide as he slowly peeled the denim down his legs, and kicked them off.

My eyes didn't know where to look because he was like a bronze sculpture standing before me in only his tight white briefs.

Unable to think of anything to say, I moved closer and, reaching out, stroked along his hugely aroused penis. I wasn't sure where my forwardness had come from, but I reminded myself that it was Rogan who stood in front of me. I trusted him. I stroked again and he hissed in response while his body trembled. Stepping up against his chest, I moaned at the feel of him against me. Nothing felt as good as that.

I tilted my face up and met his gaze offering him a smile. His large hands cupped my face, his thumbs stroked along my cheekbones. "I don't know what I'm doing," he confessed. "Except that being like this with you feels good, it feels right, like this is where I'm meant to be." He dropped his forehead to mine and searched my gaze.

My hands slid to his hips before they travelled down the inside of his briefs, pushing them over his firm butt.

"I don't want to pretend anymore, Rogan. It hurts so much having to stay away from you so this doesn't happen. We're meant to be together."

"I agree," was all he said as he lifted me into his arms, his mouth searching for mine.

We sank into the kiss as he carried me into the bathroom. I clung to him and refused to let him put me down, and we ended up fumbling into the shower. We broke from the kiss, my lips felt swollen as I licked them, wanting more of his taste.

Rogan's eyes narrowed as he watched me before he snapped out of it and sent water cascading over us.

He grinned, pressing me into the wall, the water feeling amazing on my sensitive skin.

"I'm horny as fuck because of you," he growled.

"Then I think you need to do something about it." I wiggled in his arms until he gave me some space.

He held me steady as my legs unraveled from his waist. My eyes filled with amusement as I watched his follow what I was doing. I squirted a large drop of shower gel into the palm of my hand, and rubbed them together.

I knew what he was expecting, but I decided to tease him instead. Leaning back against the wall, I rubbed the gel into my skin, my hands caressing further down. I moaned and arched—my body over-sensitive.

Rogan hissed and knocked my hands away. He cupped my breasts and ran his thumbs over my slippery skin. "I've been desperate to get my hands on these."

My body tightened, and when he licked and bit, I couldn't explain the pleasure rushing through me. I felt as though he'd overtaken my body and I was nothing more than a pulsing live wire. Rogan cursed, and guided my hands to himself, his eyes begging for my touch. I wasn't one to disappoint, so I wrapped both of my slippery hands around him. His penis looked red and painful as I stroked and learned the feel of him...how he liked to be touched.

Curiosity got the better of me and I dropped to my knees, losing his touch on my body. Rogan loudly hissed while he swelled even more against my palms. With one hand, I reached and caressed his balls that hung heavily between his spread legs.

I lifted my gaze and watched his reaction to every touch of my hands. His cheeks were flushed and his breathing was heavy and his belly quivered. Licking my lips, I held his gaze while I swiped my tongue over him.

Rogan shuddered and, before I knew it, I was back on my feet, pressed face-first into the wall with one large hand on my chest and his other searching further down. I gasped as pleasure shimmered through my body.

"Give me your mouth," Rogan hissed.

I turned my face so my lips were captured by his and it all became too much. He was everywhere at once.

A fireball started in my lower belly and sizzled through me, pleasure bursting like lightning. I groaned and gasped into his mouth while I writhed against him. By the time the pleasure became small pulses inside of me, I was panting against the wall. Rogan's gaze was fierce as he continued to hold mine and then his eyes fluttered, his voice hoarse as he grunted just when I felt hot liquid on my back. I smiled and enjoyed the feelings we'd brought out in each other.

Rogan wrapped his arms around my waist and his face became buried in the curve of my neck. He whispered, "I love you, Fallon."

"I love you, too."

A few minutes later, I turned and kissed his cheek, a smirk on my lips. He narrowed his gaze. "You have something to say?" His hands rubbed my lower back as the water helped to wash away his release.

"I was debating how wise it would be for me to admit that I once watched you in the shower."

"I seem to recall that I was the one who'd put on the display for you." He raised his brows.

I grinned. "I'm talking about before that *show*."

His eyes widened in surprise.

"You had your hand wrapped around"—I glanced down and back up—"while you stroked yourself. I couldn't move and stayed and watched to the end." I groaned. "It was really hot."

"I don't...wait a minute! Please tell me it wasn't

the time you said you needed to wash your eyes with holy water."

I giggled. "I won't then."

He groaned, his hands pushing strands of wet hair out of my face. "You're the only one I've been like this with, Fallon. I'm just as inexperienced as you are."

My brows pulled together while I thought about what he said. "I don't understand…Debra said—"

"Debra begged me to let everyone think we'd done the deed. I don't know why. But I never touched her because I wasn't interested." He gently kissed my lips. "The only person I've been like this with is you…even in my imagination, it was only you."

My eyes lit with amusement and my hands slipped around his waist, my head resting on his chest. "Tell me."

"Ugh," he groaned and laughed. "No way."

I pinched his butt and felt the reaction in his body.

"The sun lounger. The minute your fingers slipped under my shorts, I came."

"I wondered if you'd enjoyed that a little too much."

He laughed. "I'd say I enjoyed it way too much."

He kissed my shoulder, moving up to my neck and jaw before finding my lips.

His kiss was so soft, sweet, and full of love that I

knew being with him in this way would always feel right.

"As much as I hate to say this, we need to get cleaned up and get dressed. Our friends are going to be waiting."

I groaned, not wanting to leave his arms. "I know."

Rogan tugged me under the spray, and, using more gel, cleaned me up. He smirked as he patted me on the butt. "Go and dress."

"Tease," I whispered, stepping out of the shower and wrapping a towel around myself. "Are you going to do something about that?" I nodded toward his groin.

"I thought about it," he said with a cocky grin on his lips, "but no."

I took a step toward him but he shook his head. "If we didn't have somewhere to be, then I'd be yanking you back in here with me, but we can't"

"I know."

"FALLON, CHASE IS HERE TO SEE YOU," MOM SHOUTED upstairs.

It had been a while since he'd been over to the house and I was curious. Quickly moving to the landing, I looked down. "Come up."

He grinned and strolled upstairs in a lazy manner. When he reached me, he kissed my cheek as he walked into my bedroom. Flopping down on the end of the bed, he said, "Close the door, we need to talk."

"You sound serious." I did as he asked.

"Where's Rogan?"

I frowned wondering what was going on with him. "He went to the sports store with Dad."

His eyes focused on anything but me, so I stood

over him, and he was no longer able to avoid me. "Spit it out, Chase, you're making me anxious."

He tilted his head, watching me closely. "How long have you and Rogan been…um…you know?"

Blood rushed around inside my head, making a loud noise in my ears. I was too shocked to even act as if I had no clue what he was talking about.

"How?" I whispered, dropping down beside him on the bed before my legs gave out.

He pulled me down beside him and we both stared up at the ceiling.

"I was coming over last night." He sighed. "Your curtains were open and I saw you both kissing."

"Oh!" Groaning, I rolled to my side and faced him while my brain rapidly tried to think about whether or not we'd been clothed at the time, and what else he'd seen. I couldn't ask him because if he'd seen us clothed then I wasn't giving him more information.

I gazed back at the ceiling hoping Rogan got back soon because I felt out of depth.

"Awkward, right?" Chase asked. "I don't know what I intended coming here and telling you what I saw, but I'm your friend. I don't want you both getting into trouble because the wrong person saw you."

"I'm embarrassed you saw us." I frowned.

"I didn't see much if that helps. I just saw the kissing." Chase chuckled. "It certainly explains why Rogan is so pissed with me for accepting Amber's prom invite on his behalf." He sat up and stared at me. "Wait, he wasn't planning on taking you, was he? That would cause gossip."

"I wanted to go with him, but we both know that would be talked about by everyone, so don't worry about it." I gave him a side-eye. "I think you should take me."

His eyes widened. "Um, you do?"

"Yes. You don't date, and when you tried to kiss me that one time, we both agreed it was awkward, so why not?"

"Jeez, make me feel bad, why don't you?"

I nudged him. "We both know why you don't date, and why it felt odd between us." I cuddled into his side. "You'll take me, won't you?"

"I'll take you."

"Eek," I screamed and jumped up, pulling him with me. "I'm so excited."

Chase rolled his eyes. "Just promise me that you'll be careful."

My excitement disappeared as I searched his serious gaze. "I promise, Chase."

"So, I have a date to the prom with the hottest girl at school, huh?"

"What!" Rogan hissed, slamming the door as he walked into the bedroom.

He moved toward Chase, but I got in his way. "Stop, right there. He's teasing. And can I remind you, you are going to the prom with *her*. I'm going with Chase. Oh, and he saw us through my bedroom window last night."

Rogan blinked a few times as though he couldn't get his head around the change in conversation. It wasn't the first time I switched topics quickly in mid-conversation, and it wouldn't be the last.

"He saw what last night?" Rogan glanced at the window and down to the street, his shoulders dropping as he turned to his friend. "How much did you see?"

"Enough," Chase mumbled.

"Let's forget about that and make a note to close the curtains." I raised a brow at Rogan before turning to Chase. "I'm glad you told us." Chewing on my lip, I asked, "Are you okay with this? I mean, it isn't normal."

"You guys aren't biologically related, and honestly, I figured it would happen sooner or later. You've been inseparable for years."

Feeling emotional at his acceptance of us, I quickly hugged Chase. "Thank you."

He nodded and, skirting past Rogan, quickly left.

I turned to Rogan and grinned. "He's sweet." He watched me through narrowed lids, so I continued, "He is and I'm glad we have a friend like him."

"Do you know at what point he saw us?" Rogan kicked his flip-flops off and went into the bathroom to wash his hands and face.

My eyes followed him and I took a few moments to answer. "I think we may have been clothed, but I'm not sure really."

Rogan fixed his gaze on me, and my body flared with heat, coming to life all over again. Last night had been amazing and something like out of one of the books I read. He smirked and cocked his finger toward me, enticing me closer.

Of course, I followed, but only after I was sure the bedroom door was locked and the curtains were closed.

Closing the bathroom door behind me, I asked, "What about Mom and Dad?"

He slipped his palm to the back of my neck and reeled me in. "I'll be quick."

The moment his lips brushed against mine, I was

in his arms, my legs around his waist while my tongue searched to join with his.

My butt landed on the sink and then my face was cupped between Rogan's large hands as he devoured me. Our mouths melded together and there was nothing getting between us. I loved sliding my fingers through his dark hair, and holding his head so I could ravish his mouth. Just his touch made my body ache for more, like his body did when we were close.

"We need to stop."

He trailed his wet mouth down my neck to my shoulder, dipping into the front of my shirt.

"Now that we've started, I can't get enough of you," he groaned and buried his face in my neck while his breathing became easier. After a moment, Rogan lifted his head and met and held my gaze. "One day, we are going to explore each other." He paused, taking in a lung full of air. "Right now, Mom and Dad are waiting for us downstairs."

"What?" I lightly smacked him on the arm. "Why didn't you tell me?"

"I just did."

I glowered at him, he offered a soft smile, and added, "I needed to kiss you."

My heart melted. "Really?"

"Yeah."

27

ROGAN

Floating on top of the water, I stared up at the blue sky while thinking about Fallon and how she made my head spin and my body ache. She'd had that effect on me for a long time. I had a feeling we were both spiraling out of control with what we'd started and I didn't know if I could control it.

I'd been in love with her for so long, and I'd tried to stay away from her. Nothing had worked, which was why we'd already gone too far. I knew when she'd told me she had never been kissed that I was lost and I was going to give her exactly what she wanted.

Every dream I'd ever had had always included Fallon in some way. As children, those dreams would be as friends, but as I grew older, they turned into scenes from erotic novels. I smiled remembering Fallon's books I'd borrow and hide in my room. The first time I'd done it, had been as a joke, but as I'd flicked through the pages, my eyes had nearly popped out of my head while my body had heated in places. It was an eye-opener. So yeah, after that, I'd started to read them. Not that anyone knew. I wasn't even sure Fallon did.

Hearing a rustle in the tall grass at the edge of the river, I turned my head and watched as Fallon removed her clothing. She revealed a skimpy red bikini that had my blood pounding through me, heating my already aroused body. I was glad to already be in the water so as to hide my reaction. The last thing I wanted was to get caught with an erection while my shorts stuck to my body.

Fallon gave me a shy smile and slipped into the cool water, moving closer. She smiled softly as she wrapped her arms around my neck and her legs around my waist. I grunted and hissed at the feel of her body pressed against mine. It really didn't help that I could feel two hard buds poking me in the chest. Goose bumps shivered over my skin and I nearly came in my shorts.

"We're going to get caught," I mumbled, hardly able to find words as my hands grabbed her butt.

"No, we won't."

Her nails dug into my shoulders and my body trembled on the brink of losing it.

"Rogan," she moaned.

"I know. Don't move."

"We can't."

"I'm not sure I can stop," I confessed, closing my eyes before quickly looking around.

We were still alone.

"I want more." I pressed her tightly against my arousal.

Fallon clung to me, moaning when I squeezed the cheeks of her bottom. "Don't stop, please...Rogan... that feels so good."

Her moan, her frantic movement, her whispered words were all too much for me. When Fallon quivered in my arms, her head thrown backward, I let my own pleasure wash over me, sighing into Fallon's neck when she collapsed against me.

My arms held her tightly and it felt amazing to hold her in this way. I couldn't explain what it did to me, having her wrapped around me—trusting me so damn much.

I lifted my head, and when she brushed a soft kiss across my lips, the tenderness nearly unmanned me.

Her whispered, "I love you, Rogan," was what I hoped to always hear from her beautiful lips.

"I love you, too."

Hearing a cough behind the tall grass, we quickly parted, disappointment on both our faces.

Fallon swam over to the opposite bank and that was where she was as Chase, Leon, and Julia showed themselves.

Chase looked between the two of us, and I knew it had been him coughing to give us a warning. I shouldn't be happy that my friend knew how I felt about Fallon, but I was. It made things easier for me because of how laid-back Chase was. He'd always have my back and that counted for a great deal. I'd always have his.

Leon and Julia didn't notice anything going on, even though I was sure Fallon was bright red. I suffered with embarrassment at nearly getting caught and my heart had only now stopped racing.

Watching Fallon, I realized we needed to stop taking any more chances like we had. It was too dangerous to risk being with each other away from our room. Our new closeness was arousing and I found it extremely difficult to not reach for her when she was near. I couldn't shout that she was mine in the true sense of the word. It hurt me and I knew it hurt her. Having touched Fallon with no clothing between us had filled me with an intense longing to never stop. To explore more until I knew every inch of her body like no one else ever would.

Chase moved in front of me and snared my attention, followed by Julia's laugh. "I think we should sit on the guys' shoulders and play," Julia announced, being towed along by Leon.

"We're a girl short, so I think we should just swim and chill," I countered. There was no way I would be able to keep myself in check if I had Fallon on my shoulders. I'd also have to kill Chase if she climbed on him.

"Spoilsport." Julia pouted.

"Can I join you?"

My eyes immediately searched out Fallon at the sound of Amber's voice, and although she didn't look happy, she shrugged. "Whatever."

"So nice, Fallon. Are you always this cheerful?" Amber was alone, which was unusual for her.

I hated how she was bitchy to Fallon, and I turned and gave Amber a narrowed-eyed stare.

Amber swiftly backtracked. "We should get coffee sometime, Fallon. Really get to know each other."

"I'm busy," Fallon declared, shooting daggers at me.

I winced and wondered how the heck I'd gotten into this mess in the first place. It took everything I had not to laugh at the annoyed look on Fallon's face. She knew exactly what Amber was up to; she didn't miss a damn thing. I just wished Amber would change her mind and disappear.

Amber may have ended up as my date for prom, thanks to my loudmouthed friend, but I didn't have to like it.

"Rogan, please help me get in the water," Amber begged.

Well, that drained the humor from every inch of me.

"I'll help you." Fallon climbed out, giving me an awesome view of her butt. "Here, let me." Fallon's words drifted as Amber screeched seconds before she hit the water. "There. You're in!" Fallon collected her clothing and towel, slipped on her flip-flops, and stormed off through the grass.

Amber came to the surface spluttering, steaming mad, her eyes blazing fire at Fallon's retreating back.

Amber spun toward me. "You spoil her too much," she huffed, her hands smacking the water.

"Amber, why don't you understand that Fallon will always come first with me?" Climbing out of the river, I paused once I had my clothes bundled under an arm. "Sorry to bail, guys."

All I heard was Amber muttering about Fallon and me. I didn't give a shit what she thought, and I was so damn tempted to tell Chase that he could take her to prom while I took Fallon. At least there wouldn't be a chance of me being locked up for murder.

Right now, I needed to make sure Fallon was okay because I knew how much Amber got to her. She was jealous, and I got it. I was jealous of every guy to give Fallon a second glance. The only reason she hadn't been asked out by one of them was because of me. Damn straight too!

She belonged to me.

28

———————

FALLEN

STINKING MAD, I SLAMMED INTO THE HOUSE CURSING Rogan. I was being irrational and knew Amber showing up hadn't been Rogan's fault, well, not directly. But ugh! I needed to calm down and stop acting jealous. I couldn't. Rogan was mine! It ate away inside of me that we couldn't ever be together like a normal couple.

I couldn't fault Rogan. We'd both wanted what was happening between us, and we both had taken that first step together. No one held a gun to our heads.

It just got to me when I saw someone else wanting him the way I'd had him. At seventeen, anyone would say I was too young to know what my future would hold. It was something my mother would say whenever college was mentioned and what I planned to do. Where I planned to go.

The one and only thing I was sure of was that I would always have Rogan in my life. There would never be anyone who meant as much to me as he did. And even with how unacceptable it was for us to be together, I didn't care. My young heart was in love with him and there was nothing I could do to stop myself from falling deeper and deeper.

My bed was no longer my bed, but our bed. Every night we both tossed and rolled all over the sofa bed so it looked like it had been used. It hadn't, and I wasn't sure how I'd ever sleep alone again after being wrapped in Rogan's strong arms.

Glancing toward the doorway, I saw the boy who was becoming a man, standing watching me. His eyes caressed over me in a way that only he could do. My blood hummed and my breathing quickened.

"I didn't hear you come in." I licked my lips, wondering if I'd get another chance to put my hands on him.

"You were too annoyed to hear me." He closed and locked the door behind him. "We're alone, but I don't want to chance Mom or Dad suddenly walking in."

I raised a brow. "Oh, and why would that be?"

He smirked and shoved his shorts to the floor,

stepping out of them. When he stood, his large masculine body was on display for my eyes only. His thighs were thick from the sports he played, and, as my eyes drifted upward, they suddenly snapped to his when I noticed the strength of another part of him.

"It's all for you." He moved forward, his penis hard and bobbing in front of him. "And I'm going to show you how much I belong to you."

"You are?" I became nervous as he slid his hands into my bikini panties, slipping them to the floor. My bikini top followed, and then I was standing naked in front of him.

"You are so beautiful, Fallon." He reached out and cupped me between my legs with a large hand, and stroked gently. "So beautiful." His words whispered like a caress over my skin before he spread me out on the bed, his mouth going to my chest. He placed my arms over my head, and whispered, "Keep them there." A quick kiss to my lips followed. He smirked when he pulled away and I tried to reach for him. "Those aren't the lips I'm planning on kissing." He winked

Moments later, I gasped when he spread my legs and kissed my mound. He touched me with his fingers and opened me up to his gaze.

"God," he groaned. "You're really wet and swollen."

His mouth and fingers touched me in teasing strokes, which became firmer as he licked inside my tight vagina.

I groaned and writhed against his mouth, but his hands clamped on my hips so I couldn't move. I couldn't help my reaction as I arched up and came, flooding him with my release. My hands fisted the pillows above my head; Rogan never let up until he dropped his face to my belly, breathing hard.

"Fuck me, that was good," he mumbled, crawling up my body, his large hands cupping my face. "You're mine and I'm yours, Fallon." He laughed and then his lips caressed mine, the kiss deepening.

He pressed against me, giving me his full weight and I clung to him.

"You feel so good, skin against skin."

"Hmm," he mumbled, settling down with his head resting on my chest. "I could stay here forever."

The pleasure of being like this with him, without anyone else being in the house, was fun, but could get dangerous if someone decided to come home early. But I wanted to see him like this. See what no one else did. With me, like this, he was showing me his weakness, which I knew was me. He was mine too.

"I want to touch you," I admitted while enjoying his caresses over my sensitive skin.

He paused before rolling onto his back, taking me with him. He put his hands behind his head and crossed his ankles, his eyes not moving from my face. "I'm all yours—" His voice cut off when I dragged my fingernails down his chest, continuing south.

"You were saying?"

"I can't remember."

He arched upward, and pressed his large shaft into my hand, as my lips hovered over a tight nipple lightly covered in hair. I flicked my tongue around each in turn. He shuddered beneath me, wetness leaking between us as his hips moved, creating friction.

Straddling his thighs, I wrapped my fingers around his penis. I ran my hands up and down his silky, solid erection. His breathing became heavier as I held his gaze and did what I'd caught him doing to himself in the shower. I smiled as he reacted to my strokes while I jerked him off.

His hips pumped into my palm, his hands fisted the bedding at his sides while sweat coated his brows. "I can't last," he panted.

I felt a blush cover my body when I tipped slightly forward and whispered, "Do boys really get off coming over a pair of breasts?"

His eyes widened in surprise and glanced at me

breasts, and then we heard, "Fallon! Rogan! You two upstairs?"

My head swiveled toward the locked bedroom door and I felt Rogan's penis thicken seconds before a warm wetness landed on my belly and hand. "Oh fuck!" Rogan hissed, his body arched, his breathing heavy.

Our eyes met.

I grinned, delighted with how his body had reacted to me.

"You get in the shower and I'll quickly wash up in the sink and go downstairs." I kissed him, trying not to show him how much I was panicking. "Go."

The moment the shower turned on, I shouted to Mom, "Yes, we're here. Rogan is in the shower, I'll be down in a minute."

"Okay."

I watched Rogan leaning against the wall of the shower, his eyes on my body while I quickly washed up.

I blew him a kiss and left him to it.

Quickly dressing, I headed downstairs and found Mom getting the ingredients out to bake brownies. "Do you want some help?"

Mom smiled. "I'd really enjoy that. It's been a long time since you had any interest in the kitchen."

"Yeah, well, um, considering my last attempt, do you honestly blame me?" My last attempt had set the fire alarm off.

Mom chuckled. "I understand." Mom passed me an apron and asked, "What have you and Rogan been up to?"

A shiver ran over me remembering what we'd been up to, but I shook it off. "We went to the river for a short while, and then Amber showed up and annoyed me. She's so rude."

"She's your brother's girlfriend, so try and be nice to her."

"She is not his girlfriend," I snapped, and realized it was Mom I was talking to. "I'm sorry. I didn't mean to yell. He's taking her to prom, that's it. Don't be getting any ideas."

Mom gave me a weird kind of look. "Uncle Frank has found an apartment, so he'll be moving out tomorrow. Everything will be able to get back to normal then." Mom measured out the flour, always doing the dry ingredients first. "I bet you can't wait to have your room back to yourself."

"That would be good."

I didn't want Rogan to ever have his room back because that meant no more sharing. No more fooling around. The way Mom told me was as if she knew something was going on between us. But how could she know?

Mom carried on completely oblivious to the thoughts running through my mind, or then again, maybe she did know what I was thinking.

"It isn't right that you spend all your time with Rogan, and him with you. You both have your own friends, that's who you should be hanging around with." She shook her head. "I understand you're only thirteen months apart, and have grown up together, but you both need to venture out, away from each other. It isn't healthy, and people have noticed."

I dropped the sugar, making a mess. "I'll get the broom." Cleaning it up, I asked, "Noticed what?"

"How you both are *always* together." She frowned. "There's nothing, um, well"—Mom sighed and gave a false laugh—"between you both." She waved her hands around looking relieved she'd gotten the words out.

"Mom, what the hell?" Rogan came to my rescue. "Not this again." He slung his arm around my shoulders, not really helping the situation. "I love Fallon, and if some neighbors want to gossip, then let them. There is nothing wrong with us spending time together. We've grown up as best friends. People are jealous." Grinning, he leaned forward. "Brownies?"

"Yes." Mom glanced between the two of us. "I actually told your dad that others were jealous because their kids don't get along. I mean I know you two have had your differences, but, I guess I shouldn't be complaining that you're best friends."

Slipping out from under Rogan's arm, I wrapped myself around Mom. "I love you, Mom, and wherever I am in this world, I always will. I also love Rogan, and no matter who says what, that won't ever change. He's part of me." Those words were true but just had a different meaning to the two people who were listening.

"I love you both."

Rogan moved closer and hugged us both before placing a big, wet kiss, first to Mom's face, and then to mine. He grinned and shoved an apple into his mouth. "I'm going to watch the game with Dad." He winked and Mom and I laughed.

"I'll enjoy that," Dad said, walking into the kitchen. "It's been a while."

"Hmm," Rogan drawled. "We watch the game while the women make us brownies." He rubbed his belly, grinning. "I like that idea." He burst out laughing.

"We'll clean up," Dad offered, shutting Rogan up with a wince. "Before the game starts, I wanted to ask about prom." Dad glanced between the two of us. "I've heard there is a party you intend on going to, and staying until morning." He sighed. "I'm not sure that's a good idea, but your mom has persuaded me to let you both go. You only get one prom." He paused and glanced at me, and I knew it was because my senior prom was next year. "I'm going to trust you both to behave." He hesitated. "Just know that if you need me to come and get either of you, no matter the time, I will."

Swallowing hard, I threw myself into Dad's arms. "I love you, and thank you."

He kissed the top of my head and grabbed Rogan by the shoulder. "The game awaits, Son."

Mom sighed. "I don't know what I was thinking. Let's finish these brownies."

29

ROGAN

T̲HREE̲ ̲DAYS̲ ̲SINCE̲ U̲NCLE̲ F̲RANK̲ ̲MOVED̲ ̲OUT̲.

Three days since I'd been back in my bedroom.

Three days since I'd last had Fallon in my arms.

I wasn't sure either of us knew what we were doing being together, but it was something I craved.

My desire for her was wrong and forbidden. I didn't know what would really happen if we were discovered. I didn't want to know.

Softly closing Fallon's bedroom door, my eyes adjusted to the fairly darkened room. Moonlight entered through a crack in the curtains that made it possible for me to focus on the girl I was in love with. My eyes stayed on her as I pulled the covers back and slid in beside her, knowing I'd do anything to be able to keep her with me always.

Immediately, she was in my arms, a leg curled over my hip and an arm around my waist as she snuggled deeper.

Until I felt lips brush against my neck, I thought she was asleep. My hands slipped to her gorgeous bottom and squeezed, the lips on my neck curling into a smile when I did.

"I knew you'd come to me," Fallon whispered, her body warming to mine.

"I thought Mom was never going to bed." I paused and listened. "Then as I was creeping down the hallway, I half expected her to come back out of the bedroom."

"She isn't usually up so late."

"I know." I kissed Fallon on the lips and smiled softly when she followed my lips as I pulled back.

Rolling us so that Fallon was flat on her back, I quickly removed her shorts and shirt. The sight of her spread out and naked caused my heart to pound and all my blood to race into my dick.

We were both as innocent as the other and the knowledge of that excited me. Her touch on my skin was gentle and almost hesitant at first, even though we'd already been naked together.

Her eyes were heated as her hands caressed through the hair on my chest. My belly quivered and I was afraid I'd lose control when one of her hands slipped down, tangling in the hair below my belly button.

She teased me wickedly; her fingers trailed a blaze of heat back and forth along the low waistband of my shorts.

I hissed between my teeth when her hand slipped into my shorts, and sent them down my legs.

Amusement spread over her face when I groaned, struggling for control.

"We're teenagers, exploring each other and every time we touch, it feels like the first time, Rogan."

"I feel the same way."

She smiled softly. "Then will you make me feel good?"

I hid my face in the crook of her neck, and reached between us. I clamped my teeth together and moved our lower bodies closer.

Fallon sighed in pleasure, her hands on my back making sure I didn't go anywhere. Not that I would.

My body tingled as sensation ran through me at the feel of Fallon running her hands all over me, her fingernails biting into my butt.

"When?" she whispered, her gaze holding mine.

I didn't even need to ask what she meant.

"Not at the house."

She searched my face and knew I was serious, her smile fading.

I cupped her face. "I want you, Fallon. I'm desperate to make real love to you."

"Really?"

I chuckled. "You're asking me when we're together like we are?" I shook my head, amused. "Yes, really." I dropped my face into the crook of her neck, moaning as she moved against me.

It didn't take long for the passion to explode between us, her pussy lips opened and wrapped around my erection. Her excitement coated me as I rocked my hips, pressing between her thighs. Not moments later I found the excitement of being with Fallon too much and I came all over her mound and belly. I trembled when I felt Fallon come, soaking my balls in her pleasure. Gasping for breath, I climbed from the bed and grabbed a towel from the bathroom to clean us up. I then tucked us both under her quilt.

Becoming serious, Fallon held my gaze and said, "I hate sneaking around, Rogan. We love each other and shouldn't have to hide it from others."

"I wish we didn't have to, Fallon. I'm neither ashamed nor embarrassed at what we're doing, even though I think I should be. I love you, and will sneak around forever if it means being with you."

"What if you meet someone else at college?" Tears formed on her lashes. "Someone who you can be with out in the open. It would destroy me."

Fear suddenly wrapped itself around me as tightly as I wrapped myself around her. "I promise there will never be another for me. It's you or no one, Fallon." I kissed her forehead and held my lips there, whispering against her skin, "It will always be you."

"You're the only one I want," she mumbled, slipping into sleep.

I laid awake for a long time.

30

———————

FALLEN

PROM WAS UPON US AND I WANTED TO KILL ROGAN FOR agreeing to my stupid idea of keeping his date with Amber. We hadn't discussed it since, which we should have because I was eaten up with jealousy. Over the past few days, we'd stolen kisses when we'd been able to, but everything else had been pretty tame after the night we'd slept nude together. We were playing with fire and I was afraid we were going to get caught. Maybe Mom didn't exactly believe what we'd said, and she was watching. I just didn't know what to think.

Walking out of the bathroom in my robe, I heard a throat being cleared, and Rogan cursed lightly under his breath. I turned my smile to him, and caught my breath, my eyes roaming over his muscular form in a suit.

"So handsome. I can't wait for you to see me in my dress."

His eyes narrowed. "You're going to prom with Chase," he growled.

"I might be, but it was you who inspired my choice." Grinning, I grabbed the black dress bag and disappeared into the bathroom.

He had no clue what he'd unleashed along with my love. I'd discovered that I had a jealous streak a mile long. Tonight was going to be difficult to get through without giving us both away with Rogan parading around with Amber on his arm. I might be going with Chase, but it was Rogan who my heart was going to be with.

Slipping into my lacy underwear, I unzipped the bag and pulled the gown from the hanger, and stepped into it. The soft material was red and went well with my tanned skin and dark hair. I pulled the material up my body and managed to find the right straps to push my arms through. I couldn't do the zipper myself so I'd ask Rogan. The dress was fitted to my curves with a diamond shape cut out between my breasts, giving everyone a teasing glimpse of the goods.

"Fallon, we need to go."

Taking a deep breath, I opened the bathroom door and heard Rogan gasp when he looked toward me. His eyes caressed over every part of me until he finally met my gaze. He swallowed hard before he spoke. "You look beautiful."

He moved closer to where I was frozen in place. "But I think you need zipping up."

Smiling, he fastened my dress, his hands lingering on my body while his eyes strayed to my chest.

"I'm going to kill anyone who looks at you."

"You're going to behave just like I am when I see *her* with her hands on you."

He gently cupped the back of my head and pressed a kiss to my forehead. "Just remember it's you who I love, and it's you I'm going to be sleeping with tonight." He brushed another kiss over my cheekbone and then took my hand.

Downstairs, Mom was fluttering around us with a camera in her hand while Dad stayed seated in the armchair.

"Mom." Rogan got her attention. "Take our picture before the others get here." He wrapped his arm around my shoulders, bringing me into his body. I wrapped my arms around his waist and settled against him, smiling as Mom took a million pictures.

"I'll get some with your friends, who I think have arrived."

Sighing, I pulled away and greeted Julia, who was going with Leon, and then Chase and Amber walked in behind them. Chase and Amber lived next door to each other, which was why Rogan hadn't picked her up. He'd pointed out that Chase had technically agreed, so he could bring her. She hadn't been happy, and I wished I could accidentally, on purpose, stand on Amber's foot in my red high heel.

"You are up to something," Rogan whispered before turning away to greet Amber when he couldn't avoid it any longer.

"He looks like he's about to be hanged or something," Julia commented, her eyes focused on the awkwardness of Rogan.

While Mom fussed around snapping pictures, I let my eyes trail over Rogan in his suit. His navy blue slacks clung to his thighs and the white dress shirt brought out his tan. He looked good enough to eat, and I wasn't the only one to notice.

Amber trailed her hands over the front of his jacket, which Rogan soon put a stop to.

"Let's get the group photo so we can go and get this over with," he grouched.

I stifled a laugh behind a cough at the glare he

received from Amber. He even made Mom pause and catch her breath. Mom soon pulled herself together as she started to arrange us for photographs.

I smiled at Chase, and taking his hand pulled him in beside me for the photograph. Rogan was on one side with his hand low on my waist while Chase threw his arm over my shoulders, landing on Rogan's shoulder. I noticed how Amber clenched her arms around the one Rogan had in front of him. Mom frowned but took the group photograph before taking my hand and leading me into the kitchen.

"Why isn't Rogan happy to be with Amber?"

Caught off guard, I stuttered and felt a blush high on my cheekbones, but then I felt a familiar presence behind me.

Rogan laid his palm on my bared back. "Because she asked me to prom, and Chase accepted on my behalf. I didn't want to be an asshole and tell her no after she'd announced to the whole school I was taking her." He slightly rubbed my back and then moved over to Mom, giving her a hug. He towered over her. "I don't want her to get the wrong idea. She doesn't listen when I try and tell her I'm not interested." He kissed Mom on the forehead. "Don't worry."

Making his way toward me, he took my hand and intertwined our fingers, pulling me along the hallway and out of the house. Amber waited to the side and so did Chase and Leon, none looking too happy.

Rogan squeezed my hand before letting go. "We ready?"

"Where'd you two disappear to?" Leon asked, suspicion clouding his face.

"Mom wanted to talk to us for a moment." I slipped into the limo we rented for the night, tugging Chase in with me.

Amber and Rogan followed, sitting opposite Chase and me. It wasn't ideal because I felt my body heating at the lazy look on Rogan's face. And I could feel the evil glare coming off of Amber, but I avoided the girl's gaze. The silence was stifling and lasted until we arrived at the hotel and the driver opened the door for us to all pile out.

"No intimate touching," Rogan whispered, before sliding his arm around Amber's back. She preened at his touch and I swallowed my discomfort and jealously by completely ignoring them.

Turning to Chase, I grabbed hold of his hand and rested my head on his shoulder. "We're going to do this?"

"Rogan and you are asking for trouble," he mumbled, pulling me closer. "I'm only doing this because I love you both."

Smiling, I reached up and kissed him on the cheek. "I love you too, Chase, and we're going to have a good time." I grinned and got nudged in the side.

"When you two have stopped kissing face, can we go in?" Julia already sounded drunk, which made me wonder what was in the flask Leon kept passing to her in the car.

"We're not stopping you." We walked into the hotel and Chase chuckled in my ear.

He nodded toward where they had the photographer set up.

My eyes danced when I witnessed just how uncomfortable Rogan was with Amber. He didn't even know I watched him as he had to force himself to touch Amber's arm.

I'd never seen him look so awkward.

Hours later, the music sounded louder in my ears. All my friends were getting drunk around me. I wasn't sure how they'd managed to sneak in alcohol, but the punch was laced with it. Not one of the chaperones had paid attention to the fact, which I thought might have something to do with Chase's older brother flirting like crazy with Ms. Robins. He caught my raised brow and grinned, telling me to turn back to his brother.

"I think I need to tell him she's my algebra teacher," Chase grumbled.

Tugging Chase onto the dance floor, I wrapped my arms around his neck, forcing him to dance with me. "I think she's drinking the same punch that we are, so I wouldn't worry about it too much."

Chase twirled me around like a pro and I was laughing and gasping for breath by the end of the song. He reached for two glasses of punch, except my drink was taken away before I could get a hold of it.

"You know that's laced with rum, right?" Rogan growled.

"Rogan, really!" Amber staggered over in her too high heels. "It's prom, let her do what she wants. You can't babysit her all night," she continued to whine, wrapping her hands around Rogan's arm. "I want to have fun with you."

"No punch," he whispered as Amber dragged him to the dance floor.

"Um, why is Rogan being an asshole?" Julia stumbled into me, and Leon caught her around the waist from behind. "He's always watching you." She pointed a wobbly finger at me.

Coming to my rescue, Chase wrapped an arm around my neck and leered down the front of my dress. "He's just protecting his *sister.*"

I quickly turned to face Chase and he slapped a kiss to my shocked mouth.

"What?"

He winked.

"You guys break it up," Leon smirked. "Guess who has a hotel room booked for tonight?"

My eyes immediately shot to Julia, who was frowning at Leon. "We talked about this," she mumbled.

Leon grinned and kissed her fiercely. "Not me, Rogan. He's got a room booked and Amber has been trying to get him to take her there since we all arrived."

"Him and Amber?" I questioned.

Julia tilted her head.

Chase cursed.

Leon shrugged. "I don't know what the big deal is. He never goes out with anyone, so it's about damn time."

Julia hit him in the stomach, which ended in them kissing to the point that I thought they were the ones who needed a room.

A room like Rogan has booked.

My eyes filled with tears as they searched and found Rogan across the room talking to Amber and her friends. He wasn't touching her, but she was touching him—constantly. I knew I needed to pull myself together before I acted like the jealous girlfriend I was. Not that I could announce that bit of information. I was also well aware that the room key didn't have Amber's name on it. Rogan wouldn't do that to me. I was still angry and jealous, though.

Rogan caught me looking, a frown appearing on his face before he turned and headed toward me.

"Do not react." Chase grabbed my arm and spun me around to face him. He quickly wiped at my tears, and said, "Dance with me."

Chase didn't give me the choice as I was immediately in his arms. He held me tightly around the waist while we danced. My back was against his front with my butt grinding against his groin. It had no effect on Chase because I was the wrong sex, which no one else was aware of. I put my all into the dancing because I wanted Rogan to be pissed. I wanted him to know what it felt like to have to watch Chase and me, even knowing he had a room key in his pocket.

Just the thought angered me and I wanted to scream or hit him. I wanted to yank him away from Amber and tell her he was mine. Inside, I was steaming angry and upset and so close to stamping my foot like a two-year-old having a tantrum. Grabbing hold of the hands on my waist, I moved them suggestively to my hips.

Chase tightened his hold, his breath hot on my neck as he hissed, "You're going to get me a broken nose."

My eyes locked on to Rogan and the heat from his anger scolded a path straight to my heart. I burst into tears, and Chase froze behind me before leading me from the dance floor. Muttering to himself, he shoved me in front of him and out into the hallway.

His arms went around me and I clung to him, wetting his shirt with my tears. "I thought I could do this," I wailed. "I really thought I could without losing it." I looked up at Chase and then started laughing. The look of panic on his face made me laugh harder, which turned to sobs. "I don't want him to be with anyone else." I pulled away from Chase. "He has a room," I shouted.

"For us," an angry voice growled from behind me, and then cursed under his breath.

I turned and faced Rogan; his surprise as he looked at me was evident. "What—"

"Leon is under the impression that the room is, um, for Amber," Chase added.

"He's told everyone, right? That's why Amber won't stop clinging to me." Rogan ran his fingers through his hair, his eyes finding mine seconds before he pulled me into his arms.

He held me tightly with one hand on the back of my head, and the other around my waist. "I promise you that room is for us. I told you I was sleeping with you tonight." He kissed the top of my head and left his lips there. "I'm going to kill Leon."

"I know, tonight, seeing you with Amber, it hurt. I thought I'd be able to handle it because I knew your heart was mine. I can't handle it, Rogan. I can't handle seeing you with someone else, even when I know what's really going on."

Rogan sighed heavily and held me tightly.

My world righted itself once again.

31

FALLON

Looking out of the window from the hotel room there was nothing but darkness. It was earlier than Rogan had planned to bring me to the hotel. However, after my outburst at prom, we'd wanted away from there. Chase wasn't happy because Rogan had offered him up to Amber, who had been more than angry. I didn't think we'd heard the last from her, especially because she knew he was leaving to take me home.

Closing my eyes, I felt Rogan move in behind me, his fingers trailing softly along my spine. "You look so beautiful, Fallon, and tonight, as always, you outshined everyone." His lips skimmed my shoulder and I reached up, sliding my fingers into his hair.

"I'm afraid, Rogan." I turned in his arms. "What are

we doing? Nothing good will ever come of us being together." Ignoring the tears falling from my eyes, I searched Rogan's eyes as he caressed my face.

"I love you, and I'm not going to let anything stop us from being together." He kissed my forehead. "I know our relationship isn't...normal, but we belong together, Fallon. We always have."

He held my gaze as I hesitated before him, and then I was in his arms, clutching him. "Don't ever let me go," I begged fearfully.

"Never." His arms held me tightly around the waist and then we were moving. He slowly placed me on my feet in front of the bed. "I'm going to show you how much we're meant to be together." Offering a wry smile, he nervously brushed his fingers from my shoulders down my arms until our fingers intertwined. "This is the first time for both of us, and I'm just as nervous as you are." He kissed my fingers and, letting go, trailed his fingers down between my breasts to my belly button and back up.

"We don't need condoms," I whispered, my eyes met his, wondering how he'd react to my words.

He closed his eyes and swallowed before he focused on me again. "I'd hoped you'd say that because I want to feel you on me." He paused. "I came prepared, but I swear I'm healthy." He continued working his magic with his fingers.

My body trembled under his touch but the look of awe on his face gave me the courage to slip my dress to the floor. Rogan caught his breath, backing up, he dropped to his knees, removing the dress from around my feet. His hands caressed my ankles as he unfastened the high-heeled sandals, and then I stepped out of them and sat on the edge of the bed.

He moved between my legs, which was when I placed my hands on him. He'd already removed his jacket and now I helped remove his shirt, smiling when his skin was revealed.

"I love touching you," I admitted, sliding my fingers through the small amount of hair on his chest.

My fingers circled and rubbed the small, hard buds of his nipples and his body shuddered. He groaned. "I don't want to miss anything of tonight…of unveiling you." He captured one of my nipples in his mouth, sucking and licking before going in for the other.

Sliding my hands lower, his stomach quivered when I scraped my fingernails over his erection. He hissed between clenched teeth, and dropped his hands to the bed on either side of my hips, holding my gaze.

"I'm not sure I'm going to last long enough to get inside of you."

I offered him a reassuring smile. "We have all night." Moving further onto the bed, I held my hand out, wanting him to join me.

Briefly closing his eyes, Rogan got to his feet and once the rest of his clothes were removed, he joined me on the bed, kneeling between my spread legs. His eyes caressed over my nude, flushed body, his gaze unable to settle in any one place.

My eyes widened at the sight of him naked and aroused. He was magnificent. I couldn't look away as his penis grew and throbbed from the dark patch of hair covering the base of him. The tip was purple and swollen with pre-cum leaking from the slit. I reached out to touch him as he moved closer, but he captured my wrist.

"I want your touch so much, Fallon." He jerked hard. "I'm holding on by a thread right now. One touch from you and I'll come."

I was nervous knowing what we were about to do, but as I looked into his eyes, I honestly couldn't imagine being in the position with anyone else. It was reserved for Rogan and always would be.

"I'm afraid of hurting you," he admitted as he

lowered his gaze, almost as though he was as unsure as I was.

I reached out and pulled him to me. "You won't."

He swooped down, capturing my lips with his hot mouth. I moaned and wrapped myself around him, the length of his arousal pressing between my legs. His hips gently rocked and then his penis touched my opening. We froze, breathing heavily.

"You sure?" he asked, and I thought I'd die right then.

"Yes."

He cupped my head in his hands and watched my reaction as he slowly pushed the thick head of his penis inside of me. The pressure was immense and my vagina contracted around him, attempting to push him out. Rogan cursed, sweat on his brow.

"I want to feel you all the way inside of me." I clung to him, our bodies slippery.

He groaned. "Don't tell me shit like that." He panted. "I'm trying hard not to come. Having you in this way is beyond exciting. The feel of you wet and swollen, squeezing my dick is out of this world, and I only have the head inside of you."

I locked my ankles on his butt and tried to urge him on. "I'm just as excited, and feel something building. Please, just thrust inside of me."

"Fuck!" he roared, and, slowly pulling out, he thrust inside.

Pain hit me as I felt my insides burning. Rogan chanted, "I'm sorry," over and over again while his penis seemed to fill me even more, and then he clenched my hips in his large hands and came inside of me. I felt him. I felt every pulse of his penis as warm semen poured into me. It was exciting to watch him while he was at his most vulnerable. He pulled out of me slightly, and slid back in, grinding his pelvis against my clit, and then I found myself digging my nails into his ass as I joined him in pure bliss.

Rogan hissed as my body pulsated around his penis—squeezing and tugging—and, when he sucked a nipple into his mouth, I arched against him.

He cursed in my ear and I moved my arms, wrapping them around his neck as he wrapped me around his body. We gently rolled to the side and I slung a leg over his hip to keep us joined.

For the first time in my life, I felt loved in a way I'd never dreamed was possible. I'd always thought the love I'd read about in romance novels was only fiction. I knew now it wasn't.

Rogan nuzzled my ear and whispered, "I love you," his voice trembling. "I can't explain when or how I fell in love with you, but you're mine, Fallon." He brushed a soft kiss across my forehead while I felt him hardening and touching the sensitive place inside of me. "I can't let you go."

"I don't ever want you to let me go. Wherever we go in this life, we go together. Always. I love you."

Wrapped together, Rogan made love to me until I couldn't think anymore, and I knew, the night was the one I would treasure for the rest of my life.

32

———

ROGAN

Fallon walked out of the bathroom after she'd pulled herself back together, taking my breath away. Her dark hair was no longer as curly as it had been the night before, but her face was glowing. She glowed. Her happiness was clear for me to see, and it was because of me. I wanted to feel as happy as she did, but something was holding me back, and that thing was how wrong it was for us to be together.

But, I loved her. I couldn't explain why my feelings were what they were for someone so forbidden. I was waiting for something or someone to bring what we were doing out into the open, for it to crash around us.

Nothing could have stopped me from doing this for Fallon. I wanted to remember last night and have it associated with prom. We may not have gone to prom together, but, in my heart, I'd been with Fallon.

"You're thinking too deeply." Brushing her fingers through my hair, she rubbed her fingertips across my brows. "Do you regret what we've done?"

I captured her wrist and brought her hand up to my lips, pressing a soft kiss to her palm. "Here, with you, was the best night of my life." I offered her a soft smile. "I'm afraid, Fallon."

She frowned. "Why?"

"I'm afraid that when we walk out of this room, everything will change," I admitted. "I don't ever want anything to change between us, but it has. Our relationship has changed in ways it was never meant to, and that terrifies me." I brought her hands to my chest and clutched them tightly. "I don't regret anything we've done, and God help me, I want to do it all over again."

Fallon grinned and tugged her hands free. Wrapping her arms around my neck, she went up on her toes, my arms wrapped around her and held her tightly. "Last night was amazing, and I'll never forget it...but," she whispered into my ear, "I love you, and no matter how wrong this is, I want you. Only you, Rogan." She brushed a kiss across my lips. "Thank you for last night."

She stepped back and I found it difficult to remove my hands from her, so I intertwined our fingers together, refusing to let go. "We need to get home."

"I know." She sighed.

I didn't want to leave. When we did, I'd be back in my bedroom while Fallon was in hers across the hall. I hated sleeping apart from her. Neither of us had ever talked about the consequences of being together. I was thinking the trouble wouldn't happen to us—to other people, yes, but not to us. It was naive of me, of us. I only hoped that one day it wouldn't come back to bite us on the ass.

Fallon slipped her other hand into mine and backed toward the door. "We need to get it over with and, hopefully, I won't blush."

Grinning, I moved closer until her back was up against the door, and captured a quick kiss. "You'll blush," I whispered, knowing that she wouldn't do anything else as I unlocked the door. "I'll get the car. Give me fifteen, twenty minutes."

"OH," FALLON MOANED, SLIDING DOWN IN THE SEAT AS I pulled into the driveway. Mom was out front pulling weeds while Dad came around from the back. It made me twitch having to face them and I felt like a younger version of myself about to get in trouble for something.

Without looking at Fallon, I climbed from the car and hugged Mom.

"Did you have fun last night?"

If only she knew!

"The best night," I admitted, and smiled over the top of the car at Fallon, who, as predicted, had gone bright red.

Mom rushed around and scooped Fallon up in her embrace. "Did you too?"

"Yes, Mom. It was amazing."

I grinned like an idiot from behind Mom before straightening my features and turned toward Dad, who was watching us both closely. Dad didn't say anything but a frown appeared across his brow as we headed inside.

"I'm going to get changed," Fallon stated, trying to make a quick escape.

She wasn't quick enough.

"Can I talk to you both in the kitchen?" Dad asked in a tone that meant no argument.

Fallon glanced at Mom and Dad while we waited for her to come back downstairs. She looked scared, so I wrapped my arm around her neck and kissed the top of her head, not caring what anyone thought right then. She was mine to protect and that was what I was doing.

"Where did you go last night?" Dad asked before our butts hit the chairs.

"You gave your permission for us to stay out?" I questioned, confused.

"Rogan, your dad wants to know exactly where you stayed because Chase turned up here looking for you. The both of you." Mom fidgeted and took the seat across from us, showing a united front with Dad.

Chase knew where we were, so why the hell would he show up at the house? That didn't make sense, which meant either Mom or Dad were lying to trip us up, or Chase really had shown up after prom.

Fallon continued to fidget, so I slipped a hand over hers on her lap and squeezed.

"The truth is I ditched Amber not long after we arrived. I didn't want to be there with her, and she came out with a load of stuff about Fallon. We left and went to the park while the prom was still on, then afterword, Greg Flynn had invited us back to his place. We crashed there, as originally planned."

"I don't like the idea of you both spending the night together," Dad muttered, shaking his head.

Mom looked startled and glanced between us both.

"We spent last night with about sixty other people," Fallon added.

She hadn't exactly lied either considering the motel had thirty rooms, and it was prom. At least I'd had the sense to actually leave my car outside of Greg's house. It was a ten minute walk through the trees at the back of his house to the motel.

"Frank did say he saw Rogan's car parked outside one of those large houses on the other side of town." Mom turned to Dad.

Thank you, Uncle Frank.

"Are we done here? I know I want a shower and my own bed. Fallon probably does too." I hauled her up and nodded toward the stairs.

I waited until she'd disappeared and then turned to our parents. "What is this about?"

"It doesn't matter now," Dad muttered.

Mom wouldn't meet my gaze and finally got up to do the dishes.

"What did you think?" I placed my hands on the table in front of Dad, who didn't even flinch. "Dad, you always get to the point. Why not now?"

"I'll tell you why," Dad shouted, leaning toward me, "because I don't even want to think about it."

"Think about what?" I yelled back, having no idea why I pushed him to answer. I didn't want them to know anything. I didn't want it to be spoken about. Was it my guilt talking?

"Are you sleeping with Fallon?" Dad actually asked and I felt like I was going to puke.

I was stunned at Dad's outburst. Thank God, because it saved me from giving myself away.

"Who told you that?"

Mom snapped, "I've had enough of shouting in the house. This isn't like us."

"Who put that into your head?" Dad winced at my tone, and I laughed. "Let me guess, Uncle Frank." I shook my head. "You do realize he'll do anything to cause trouble between us all. He's always been jealous of the happy family you have." I turned away, and said over my shoulder, "Let's not forget that it was because of him *you* put Fallon and me in the same bedroom. So, of course, doing that would make his tongue wag."

Hitting the stairs hard, I slammed into my bedroom. I stripped and took another shower, feeling a deep-seated sadness as it started crawling through my body. Why did it have to be so wrong for Fallon and me to be together? Why?

Tears of anger fell as quickly as the water pounding down my back, and then they changed into tears of anguish. Our being together would cause too much pain, and even then, I wasn't sure I'd last it out. I may only be eighteen, but I knew I'd always want Fallon by my side. The thought of anyone else made me sick. I didn't need anyone else, just her.

But would I always have her?

33

FALLON

After being confronted by our dad, it had made us realize just how close we were to being caught. But it didn't matter to us. We couldn't stop; we just made sure to never touch at the house anymore. There was no more sneaking around. It had become too risky.

We now had our own private place close to the river where we could be alone. It was where Rogan had made love to me numerous times.

It had been here while I'd lain, secure in his arms that I'd realized summer was moving too quickly for us. We spent lazy days here or further along the river with our friends, Chase having not turned up at the house the night of prom looking for us. But before we knew it, we'd have to say goodbye. I didn't want that.

I wanted to cling to Rogan and beg him not to leave, or to take me with him.

"A nickel for your thoughts," Rogan whispered, a long blade of grass between his lips.

I rested my chin on his chest and held his gaze. "I'm thinking about you and college and how I don't want to say goodbye to you."

"I'm only going to be a few hours away."

"Ten hours round trip," I added miserably.

He ran his fingers through my thick hair. "Me going to college isn't the end of us, Fallon. You know that, right? Nothing will ever stop me from being with you."

"I know." I chewed on my bottom lip. "I've been thinking about driving again." It was the truth but it made me sick to my belly thinking about it. I hadn't driven since the accident.

Rogan's hands massaging my scalp paused. "Don't push yourself. Wait until you feel ready, and not because you feel that you have to."

Sighing, I rested my face against his chest, comfortable in his embrace. "I'm afraid, but I'm also angry at myself for not getting right back into driving as soon as I was well enough. I've left it too long."

I felt him shake his head in the vibration from his

body. "One day you'll suddenly get the urge to drive. I really believe that will happen."

Silence surrounded us for a long time and I was in the middle of a brief nap when Rogan said, "I want a house by the ocean, and I want to share it with you and a dog." He chuckled. "Cats too, if you want."

I smiled. "What brought that on?"

"I've been thinking a lot about our future. To have a relationship out in the open, we'll have to move away from here. We'll make new friends. He sat up, keeping me straddled over him. "I have it all planned."

"Really?"

"Yes." He grinned. "I promise you, Fallon," he said, excited, his eyes alight. "One day, we'll be together the way we should be."

Listening to Rogan talk about our future made me lighthearted and filled me with joy, but there was also fear buried just below the surface. Fear of the unknown; fear that, one day, our lives would come crashing down around our ears.

"I don't want to go anywhere right now, but the others will be at the house soon."

"Hmm," I mumbled, wanting to stay in our secret place, too.

JULIA WAS QUIET IN THE BACK GARDEN WITH THE GUYS. They were sitting on lounge chairs talking, and I was afraid to join them in case they were discussing college. I wasn't naive. I was well aware of what college guys got up to and that scared me. Not because I didn't trust Rogan, which I did, but because he's a hot looking guy and the girls are going to be all over him. So I certainly didn't want to hear Leon and Chase's plans for any of it.

I caught Julia's quick glances toward the house and was sure she'd figured out that I was using the excuse of making drinks for everyone to hide. Julia would be right too.

On a heavy sigh, I turned and picked up the tray with the homemade lemonade, along with sliced pound cake.

Nothing felt real as I walked across the lawn and it hurt that I couldn't show how much I loved Rogan. He looked so handsome relaxing on the lounger wearing his long-sleeved tee and sweat pants. I wore yoga pants and one of Rogan's sweatshirts.

Placing the tray down on the table, I felt Rogan's eyes on me while everyone else dug into the refreshments. So I gave in to what I wanted and climbed on the lounger with him. I curled up against him and sighed when his arm wrapped around me. He kissed the top of my head and I didn't move. The silence from our friends didn't even bother me.

"You two are weird." Julia sat on the lounger facing me. "You need a boyfriend."

Rogan tensed against me at Julia's words and his hand on my waist dug in before he realized what he was doing.

"And you"—she pointed at Rogan—"need a girlfriend."

"Julia, I'm eighteen and in no rush." He hesitated. "Besides, if anyone came sniffing around Fallon, I'd have to kill them." He grinned. "So don't go getting ideas about setting her up, or me for that matter."

Leon kicked the bottom of the lounger. "You act like lovers," he grouched before joining Julia.

"Get off their case," Chase said from behind us. "Things are changing and we'll be college freshmen while the girls will be back here finishing high school."

"Thanks for that reminder," Rogan complained.

"I'm planning on having the whole college experience," Chase continued. "This is why I'm not attached like you guys."

"What?" Leon jerked his gaze toward Rogan and me. "You need to tell us something?" He narrowed his eyes.

"Okay, bad choice of words," Chase muttered. "You have Julia, and Rogan and Fallon are always together is all I meant." He trailed off into silence. "Jeez, lighten up."

"Not funny, man." Leon stood and tugged Julia with him. "We're heading out. Have fun, assholes."

"I'll call you later," Julia shouted as Leon dragged her behind him.

"Sorry. Now I really feel like the odd one out," Chase added.

"Don't worry about it," Rogan said. "They'll forget about the time I spend with Fallon once we've separated." He tightened his hold. "I won't, though." He placed another kiss on the top of my head.

"What's going to happen when you're gone? I mean…" Chase trailed off.

Rogan moved us into a sitting position, me between his legs with my back against his chest. "I can't switch off what I feel because what I'm doing with Fallon isn't allowed. I love her. No distance is going to change that." He looked at me snuggled in his arms. "I'm probably going to be an asshole when we're not together, but you'll get used to it," he said to Chase.

Rogan held Chase's gaze, and I felt him sigh. "Mom and Dad are home."

Groaning, I reluctantly moved to sit beside him with a small gap between us. "I hate this." The tears on my lashes slowly fell as I listened to our parents moving around in the house.

"You're staying for dinner, right?" Rogan wasn't really asking Chase, he was telling him that we needed him to stay.

"One of these days"—Chase lay back on the lounger—"you're going to get caught and I won't be around to act as a buffer." He glanced between us. "I love you guys and I consider you both family, so please, if for no other reason, be careful."

"We try to be." I said so quietly I wasn't sure they heard me.

"Try harder," Chase replied. "The thing is, if anyone is really looking at you both, they'll see what I do."

Rogan tilted his head at one of his best friends.

"I see the connection you share, and I see that it goes a lot deeper than it should. I've seen it for years. Since before either of you knew yourselves. Just be careful."

Rogan's fingers slipped over mine and I smiled at the feel of his touch. Anyone looking wouldn't know we held hands, but we did, even if it was brief.

Standing, Rogan brushed my thigh with his

fingers and I joined him, along with Chase, whose stomach loudly rumbled. Laughing, I teased, "You planned on staying for dinner regardless of Rogan's command, huh?"

"I distinctly remember hearing your mom state that it was burgers on the grill tonight." Chase grinned. "No way am I missing your dad's burgers."

I winked at Rogan and then wrapped an arm around Chase's waist, his arm wrapping around my shoulders. He kissed me on the top of my head just like Rogan always did. It didn't feel the same, but Chase offered Rogan a wicked grin. "She likes me more than you."

"Don't tease him." I poked Chase in the stomach.

He caught my hand. "No tickling."

I rolled my eyes and caught the look exchanged between Mom and Dad as we approached. I knew they thought something was going on between Chase and me, and I didn't mind them thinking that. Even Chase didn't mind because it helped keep the speculation off of him.

"We got you some bedding and things for college today." Mom grinned, pulling Rogan to her for a hug. "I'm going to miss my baby."

Dad rolled his eyes behind Mom's back. "Don't

worry, you will still have Fallon." He grinned wider when he noticed the look of horror on my face.

"I'm more than capable of looking after myself." I moved over to Dad and smiled against his chest as he pulled me in close.

"I know you are, sweetheart." He kissed me on the cheek. "It's going to be strange for you as well with Rogan being away."

Tears formed on my lashes, which I rapidly blinked away, not wanting anyone to see how upset I really was.

I dreaded the day he left, knowing things were going to be different between us no matter how much Rogan insisted we'd always be the same.

IT WAS DOWN TO MINUTES BEFORE ROGAN LEFT FOR college, and I still didn't know how to say goodbye to him. He'd be home for Thanksgiving, but it wouldn't be the same as having him with me all the time.

My hands trembled as I heard a soft knock on the bedroom door before Rogan slipped inside.

The moment our eyes met, I knew he was just as upset.

Tears welled in my eyes as he reached for me, his

face burrowed into my neck. His arms held me against his warm body.

Everything inside of me hurt to the point that I was afraid I would fall to pieces. My throat ached with anguish as I tried to hold back until he'd left. I didn't want him to witness how heartbroken I was.

Rogan pulled away, and cupped my face, searching for something and that was when it happened. I smothered a sob and fled, hot tears slipping down my cheeks.

Rogan pounded downstairs behind me, but I didn't stop. I couldn't. I flung the backdoor open and ran out into the heavy downpour currently water logging the footpath around the edge of the garden.

My feet splashed in the water while my tears continued to blind me. I knew exactly where I was going as I ran away from Rogan leaving me.

By the time I arrived at our place by the river, I was drenched to the skin, my hair dripping.

Rogan burst through the tall grass just as drenched, his breathing fast and heavy.

"Do you think this is easy for me?" he shouted, moving closer, angry. "I'm going off to college without the girl I love and it's killing me." His voice broke and a tear rolled down his cheek. "I don't want to go, but if we want a future together then I don't have a choice, and neither do you."

"I love you," I sobbed, throwing myself into his arms, searching for his lips.

My lips smothered his groan, as his firm mouth demanded a response from mine. His tongue sent shivers of desire racing through me, warming me through to my broken heart.

Our tears fell together under the tree we'd claimed as ours at the beginning of summer. We slowly parted and stared at each other, we knew things were changing in our lives and that we had no control over it.

Rogan cupped my face and brushed at my tears with his thumbs, smiling through his own. "Tears in the rain," he whispered, placing a gentle kiss on each of my eyelids and the tip of my nose. "I love you, Fallon." His last kiss was placed on my forehead where he lingered.

"I love you, too." I forced myself to smile as he slowly backed away and disappeared from view.

I raised my face to the sky, letting my tears fall with the rain.

34

ROGAN

Being a freshman in college sucked big time when the girl I was in love with was back home. I knew she was just as miserable as I was, but I was relieved her tears had stopped. Every time it had rained since I'd left, it had reminded me of Fallon and her tears in the rain. It was heartbreaking, but she had been so beautiful standing in the rain, soaked to the skin and clinging to me. It had killed me to drive away, knowing Fallon was alone by the river. Mom had looked worried when I'd asked her to check on Fallon after I'd gone.

As for school, I managed, even if I missed Fallon on a daily basis. We talked every morning when we woke up, then again every evening before going to bed. It wasn't the best but it also wasn't too bad. As time went on, I knew it would become harder and harder to be away from her.

Leon surprised me because he really was missing Julia. He flirted with the girls on campus, but nothing serious. I would laugh if one of them took him up on the teasing because I knew Leon, and my friend would run a mile back to Julia. Theirs was a relationship I'd never seen happening.

My dorm room was for single occupancy, so I was lucky enough to get Chase on one side and Leon on the other, which was good. At least we didn't have to go too far to meet up. It was the girl opposite who was a pain in my butt, and I had Leon to thank for that. With Leon not being in the know about Fallon and me, he'd flirted with Tiffany on my behalf, and now she had it in her head that I was shy and interested. Not the case. Chase found it amusing, but that soon changed once he caught the eye of Rome.

Leon was no longer under the impression that Chase was dating Fallon. I was just glad he hadn't made a scene now that he was aware of Chase's preference.

I still waited for Leon to ask me about Chase. He knew we'd hung out a lot back home while he was off with Julia. He was going to put two and two together and come back with five. So yeah, I actually looked forward to that.

Leon was currently slumped on the end of my bed with his phone glued to his hand, a smile on his face. Only Julia could make that happen.

Hearing Leon's stomach growl, made me crave the burgers Dad cooked on the grill. Tonight, I thought a trip to Wendy's might be in order. They weren't as good as home, but they'd fill the hunger until I was back there.

Nudging Leon with my foot to get his attention, I smiled as he gave me the finger.

"I need a burger."

Leon's eyes popped wide. "Why didn't you tell me you were hungry?"

"I did." I shoved Leon off the bed. "Let's go get Chase and eat."

"What about a movie afterward? We don't have anywhere to be tomorrow."

"Pick something." I paused. "Nothing girly to remind you of Julia."

"Yeah, right, asshole! At least I have a girl. Can't say the same about you and Chase." He frowned. "Forget I mentioned Chase and girl in the same sentence."

I ignored Leon as he shot a message off to Chase.

Seconds later, he got a reply when Chase barged in. "Let's go."

I watched Leon and Chase, and I was glad nothing had changed between us. That was what true friends were. I just hoped when it came out about Fallon and me, that I'd still have that with Leon. Chase wouldn't be an issue.

"Wendy's?" Leon asked, not looking up from his phone.

I rolled my eyes at Chase and shook my head. Chase just grinned and climbed into my car. "When we go home, do you think your dad will grill?" Chase asked.

Laughing, I replied, "The next time we're home is Thanksgiving, so it will be snowing."

"That sucks."

After eating, we walked to the movie theatre and I couldn't help the groan of annoyance slipping from my lips when I spotted Tiffany and a friend waiting near the ticket office.

Leon was the only one who didn't look surprised.

"What did you do?" I growled.

"Look, you're single. She's single and interested." Leon, the *asshole*, grinned and sauntered up to the girls.

I narrowed my eyes at Chase, who shook his head

and moved away. "I had nothing to do with this. You should know that."

Running my hands through my hair, I cursed and glared daggers at Leon. "I'll get our tickets but the idiot can sit with the girls." Stomping off to the ticket counter, I ended up getting Leon's ticket, even though I was irritated with him.

Chase was struggling not to laugh as I shoved Leon and gave him his ticket.

"You get the girls a ticket?" Leon had the balls to ask.

It stopped me mid-step and I slowly turned toward my idiot of a friend. "I didn't invite them, so no, I didn't."

Turning my back to them, I headed into the theatre and found Chase chuckling behind me. "You are so awesome when pissed."

"You better be sitting next to me or I'm leaving," I grumbled.

"How old are you, six?"

Ignoring my amused friend, I slumped in the seat right up against the wall and glared at Chase when he moved to sit along the row in front. "Are you kidding me?"

He smirked.

Leon and the girls appeared. Tiffany slid along

until she was in the seat next to me. Her gaze immediately went to my angry face and her blush deepened, making me feel like a shit for being such an asshole.

Inhaling, I turned to Tiffany and admitted, "I'm sorry Leon keeps doing shit like this. It isn't you, okay? It's me. I'm just not interested because I'm already in love with someone else. So please stop because I know Leon won't."

"He said you've never had a girlfriend," she whispered back. "I thought you two were best friends."

I rubbed at my brow where the headache was starting. "We are, and Leon doesn't know everything like he thinks he does. I'm not interested, okay? Ignore Leon in the future."

Within minutes of me being honest with Tiffany, she was cuddling up to me as the movie started. So I did the only thing I could and climbed into the seat behind everyone.

Chase was oblivious, but the others glared at me, especially Leon who narrowed his eyes. I shrugged. "You arranged this."

Retrieving my phone from my back pocket, I unlocked it and immediately saw a message from Fallon. It was only a smiley with a love heart over the lips, but it said more than words.

All tension drained from me.

Rogan: I miss you <3

Fallon: Miss you more <3

Rogan: How was school?

Fallon: Boring!

Her usual reply.

Rogan: What you doing?

Fallon: Lying on my bed, thinking of you.

My heart pounded as it always did.

Rogan: I'm always thinking of you.

Fallon: <3

Fallon: What are you doing?

Rogan: At the movies with the guys.

I wasn't even mentioning the girls Leon had arranged to join us, or rather me.

Fallon: What are you watching?

Realizing I had no clue, I laughed.

Rogan: IDK.

Fallon: lol

Rogan: I love you.

Rogan: I miss you.

Fallon: Forever my heart <3

Rogan: Goodnight! Sweet dreams! <3

After the movie, Leon confronted me, so I set him straight. "You need to stop trying to fix me up. I'm not interested."

"You...um...and Chase—" Leon didn't finish and I noticed an actual blush on his cheekbones.

Chuckling, I grinned so wide my face hurt. "I can assure you that my preference is of the female variety." I shook my head. "Please stop, Leon. If I wanted to be with someone, then I'm sure I could find my own girl. I'm just not into anyone, so leave it."

Leon added, "You really don't want to mess with Tiffany?"

I gritted my teeth together, trying to find calm when I really wanted to knock Leon's head off. Maybe he'd listen then. "Listen clearly. No, I am not interested in *messing* with Tiffany or anyone else you can think of. If you do this again, I'll make sure Julia knows about it."

Leon cursed and I thought I'd finally made my point.

"I'm leaving, so if you or Chase want a lift, get a move on." I made my way to my car and waited.

With my phone in hand, I opened up my photographs and smiled as the images appeared of Fallon. Her black hair flowed down her back and was so thick and shiny that it seemed endless. I loved losing myself in those waves as I'd run my fingers through the thick tresses. She was the most beautiful girl I'd ever seen and I was completely obsessed with her. The way she moved would cause me to lose my every last thought. The way she looked when she hovered above me, her silken strands caressing my body. But my favorite part of Fallon was her smile. She lighted my heart when she smiled, and it was only for me—a secret tilt of her lips whenever she noticed me. It was something I missed.

You could only have so much through the phone or via computers, and even though I hadn't been gone that long, I missed the physical contact. Just being able to hold her hand would satisfy me.

She said everything would change once I went away to school. She'd been right in some ways. Things had changed and continued to do so, but the one thing that had stayed the same was my love for the girl I'd left behind.

PART III

Rogan, 19 / Fallon, 18

35

FALLON

Sitting in the new window seat in my bedroom, I watched as the rain fell in large, thunderous drops. It was almost pretty, but, right now, it matched my mood—dark. I missed Rogan so much and the daily calls and texts were not really the same as being with him. I felt cold without his arms around me. Sad without his smile to brighten my day. I desperately wanted to talk about him and my misery with Julia, but I couldn't.

Julia was just as miserable with Leon being in college with Rogan and Chase, the guys having decided to stay together. It was good for them, but not for the ones left behind, missing them. I wasn't being fair because I knew Rogan was missing me. He didn't have to say anything because I could hear it in his voice whenever we hung up. I could see it on his face after we'd video chatted.

It had been strange with him gone from home. The summer before he'd left for college had been bittersweet because we'd known he was leaving. I'd gotten the feeling he'd wanted me to beg him not to go, but as much as I'd wanted him to stay, I couldn't do that. I loved him too much to be selfish.

In the last six months, he'd only been home for Thanksgiving, Christmas, and my eighteenth, and his nineteenth birthday. I wondered, occasionally, if our parents still suspected something between us. Our parents hadn't said anything recently. Even if they had, I knew I couldn't stop. Neither could Rogan.

I knew what I felt for Rogan was real, and I'd do anything to keep him close. I hated the thought of him being away at college with all the girls I knew would be looking at him. The thing was trust, and I did trust him. It also helped that Leon was constantly complaining about Rogan's lack of female companionship, as in nothing happening on that front. So yes, it was good to have that reassurance.

But I missed him.

"How long are you going to sit there lost in your own thoughts?" Julia asked, not even making me jump at my friend's sudden appearance.

Turning my head, I found my bedroom door was closed and Julia spread out on my bed. "How long have you been here?"

"About five minutes." Julia smirked. "You weren't really here." She waved her arms around.

"Sorry," I mumbled, stretching as I got to my feet. "I can't shake this gloom that's hanging over me."

"Do you have plans?"

"You mean like staying in my room, missing Rogan?"

"I mean like packing a bag and coming with me to see the guys."

My heart missed a beat at Julia's words and my eyes searched hers to see if she was lying to me. "Please tell me this isn't a joke."

"No joke." She grinned. "I begged Leon to drive home yesterday while he had no classes so he could take us back with him." Jumping from the bed, Julia quickly hugged me, and shoved me toward my backpack. "We need to be quick," Julia added, "he's already been waiting while I waited for you to notice me."

"Does Rogan know I'm going back with him?"

"No! I can't wait to see his reaction. According to Leon, he's a miserable asshole, and that's a quote." Opening the top drawer of my dresser, Julia glanced at me. "What do you want to take?"

"I'll pack, you go and tell Leon I'll be down in five minutes." My lips twitched up into a smile. "We're really going to see the guys?"

Julia nodded and I threw my arms around her shoulders. "Thank you."

"Hey, I'm not just doing this for you."

I rolled my eyes. "Yeah, I've already figured that one out."

"Move it." Julia smacked me on the butt and then she was gone.

Not wasting another moment, I tossed a set of clean clothes into the bag and then I was running downstairs, texting Mom to let her know where I was going. I grabbed a raincoat on my way out before running to the car.

Hours later, we pulled up outside the dorms and my stomach was in knots. What if he didn't want me here? He had never asked me to come up for a weekend. Maybe he wanted to stop what we'd started? Doubts, and more doubts ran through my mind as I followed Leon and Julia into the building.

I didn't pay much attention to the other students we passed in the hallway because I just wanted to get to Rogan.

Coming to a stop, Leon pushed a key into a lock

and softly opened the door. "He's in there," he whispered. "I think Chase is with him."

Leon took Julia's hand and led her down the hallway to the room next door to Rogan's.

A girl opposite the door openly stared, making me feel uncomfortable as she looked between the door, back to me, and the door again. Just as I was about to enter, the girl took a step closer, so I quickly slipped inside and let the door close in the girl's face. Something told me I wasn't going to like her, whoever she was.

Before I made my presence known, I heard, "Chase! Stop getting on my butt. I'm not bothered about what girl has her eyes on me." Rogan cursed. "The only girl I will ever want is waiting for me back home. She's mine and I belong to her, so stop. Shit, tell everyone I'm gay or something. Just back off."

I was frozen just inside of the doorway feeling my heart swell and any doubt I had dwindled at his words.

"You need to be careful," Chase stated, more serious than I'd ever heard him. "Real careful."

"I don't know what I'm doing, but I love her. I always have. I know it's wrong. I also know that I'll never want anyone else the way I want her. She's part of me, and this may be selfish, but I love her too much to ever give her up because I won't survive if she's ever with someone else."

"That will never happen," I said, surprising them both. "I love *only* you, Rogan."

Rogan blinked a few times. "You're really here?"

I nodded, tears swimming in my eyes. "Yes."

"Thank God." Rogan rushed forward and swept me up into his arms. My legs automatically curled around his waist while my mouth searched for his. "I've missed you," he whispered before he devoured me.

I vaguely heard, "I'll go," and then the door closed.

Panting against my mouth, Rogan said, "Let me lock the door so no one can get in."

My legs and arms tightened around him and I kissed and licked his neck, sucking on one of his earlobes as I heard the lock engage.

Rogan growled, pinning me to the wall with his hips. "You overheard everything I said to Chase?"

I nodded.

He paused. "Good."

His mouth came crashing back down, passion and desperation hitting us both. Our clothing disappeared, and then I shoved a hand between us, wrapping it around his large penis.

"Inside you," he groaned, and then grunted when he slid all the way inside. "So good."

I arched, stretching up to the ceiling, enjoying his hands on my butt as his mouth sucked and nipped at my breasts. Then he started hammering between my thighs. He was really thick and long, I felt every single inch of him as he brought me higher and higher toward release.

"I can't go slow." He trembled.

The angle of his thrusts changed slightly and, without warning, my orgasm rushed through me. Rogan mouthed my neck while my body pulled every ounce of semen from his flesh.

"I've missed you," he mumbled into my neck.

Chuckling, I tugged his face up to mine. "I've missed you more."

"Not possible."

I brushed the hair from his forehead, and trailed my fingers down his face. "I wish I could stay here with you."

"You're here until Sunday, right?"

I nodded.

"Then you're not leaving my sight the whole time." He rested his forehead against mine. "It won't be long before you start college and then we'll be able to live together."

"Only if Mom doesn't get her way and has me in the dorms."

He shook his head. "No way will that happen… even if it does, you won't be staying there."

Grabbing my waist, he lifted me off of him and my eyes rolled, my teeth chewing on my bottom lip at the sensation of him sliding out of me. Rogan hissed when he popped free, and I was back on my feet. My eyes roamed over him and I couldn't hold the amusement in when I saw his sweats wrapped around his ankles.

He followed my gaze and smirked. "What can I say?" He wrapped a hand around his wet penis. "I missed you."

My body trembled as I watched him stroke himself, but then he spoiled my viewing pleasure by turning and kicking off his sweats. He grabbed up all our clothing, then he kissed me on the nose. Holding out his hand, he said, "Come and sleep with me. I want to feel you in my arms all night."

I didn't need asking twice as I moved forward and took his hand. He put me into his bed and climbed in behind me, spooning.

"I've missed you. I find myself turning to ask you something and you're not there. The other weekend there was a band in the park and I wanted you to come listen to it with me. With you, I enjoy the silence, too. Just spending a day in the same room is enough for me." I felt him smile against the back of my neck. "But of course, I love being able to hold you with no barriers between us."

I turned in his arms and wrapped myself against his warm chest. "I don't want to leave," I whispered. "I want to stay here with you. I'm so unhappy at home."

"I know." He kissed me on the forehead just as sleep and exhaustion took me under.

ROGAN SLEPT DEEPLY NEXT TO ME. SOMETIME DURING the night, the covers had been kicked off and he was on complete display with his legs spread and his arms bent over his head. He looked so damn cute like that, but all those thoughts fled when my eyes caressed over his body.

My heart pounded when my eyes focused lower on his body. He certainly wasn't asleep there and he was too tempting not to touch with my hands and mouth.

I gently moved between his legs, and nearly face-planted into his balls, my breath teased across the big looking things. I stifled a giggle at the thought that he was big all over, and kissed at the base of his erection. He jerked at my touch.

"I'm going to come all over my stomach if you keep doing that," his rough voice announced.

My eyes shot up to his and I held his gaze as I licked him from base to tip, swirling my tongue around the leaking crown. Rogan panted and dug his fingers into the mattress, releasing more pre-cum onto my tongue.

"Fallon," he groaned, his body taut and his penis rigid with need.

"You're not going to come on your stomach," I teased, his eyes darkening with lust. "You're going to come in my mouth."

I slowly slid my mouth down the length of him, going as deep as I ever thought possible, until my nose brushed the hairs at his groin. Rogan groaned, his hips moving helplessly beneath me.

His hands slid through my hair and held me down on him, until he got a fist of hair and made me rise. When I did, his penis glistened from the wetness of my mouth and when I glanced at Rogan, he snapped his eyes closed at the sight. He was so damn close that I didn't know how he held himself in check.

Gliding back down on him, I slid my hands over

his hips to his butt and held him inside of my mouth. I dug my fingernails into his flesh and sucked—hard.

"Oh fuck! *Fallon*... Oh God! I'm gonna... Oh God... *Oh God! FALLON*," he finally roared with release.

"Stop. No more," he panted. "Fuck, Fallon." He tried to move my head, but I wouldn't be moved. He hadn't let me do this before so I wasn't wasting a moment that I was down on him.

He grunted and came one last time before he started to go soft in my mouth. I made sure I'd gotten every single drop before I lifted my head from his lap. His eyes were soft and relaxed as he tugged me up his body. He wrapped his arms around me and then rolled to the side.

"You've wanted to do that for a while."

"You wouldn't let me."

"I wanted inside of you too much to let you." He rolled me to my back and slipped a hand between my legs. "I want to see what blowing me did to you."

He dipped a finger between the swollen lips between my thighs and then lifted that finger to his mouth, his tongue coming out and wrapping around the digit. "Tasty."

My breath caught and then I couldn't breathe

when he buried his face between my legs. The pleasure from his mouth was unbelievable.

I was burning up and a tight coil in my stomach felt like it was about to unravel. The minute he fingered me, and sucked, I flew apart, screaming his name. Pleasure had me rubbing against his face—I couldn't stop. So…so good!

His face appeared in my line of sight and the heated look in his eyes told me he was aroused. "I need you." He thrust hard and I came again while clutching at him. Rogan grunted and ground down as he took his pleasure. A grunt and hiss was the sign he'd finished as he collapsed on me. "Need a nap."

Chuckling, I slid my feet over his ass and between his legs. "You're really comfy in this position."

"Hmm," he mumbled, his face between my breasts. "I could stay like this forever." He looked up at me and wiggled his brows before becoming serious. "You're going to be sore," he commented, pulling out of my body. He kissed the tip of each breast before rolling to his side, his hand searching for mine.

Holding each other close, I asked, "Are the girls really after you?" I wasn't sure where that question came from but it was out now.

Rogan rested his hand on my hip. "Yeah, they come on to me, but I don't take them up on anything."

He shrugged. "Leon keeps trying to get me to look, but that won't ever happen. I love you, Fallon. I know it's wrong. But when we're together, it feels right."

I snuggled into his chest, and whispered, "I love you, Rogan, and it would kill me to see you with someone else."

"That's how I feel." He kissed the top of my head and I fell back asleep.

NOT SURE HOW LONG I'D SLEPT FOR, I CAME AWAKE suddenly to Rogan when I heard him growl, "She's sleeping, Julia, you're not going into my room."

Glancing at the digital clock at the side of the bed, my eyes widened in surprise. I'd slept till eleven in the morning! I hadn't realized just how tired I was.

Yawning, I stretched and decided I'd better find something to wear before Julia got her way and found me naked in Rogan's bed. I did get a weird look from Julia now and again, but I wasn't sure how to take it. She had said it was her "thinking look," but it worried me.

"Leon, do something about your girlfriend," Rogan shouted. "You are going to wake her up."

"Don't tell me what to do, Rogan Scott. Fallon is my best friend and if you've hurt her I'll…I'll kill you!"

Rogan laughed and I smiled at my friend. Julia could be difficult when she wanted to be, but I wasn't sure why she was so adamant that I needed waking up.

The shaking of the doorknob drew my gaze, so I grabbed the tee Rogan had on last night and made a dash for the bathroom, just closing the door as the dorm room door swung open.

I sagged against the cool tile while I sorted his tee out, finally covering my nakedness. It was black, which was good, but I wished I'd had time to grab a pair of panties from my bag or even a pair of Rogan's shorts. Smiling, I spotted three pairs drying over the shower rail. I chose the black ones covered in red kisses, which I'd bought him for his birthday, amongst other things.

It took me a few minutes to finish in the bathroom, and then I opened the door and found four pairs of eyes on me: Rogan, Julia, Leon, and Chase.

Rogan slipped toward me and wrapped his arm around my shoulders. "I told you I didn't kill her."

Julia rolled her eyes.

Rogan asked, "You sleep okay?"

"Like the dead, until I heard shouting." Raising a brow, I glanced between Julia and him. "Keep it down next time."

"You never sleep this late." Julia pouted, watching Rogan and me from beneath her lids.

Rogan moved closer and took my hand. "You okay?"

"Yeah. For a minute there, I thought she would find me tangled in your sheets." No sooner had the words left my mouth, had I realized how stupid they were. It was obvious I'd slept in his bed.

Rogan pulled me down beside him on the unmade bed, so I curled into his side and found all eyes on us.

"I'm not sure I want to know this," Julia started. "But it's been on my mind on and off over the years, as I know it has Leon's." She inhaled. "What exactly is going on between the two of you?" She waved her hand between us. "You're wearing his shirt, and you slept in his bed."

My stomach felt weird as all color drained from my face. Realistically, I knew this day would come. I wasn't ready and didn't think Rogan was either. It could be worse—it could be our parents standing in front of us.

Rogan gripped my hand and slowly kissed my knuckles while holding my gaze. "We have this."

Facing Julia and Leon, he admitted, "Fallon is the reason you don't see me with anyone else."

"No way," Leon cursed and laughed, looking between us all. "This is a joke, right?"

"I don't think it is," Julia said, tilting her head, watching me closely.

With tears on my lashes, I clutched Rogan's hand as though he was my lifeline. I was scared, but I was also relieved to be able to admit to Julia how I truly felt about Rogan.

Holding Julia's gaze, I admitted, "I'm in love with Rogan. Really in love with him." I smiled at Rogan through my tears. "We never meant for anything to happen between us, and we really tried to stay away from each other." I turned to Julia. "Except...we constantly were drawn together until we couldn't stay away any longer. He's all I want. We both know how wrong it is, but we can't help who we fall in love with."

Silence surrounded us, and then Leon sank to the floor, leaning against the wall beside the door. He whispered, "You're really in love with your...your... *Fallon?*" He laughed. "I can't even say it." He shook his head.

"She's mine, Leon. Always has been and always will be, so yes, I *really* love her." Rogan let go of my hand and pulled me completely against him, holding me tightly. "We didn't want you to find out like this, and I'm not even sure if or when we planned on telling you. But it is what it is. I love her."

"And I love him," I whispered, my voice failing.

I looked at Julia and saw the disgust on her face, which brought tears to my eyes. Out of anyone, I had always thought Julia would accept Rogan and me. I'd been wrong.

"You knew," Leon accused Chase, his voice angry to match his darkened mood, as he climbed to his feet.

He stepped into Chase and got in his face. "You're okay with what they're doing? Been doing?" Leon threaded his fingers through his hair and tugged, clearly agitated.

"I always knew you had a close relationship, I just never believed it was anything but friendship." Julia moved to Leon and took his hand, her sadness seeping over me as I held her gaze. "Once or twice, I did think there might have been more going on, but I never imagined—" Her eyes filled with tears. "How could you? What about your parents, this will destroy them?"

What color was left drained from my face.

Rogan stood.

"You can't say anything to anyone," Rogan begged, his fists clenched tightly. "If we ever meant anything to you, please forget about this."

Leon glared while Julia continued to stare at me.

"Julia?" I held my hand out.

Julia glanced at my hand, and then slowly shook her head. "I can't right now. You're my best friend, Fallon, but what you're doing is wrong." She lifted her face to Leon. "Can we leave?"

His jaw tightened, then he wrapped an arm around Julia's shoulders. "Let's go."

They refused to look at us as they left.

"That went well." Chase slumped on the bed, and reached for my hand. "You both had to have known not everyone would be okay with this?"

"I thought Julia would be." I lifted my gaze to Rogan. "I was stupid thinking that." I let the tears slowly slip down my face. "Why can't they be as easy-going as Chase?"

Chase snorted. "I accepted you both easily because you accepted me." He shrugged. "Hopefully they'll come around in time."

Rogan crouched in front of me and took my hand from Chase before capturing my other, holding them tightly. "I don't regret anything, Fallon. Nothing and no one will make me regret anything. Remember that always, okay?"

My watery gaze searched Rogan's as panic started to build. "What? Why are you saying that to me? We are not over. We'll never be over." I climbed into his lap, sending him backwards.

I vaguely heard Chase as he left.

"Tell me you are not breaking this off!" I pushed.

Rogan was so damn quick, I didn't have time to catch a breath as he flipped me to my back. "I am not breaking this off." He breathed heavily. "I'm worried about Leon and Julia, and whether or not they'll stay quiet. I'm worried about Mom and Dad finding out from them, or someone else, before we're in a position to be together independently of them. It just all of a sudden became important to me that you know."

I burst into tears, surprising us both.

"Don't cry." Rogan sat up, bringing me onto his lap, and cupped my face in his hands. "I love you, Fallon. Please don't cry."

I wrapped my arms around his neck and clung to him while my tears flowed, and then I glanced at the window and realized it had started to rain hard. My tears turned to a wry smile as I leaned back and held Rogan's worried gaze. "It's raining, and I'm crying."

He smiled and brushed my hair back from my face. "It doesn't count, my tears in the rain, because it may be raining outside, but we're inside and nice and dry."

36

———————

ROGAN

I LAY NEXT TO FALLON AS SHE SLEPT CURLED INTO MY body. Her soft breathing washed over me on each exhale and my heart ached. I didn't ever remember seeing the look of devastation on her face like I had earlier when her best friend walked out the door, with one of my best friends. I wasn't sure what we'd both expected—understanding, compassion? I really didn't know. It had hurt us both watching our friends leave. Worry followed because they could ruin everything between us.

Fallon and I loved our parents and neither one of us would want to hurt them because of our relationship. I wished I had the answers. When Fallon woke up, I wanted to be able to tell her that everything was okay—that everyone who was important to us knew and accepted us together. Unfortunately, that wasn't going to be the case. I didn't have answers. I didn't know whether Leon and Julia would go to our parents and tell them what Fallon and I had been doing. How would I answer our parents?

My vision of the future had only ever included Fallon. My mind had always blanked the idea of anyone else knowing about us. Fallon and I would live in our own little world, thousands of miles from anyone who knew us—that had been my vision. Not this.

Her slight body moved gently against mine. The ache in my heart for her complete happiness overwhelmed me. I brushed a lock of hair over her shoulder, loving the way she fit perfectly against me. I loved the fact that she was comfortable wearing my T-shirt and boxers, and I had to say they'd never looked better.

My hand rested on the curve of her hip and my fingers caressed back and forth on her hipbone. I desperately wanted to slip my hand inside and touch her skin, but I wouldn't. She needed to sleep after the wakeful night we'd both had and then the stress of earlier.

Hoping sleep would claim me, I closed my eyes, only finding them snapping open five minutes later when I heard a soft tap on the door. While I wondered whether or not I'd actually heard the sound, a louder knock hit the door.

Grumbling to myself, I reluctantly slipped out of the warm bed and tugged on a pair of sweatpants, ignoring the fact that they were too big and hung low.

Tugging the door open, I was surprised to find Tiffany with her arm raised to knock once more. Her eyes trailed over my body, lighting with mischief. She raised a finger and reached out to touch my chest, but luckily for me, my reflexes were more awake than I felt as I ducked her touch.

"What do you want?" I whispered, impatience clear in my voice, making sure she couldn't see into the room.

I heard the rustling of covers behind me as Tiffany asked, "Can we talk in my room a minute?" A teasing smile spread across her face.

There was no need to ask why, when her face said it all.

"What's going on?" Fallon wrapped an arm around my back and ducked under my arm, which I wrapped around her waist to keep her pinned to my side.

I glanced down and the sleepy girl in my arms made my heart turnover with love. I offered her a soft smile. "I'm not sure." I kissed her sweet lips, unable to stop myself. "Tiffany just knocked."

"Hmm," Fallon mumbled and offered her hand to Tiffany. "We haven't met, I'm Fallon."

Ignoring Fallon's hand, she smiled. "I'm Tiffany."

"So, Tiffany." Fallon pinched me on the butt, her smile still in place while she talked to the other girl, except I was having problems keeping my reaction to Fallon contained. "We don't have any secrets between us, so why don't you say what you have to say to Rogan here?"

"He didn't answer his door last night after *you* arrived, so I waited until now." She smiled at me. "I have something to show you."

Fallon's arm loosened from around me and I felt her pulling away, which I was having none of. "Oh, no you don't." I gripped her fiercely. "You're mine, babe. Deal with it." I smacked her on the butt, ignoring the narrowing of her eyes.

"What does she want to show you?"

"I have no idea," I answered, truthfully. "Tiffany, why don't you tell us? Because I don't keep secrets from Fallon, and right now, she's presuming the worst."

"You tell your *sister* everything?" Tiffany raised a

brow while her eyes filled with mischief. "And why should it bother her if we're dating?"

My muscles tensed as I heard Tiffany's words and felt Fallon's stillness. My heart threatened to beat out of my chest while the silence in the room went on and on, until I snapped. I was angry now. Angry that Tiffany thought it was her right to come over here to my room and pretend shit that wasn't true. I blamed Leon for that and putting the idea in the stupid girl's head.

"Get out," I hissed between clenched teeth, barely containing my anger. My eyes narrowed as I focused on Tiffany. "You got Leon to arrange for me to show up at the movie theatre thinking I was meeting him. I told you when I arrived that I wasn't interested. I left. End of story. Stop trying to cause trouble."

Fallon buried her face against my bare chest and I felt wetness from her tears. That angered me all the more. "Get out, Tiffany. I won't ask you again."

She glanced between us, an evil smile on her face. "I won't forget this." With that, she turned on her heels and disappeared.

Taking deep, calming breaths, I cupped Fallon's face. "I promise you I have remained faithful. I haven't so much as gotten coffee with another girl, let alone gone on a date with one. It's you, Fallon. Always you."

I was standing in the middle of my dorm room with Fallon wrapped in my arms, and I was terrified our relationship had just changed. I was terrified there would always be someone trying to push their way between us. Someone trying to make trouble. Trying our loyalty to each other.

We should have our whole lives ahead of us. We should be excited to meet new people and to experience what the world had to offer. Yet, here we were, trying to cling to the dream of being together for the rest of our lives, when I was slowly starting to realize, that *that* might not happen.

A deep sadness overwhelmed me as I clung to Fallon wondering what would happen when she left on Sunday.

I put on a brave face, but Fallon knew I was suffering as she was. Until Leon and Julia discovered our secret, we were happy to carry on the way we had been, now though, I wasn't sure what was going to happen.

37

FALLON

I curled my arms around Rogan's neck and held on tightly as he carried me to the chair and settled me onto his lap. The chair supported us both and I felt warm and languid with his body heat surrounding me, as though nothing could touch us. If only it was that simple. Tilting my face up, Rogan smiled and placed a sweet kiss to my lips.

"What's going on in that brain of yours?" I asked, ruffling his hair, enjoying the slide of my fingers through the silky strands.

"I'm wondering what we're going to do about Leon and Julia," Rogan admitted. "I don't like that they walked away from us." He paused. "And I'm really hoping they come around and understand what is between us is here to stay."

I returned Rogan's heavy gaze and I couldn't stop the worry from being etched across my brow. Rogan reached up and lightly rubbed with the tips of his fingers. "You take my breath away," he whispered.

"I love you so much." I searched deep in his gaze. "I'm afraid," I murmured with tears in my voice. "I'm so afraid I'm going to wake up one day without you in my life."

Rogan crushed me to him, unable to hide how much he trembled against me. His breathing became heavy as I felt his panic rapidly growing. I wished I had the words to reassure him that we would always be together. I wanted to—desperately. Losing him was a real fear and deep down in a very dark place, I knew there would come a time in the not too distant future where we would have no choice but to go our separate ways.

Instead, I drew slightly away from the boy I loved and cupped his handsome face between the palms of my hands. A slight smile lifted my mouth before I took my time pressing small light kisses to his cheeks, his forehead, and both eyes before I finally hovered over his lips. "Make love to me, Rogan. Slow, sweet love." My lips captured his in a deep kiss that left us both trembling as our clothes slowly fell to the floor.

With his strong arms wrapped around me, I held

on as he laid me on his bed. I kept my arms around his neck, not willing to let him go anywhere other than to cover my body with his.

He settled on top of me, his chest teased my nipples, and his hips settled between my legs. The thick hard length of his penis throbbed against me, wetting my belly with his excitement. He shivered and wrapped his arms around my back, so not an inch separated us.

"Let me know if I'm too heavy," he breathed deeply into my ear.

I dug my nails into his shoulders, and wrapping my legs around his waist, arched up, rubbing against his erection. "I love having you holding me exactly like this." I wiggled. "But I love feeling you filling me up as well."

"I'm trying not to ravish you," he panted. "Feeling you naked and aroused against me is such a turn-on."

I was pretty sure my eyes burned with fire at hearing his words. Desperate to have the fire inside of my body extinguished, I raised my hips, rubbed and wiggled against him…and then, the tip of his arousal was at my entrance.

He paused and held my gaze while he slowly slid inside me. I thought my heart was about to burst from my chest with how much love I felt for him at that very moment.

He was my world.

Unable to keep my eyes open another moment, I let them fall closed and held onto to Rogan. My feet slid from his butt and landed between his legs, which tightened my vaginal walls around Rogan's penis. My eyes snapped open in surprise at the feel of him and the rapidly growing orgasm that had started to coil in my belly.

He growled. "I can't go slow. You lit the fuse with that move," he panted into my neck, his body glistening with sweat.

I held his gaze once more. "I love you, Rogan Scott." I arched my body and reached above my head. Rogan sucked on a breast and I came apart around him.

The keening noises I made in the throes of passion completely undid Rogan. He thrust hard and ground into me, coming in a long burst of pleasure. I reached for him and dug my fingernails into his butt, keeping him against me. Rogan grunted and sweated with every hard throb of his penis as he released semen inside of me. I loved the feel of him coming so deeply and it made my pleasure last far longer.

We held each other close until we could breathe

again. I watched Rogan withdraw from my body and licked my lips at the sight of him nude and swelling rapidly with my eyes on him.

Rogan rolled to his back and pulled me into his arms. I curled into his side, but found I couldn't keep my eyes off his beautiful body, he noticed too. "You like what you see?" he said, the smirk clear as day in his voice.

"Mmm." I trailed my fingers down his chest and trailed the tips along his hardening penis. He sprouted from dark hair, which I ran my hand through to cup between his legs.

"That feels good," he moaned, thickening even more.

I gave a dirty laugh. "I can see that." I leaned over him and bit down on a nipple.

Rogan shot up and pinned me to the bed. "As much as I want to make love to you all over again, I think we need to head home and find Julia and Leon." He sighed and moved to sit on the edge of the bed. His shoulders drooped and his head dipped. "I'm worried about what they're going to do or say," he admitted.

An uneasy feeling built in my belly as I moved and straddled Rogan's thighs. His large hands grabbed my bottom and brought me snug against him, and I wrapped my arms tightly around his shoulders. I rested my head on his shoulder and sighed. "I wish we could go away somewhere and not have any of this to worry about. I just want a life with you."

Rogan moved his hands and caressed along my spine before he hugged me close. "I want that too, but we both knew we'd have to deal with our friends at some point." He let out a heavy sigh. "Our parents are going to be the biggest hurdle."

Tears popped into my eyes as I moved and pressed my forehead against his. "I can't deal with them as well as our friends right now." I sobbed. "Please, Rogan. I can't."

Rogan kissed my cheek. "I agree." He kissed my shoulder. "One couple at a time."

I leaned closer and captured his lips in a kiss so powerful, we moaned unable to break the connection.

Moments later, I pushed Rogan down to the bed, and then with his hands on my hips, I took his swollen penis into my body. "One more time before we leave."

I couldn't hold my tears in as I rocked on Rogan, because something told me that once we arrived home, things were about to change.

38

———

ROGAN

IT HAD BEEN LATE WHEN WE'D ARRIVED HOME, SO WE hadn't talked to Mom and Dad, instead we'd gone straight to our own rooms. I'd passed out the moment my body had landed on the bed.

The clatter of pots could be heard from the kitchen, directly beneath my bedroom as I lay there and wondered about the day ahead. Was Fallon up? Had she heard anything from Julia? I hadn't heard anything from Leon, which I checked again by reaching for my cell phone. It sat on the bedside table and lit up as soon as I touched the screen. Nothing from Leon, but Chase had sent me a thumbs up emoji. Fallon had sent me a red heart, and another message telling me she was up and heading down for breakfast.

As much as I wanted to see Fallon, I didn't want to get up. If I stayed in bed, then I wouldn't have to face anyone. I could stay in my own world. As sensible as she was, I knew Fallon would stay with me. Neither of us wanted to venture out to find our friends because we both knew something was about to change. I didn't do well with change. I hated it. So did Fallon. She was a stickler for routine, at least during a school day.

The thud of feet on the stairs drew my gaze to my bedroom door, and seconds later it slammed open and Fallon came flying in, and dived onto my bed. She bounced once and then twice before she crawled further up to rest her head on the pillow beside mine. "Mom said to wake you up." She grinned and turned onto her side. "I didn't need asking twice."

Amused, I reached out and moved a lock of hair behind her ear. I let my finger linger and slowly caressed her plump bottom lip before I forced myself to move my hand. "I missed waking up with you."

Her eyes darkened and a light flush covered her cheekbones. "I missed that too. It was so different than yesterday morning, in more ways than one."

"I'd have done everything to prevent that from happening if I'd known."

Fallon traced my lips with the tip of a finger. "It's

happened and it's something we have to deal with, no matter how nauseous it makes me." Sadness slipped onto her face. "I still can't believe how Julia reacted. She's known us both for years, and knows our history."

"I thought"—Mom made us both jump in surprise—"that I sent you," she glanced at Fallon, "to wake your brother up?" Mom raised a brow.

"I'm awake." I groaned and stretched. "I miss my bed when I'm at college." I quickly glanced at Fallon and realized Mom had witnessed it when she frowned and her eyes moved between us.

Mom cleared her throat. "Well, breakfast is ready." She frowned again and moved away from the doorway. "Five minutes," she shouted.

"Ugh," Fallon groaned. "I really don't want to face today."

I knew how she felt. "We need to get it over with." Dropping my legs over the side of the bed, I added, "We need to have the confidence that it will all work out. It's the only option." I reached out and squeezed Fallon's hand before heading into the bathroom.

It didn't take me long to finish getting ready and when I joined my family in the kitchen, I could have sliced a steak knife through the silence it was so thick. I briefly glanced at Fallon, who kept her face buried in the bowl of Froot Loops cereal she ate. I winced.

Toast and coffee was all I could stomach this morning, and I hoped there was some jelly left, otherwise it would get stuck in my throat. It appeared tension was high in my family, and I was nervous to ask what I'd missed. Fallon would tell me once we were alone, but I wanted to know while I ate my breakfast so I was prepared—at least some sort of hint. It wouldn't happen, though. I could see that clearly.

Dad drew my attention and after a large sigh, kissed us all on the top of our heads like he did when we were younger, before he left the room.

I breathed easier once it was only Mom and Fallon in the room.

"More coffee?" Mom asked, jumping up from the chair. Her actions were nervous, as though she didn't know what to do with us.

Fallon twitched beside me and I knew without looking that she too realized Mom was acting oddly. Instead of keeping her mouth shut, she asked, "What's going on?"

Mom froze and looked like a deer caught in headlights. "I don't think I want to know the answer to the question that I need to ask." She took a deep breath.

"So, I'm not going to ask it." She turned her back and busied herself with the breakfast dishes.

I felt Fallon's eyes on me but I kept mine on Mom, a frown crossed my brow.

Before I had time to think about what to say, Mom said, "Julia and Leon are outside. Looks like they're arguing." She leaned closer to the window. "Definitely arguing. They've disappeared into Leon's house."

While Mom was distracted, I grabbed Fallon by the arm. "We're going out." I tugged her with me and instead of heading to Leon's house to talk to our friends, I intertwined my fingers with Fallon's and took her to our spot at the river.

39

FALLON

"Leon finally replied to my message." Rogan winced and passed his phone to me.

Leon: Julia needs time.

I wanted to rage that it was unfair, that we both should be allowed to be together, regardless of how right or wrong it was.

Feeling lost and uncertain of anything anymore, I turned my sad gaze to Rogan. No words were spoken as he laid me down on the blanket and wrapped himself around me. The warmth of his body and the beat of his heart put me into a safe place. The sounds around us also helped calm my racing heart. Frogs croaked, birds squawked, insects buzzed, and the light sound of turtles as they plopped into the river settled me.

We were surrounded by tall grass and wildflowers, which looked so pretty with the sun shining through the trees, creating patches of bright light. The place we'd made our own was beautiful and special and a love like no other was sheltered from prying eyes.

"I want to leave with you," I whispered against Rogan's chest. "Mom and Dad won't let me, though."

"No they won't." Rogan tilted my face up to his and pressed a sweet kiss to my lips. "You know how much I love you, Fallon." He kissed me again. "We have to make sure we get a proper education so that we're capable of supporting ourselves. We have to. It's important."

"I'm aware of that. I'm just afraid that if we don't stay together we'll end up going in different directions. That you'll meet someone at college." My breath caught and I swallowed hard before I continued, "There is Tiffany waiting in the wings." I hated him living in a co-ed dorm. "She'll trick you into something. I just know she will. I don't like her."

"Fallon, I'm trying to not get offended that you'd think I'd cheat on you so easily. I might be a horny guy with a dick, but I can assure you, it's all yours, babe."

I burst into tears, much to Rogan's shock. I knew he'd tried to lighten his words. He'd wanted me to smile; he hadn't expected it to backfire. That made me cry harder.

What was wrong with me?

He held me tightly and soothed me with soft strokes of his large hands down my back until my tears became soft hiccups. I wiped my face on my discarded sweater before letting it drop beside us. "I'm sorry." I nuzzled into his neck. "I do trust you, it's just difficult to trust us. Chase is the only one in our corner, and I'm terrified that the moment Mom and Dad know for sure about us, that they'll make it nearly impossible for us to be together."

Rogan sighed. "I can't look into the future; however, I do know that I will always love you. You're the only woman I want by my side, and it will happen. How we finally get there, I don't know. Don't ever lose hope." He kissed the top of my head and kept his mouth against me.

Time stood still until Rogan started to move and pulled me up with him. "I really don't want to leave you, but I have to get back to school."

My lips started to quiver, which I was unable to

hide. Rogan tugged me to him and held me so tight I could hardly breathe. "I love you, and I'll be back to see you before you know it."

"I love you too."

With reluctance in every move, Rogan finally released his hold on me and ran back to the house. As usual, I was left standing by the river as silent tears fell down my face. The anguish I felt would be written all over my body—the slight slump of my shoulders, the sad eyes, pale complexion.

My legs gave way and I slumped down and cried into my drawn up knees, which I hugged close to my chest.

I didn't know how I knew, but nothing was going to be the same.

And then the heavens opened and it rained down on me while I cried tears of heartbreak.

"CAN WE TALK?" LEON ASKED AS I OPENED MY CAR door.

I sighed and turned to face him just as a heavy shower dropped from the sky.

I'd left Fallon by the river and it had left me raw and hurting; the last thing I needed was an argument with one of my best friends.

"Please, Rogan?"

With a nod of my head, I agreed. "I'll meet you at the back of the diner's parking lot."

"Okay." Leon got behind the wheel of his car and took off.

I was weary as I climbed into my car and turned the key in the ignition. As I started to reverse down the driveway, I spotted Fallon watching me from the side of the house. I wanted to go to her but I forced myself to pull away from the girl I loved and headed to where Leon waited for me. I'd be back for her, but it hurt too much to say goodbye to her. I wished my life away with wanting us both to have finished college so that we could be together.

It just hurt every time I had to leave her.

Sighing, I spotted Leon parked at the back of the lot. We'd parked there so many times over the years that I supposed it was habit to arrange to talk to Leon in our spot. I hoped that Leon accepted my relationship with Fallon because I didn't know what I'd do otherwise. I needed him on board.

Moments later the passenger door opened and Leon climbed. "Didn't know if you planned on getting out or not." He shrugged and stared out of the front windshield.

"I didn't know either," I admitted, gripping the steering wheel. I forced myself to relax and drew my hands from the wheel to rest on my thighs. "You're one of my best friends." I cleared my throat. "I don't want to lose you because of Fallon."

Dark eyes focused on mine and made me cringe. "You'll walk away from me if I don't accept you with her." Leon shook his head. "You'd throw years of friendship away for a piece of ass?"

"Get. Out. Of. The. Car," I said slowly between gritted teeth. "Now." I slammed out and met Leon at the front of my car with my fists. Leon had expected it and managed to duck out of the way, which infuriated me all the more. "You don't fucking talk about her like that," I yelled, so angry that I crouched and tackled Leon to the ground. Grit spread and flew around our furious bodies as we traded punches. I couldn't stop, and the more Leon fought, the more I wrestled to get control.

Water hit us in the face so suddenly that we broke apart, spitting water from our mouths. "No fighting in my parking lot!" Gladys huffed in a furious breath. "You two have been friends too long to be fighting like punks. Pull yourselves together." She placed her hands on her ample hips. "You hearing me, boys?"

I replied, "Yes, ma'am. I apologize."

"Hmm." She turned her attention to Leon. "What about you?"

"I'm sorry too, Gladys." Leon sighed. "It won't happen again."

"It better not or I'll be calling the Sheriff, regardless of how much I like you both." Gladys gave us both a pointed look before she turned her back and made her way inside the diner.

Out of the corner of my eye, I caught Leon giving

me the side-eye. I rolled my eyes and got to my feet, shaking like a dog would do after a dip in the river. Leon did the same.

"I know Fallon is a lot more to you than…what I said, so I'm sorry. Okay?" Leon grunted and perched on the front of my car, rubbing at his bruised jaw. "I can't get it out of my head that Fallon is your sister. All my life I've known that, so finding out she's a lot more is difficult to handle. It's wrong, Rogan."

I sat beside Leon and hoped my friend wouldn't say anything else to make me angry.

"We both have different parents, Leon. We're not related really."

"You both grew up together from being little kids. Nothing should ever happen between you. It's wrong, dammit."

"Best friends fall in love all the time. That's what we've done."

Leon jumped up and started to pace. "Why can't you see what you're doing?"

"What are we doing?" I got in Leon's face. "Tell me, as you obviously know so much? What are we doing that affects you?"

"It doesn't just affect me," Leon bit out. "It affects, Julia, Chase, and what about your parents? Do you think they'll be so accepting?" He threw his head back.

Anger had me clenching my fists with the need to punch him again; however, I closed my eyes tightly and inhaled and exhaled real slow. Tears of frustration, anger, and despair burned behind my tightly closed eyelids.

"Look," Leon said softly. I opened my eyes and stared into his, and he continued once he had my sole focus. "I know you love her, okay?" He sighed. "I might not like it but I know it's how you feel. For just once, think with your head instead of your heart. Think about Fallon and how it's going to affect her if news of your relationship gets out. She's going to be here, all alone, while you're away at school. You're not going to be able to protect her."

I breathed heavily, not wanting to hear a word Leon said. Unfortunately, I heard every word.

"What do you want me to do?" I asked, my heart heavy and aching.

"It's not what I want you to do, it's what you *need* to do. It's what you have to do for Fallon. You need to give her a chance without you." Leon squeezed my shoulder and left me standing in front of my car as he climbed into his.

He shouted, "I'll see you back at school," and drove off.

Hot tears slipped from my eyes and slid down my cheeks while I stood in the parking lot, knowing I couldn't go back to the house to see Fallon. If I saw her, I wouldn't be able to tell her it's over and to get on with her life without me. I wanted to be pissed at Leon, but the truth was, he'd only spoken my thoughts and worry aloud. But could I actually leave her alone? Did I have the courage to walk away? To leave her open for someone else to take my place?

Angry at how much I was hurting and eaten away with jealousy over someone having what's mine, I slumped into my car and hit the steering wheel with my fists. A sob tore threw me, and then another as my shoulders dropped and my forehead banged against the wheel in front of my face. Sobs came faster and faster, my whole body shaking with anguish over losing the one person who I loved with all my heart.

You don't have to lose her...

"I do. I need to be the one to let her go," I whispered into the silence of my car.

I knew in my heart that Fallon would never be the one to walk away from me.

I had to walk away from her.

41

FALLON

I HATED SCHOOL.

Everyone ran around me getting ready for prom, crying because they'd soon be leaving high school. Me, I couldn't wait to leave and get as far away from home as I could. The past three months without a word from Rogan had taken a toll on me. He'd made his choice to leave me without a word and it hurt beyond belief. I felt anger toward him too. He could have spoken to me about what was going on inside of his head, but he hadn't. He'd decided that we'd no longer be together and that was that. *Asshole!*

Julia caught my eye as I sat alone in the cafeteria, but I ignored her. She'd tried to talk to me after Rogan had left but I had no interest. She'd told me that Rogan leaving was for the best, and I hated her for that. It wasn't what I wanted to hear. I couldn't help thinking that Leon had something to do with Rogan continuing to ignore me, and I blamed Julia for that too. We'd been friends for years and she hadn't been able to stand by my side when she'd found out about Rogan and me. That had hurt me deeply, but not as deeply as losing Rogan.

Blinking back tears as I stared into my soup, I felt someone take the seat opposite me. Daniel. I swallowed around the lump in my throat and slowly raised my face. He offered me a large smile, so I gave him a tentative one back.

"Do you want to go watch that new action movie Friday night?" he asked, and took a bite of his sandwich. "It's supposed to be really good."

I tilted my head and watched him. I'd known Daniel since middle school and he'd always been in the background, apart from the past few months when we'd started hanging around together. I wasn't even sure how it started. Daniel hated attention and had finally admitted that it had taken him a long time to work up the courage to talk to me. I'd been surprised because I'd never considered myself a difficult person to talk to.

"So, you going to come with me?" Daniel asked, solely focused on me.

Slowly nodding my head, I smiled. "Okay."

He laughed. "You could sound as though you actually want to go to the movies with me."

"I do want to go to the movies with you. I just have a lot on my mind." I shrugged, and pushed my tray with the soup away. My appetite had long since deserted me, along with Rogan.

I knew Mom and Dad worried about me because I'd lost weight. They'd worry more when they discovered I'd applied to colleges on the West Coast. Far away from home and the boy I loved.

"I'm a good listener." He didn't look at me, but switched his empty sandwich plate with the dessert one.

"I don't think I know what I'm doing anymore. The friends I've grown up with are no longer around, my parents are constantly watching me because I never leave the house other than to come to school. I'm also worried about telling them I've been accepted to a school on the West Coast." I stared at the poster behind him and added, "I've also had enough of my mom constantly telling me that I have to go to prom when I really don't want to. I went last year, so I don't see why I have to go again."

"Where on the West Coast?"

"What?" I couldn't remember what we'd been

talking about. I rubbed at my brow and wondered what the heck was going on with me.

"School. You said you'd been accepted on the West Coast. Where?" Daniel said, shaking his head. His smile never really left his face and he always seemed happy and full of life. I needed some of what he had. "Because I've been accepted at a school out there too."

My eyes widened. "Really?" I grinned, liking the idea that we could be heading to the same college. "San Diego."

Daniel cheered and pumped his fist in the air. I felt my cheeks heat with embarrassment, and quickly leaned over and grabbed his sweatshirt. "Everyone is looking at us."

He rolled his eyes. "Let them." The chair creaked as he dropped into it. "For once I'm not bothered about being watched. I have the most beautiful girl in the school sitting with me...going on a date with me...going away to school with *me*."

I chuckled. "Let's not get carried away." We had another twenty minutes before lunch period was over and I wanted to get some fresh air, so I grabbed my things up.

"You're leaving?"

"I'm going outside." I turned to head away and then turned back. "Want to join me?"

He quickly grabbed his backpack and caught up to me. An arm went around my neck and he whispered, "I think we should go to prom together."

My breath froze in my lungs and a wave of dizziness washed over me. While I'd been talking to Daniel I'd forgotten about Rogan and how much I missed him. With Daniel asking me to prom, I couldn't think straight. My first thought was to refuse. I couldn't go with anyone but Rogan. Except, Rogan had chosen to step away from me, and what we'd shared. Would he be hurt even now if he discovered I'd gone to prom with Daniel? Would he even care?

Sucking in a deep breath, I mumbled, "Prom sounds good."

"Um, did you just agree to go to prom with me?" He pulled me to a stop on the steps outside of the school and turned me to face him. The wind caught my long hair and whipped it around into my face, so Daniel reached up and gently tugged it away and looked into my eyes. "You really mean it, Fallon? You'll go with me?"

As I stared at Daniel, I knew I'd go with him. How could I not go? He wanted me when no one else did. He was sweet and kind, and it had taken a great deal of strength on his part to befriend me when I was so alone. "Yes, Daniel. I'll be your date for prom."

The bell announcing the end of the lunch period sounded loud in my ears with us standing beneath it. Daniel quickly hugged me, and whispered, "Thank you," in my ear before he took off to class.

My feet stayed stuck to the path as the bell continued to shrill overhead. So suddenly I felt as though I was being watched, as though Superman was using his X-ray vision to see through me. I glanced to the road out front of school and my heart dropped to my toes. There stood Rogan, leaning against his car with his fists clenched at his sides.

Before I could think, I found myself moving toward him but the look on his face gave me pause. He looked angry and as our eyes met and held, he let me see the hurt. Neither of us looked away, even when I stopped directly in front of him. I couldn't.

"You didn't wait long to replace me," he bit out.

His jealousy made me angry. "You left me, without one word, without answering one of my messages or calls." I stepped into his space. "So you don't have the right to accuse me of anything."

Rogan moved in so close that I had to tip my face up so I could look at him. I wished I hadn't. He wasn't only hurt and angry, he was furious. "He touched you."

My eyes widened and I took a step back at the

venom in his tone. I swallowed hard and hissed, "At least he wants to touch me."

He stared at me for a long time before he moved and tugged on his hair. "We need to talk," he whispered, and I don't think I'd ever heard him sound so broken. "Will you come for a drive with me?"

I stared into his eyes and I knew I wouldn't refuse him. At least the drive. Anything else and I'm going to have to stay strong. He hurt me badly when he ended things without actually saying anything. I couldn't be hurt like that again, and Rogan was the only one who could do it.

"As long as you tell me why I'm no longer yours, then I'll come for a drive."

He swallowed hard and nodded. My words had hurt him.

I climbed into the passenger seat of his car and I told myself I had to be stronger than I'd ever needed to be before.

42

ROGAN

NO ONE ELSE WAS AROUND DURING THE MIDDLE OF THE day as I parked my car overlooking the river. I wanted to avoid bumping into our parents, and I couldn't imagine being in our private place while there was so much hurt between us.

I'd stayed away and thought I was doing well, until Dad had called and asked me to come home and talk to Fallon. Our parents were worried about her. Looking at her, I knew why. Her complexion that had once glowed had paled. She'd lost weight, but her curves still made my mouth water. Dad told me she'd been accepted to a school in San Diego, which she had no clue that Mom and Dad actually knew about, so Dad had asked me to keep it to myself. They wanted me to make right whatever had happened between us, so that Fallon stopped walking around looking so unhappy.

If only it was that easy.

I'd taken the easy way out because I knew I wouldn't be strong enough to tell her exactly what was going on, or where my thoughts had landed. It was the coward's way out and it had bothered me ever since.

Not a day had gone by that I didn't regret walking away from Fallon, and now it was time to explain, and hopefully help her in my own way. At least that was the plan. Fallon being in my car while she looked so sad and forlorn was going to end up unraveling everything I'd tried to accomplish by walking away.

My eyes continued to travel over her gorgeous curves, down her tanned legs and back up to her face. She had tears swimming in her eyes while she tried to avoid my gaze. I was a bastard and wouldn't let her. I reached out and grabbed her jaw, turning her beautiful face to me.

I caught my breath when she lifted her eyes to mine and my breathing became heavy. "I can't be yours anymore, Fallon."

I never in a million years wanted to hurt her. I loved her. I always would. I couldn't say that now because I had to make her understand why I'd left her alone.

Instead of doing what I really wanted to and take her in my arms, I forced myself to only rub her back. I had to give her some sort of comfort, even if it wasn't what I knew we both needed.

"Fallon?" I whispered. "You need to listen to me."

She shook her head.

"Yes, you do. I should have had the guts to talk to you before I left that day. I know how I went about cutting you out of my life hurt you. It hurt me too. I never wanted to do that, but I had to." I turned her to face me. "I had to, Fallon. We lived in a bubble that only enclosed us both, and that was dangerous. If Mom and Dad ever found out about us, and they would have, our relationship would have had far reaching consequences. You'd have been left in town having to face everyone, not just our parents. I'm away at college and wouldn't be able to help you. All I've ever done was for you."

Fallon shook her head and pulled away from my touch. "You never asked me what I wanted, Rogan. *You* are the one who decided to leave me. I didn't have a choice. Yes, you hurt me. You hurt me more than anyone, and I don't know how to recover from it. You damaged my heart when I thought I'd always be able to rely on you to keep it whole. You let me down and I'm dealing with it. It isn't easy, but I'll get there in the end."

"We damaged our friendship by having sex." I winced the moment the words left my mouth. I hadn't meant to say that, especially as bluntly as I did.

Fallon gasped. "It was never only sex," she hissed between clenched teeth. "I'm going away to college. So far away from you that there won't be a chance of seeing each other. You'll be glad when I'm completely out of the way. No chance of bumping into me on campus."

Her words sent panic into my gut and I cursed. "Fuck, Fallon! Do you seriously think I want you out of my life? You don't have eyes in your head if you do." I threw my hands up and climbed from the car before I broke my own promise of keeping my mouth shut. Fallon had always been the one to bring out my anger like no other. I stared off over the river wishing I could go back to my last summer home before I left for college. Those days had been perfect.

"Rogan," she softly whispered, her hand curling around my arm as she stood behind me. "I'm so confused."

I closed my eyes and breathed deeply. "What I did was for you. I wanted you to go on without me. Leon thought if we weren't together, then we might get over whatever was going on between us." I offered a mirthless laugh. "He knows nothing! You think I'm not hurting, well I am. So fucking much, Fallon." I turned and cupped her face. "I will always be available to you, but I refuse to carry on with you like we were. As fucking jealous as I am with Daniel touching you, I want you to experience everything without me around. I want you to be so fucking happy." I yanked her to me and held her while my mouth slammed down on her plump red lips. I pushed my tongue into her mouth and invaded.

God, I'd missed *my* girl. I couldn't get enough as I plunged, giving and taking everything she allowed me, and more. The deep moan in her throat made me press harder, our teeth clashed before I forced myself to ease up. I couldn't catch a normal breath with her taste in my mouth and with her lips touching mine. My body had missed her too, and the thick blood coursing through my veins all centered in my groin. My dick throbbed and hurt so damn much squished in my jeans. But today wasn't about sex, it was about setting straight the reason why'd I'd abandoned her in the hope that she finally moved on and started to enjoy life without me.

My sadness crept along my spine and I slowly

calmed the kiss down and put Fallon away from me, when all I wanted to do was pull her even closer. She stared at me in surprise, her fingers stroked over her lower lip while her eyes searched mine.

I couldn't continue to hold her gaze, so I moved toward the car. "I'll take you home."

Fallon didn't speak but climbed into the car and fastened her seatbelt.

I'd always love her, I just wished I could tell her.

43

FALLON

Dressed for prom, I didn't feel like I had last year when I'd known I was going to be spending the night with Rogan. My dress was simple in a black silky fabric to match my recent mood. I'd yet to slip my feet into the high heels that went with the dress because my heart really wasn't in it. I wasn't going to let Daniel down, though.

He was a handsome boy who was my age. He had light blond hair and a slight build, and he always appeared happy. I was afraid I was leading him on by being his date to prom, and how our friendship was progressing. I didn't want him to get the wrong idea about our friendship, and wondered how I was going to tell him. I liked spending time with him and he took my mind off my screwed up life.

The sound of footsteps clunking upstairs caught my attention. I knew it couldn't be Mom because she had slippers on, and it certainly wasn't Dad. It sounded like someone else in heels. A slight knock sounded at my bedroom door and my heart sank. There was only one person who would be in the house with heels at this time. *Julia.*

Resigned, I opened the door and met her curious gaze. "Why are you here?"

Julia pushed her way inside and dropped to the edge of the bed. "Close the door."

I bit the inside of my cheek and ignored her comment and left the door opened slightly. She watched me as I finally put on my shoes.

"Fallon, can't you put everything behind us and make up with me?"

Swallowing hard, I shook my head. "It isn't easy. Every time I look at you, and see you with Leon, I remember everything I had until you both ruined it for Rogan and me. I know you couldn't help the way you reacted, but Leon got involved and now all I'm left with is a broken heart. I hate you both for that."

A tear slipped down Julia's cheek. "I don't understand how neither of you could see how wrong it was for you to be together. I know you don't share blood, but it's weird. It's not right what you were doing."

Anger started to seep through my blood as I listened to her. "It was my life, Julia. It was Rogan's life. Neither of you had any right to interfere."

"Fallon, please. I hate us not being friends. I can't be sorry for the way I feel, but I am sorry my feelings hurt you. I never wanted that, and neither did Leon." She shrugged. "If it helps, Rogan is having a hard time too. Leon said he barely talks anymore and he has no interest in anything or anyone other than his classes."

"It doesn't help," I snapped. "It hurts." I glanced at my partially opened door and nodded. "I want you to leave. Daniel will be here soon."

Julia stood and wiped at her eyes. "You can't continue to ignore me." She paused and I didn't say anything more.

Unable to move, I placed a hand over my chest, afraid my organ was going to beat right out of my chest. I was in the same position when Mom entered my room, not a few moments after I heard the front door close. Mom looked pale and worried as she closed my door behind her. She leaned against it and looked up to my ceiling while she gathered her thoughts. When she was ready, Mom took my hands and sat me beside her on the bed.

"Mom?" I questioned softly, afraid of what she was about to say. "Dad's okay, right? Rogan?"

"Oh, honey, they're both fine." She squeezed my hands and kept hold. "I heard the tail end of your conversation with Julia." Her eyes filled with compassion. "I've wondered for a long time if there was more between Rogan and you." Her voice quivered and she paused. "I never really wanted to know, so I never asked. After prom when Dad asked, I wanted to forget the look on both of your faces when you arrived home. I pretended I hadn't seen anything because it was easier than having to have a conversation with you both."

I winced. "Mom."

"Oh honey, I failed you, and I failed Rogan." Tears appeared in her eyes and I watched as they slowly slipped down her face. "I knew for sure the day Rogan left for school. It was hard for me watching your heart break. You were so torn up that I was tied as to whether or not I to say anything. Instead I stayed silent. I figured you had enough on your mind without me telling you what I knew."

"I'm sorry," I cried and sagged against her.

Her arms came around me and held me tightly while I sobbed into her chest. Her hands gently stroked down my hair, which she'd curled for me for prom.

"Why are you sorry, Fallon?"

Confused, my brows drew together and I raised my tearstained face toward her. "I don't know what you mean."

She smiled softly. "I think you do." Her cool fingers ran over my temples and she brushed loose strands of hair away from my face.

"I really don't know why I'm sorry. I'm not sorry for how I feel about Rogan. I'll never be sorry for loving him." I swiped at a loose tear. "I am sorry that I've hurt you because of him."

"You still love him?"

"I always will," I whispered, searching her gaze. "He wants me to get on with my life without him, and I can't." My chest ached from holding my heartbreak inside. I gulped and hiccupped until the tears came. Great big racking sobs that shook my body. Mom never once loosened her hold around me. She held me while I cried my eyes out until the hiccups became worse and she finally put me away from her.

"Here, drink some of this." Mom offered me a bottle of water.

Unscrewing the cap, I hoped I wouldn't choke on it.

I didn't.

She watched me while I could see her thinking

and contemplating what to do or say next. There was something that I needed to know, though.

"Doesn't it make you angry or disgusted?"

"You're my daughter, Fallon." She offered a wry smile. "I love both you and Rogan, and I don't know what to think. I hid my head in the clouds when I suspected because I really didn't want to know. Your dad had his moments of suspicion and I told him it was all in his head, just like I wanted my suspicion to be." She sighed. "It's over with, so no more talk about it. No matter what the future holds, *he* is still your brother and you are still his sister."

Mom briefly squeezed my hand and let go and I had to fight not to cry all over again because she really didn't understand. She knew about us, but didn't want to think about us being together. I got that, but I wanted Rogan.

"You're going to San Diego, huh?"

My eyes snapped to hers. "I haven't said anything." I frowned.

"You left your acceptance letter under your pillow. I didn't snoop, I was changing your bed sheets." She turned and held my gaze. "I don't want you being so far away, but at the same time, I don't want you at the same college as Rogan. So we'll support you going to

California." Mom moved forward and kissed me on the forehead. "Let's not tell your dad about you and Rogan." She stood in the doorway and turned back to look at me from over her shoulder. "You need to get cleaned up. Daniel will be here soon." She smiled. "He's a nice boy." With her final words she left.

There had been a slithering piece of hope that she would tell me everything was okay and that she was good with me having a relationship with Rogan. I was wrong. She wouldn't even talk about it properly other than to tell me to not say anything. I hadn't planned to but it hurt.

With a deep sigh, I caught a glance of myself in the mirror across the room, and it wasn't a pretty one. My makeup had streaked down my face and I was a mess.

My heart wanted to toss my clothes off, scrub the stuff from my skin and spend the night in bed with a movie or a good book to take my mind off of Rogan and the reasons why we couldn't be together. What I did instead was pull myself together and washed my face. I applied fresh makeup, more than usual to cover up my ragged face. I then stood in front of my full-length mirror and smiled.

The dark dress fitted my womanly curves and especially clung to my above average breasts. They were high and perky, something Rogan couldn't get enough of. Well no more, I was going to prom with someone else. My mind needed to focus on Daniel. At least he wanted me.

I was going to prom with Daniel and I was going to have a good time!

44

ROGAN

MY FISTS CLENCHED TIGHTLY AS I WATCHED FALLON IN the sexy black dress be escorted inside of prom with Daniel's hand resting low on her back. She couldn't see me from my spot at the end of the hallway, no one could. Staying away hadn't been an option, although it should have been. The need to see my girl with another guy had eaten away at me until I'd found myself behind the wheel of my car.

She punished me with him and it hurt so much. I wanted to go over there and pull her from his arms. I wanted to beat the crap out of him for daring to touch her. Instead, I did nothing. My feet kept me rooted to the spot long after they'd disappeared inside the ballroom. It was a physical ache being so close to her and not being able to talk to her, to touch her. As much as I loved her, I couldn't do that. I couldn't confuse her the way I'd confused myself.

Some days I knew that I'd made the right decision by letting her go, and others, I wanted to drive home, climb into her bedroom window, and take her back to college with me. No matter the distance between us, I would always love her. She'd always be mine, except because of my actions, I had to share her with someone else.

The thought of him touching her the way I had drove me insane and caused my breath to get stuck in the back of my throat to the point that I doubled over. I rested my hands on my knees and concentrated on breathing, and eventually it became easier. Jealousy was an ugly emotion and I wished to God it would leave me. It would be so much easier for me if it would. Unfortunately, where Fallon was concerned, I didn't think it ever would.

I'd told her to get on with her life and she'd finally listened.

I needed to listen too.

PART IV

Rogan, 20 / Fallon, 19

That's all I had now, tears in the rain,
all because I fell in love with a boy.

45

FALLON

Sophomore year was well underway and I was so glad to have classes to occupy my mind. I loved San Diego and although I'd stayed here over the summer, waitressing at a local hotel, I missed being home. I missed everything familiar, including Rogan. My heart still ached when I thought about him, and I knew it was because of that that I hadn't been able to move forward with Daniel.

I'd spent my freshman year hanging out with Daniel and I hated that I'd hurt him because I knew he wanted me. I hadn't been able to bring myself to be with him, although we had tried. Once. I'd panicked and told him I wasn't ready. He thought I was innocent and I hadn't said anything to the contrary. It played on my mind and I didn't know what to do. I was being selfish because I was afraid he'd leave me when he was the only friend I had. I liked him and found him attractive, but I didn't want his hands on me. No one other than Rogan had ever touched me deeply and I couldn't bring myself to let anyone else have the same claim as Rogan.

At times I wanted to, and I'd even thought about doing it with Daniel and then making sure Rogan found out about it. But I'd be using Daniel, and I'd have to let him touch me in order to accomplish that. So I'd let it go.

The biggest surprise once students started turning up for the beginning of the school year was Julia. I hadn't spoken to or seen her in over twelve months, and now she'd started classes here. Coincidence, I didn't think so. Not when everywhere I went she appeared. She'd spent her freshman year with Leon, so I was curious as to why she'd obviously transferred to San Diego. Had she broken up with Leon? But why come here? I wanted to know and in truth, I'd desperately missed my friend.

With time between us, I realized how I'd acted toward Julia was wrong of me. Instead of pushing her away, I should have kept her close and let her be there for me. I didn't give her a chance. In a way she put me on edge because I knew it was only a matter of time before she confronted me.

And when I heard the banging on the door of my room, I knew that time was now. Julia had always done things with a lot of noise.

I couldn't prevent the smile from slipping to my lips as I slowly opened the door and found Julia with her arms crossed over her chest. "Are you going to invite me in?"

Swallowing hard, I moved out of the way and waved my arm toward my room. "I was just wondering when you'd come knocking." I winced. "That was horrible. I'm sorry. I'm actually glad you're here."

As was the norm, Julia had dropped to my bed. Her eyes watched me and made me slightly uncomfortable, so I sat at the desk, shutting my laptop screen.

"Why are you here and not with Leon?"

Julia looked uncomfortable, and answered my question with one of her own, "Are we just going to ignore the elephant in the room?" Her eyes narrowed.

I owed it to her to explain. "I don't think I'll be able to explain to you how much I broke when Rogan left. He was everything to me. My world. And then he was gone because he'd listened to Leon. I miss Rogan every day, Julia. He wanted me to get on with my life, and although I have with schooling, I haven't with my personal life because the only guy I want is thousands of miles away in Boston. I don't see that changing."

Julia watched me carefully with a tilt to her head. "I'm sorry," she said quietly. "I never wanted it to all blow up. I don't know what I expected, but I didn't think I'd lose my best friend." She swiped at a tear, as did I. "I didn't understand how much you were entwined with Rogan." She shrugged her shoulders and laughed. "I should have. I'd seen you both together since before we became friends. It stared me in the face as to how much in love you both were."

"No matter what anyone says, Julia, he will always be in my heart. I'll always pick up my phone to call him, and remember why I can't. He'll always be the first person I want to share in my accomplishments. I can't just click my fingers and have my past with him wiped clean, although it wouldn't hurt as much if I could."

Julia glanced away and sighed. "You're friendly with Daniel?"

"Not as friendly as he'd like," I admitted. "He's a good looking guy, but I just can't be with him the way I know he wants me to. The thought of someone else putting their hands on me makes me cringe."

"I'm so sorry," Julia cried, crumpling into tears. "Forgive me?"

Momentarily surprised, I paused and then went to my friend. I wrapped my arms around her shoulders and brought her against my chest. She sobbed while I whispered, "I forgive you, but only if you'll forgive me."

She nodded her head.

After what felt like a long time, Julie subsided into small hiccup tears, so I asked, "Why are you here and not with Leon?"

She lifted her face and her eyes filled with more tears. "He hates me."

"No way." I shook my head. "That boy loves you, Julia."

Sat facing each other, she admitted, "I told him I didn't want to be with him anymore and that I was moving here to be with you."

My eyes widened at her confession, but something wasn't right. No way would Julia break things off with Leon. She loved him. "Tell me what's really going on."

She swallowed hard. "I'm pregnant."

I opened my mouth but no words came to mind. I was too surprised. My mind ran off wondering why she'd leave Leon because of a baby. Wouldn't she need his help? Then I really looked at her and I realized why. "Leon doesn't know about the baby, does he? You left before he could leave you."

Tears started falling from her eyes. "We're still in school. I don't want to burden him with me and a baby." She glanced away.

"You are a good person, Julia, but sometimes you are an idiot. You wouldn't be burdening Leon with you and a baby. Leon loves you, and he would love any child you had together. No way would he bail on you. He wouldn't consider any other option but to stand right by your side." I snickered. "I can imagine him panicking to begin with, but he'd be there for you."

"You really think so?" she asked in a small voice.

I clutched her cold hands in mine. "Julia, answer me truthfully, is it the fact that you think Leon would desert you, or that you're scared shitless as to why you left?"

"Both." She shuddered. "My parents will disown me when they find out. You know how they are. They've never been supportive and I've had to fight for everything I have. I don't know what to do, so I ran to you." She bit her lip. "You're the one person I trust with this. You don't hate me, do you? For showing up like this?"

"No." I held her gaze. "You have to tell Leon."

"I can't."

"Yes, you can, and you know you have to. Give him a chance, Julia. Leon may act the group idiot sometimes, but he loves you." I paused. "How pregnant are you?"

"Four months."

"What?" I stared at her belly and reached out with my hand. I gently pressed against her and felt the hard lump she'd hidden behind a baggy sweatshirt. "Oh, wow. How did Leon not notice this?"

"He joked that I had put on weight. I laughed it off. He looked at me funny but then got interrupted with a phone call."

"Call him, Julia." I grabbed my cell and held it out to her. "Call him, now. I'll stay with you if you want."

"I need to tell you something else, which I hope you won't hold against me because I really need you."

My heart sank. "Tell me."

"Rogan is dating Tiffany." Julia gulped and rushed on, "I didn't want you finding out through anyone else. It's weird because sometimes I don't think Rogan actually likes the girl, but other times, especially when he knows I'm watching, he's all over her." Her brows drew together. "I've wondered whether it's all for show." She met my watery filled gaze. "A bit like you and Daniel, except Rogan is putting on a show for my benefit in the hope that word will get back to you."

"You need to call Leon." I nodded toward my phone clutched in her hands.

No other words came to mind. I felt numb at the thought of Rogan with another girl. Through all the time we'd been separated, I'd never thought of him being with someone else. It hurt and made me wonder if there had been more going on when I'd visited him at school. I was too sad and worn out to let his actions play on my mind like they'd always done.

Until Julia had showed up, I'd been doing well with carrying on with my life. I had a part-time job that I actually liked, I had a good friend in Daniel, and I enjoyed my classes. I didn't want to go back to the never-ending days when I couldn't switch off, and the nights where I'd wake in a cold sweat and panicked.

"I have my own phone." Julia placed mine down beside her on the bed and reached for hers in her back pocket. She spent a few moments on her phone and then winced. "I texted and asked him if he could visit me here. I told him we needed to talk, and that I missed him."

Julia's phoned buzzed.

"What did he say?"

"He's getting the next flight he can. He'll let me know what flight he's on."

I offered her a small smile. "I told you he loved you. Don't hurt him, Julia. Give him a chance to be there for you both."

She smiled through her tears. "Thank you for being here, even though I don't deserve you."

"I'm always here for you, and I'll help you in any way I can. I hope you know that."

"I was so stupid and naive about Rogan and you. I really am sorry."

Rogan had to be a topic that never got discussed, otherwise my life was going to be hell.

46

ROGAN

"LEON, YOU ASSHOLE. WHY COULDN'T THIS WAIT UNTIL morning!" I hissed at one of my best friends. He'd been out to San Diego to make up with his girlfriend, and it had killed me to watch him go, knowing that he'd also see Fallon. I hadn't seen her in over sixteen months.

"It is morning." Leon paced back and forth in the small apartment we rented between Chase and us.

The apartment was much quieter than the dorms, and the privacy was welcomed. The only drawback was having Leon waking me at three thirty in the morning. "Spit it out so I can go back to bed."

"We're pregnant." He grinned. "And engaged."

I blinked. "What?"

"Julia. She broke up with me because she thought

I'd break up with her when I found out. Stupid girl. I love her like crazy. She's mine and I'm not going anywhere, but to San Diego to be a daddy." He grinned like a fool while my brain tried to catch up to him.

While he paced, I switched the Keurig on and brewed a dark coffee to help me wake up and be able to think properly. "You're transferring?"

He rolled his eyes. "Is that all you got out of that? I'm going to be a dad!"

I laughed because Leon's excitement was amazing to see. "I'm happy for you. I really am. I'm just surprised and wow. Julia's pregnant."

"Fallon is going to help her until I'm there permanently."

My heart clenched at hearing Fallon's name.

"I saw Daniel while I was there. He seems like a good guy. Only has eyes for Fallon," he commented.

My gut clenched and jealousy hit me hard. Fallon would always be my girl and hearing that Daniel was still in the picture ate at me. Had she allowed him to be intimate with her? Leon glanced at my clenched fists and added, "Fallon never returned his look, if it helps." He ran his hands through his hair. "You and Fallon need to talk and sort shit out because you're my best friend and Fallon is Julia's. We're having a kid together and we want you both in our child's life."

"I walked away because it was the right thing to do."

"You walked away because I talked you into it. It had already been on your mind, which is why you allowed me into your head. From what I saw in San Diego, and from what I witnessed between you and your stalker, is that you're both as unhappy as the other." Leon sighed. "The truth is, I don't feel your relationship with Fallon is as wrong as I used to do. Maybe it's because we're not at home anymore. Or maybe it's because I've witnessed firsthand how much you miss her. I don't know, but you're both as miserable as the other."

"I can't remember the last time we really talked." I laughed. "Actually, I can."

"Yeah, me too. My jaw hurt like a bitch for a month." Leon snickered. "Yours did too, even though you denied it. I saw you rubbing it a few times."

"I miss her, Leon," I admitted quietly. "Stalker Tiffany has been useful in what I wanted Julia to see, but I should never have encouraged the girl. She won't leave me alone and has it in her head that I'm into her. She knew upfront I wanted Julia to see me all over her and she was only too happy to agree. I should have realized then what a mistake I was making."

"Right now I should be saying, I told you so, but I won't." He smirked. "Because I did."

I thumped him in the arm, and changed the subject. "So, when is baby Leon due?" I groaned. "I think I'll hope you have a daughter. One of you is enough."

"Hey!" He shoved me. "I don't give a shit what she has as long as Julia is okay, and the baby of course." He guzzled the rest of my coffee. "She's four months along."

"How the fuck did you not notice?" I asked, surprised.

"I noticed she'd put weight on." He rubbed his chin. "It flittered in my mind that she might be pregnant but she was convincing. She was scared, and ran. I'm still annoyed she broke up with me and left. It fucking hurt."

"I saw."

He watched me from the corner of his eye, so I raised a brow. "What?"

"Fallon seemed sad at times when I saw her looking at Julia's belly. At first I wondered why, then I remembered the accident and that Fallon couldn't have children. It must hurt."

"Yeah," I agreed roughly, and cleared my throat. "When are you going back?"

"I'm going to go and talk to someone over at administration later and find out how I can transfer to San Diego. Julia doesn't want to come back here. Her parents won't talk to her, but I'm hoping for her sake that they'll come around." He shook his head and ran his hands through his hair. "I'll drive when I do go because I have too much shit to fly. We can do a road trip." He grinned.

My heart didn't think it could take seeing Fallon when I could no longer be with her. I just agreed. "That would be good. Chase loves road trips."

"Don't think I don't know what's going through your mind right now." Leon smirked, which turned into a frown. "You have no plans to help me move," he stated. "But you and Chase are my best friends, so you don't get a choice."

I collapsed back onto the couch and wondered when my life got so complicated.

When you fell in love with Fallon.

"Tiffany." Leon sat forward and put my empty coffee cup onto the messy coffee table between us. "You need to come with me to get away from her."

"I can handle Tiffany without running away." I ran a hand through my short-cropped hair. I kept it that way now because I knew how much Fallon liked it longer. "Tiffany is—"

"Stalking you!" Leon banged his fist on the table. "Admit it, Rogan. The woman has been after you since we started freshmen year. Since the ruse for Julia to report back to Fallon—even though I told you they weren't talking—that girl has been everywhere. Jeez, even I can't turn round without her watching me. It's damn creepy."

"Maybe she is a bit over the top." I sighed. "I'm going to try and get some more sleep." I raised a brow. "I'll find her tomorrow and tell her to stop."

Leon snorted. "You won't need to find her because she'll find you within ten minutes of you leaving here." A frown appeared. "You be careful with her, okay? I wasn't joking when I said she scares me."

"I promise to be careful."

I grabbed my cell phone from where I'd left it charging and settled under the quilt. I opened my photo app, and there she was. My girl. My heart ached and I reached up and pressed against my chest in the hope that the pain would dissipate. The photograph album I have of the two of us hasn't been viewed that often. I had to force myself not to look at first and then it became routine. I knew the photographs were there, so it eased the pain. But when I did look at them, the pain tore through me and I found myself in agony. Unbeknown to me, tears ran down my face as I looked through my collection. I swiped them away but couldn't move my eyes from the smiling face looking back at me.

In the picture Fallon smiled, full of arousal. She looked sexy as fuck with the come-hither gaze. I'd just gone down on her and refused to let her come. I'd wanted her release to be wrapped around my dick. As soon as I'd taken the photograph of her, I'd thrust inside of her tight heat and given us both the release we'd craved.

My dick had throbbed into a rock hard erection with the remembered images in my head of that day. As I fastened a fist around my flesh, my ass clenched and my hips pumped into my fist. I still held my phone with the sexy image of Fallon and I remembered the way her dark hair had spread beneath her. I remembered how she had looked at me. Touched me. My legs spread as I pumped faster, harder, tighter, into my fist, the image of Fallon and the small gasps she'd made as she came fresh in my head. Her pussy had quivered and pulsed in pleasure, and I hadn't been able to hold myself back for another moment.

I dropped my phone to my chest, arched up with my head thrown back, and I came. I panted hard and pumped my release all over my belly, chest and hand. I was a mess. Inside and out. I missed my girl like fucking crazy, and the temptation to go and get her back was so close to the surface that I thought I'd break. I couldn't. I had to stay strong. It was for the best.

Why didn't I believe that?

47

FALLON

"My back is killing me," Julia moaned, as she tried to reach around and press into her lower back.

I smiled because my best friend was huge and she blamed Leon for the size of their baby. Both Leon and I worried that she was too small to give birth the natural way, but so far her OB wasn't.

"Go and lie on your side on the bed and I'll massage it for you." I slipped my hand into hers and led her through to the bedroom she now shared with Leon.

Things had rapidly changed once we became friends again and Leon arrived. I moved out of the dorms and into a small two-bedroom apartment, and between Leon and me, we managed with the rent. They wouldn't have been able to manage alone, so I'd offered. I hadn't known at the time that they'd presumed I was moving in with them anyway, not because of the money, but because of our friendship.

"Fallon," Julia moaned, ending my wool gathering. "It really hurts, please press on my back."

Was Julia in labor? She wasn't due for another three weeks, which was why Leon had quickly popped home to visit his parents, his father being too sick to travel here.

Knelt behind Julia, I pressed into her lower back where her hands had been trying to reach. The deep sigh she released told me I was working my magic.

"Oh!" Julia hissed. "Fuck, I think I might be in labor."

Blood gushed around in my head as I panicked. I was so not ready to help her with this. "This is Leon's fault," I cursed. "If he hadn't put his dick inside of you, then I wouldn't be here freaking the heck out because my best friend is in labor and I don't know what to do!"

"Fallon, stop and take a deep breath," Julia hissed, and started her breathing exercises. I copied her, which surprisingly put my head back on.

"I'm calling an ambulance because there is no way I can get you to the hospital, not even in a taxi."

Julia didn't argue, which had me worried. She

argued about everything lately. So before she had time to realize what I'd said, I grabbed my cell and called 911. Help would be arriving in five minutes. At least we only have two blocks to get to us. My next call was to Leon, whose phone immediately went to voice mail. So did all the other times I called and left him messages on the way to the hospital. He still hadn't called me back or answered my other calls when Julia was wheeled into a delivery room.

Julia grabbed my hand and the tears that ran down her face hurt me to see. I wanted to take the pain away for my friend. "He's flying back, remember?" she whispered. "Send him a text and tell him where I am and not to worry." She moaned and grabbed her belly while breathing heavily. "Tell him his baby isn't coming into this world until he gets his ass here."

"Now, Julia Quinn, I can assure you that your baby will arrive when he or she is ready, and not because you decide it's not time." The labor and delivery doctor appeared with a stern look on her face. The slight tilt of her lips made me grin. She obviously found humor in Julia's words. "I'm going to examine you to see how far along you are. Your contractions are close together, so I think things are moving quickly. I want to be certain."

The doc turned to me. "If you're staying, can you

suit up?" She nodded off to the side where a small neat stack of blue gowns waited in plastic wrap.

The gown hung off me it was so big, but fidgeting with it gave me an excuse to avoid the examination the doctor was doing on Julia. Blood never bothered me, but the thought of seeing my best friend down there made me faint.

"She's covered up," the doctor said, a grin on her face.

"Thank you." I cleared away my embarrassment and asked, "How is she doing?"

"I think she's going to become a mom within the hour."

My eyes widened and panic flittered in my belly.

Leon, where are you?

"Baby daddy in the picture?" she asked.

"Yes. Leon Davies. He made a quick trip home to see his dad, who is really sick. We thought there was time, with Julia, not his dad. He's on his way back, which is why I can't get him on the phone. He knows to come straight here when he lands." I really hoped Leon got his messages. I'd also risked a message to Rogan telling him to get ahold of Leon, and the reason why. He hadn't replied.

I'd slept on the sofa at Daniel's apartment when Rogan had helped Leon move to San Diego. I was terrified of seeing Rogan, and wasn't sure how he would react. I missed him every day, but I managed to get through the days without crying now. I hadn't wanted to go back to the days where I felt dark clouds permanently hung over my head. So instead of facing him, I'd escaped to Daniel's place.

From all accounts, Rogan had been resigned to me not being around, but when Julia had let slip that I'd gone to Daniel's for a few days, he'd been hurt and upset. He'd gone off on his own for a few hours, and he'd barely spoken to anyone for the rest of the weekend.

I'd been tempted to get in touch with him and tell him there was nothing intimate between Daniel and me, but I hadn't. Rogan had been the one to tell me to get on with my life, so I'd decided to let him stew.

"Earth to Fallon," Julia whispered between bouts of pain.

"I'm here." I grabbed Julia's hand.

"I'm scared."

"Julia, don't think like that. Very soon you are going to be holding your beautiful baby, and everything that you're going through now will be worth it." I smiled through my tears. "Leon will get here eventually and we have to make sure he knows that you don't hold it against him for not being here. You practically shoved him out the door to go and see his dad."

"His dad only has a week or two at the most left. He had to go. I wanted to as well."

"I know." I kissed her wet cheek and let her squeeze my hand as another sharp pain tightened her body. As she relaxed, exhausted against the pillow, I added, "We can do a video of your baby and send it to Leon's mom to show his dad." I smiled. "He'll get to see his grandchild. Everything works out for a reason."

"What about you?"

"What about me?"

"Fallon, how is me being pregnant with Leon's baby affecting you? You never talk about it with me."

I knew exactly what she meant, but I tried to be funny. "I've never wanted to have Leon's baby."

She started to reply until another pain ripped through her body. "Idiot," she moaned. "I meant—"

"I know what you meant." I sighed, and swallowed hard. "It's something I try not to think about, more so since you've been pregnant." I glanced away and then held her gaze. "The only boy"—I smiled—"man that I've wanted to spend my life with is Rogan. I can't see beyond him. No matter how much I've tried, even with Daniel, it's always going to be Rogan. He doesn't want me, though, so worrying about not being able to give him a child is a moot point."

"You didn't see his face when I let slip you were at Daniel's place." She shook her head. "I saw his pain, Fallon, and I don't ever want to see either of you hurting like that again. I want you to tell him about Daniel."

"He has Tiffany." I glanced away again and quickly turned back to Julia when she cried out in pain, and right on cue a delivery nurse walked into the room.

Julia grabbed my wrist. "He only did what he did with Tiffany in front of me because he wanted me to tell you he'd moved on, so you would. Leon told me Rogan set it all up for my benefit. Except, the girl is stalking Rogan now. He can't go anywhere without her showing up. Leon and Chase want him to go to the cops, but Rogan thinks she'll eventually give up."

Julia paused and sucked in a breath. "Oh God, I need to push," Julia screamed.

"Not yet," the delivery nurse said, utter calm in her voice. "Breathe through the urge. I'll tell you when to push or pant."

"I want Leon," she cried.

"I'm here." Leon rushed into the room and straight over to Julia.

Julia started crying and Leon cupped her face and

kissed her on the forehead. "I love you, babe. I got Fallon's messages the minute we landed and I switched my phone back on." He kissed her again.

The doctor walked in and finished helping the delivery nurse get everything ready. "We have a baby to deliver." She glanced at Leon. "Dad, I presume?"

"Yes."

"Good, this is how you can help your girlfriend…"

I tuned the doctor out and stood at the back of the room so I wouldn't get in anyone's way. I wished I could lie and say I wasn't nervous, but I was. My friend was in so much pain, and the fact that they were letting her have a vaginal birth terrified me, as it did Leon.

Leon followed the doctor's orders and within twenty minutes a wiggling baby was placed on Julia's chest.

I burst into tears at the sight and noticed both Leon and Julia cried too. Leon cuddled Julia to him while he cradled their daughter against her mom. My heart felt so full as I watched, and it did hurt knowing that I would never experience the joy of bringing a child into the world. It hurt more than I'd cared to admit to Julia, which was why my tears refused to stop as I watched them from the back of the room.

Leon turned his head and indicated for me to

come closer. I didn't want to move, but I forced my feet forward. "Fallon, meet Poppy Gerri Davies."

My tears continued falling and I didn't care. Little Poppy was gorgeous with a head full of dark blond hair. I leaned in and kissed their baby on her small cheek before kissing my best friend on her forehead.

"I'm so proud of you Julia." I smiled and turned to Leon, whom I pulled into my arms for a long hug. I whispered, "I'm so proud of you too. You're going to be an amazing dad." I kissed his cheek.

"I'm going to leave you two to get to know your daughter." I moved toward the door and removed the blue gown I'd had to wear.

"Will you tell Rogan about Poppy? Tell him I'll be out soon."

I froze and shot my gaze to Leon's, who hadn't noticed my reaction.

"Okay." I left and leaned against the wall directly outside of the room. I hadn't been prepared to see Rogan, but he was here and I had to go and talk to him. I felt emotionally drained and probably looked as much. I didn't have it in me to sneak away. I knew how much Leon meant to him, and he'd be worried.

I could do this.

Head turned toward the entrance to the delivery suites; I forced my body to move. Albeit slow. The moment I saw Rogan through the small window in the door, his head snapped up and our eyes met and held. I couldn't look away. I didn't want to look away. The tears that I'd managed to get ahold of started to flow freely.

As if in slow motion, Rogan stood and moved toward me, and I exited through the door and moved toward him. Only before we reached each other, strong arms wrapped around me and pulled me into a hard male body. I was startled until I heard Daniel's whispered, "Are you okay?"

Rogan came to a sudden stop, his eyes never left mine while Daniel hugged me close. I kept my eyes on Rogan, wishing it were him who held me. I let him see everything I was feeling on my face, which I think surprised him. I pushed out of Daniel's embrace and offered him a small smile before my eyes found Rogan again. I'd always find Rogan, no matter how crowded a room would be.

"Oh, I didn't know your brother was here," Daniel said, wrapping an arm around my back and propelling me closer to Rogan.

I swallowed hard and cleared my throat. "Poppy Gerri Davies has arrived and has a head full of dark blond hair. Mother and baby are doing fine."

"And Leon?" Rogan asked between his teeth, his anger leaking out.

"He surprised me and never let her down." I felt uncomfortable with the looks Rogan and Daniel exchanged, so I added, "I'm going to go home and then I'll come back at visiting time."

"I'll come with you," Daniel stated.

Rogan's jaw tightened. "I'm waiting here." He turned around and went to stand in front of the window, his back to us and his hands rested on the windowsill. His fists clenched around the wood while his head dropped.

I wanted to go to him, except I was pulled toward the elevator. I didn't want to leave with Daniel, I wanted to stay with Rogan. Daniel didn't talk the whole way down, and it was only as we left the hospital that he said, "It's true, isn't it?"

"What is?" I asked, confused.

"Rogan and you." He shook his head in disgust. "That's why you've never wanted anything more with me. You really are in love with *him?*"

Silent. My mind went numb the moment I heard "Rogan and you" and all thoughts fled. I couldn't form words to defend us because Daniel spoke the truth.

"How?" I asked softly.

"You are so blind where he's concerned that you never noticed the whispers at school." He shook his head and slammed his fist on the steering wheel. "Everyone talked about you both. About the way you'd look at each other. About the way that neither of you dated. About the way you went off with Rogan at his prom. I listened to it and wondered, and until now I never truly believed the gossip. I realize now that I didn't believe it because I like you. You're so damn nice and easy to talk to. I *really* liked you, Fallon."

I stared out of the window in shock at his words. I was clueless it would seem. Everyone knew and yet I hadn't known. Had Rogan? Had the gossip at school gotten to Rogan somehow and that, with whatever Leon had said, had forced him to walk away from me? It made me wonder.

At my apartment building, I made no move to climb from his car. I wasn't sure my legs would hold me up.

"I'm sorry," Daniel murmured. "I shouldn't have said all that. It just ticked me off seeing the way you looked at him when you've never looked at me like that. It hurt, Fallon."

My face was covered in tears as I turned toward him. "I'm sorry. You know I never meant to hurt you. I do like you and consider you a friend, but"—I inhaled and slowly exhaled—"my heart will always belong to someone else. I can't help who I fell in love with, no matter how right or wrong it is. I've always loved him, and I'm so sorry I've hurt you."

Daniel sighed. "Come on. I'll take you up to your apartment."

I was too tired and upset to refuse, even though I knew I hung on to my emotions by a thread. I felt raw and bleeding and I didn't know how to make it stop.

48

ROGAN

I SAID THAT I WAS STAYING AT THE HOSPITAL, BUT I couldn't. Once my anger and jealousy had calmed down, I started to remember small things when Fallon had first seen me in the waiting room. Her eyes had shone brightly with tears, but when she'd seen me, I witnessed the change come over her. I didn't think she realized it, but her watery eyes had lit up as she'd made her way toward me. I saw relief mingled with love on her face.

Then Daniel had gotten between us and I'd come close to punching him. How dare he have his arms around my girl! Fallon had been frozen and hadn't returned the other guy's hug. It had been me she'd wanted to hold her. I saw that clearly now that I wasn't so eaten with jealousy. She'd let him take her home, but that thought gave me pause, and then made me act.

Grateful I had Leon's car keys in my pocket, I turned and dashed to the parking lot. No way could I wait a moment longer to talk to Fallon. I'd tried to live without her and that hadn't gone too well.

It took only a few minutes to arrive at her apartment at this time of night. Nothing had changed from when I'd helped move Leon here, except this time Fallon wouldn't be going to Daniel's place. No way. I'd given her space, but all it had taken was the look on her face back at the hospital and I knew she still loved me. Only me. That wasn't even a question I needed to ask her because I knew.

I typed in the security code for the outer door, and then my legs ate up the distance between us, but I paused once I was outside of her apartment. I really hadn't thought it through. What would I say to her? What would I do if she ignored me? Slammed the door in my face?

Only one way to find out. I rapped on the door and waited.

My jaw clenched tight when Daniel answered. The other guy gave me a resigned look and stepped back so I could enter.

"I should have known you'd follow her," Daniel commented.

I raised a brow.

"She's in the kitchen." He glanced over his shoulder. "I'll leave you alone. It isn't me she wants here."

He left and I wanted to punch him all over again. Why would he leave his girlfriend so easily?

The clatter of cups led me toward where Fallon was. She looked small and delicate as I watched her move around the small kitchen. Her body slowed and she turned as though she was afraid.

Our eyes met and I couldn't look away. Fallon had always been a beautiful girl and she'd become so much more as she'd grown into a beautiful woman. She took my breath away.

Regardless of the hurt I'd caused by leaving her, I moved forward and wrapped my whole body around her. Fallon only paused for a moment and then I felt her sink into my embrace. Moments later her body started to tremble and I felt the hot tears she released through my shirt. I picked her up in my arms and sighed into her neck when her legs automatically wrapped around my hips. She clung so tightly to me that I never wanted to put her down.

The couch looked good, so I dropped my bulk onto it and managed to hold onto Fallon. She settled against me, her face buried in my chest. I dipped mine and brushed my nose along the arch of her neck, capturing her scent that was so familiar. I was a fool to give her up. I did it for the right reasons, but it had hurt us both badly.

Not sure how long I'd held onto her and offered her comfort, she lifted her gaze and the first thing she said to me was, "I've never had sex with Daniel." I winced at the bluntness but deep inside I felt relieved, and she continued, "I'm not going to lie to you and say I never thought about it because I did. Except, the moment Daniel kissed me and touched me, I pushed him away. I hated myself for being cruel to him when I knew he liked me a lot more than I liked him. The thing is, I only want you, but you don't want me anymore."

Fallon tried to bury her head back into my chest but I refused to let her. She needed to hear what I had to say. "I was sick with jealousy when I found out about Daniel."

"Just like I was when I found out about Tiffany."

My blood ran cold at the mention of the girl's name, and I felt uncomfortable. "I never did anything with *her* or anyone else. In fact, I regret asking her to help me out." I closed my eyes and tipped my face up to the ceiling. "She's nuts, Fallon. I can't go anywhere around Boston without her showing up. It's damn spooky."

"She's stalking you?" Fallon tilted her head to the side and searched my gaze. "I had her pegged as a stalker when we met."

I smiled and rolled my eyes. "No, you didn't." I pushed her head back to my chest. "You were eaten with jealousy, the way I am when I think about you with another guy."

She sighed softly into my neck as her face slowly moved up and nuzzled into my neck. "We're a right pair, huh?"

My fingers wrapped into her long curls and I stroked and played with the soft strands. "I wished I'd never let you go. I ruined us both, Fallon. Don't for one-minute think it was easy to walk away from you because it was hell. I thought I was doing what was best, and I still do. I'm not sure anymore if it's healthy for us both to stay away from each other. I thought because you're young that you'd find it easy to move on, and then maybe if I saw that, I'd be able to do the same. Except it didn't work out that way. I don't just miss my girlfriend, Fallon, I miss my best friend."

"I missed you too." She sniffled against me. "Please tell me we can be friends again. I don't ever want to spend another day not talking to you. Something broke inside of me when I lost you."

My own tears threatened to fall and I quickly swallowed them back and concentrated on breathing. I held Fallon in my arms and she felt amazing. I never wanted us to move. Her scent washed over me, and my heart was finally soothed.

"I can't believe Leon is a dad," I commented. "Was he really strong while Julia brought his daughter into the world?"

Fallon sat up and wiped at her face, a smile slipped across her lips. "He really was. Didn't you see them before you left the hospital?"

"No." I sighed and urged Fallon to rest back down on me. "I left soon after you did. I didn't want you alone with Daniel, if I had anything to do with it."

"I'm glad you're here. I wish I knew how I was going to explain everything to Daniel."

"I'll help you."

She laughed. "He knows about us, Rogan."

My breath caught and her fingernails dug into my chest.

"Don't claw me to death." I captured her hand and wrapped mine around it. "And explain?"

"We weren't as secretive as we thought we were." She shrugged. "I really don't care about high school anymore. It's in the past and Daniel is the only one from there that I see." She paused and I knew there was more that she wasn't telling me. I waited, but Fallon stayed silent.

"You're not telling me something. Trust me, Fallon." I kissed her cheek and lingered. "Trust me."

"Mom overheard a conversation between Julia and me on prom night."

"The prom you went to with Daniel."

"You weren't around."

"I was there," I admitted.

The dark lashes that shadowed her cheeks flew up and seconds later she stood, shocked. I felt the immediate loss of her warmth. "You were there? At my prom?"

I stood and captured her face between my warm hands and held her still. "I was there because I couldn't stay away. I watched. I saw you enter and I saw you leave. Daniel took you straight home."

"I don't know how I should feel about you watching me."

"I wanted to be the one who led you to prom. Me, Fallon," I shouted and made her jump. "But I screwed it all up." I felt like a caged lion as I prowled around the small apartment. "I ruined everything."

"No way." Fallon got in front of me and grabbed

my arms. "You did what you thought you had to do *for me*. I know why you did it, it didn't hurt any less knowing that, though." She sighed and pushed me to the couch and straddled me, her finger pressed against my chest. "Mom said she'd always suspected there was something more and that she'd always distracted Dad when he was on our scent." Tears hovered on her lids. "She was happy that you'd walked away, even though she'd wished I wasn't sad." She burst into a fresh set of tears. "What are we going to do?"

"We are going to take everything slow until we graduate. We're not going to give our parents anything to suspect. Not this time. We're older." I smirked. "And someone is a year older tomorrow."

"Ugh, don't remind me." She grinned through her tears. "It also means that you're twenty-one in a month."

"Hmm." I laughed. "You're going to help me celebrate, right?"

"I'm afraid, Rogan."

"I'm here, and after the hell I've put us both through, I have no intention of doing that again. We're going to hang out together whenever we can and once I've graduated, which isn't too far off, I'm going to move out here to you." I kissed the top of her head. "I've applied to the fire department's training center here." I grinned at the look of surprise on her face. "I also have an interview in four days."

"I, um, wow!" She laughed and cupped my face. I felt her touch all the way to my toes. "So you'd already decided what you wanted to do and where you wanted to be before you saw me?"

"Yes. You've always been mine, Fallon. That's never changed, even though my actions said otherwise."

"You've made me happy, but I still have this knot of fear in my belly. It's hot and feels stuck inside of me. Mom won't be happy to see us together, and will take some convincing that we're friends, and only friends."

"We're going to be a lot more than friends, Fallon." My eyes darkened as I watched the blush on her cheeks.

"I know, but Mom and Dad can't know, Rogan. They just can't." Her panicked words had me worried, and I didn't want to think about our parents.

"They won't know if we don't tell them or give them anything to suspect." I squeezed her around the waist. "So, Poppy Gerri Davies, huh?"

She chuckled. "She's gorgeous, Rogan. I can't wait to go and visit tomorrow and be able to hold her."

"Me too. I'm glad they managed to incorporate Gerry's name with her being a girl. Leon's dad will love that touch."

"I know. It's sad he may not be around to hold his granddaughter, but he'll get to see her on Facetime, and see how happy his son is with his own child, and Julia."

"Dad is helping, and he's said if he can do anything to help get Julia and their baby home to see Gerry, then he'd help."

"We all will." She yawned. "I think I'm going to be asleep on you soon. I haven't slept well for a long time and worrying over Julia, then the labor, and then seeing you, it's all too much."

"Will you let me hold you while you sleep?" I asked. "I promise I'll behave. I just want to feel you sleeping in my arms."

"I'll probably sleep better than I have since you left if you hold me."

I pushed up from the couch and carried Fallon into her bedroom. My feet stopped moving when I caught sight of the photograph of us she had on her nightstand. "Jeez, Fallon. I have that photograph on my nightstand."

She smiled against my neck. "Soul mates," she mumbled as I laid her in bed.

I stood watching her for what felt like an age before I slowly pulled my clothing off, but kept my boxers on. I hadn't lied to Fallon when I said we'd go slow. The need inside of me was there and my body ached for her in a way I knew it always would. She was my beautiful Fallon.

Before climbing into the bed beside her, I carefully undressed her to her underwear, and regardless of how hard my body became, I eventually settled beside her. She rolled into my arms and I held her. My dick throbbed and my heart pounded with our bodies pressed tightly together.

No matter how much I hurt, I held her all night.

49

FALLON

Rogan's warm body surrounded me and I didn't want to leave him. But I needed to pee. Still, I could take a few moments to look at him while he slept. My eyes slowly caressed his body, which had changed even more in the time we'd been apart. He was a man now. A big strong sexy man. His thighs were muscular and covered with dark hair while his abs were more defined. The part of him that my eyes struggled to move on from was his penis. He was thick and long trapped in his fitted boxers. The plump head poked from the waistband with a pearl of liquid at the slit.

"If you touch me, I'm not going to be held responsible for what happens next," he growled.

My eyes popped to his and I smirked. "Is that so?"

His eyes darkened and in the next moment, I was on my back with Rogan over me.

"Happy birthday, Fallon. I'm so happy I get to spend today with you." He leaned down and pressed a sweet and soft kiss to my lips.

"I'm happy too, Rogan. For the first time since you left me, I'm happy."

"I never meant to hurt you. I'd have given anything not to have. At the time I honestly thought I was doing the right thing." He paused. "It hurt me too."

"I know." I reached with my arms around to his back and he shuddered when I dug my fingernails into his skin. I trailed my fingers into the back of his boxers, shoving them over his firm ass while I held his gaze.

"Fallon," he warned, but his hands went to my panties and he tugged them to my hips. They wouldn't go further because he was pressed between my legs, and showed no signs of moving. He paused and breathed heavily, his gaze going to my breasts that felt swollen, achy. "What are you doing to me?"

I smiled. He'd get over my devious plan to seduce him because I needed physical contact with him. I couldn't explain it, but I needed his touch on my skin. I needed to touch him. My legs wrapped around his hips and when I tightened them, I felt his penis pressed between my legs. Well, the base of him had slipped between me and where my panties stretched. He pressed in a really good place between my legs, but the tip poked up between us.

Rogan hissed and looked down between us. "Fucking hell, Fallon. I'm going to blow watching us." He breathed deeply and moved his gaze to mine. His eyes caressed my face while he rubbed against me with deliberate ease. It was as though his hips had a mind of their own.

I could tell Rogan didn't know whether to continue with the slow torture, or to get rid of my panties altogether, or whether to move away from me. I watched as his mouth moved closer to mine. He licked his lips, and then someone started banging on the door. I wanted to cry in frustration.

"Hell!" Rogan panted, his hips rubbed faster. Harder. The friction against my core was delicious, but the friction of his penis against the soft hair covering my mound with some trapped in my panties made me dig my nails into his skin.

It had been so long since he'd loved me that I didn't care someone was trying to bang my front door down. Neither did Rogan. I clung to him and frantically moved my hips with him. The moment he captured my lips with his and thrust his tongue into my mouth, pleasure rippled through me. I quivered in his arms and moments later, I felt thick wet heat land on my lower belly. Rogan didn't stop kissing me, even when we heard Chase shout through the door. His hands tangled in my hair and he kissed me like a starving man. Even when he pulled away so we could both catch a breath, he continued placing small kisses all over my face and neck before he reached my lips once more.

"I love you," he breathed against me.

"I'm going to set your apartment on fire if you don't open this door!" Chase shouted.

I gripped Rogan to me and laughed. Rogan kissed me deeply, and whispered, "I'll go let him in while you go and get cleaned up." He lifted off of me and I nearly swallowed my tongue when he kicked his boxers off and used them to dry himself. He winced and offered me one hell of a sexy smirk. "I'm all yours, babe." Naked as the day he was born, Rogan moved to the side of the bed and gave me a slow kiss. "Get your ass in the shower."

He grabbed his jeans while I watched the shear perfection of Rogan Scott shove his toned legs into his jeans, sans boxers. "You're going to be naked in your jeans?"

"I'm calling the cops," Chase yelled.

"Give me a minute," Rogan shouted to Chase. "And, babe, anytime you want to see what's inside of my jeans, you only need to ask." He winked and left me laid out on my bed with my panties digging into my hips and his release all over me.

It wasn't a pretty sight but it had felt wonderful having Rogan in my arms again. I'd missed him a lot. He hadn't only been my love, he'd been my best friend. I could talk to him about everything and anything, and I hadn't had that for a long time.

"I hope she's dressed because she has a visitor," Chase shouted from the other room.

"Stop being a pain in the ass. Fallon's in the shower. She'll be out soon."

I smiled and dived into the small bathroom that was called an en suite. It was *really* small. It had a sink, toilet, and shower with no spare space. The door could only just close with me inside the room.

It didn't take me long to shower and dress and tie my hair in a band. The smile was still on my face as I left the bedroom and found Rogan and Chase drinking coffee at the breakfast bar. I snuck up on Chase and wrapped my arms around his neck, plastering a big wet kiss to his cheek. "I've missed you."

Chase stayed silent but quickly moved from his

seat and wrapped me in a strong hold, which felt like home. Tears sprung into my eyes, and I rapidly blinked them away. Rogan caught them, though.

"Happy birthday," Chase whispered, and cleared his throat.

"Thanks, Chase."

"So you two are back together, huh?" he asked, pulling me down beside him.

"We still have some things to work out, but yes." I smiled at Rogan.

Rogan brought me a cup filled with coffee and kissed the top of my head as he placed it in front of me. His hand caressed down my arm and our fingers intertwined. With a slight tug I was up and being tugged to the couch. Rogan dropped his butt down and pulled me onto his lap, his arms around my waist.

"Bring the coffee over, will you?" he asked Chase.

Chase smirked. "Of course, oh master!"

"I've really missed being around you," I said to Chase.

Rogan squeezed me and nuzzled into my neck.

"As far back as I can remember, you, Leon, and Rogan have been friends, and I was always the one tagging along. When Rogan left me"—I glanced at his face filled with sorrow, and continued looking at Chase—"I didn't just miss him, I missed you too." I offered him a watery smile. "I'm glad we're all together for Leon and Julia."

"We missed you too, Fallon," Chase whispered choked up. "And who knew it would be Leon becoming a father to bring us all back together."

"I need to disagree with that." Rogan tilted my face toward him.

"You got the kick up the ass you needed to make it right with Fallon." Chase chuckled. "But we're all together and I'm happy."

"Thanks for that, Chase," Rogan grumbled and brushed a kiss across my lips. "What I was about to say before Chase interrupted, was that I'd planned on coming for you the day I took my last exam at school." He paused. "I wasn't even going to tell you about the interview with the fire department until I made the cut. I wanted everything in place to come to you and beg forgiveness."

I chuckled. "It didn't take much for me to forgive you. I understood, even though it hurt so much. Don't ever do that again."

"That's it, tell him." Chase made himself at home on the other couch. "He's been no fun to be around. I know Leon is sorry for what he said, not that he'd ever admit it. I mean, the asshole always has to be right." He moaned. "This couch is so comfy. I'm going to sleep here while you two go back to the hospital. I know they can't wait to see you."

After I quickly dropped a kiss to Rogan's cheek, I stood and grabbed a throw from the back of the couch. Chase grinned but kept his eyes closed as I tucked him in. He whispered, "Thank you."

"Let's grab some coffee and breakfast on the way to the hospital. I want to stop for some gifts too."

"In a minute." Rogan took my hand and led me inside my bedroom and closed the door. He turned and pressed me against the solid wood. "Not a day went by that I didn't think of you. That I didn't miss you like crazy. No matter what happens, we have to stay together. We're stronger together." He pressed his lips to mine and I immediately opened my mouth and pressed closer. The kiss deepened and I felt Rogan's reaction in the press of his erection against my belly.

"We need to leave," I breathed against his mouth.

"Hmm." Rogan gripped my butt in his large hands. "In a minute." He grunted the words into my mouth as he hauled me up the door and pressed directly between my legs. "I need a minute."

My eyes darkened and I leaned forward and bit his neck. He cursed and quivered against me. With strength I didn't know he had, Rogan held my hips and placed me back on the floor. He took a step back and closed his eyes while he breathed heavily.

His eyes opened and the swirl of desire for me was there, along with his love.

My heart thudded loudly that I was surprised Rogan didn't hear it. I went up on tiptoes and wrapped my arms around his neck. "Together, Rogan. From here on out, we're together. I promise."

My big strong man had to rapidly blink to clear his eyes of the emotional tears that hovered.

50

———————

ROGAN

LEON BENT MY EAR ABOUT SOMETHING; HOWEVER, I paid him no attention. My gaze was solely focused on Fallon as she cuddled Poppy in her arms. She snuggled beside Julia on the bed and they both had tears on their cheeks. My heart broke as I watched Fallon because I knew she would never get to experience becoming a mother. I wished I could turn back time and not screw up so badly that she went off by herself in that car. If it hadn't been for me, she wouldn't have been driving that night. We'd have been home after dinner and watched a movie in her room.

I'd never admitted to Fallon that I blamed myself for what had happened to her. I thought she knew, but it wasn't something we'd talked about. I wanted so badly to give her a child of our own, and

446

it made me sad that would never happen. I didn't love her any less, and if it meant growing old with the woman I loved, then everything else didn't matter.

"That's an intense look on your face." Julia observed.

"Just thinking." I met Fallon's gaze and held her beautiful eyes with mine.

My feet took me to the chair beside the bed, which I moved closer and leaned in. I nuzzled into Fallon's arm and rested my face there watching Poppy. The baby was sweet and content lying in Fallon's arms. Julia had fed her daughter before we arrived, which probably explained the silence in the room from the baby.

"You did well, Julia."

"Hey, *Rogan!* I'll have you know it was my swimmers that did good." Leon grinned.

Julia laughed. "I think Leon is going to need therapy after seeing my vagina in a whole new way."

Leon winced. "Let's not talk about that."

"You know I'm proud of you, right?" I looked at Leon. "You never once panicked over Julia being pregnant. Not once. You've been there for her, and now you're a dad. You've both done good."

"Jeez." Leon blinked and pressed his thumb and

finger into the corner of his eyes. "You know how to unman me."

I rolled my eyes at my dramatic friend. "Babies have a habit of making grown men cry."

Leon smiled. "I agree with you there." He sighed and perched on the edge of the bed beside Julia. "I don't mind admitting that I cried like a baby when Poppy was born. It was from relief that Julia was okay, and meeting my daughter for the first time. Seeing how much she looked like her mom." He dropped his face to Julia's chest and stayed hidden while he got his emotions under control.

"We have something to ask you both." Julia waited for Leon to lift his head, and she continued, "We'd like you both to be Poppy's godparents. So if anything ever happens to us, God forbid, you'll be there for her. We need to know she'll be taken care of by the two people closest to us."

Fallon dipped her head and sniffled, which alarmed me. I quickly moved and indicated for Julia to take Poppy. I pulled Fallon up and into my arms and held her tightly while she cried.

"Fallon?" Julia asked.

"She'll be okay. She's overwhelmed." My arms tightened around her as she clung to me.

"I have you," I whispered into her ear. "I'm not going anywhere."

Fallon nodded and finally managed to calm down. I passed her tissues Julia had passed me.

"I'm okay."

"I'm here, just remember that, okay?"

She nodded and let me pull her onto my lap.

"I'm sorry for my meltdown. I'd love to be Poppy's godmother. I'd consider it an honor." She smiled through her tears that continued to leak. "It isn't something I ever want to think about, you both not being around, but I promise you that Poppy will be loved and well cared for if anything were to happen."

I swallowed around the lump in my throat. "That goes for me too. I'd be honored."

"We're going to ask Chase to be her uncle." Leon rolled his eyes. "Julia's idea so he won't feel left out."

"That's really sweet." Fallon kissed my cheek. "Chase is currently crashed on our couch."

"He said he was heading there when he left here." Leon smirked. "He cried too!"

I chuckled and stood, but kept Fallon in front of me with my arms tightly around her belly. I dropped my chin to her shoulder and let my friend see how amused I was. "Because you cried, everyone has to know who else did, huh?"

"Damn straight. I don't want to be the only pussy."

"Leon!" Julia shoved him in the chest. "Watch your mouth around Poppy."

"And on that note, we'll go and let you have some time alone. We'll we back tonight, though, so behave." I slung my arm around Fallon's neck and moved her with me to the door.

"Wait," Leon said.

We turned to face our friends.

"I just wanted to say I'm sorry for what I said about you both being together. I never wanted to see either of you hurt. At the time I couldn't understand how you both could be together." He paused and moved toward us. "After seeing how you both were alone, I regret what I said. I should have tried to understand more back then. I'm sorry."

I had no words for Leon because I felt what he said to the bottom of my heart. Moving out from behind Fallon, I grabbed him by the shoulder and tugged him into my arms, and hugged the hell out of him. "I know you did it for the right reasons, so no need to apologize." I nodded and then with a second thought, I grabbed his head and slapped a kiss to his cheek. "Love you, man." I shoved him away. "Go be with your family. We'll be back later."

I wrapped my arm around Fallon, who grinned so

wide, and I kissed her on the nose once we left the room. I didn't really like hospitals, especially after I'd spent over a month inside of one waiting for Fallon to wake up. But once we got outside and the sun warmed me, all was good. I paused and turned my face up to the sun and let the rays soak into me.

"It's nice always having the sun to wake up to." Fallon rested her head on my chest while I enjoyed the heat.

"Fallon?"

Her head snapped up at the sharp tone in the voice.

Daniel.

"Seriously? You picked up where you left off? I shouldn't have left last night." He fumed. "He is your *brother*," he snarled, getting too close to Fallon for my liking.

I stepped in front of her and pushed Daniel away. "Get the fuck away from her." My fists clenched.

"Is there a problem here?" a security guard asked, coming up fast.

"I don't know." I glared at Daniel. "Is there?"

Daniel wanted to say a lot more, but instead he tightened his jaw, and hissed, "No," before he headed inside the hospital.

Fallon gently wrapped her hands around my fists

and opened them up. She pressed her palms against mine and intertwined our fingers. "I want to take you to my favorite place to think. I don't want to think about anything bad today, okay? I just want to have a picnic with you, and be alone without any worry about others finding out about us."

I leaned in and captured a quick kiss. "I've always been yours, Fallon, so lead the way."

Her smile lit her whole face and it was infectious as she directed me to her favorite spot out here. I couldn't help worry about leaving her when I went back to Boston to finish out the school year. I didn't have long left, which was good, but who would be here to look out for Fallon. I worried after Daniel's outburst. I knew he was eaten with jealousy over her being with me.

It didn't help that he was from our hometown, so he could easily spread gossip about us before we had a chance to be open with Mom and Dad. I didn't believe he'd hurt Fallon, but I wouldn't put it past him to cause problems for us.

THE BEACH.

Rogan had been surprised when I directed him here, and considering how much I enjoyed my privacy, I knew he would be. This part of the beach was always quiet and I'd often sat here and stared off into the horizon and imagined what it would have been like to sail off with Rogan—to have no problems hanging over our heads because of our love for each other. It was a permanent ache wanting to be with him and knowing that our parents wouldn't approve. We both knew they loved us. But having us together was never what they would want.

"I see why you like it here." Rogan munched on a sandwich and allowed the silence to go on. He then added, "It's you. You've always been drawn to water. I have too, which is why I love getting down to Boston Harbor when I can. If you know the right spot, you can avoid tourists and spend hours alone."

"It's like that here. I love this spot." I laid down on the throw blanket beneath us, and enjoyed the closeness I feel with Rogan. He knew me better than anyone. Even our parents. Even Julia. Rogan knew me inside and out. Just like I knew him. Which was how I knew he tried to hide how worried he was.

I touched his hand and when his gaze landed on me, he smiled and settled on his side next to me. "You look good enough to eat," he whispered.

"You've changed," I commented, letting my fingers slip beneath his T-shirt. His belly quivered at my touch. I felt brave and slipped my hand beneath, my palm going flat over the light sprinkle of hair on his chest. "You've always been mine and hot, but now, you've grown into a sexy man." I teased the waistband of his jeans. "You're firmer, and bigger."

He burst out laughing. "Bigger, huh?"

I rolled my eyes, a smirk on my lips. "Don't let my observation go to your head." I pinched his belly. "I want to touch you everywhere."

He groaned and captured my hand, removing if from his shirt. "You have no idea how much I want that, but not yet." He winced. "I can't believe I'm saying no to you." He pulled me into his arms and tucked my head under his chin as I settled against his chest. "Will you come out to Boston when it's my birthday? Spend the weekend with me?"

"Yes."

He laughed. "You don't need to think about it?"

"Hell no! I've waited nearly two years to be with you. To make love with you again. So I don't need to think about it. My answer will always be yes."

"I hope I have the control to behave while I'm here because I have to say, you've changed too. You're hips are wider."

"Hey!" I shoved him in the belly with my elbow. "You're not supposed to comment on women's expanding parts."

"I think you are really sexy. I think the shape of your hips is slightly more defined and I can't wait to sink my teeth into each one."

"Oh," I moaned, my breath became heavy. "Go on."

His eyes lit with amusement and longing. "Your breasts are plumper and my mouth waters to lick and tease them. To tease your dark nipples into hard buds while I have my cock buried deep inside of you. I remember playing with your nipples and the sharp tugs your pussy would do, thickening me." He panted. "I don't think this was a good idea."

I slipped a knee between his legs and we both groaned when I pressed against his heavy erection. "That feels really good." I writhed on him until I felt his hands clamp down on my ass.

"Please stop moving," he moaned. "I'm really turned on with you being in my arms. It didn't help remembering what it used to feel like to be naked with you."

"Stop remembering then," I offered.

"I can't." He gave a hard thrust against me. "I need a cold shower."

"Or relief." I slipped my hand between us and glided straight down into his jeans. "Mmm, how could I forget you had no boxers on?" I wrapped my hand around him and his penis twitched and jumped against my palm.

"I'm going to really embarrass myself by coming in less than thirty seconds," he growled.

I hovered over his mouth with mine and whispered, "Imagine it's my mouth sucking you off instead of my hand jerking you off," before I sealed my lips over his. He consumed me with his tongue, and then he gasped and grunted as his penis throbbed hard, and warmth poured into my palm. "Um, you were right. You came in under thirty seconds."

He laughed, and turned it into a growl when I

reached lower and cupped his hairy balls. "These are bigger than I remember too." I massaged and grinned when his eyes rolled into the back of his head, his penis swelling against my wrist.

"You need to stop."

"I'm not sure I can." I wiggled closer, trying to ease the ache between my legs. "It turned me on, touching you."

He gulped hard and removed my hand from his jeans, wiping me down with a wet wipe from the picnic basket. He grabbed another and shoved it into the front of his jeans. I chuckled.

"I don't want to be walking around with a mess in my jeans." He kissed my cheek. "I'm going to make you scream my name."

I opened my mouth to ask what he intended, but he didn't give me chance. He kept my leg trapped between his and pressed his fingers between my legs. I sucked in a sharp breath, panting from pleasure. I grabbed his biceps and dug my nails in, unable to move from the tingles running down my spine and to the tips of my breasts.

Rogan noticed how hard my nipples had gone through my bra and shirt. He quickly glanced around us and put his mouth to me at the same time as he wiggled a finger inside of me. My vagina pulsed around that digit but the way he overwhelmed me, had me shaking apart in pure bliss.

He left me panting hard as he slipped his hand free and brought it up to his mouth. "I've missed your smell." He sniffed his finger. "And I've missed your taste." He licked his fingers clean. "We shouldn't have started this here where I can't strip you naked and put my mouth everywhere."

I wrapped myself around him and held him to me while the lust and need for this man ran through my body. I didn't care that we were on a stretch of beach, out in the open for anyone to see us. I wanted Rogan and I knew he wouldn't make love to me until his birthday in a few weeks. That's what he was waiting for and I had an idea as to what he planned.

52

ROGAN

FALLON WAS AT THE CAMPSITE WITH ME AND I FELT more nervous than I had in a long time. Right where she stood was my dream to build a log cabin for the two of us. It felt like a lifetime ago that I'd started to have big dreams where the two of us were concerned. They hadn't changed much in the past few years. Maybe they went a bit off track, but they were formally back in place.

The sunset over the lake had cast Fallon as a silhouette against the beautiful background. It's an image I captured with my cell. She was the beautiful one. Her smile and the way she always listened to me were special. The way she'd touch me and made me believe that I was the only one for her made my heart turn over. I'd loved Fallon for as long as I could remember, and now I had her back with me.

As I tossed my cell into the tent, I removed my jacket and made my way to the girl I loved. She turned on my approach and held her hand out toward me. A gorgeous smile on her beautiful lips.

My arms wrapped her against me and my hands caressed down her back to her bottom. "I love that you brought me here." She said against my neck before she laid a kiss in the curve. "I want you to make love to me, right here. By the lake with nothing but nature around us." Fallon stepped out of my arms and tugged her dress over her head. I nearly swallowed my tongue at the sight before me. Her nude body glistened in the moonlight, and her curves stopped my breath.

"When did you remove your underwear?" I asked, my eyes focused on her swollen breasts.

She offered me a dirty laugh. "When I cleaned up after dinner." She tilted her head. "You have too many clothes on."

"I was just thinking that."

"No, you weren't." Her eyes lit with mischief. "You couldn't decide whether to stare between my legs or at my breasts."

"Ugh," I groaned. "You caught me." I grinned and

made quick work of my clothes. I tossed them down to the ground so I had something to lay her down on. My body ached to join with Fallon, and my dick throbbed and twitched it was so hard and ready. I wrapped my hand around my flesh and slowly stroked with the heat of Fallon's gaze on me.

"Don't stop doing that." She moved to stand in front of me and then dropped to her knees. Her hand covered mine and started moving back and forth when I stopped. "Do it."

I couldn't catch a breath at the heat running through me. Every part of my body tingled with need for this woman. Her hands gripped my thighs and when she opened her mouth and closed around the head of my cock, I nearly fucking unloaded. The sight was hot and I didn't want it to end so quickly.

Pinching my dick to stop my pending orgasm, I pushed her back on my clothes and followed her down. I caught a quick breath and kneeled between her thighs. I raised one of her legs over my shoulder and pressed kisses along her thigh until I got to her pussy. In the darkness I could see how wet she was and it made my dick throb and leak at the sight. "So beautiful," I whispered and dipped my head. My tongue swiped through her soaked folds, her moan nearly undid me.

Not sure how long I would be able to last when I wanted to savor every taste of Fallon, I pushed my tongue between her swollen lips. I felt elated when she arched, rubbing her pussy on my mouth. She moaned and grabbed at my hair, tugging me away.

"Inside me."

Tempted to bring her to completion with my mouth as the entrée, my own body was on fire to be inside of her. I couldn't wait.

My dick swelled more as I held it and moved my body into position to enter her. The crown breached the entrance and I couldn't stop, even if there was an earthquake. My hips thrust forward and I was home. Fallon moaned and wrapped herself around me. Her amazing breasts with tight nipples pressed into my chest, and her vagina squeezed and pulsed around my dick so tightly that I saw stars.

I felt every ridge of my dick as I slid all the way out of Fallon's pussy. As the head popped free, I slowly slid deep. I repeated this over and over again with no clue how I managed to do this without hammering her into the ground. It felt delicious. I rose up slightly so I could lick at her nipples, which drove me crazy. She had dark nipples that got deeper in color the more aroused she was. Right now they were *very* dark and begging for my mouth.

Her chest heaved and Fallon panted as she saw my destination. I captured a dark cherry nipple between my teeth and gave it a little tug. I felt her reaction around my dick as she contracted around me, becoming wetter. I turned my attention to the other and felt the same reaction around my dick.

Fallon called my name and arched her back while I felt every tiny tremor inside of her around my pumping flesh. I grit my teeth and forced myself to keep it slow, but I was rapidly losing the strength not to pound into her.

The pleasure wrapped around my cock was too much. Fallon was too much. Naked and under me. The moment I felt her orgasm wrap around me, I grabbed her hips and pumped into her. I couldn't control the thrusts anymore. I was beyond anything but pleasuring us both. Sweat dripped off my forehead and I felt it on my back in the way Fallon struggled to get a hold on me. She had no trouble digger her fingernails into my ass, which detonated the fire in my balls. I tightened my ass and thrust hard inside of her sweet pussy, and let my orgasm overtake me. Fallon ground on me and my eyes near rolled into the back of my head at the feel of her pussy sucking and tugging my release from me.

Never had anything felt so good.

"When I can feel my legs," I panted into her neck, "I'll carry you into the lake." Not wanting to crush her, I rolled us so she was straddled above me, her gorgeous tits in my face. I groaned and arched my hips, which lifted Fallon slightly. It certainly made me hard in record time.

"You like looking at me?" Fallon wiggled on my dick and when she was comfortable, her back arched as she raised her arms above her head, taking her long dark hair with her.

"I love looking at these." I cupped a breast in each hand and rolled her nipples with my thumbs.

She shivered.

"So responsive," I murmured, sitting up and tonguing one of the delicious buds.

"Hmm, you're so deep." Fallon wrapped her legs around my waist and I groaned at the pressure around my cock. Her small hands cupped my face with a day's worth of whiskers, and as her mouth hovered over mine, she whispered, "Happy birthday," before her lips captured mine.

53

FALLON

"So tell me"—I snuggled into Rogan's arms around the small campfire he'd made for us—"when are you moving out to San Diego?"

He grinned into my hair and I felt his lips before he answered, "I have exams in two weeks, then I'm all yours." He squeezed me around the waist. "I've told Mom and Dad that I got the job with the San Diego Fire Department. They weren't pleased and tried to talk me into staying in Boston." He sighed. "I replied that we're friends again and that I want to be where you and the others will be."

"Mom will know we're together. You know that, right?"

"I know. I could tell from her tone that she knew." He sighed.

Silence followed, and then Rogan said, "We won't be able to keep our relationship silent forever."

"It worries me is all."

"We have each other, Fallon. They love us both, so we have to hope they will accept us being together eventually. It just might take a while."

"Oh!" I remembered something and raised my face to look into Rogan's. "I forgot. I caught a glimpse of Amber at Boston Logan."

He gave me a bland look.

"Oh my God! Rogan Scott, how can you not remember her? Prom."

"Oh!"

"Yes, oh!" I laughed. "I haven't seen her since I left home. She looked the same. A bit older."

"We're all a bit older, Fallon."

"Hmm, especially you." I teased. "I can't believe you're twenty-one. The last time we were here you were seventeen."

He snorted. "The last time we were here, I was so hard I could have pounded nails."

"Nothing has changed then?"

"I'm serious. When we swam in the lake, my cock was rock hard and I thought I wouldn't have a choice but to climb out and then our parents would get to say 'Hello, big boy!' Luckily the seriousness behind Dad's words when he wanted to talk helped me rapidly deflate."

Laughter filled me and I could no longer hold it in at the serious look on his face. Tears trickled from my eyes as I laughed. What made it worse was how embarrassed Rogan appeared, which endeared him all the more to me. I slipped my fingers through his hair and massaged his scalp. "That was our last trip here. Our last summer before everything changed."

"Do you regret anything, Fallon?" he asked so quietly.

"My only regret is listening to you when you walked away. I should have gone after you. I don't regret being in love with you. You're my everything, Rogan. I can't go on without you in my life. I tried and it sucked. Big time. We were always meant to be together." I stared into his eyes and admitted, "I worry that one day you might hate being with me because I can't have children." I swiped at a loose tear as it slipped down my cheek. "I see your face when you watch Leon with Poppy, and it hurts. I want to be able to give you a son or daughter and we both know that isn't possible. I crave what they have."

Rogan reached for me and wrapped an arm

securely around my waist while his other hand cupped my face. "I love you. We are going to be the best godparents in the world to Poppy. She's only a month old now, but as she gets older, maybe she can come stay with us from time to time and give Leon and Julia some alone time." He made sure I was listening to him. "I would rather spend the rest of my life with you and no children, than with someone else. I love you. I always will."

"Promise?"

"I promise, babe." He kissed me on each cheek and tucked my head beneath his chin. "I'm excited, Fallon. Very soon we're going to be together, but one last thing." He rooted around in a pocket on his backpack and brought out a velvet pouch.

Rolled to my back. Rogan hovered over me, and took my left hand. "I know our being together might cause problems, but no matter what happens, I'd be honored if you'd wear my mother's ring as a token of my commitment to you, and yours to me. And one day, I'd love for you to be my wife. I've loved you since before I was old enough to know what love is." His eyes glistened with unshed tears as he slipped the beautiful diamond shaped ring on my finger and then brought my hand up to his lips and kissed my fingers, over the ring.

"I'd be honored to be your wife, and knowing the ring is the one your dad kept all these years for you to give to your wife, it means so much more to me."

"It's where it's always belonged."

"I love you, Rogan Scott."

"I love you too, Fallon Scott."

PART V

Rogan, 25 / Fallon, 24

FALLON

"Mmm," I mumbled, stretching like a cat. "Good morning."

"Morning, babe." His hands continued caressing my body and his mouth moved from my breasts to my belly button while Rogan tugged my panties off my body. "I need you." His whispered words were followed by him rising up and sliding inside of my body. Rogan wrapped me in his arms and held me tightly while his hips rocked, creating a delicious friction between my legs.

Our lips met in a soft kiss that became heated the faster Rogan moved in my body. He used his knees to spread my legs wider and then I really felt him. He angled his body differently and I gripped him hard. "Oh! Right there."

"I felt you clench around my dick," he panted. "What you do to me."

His hips pounded and within seconds, I was throwing my head back and arching into him while my core pulsated hard around his throbbing penis as I felt him release.

Rogan grunted above me and he finished coming, I tugged him into my arms. From the get-go I'd always enjoyed having his weight on me. It felt good having him pressing me into the bed. He shivered as I ran my fingernails along his spine and pinched his ass.

Groaning, he withdrew and rolled to his back. "I can go to work now with a smile on my face."

I nudged into his side. "You always have a smile."

"That's because I have you in my life." He moaned like an eighty-year-old man as he rolled to his side and climbed from the bed. I raised a brow and smirked. "You make me ache."

I offered him a dirty laugh and glanced down his body. "I think you have time to get yourself back in this bed."

"Don't tempt me. I have a meeting this morning before my shift starts, and"—he leaned over and kissed me—"Poppy will be bouncing in here anytime soon."

"I'll just enjoy watching you get ready for work. I think you look sexy in your firefighter's uniform." He blushed at my words.

"Hold that thought." He dived into the bathroom and then I heard the shower go on. He'd be quick. He always was unless I was in there with him.

I cuddled into Rogan's pillow so happy I could cry. The past four years had been wonderful to us. First Rogan's training and job with the San Diego Fire Department, and then last month his new job with the Newport Fire Department. He loved fire investigation, which is where he managed to gain employment here on Rhode Island. We are closer to home than we were out in San Diego, yet neither of us had visited together, and when we did go, we removed our wedding bands. It made me sad that we'd both been living our lives and yet our parents didn't know that we were *really* together. We married three years ago in a beautiful ceremony on the beach of Maui. Our first real vacation as a couple had ended with us becoming man and wife.

We both suspected that our parents knew about us, considering we lived together and were never with anyone else. We'd just kept the words to ourselves, and I didn't think they wanted to know the truth anyway. They visited once for a day and had seen Rogan's room, and mine, but they also saw the guest room that we let them believe was mine. But after eight years of being with Rogan, it was time to tell them both the truth. It wouldn't be easy but it needed to be out in the open. So when we took Poppy home to her parents, we'd speak to our own.

Poppy was a delightful four-year-old who seemed older than her years. She loved staying with us in Newport because she got to see the ocean, the harbor, and lovely stores—the bouncy four-year-olds favorite things. Leon had moved his family home to be closer to his mother, who wasn't doing too well. But the past week had given Leon and Julia freedom to celebrate his new job at the sheriff's department. Who knew Leon would have been a cop? I hadn't seen that coming at all.

My eyes snapped to the bathroom as Rogan walked out in his tight black boxers. "Mmm." His eyes met mine and he paused mid-step. "You get sexier with age."

He dived on top of me on the bed and wrapped me in the quilt. "Says the woman who makes me ache from the sound of her voice." He gave me a long and serious kiss, his eyes unmoving from mine. "Don't worry about the weekend. Whether or not our parents accept us being together, nothing is going to tear us apart." He dropped his forehead to mine. "I've booked us into the hotel in town so we can stay together. I have no intention of being separated from you anymore when we visit. We'll respect our parents' home, but that's it. I'm through pretending I'm not in love with you." He kissed my nose.

I reached up and caressed the side of his face. "I love you. Please be safe out there today."

"I love you more, and my reason for breathing is currently naked in our bed." He groaned. "I also hear little feet heading this way." He rolled from the bed and placed his back to the bedroom door just as Poppy came running in. Her little arms pumped at her sides as she flew onto the bed.

My arms wrapped around her and I hugged the second love of my life to me. Rogan came into my line of sight wearing his navy work pants and nothing else. It wasn't my fault if my eyes narrowed as I admired the man I loved, the first love of my life. He wore a cocky grin on his handsome face because he knew exactly what I was thinking. He was hot. He had no shame either.

Rogan slipped his T-shirt over his head and tugged it down his flat stomach before he lifted his gaze and gave me a dazzling smile. He shook his head and tossed my rob onto the bed.

"Poppy, let's go and get you some juice while Aunt Fallon gets dressed."

Poppy was off the bed and into Rogan's arms before I could blink or comment that he'd be late. He winked going out of the door. I wanted to roll over and go back to sleep but that wasn't in the cards today. I'd promised Poppy a trip to the museum followed by lunch and ice cream. I knew she hadn't forgotten about our plans. The child had a better memory than me.

It didn't take me long to quickly shower and dress, and as I walked down the hallway in our apartment, I heard Poppy ask, "Why can't I watch them from the window?"

"Because it's not right to spy on people."

"But that's not fair. I'm not spying on people. I just want to spy on that boy and his puppy."

Laughter burst from my lips.

"Just like your mother."

"I was about to say, like her father."

Rogan rolled his eyes and dashed over to me. "I really have to go." He quickly kissed me. "I love you." He kissed me again and then kissed Poppy on the top of her head. "I love you too, squirt." He shot out the door.

"Aunt Fallon?" Poppy asked in a way that I knew

something cheeky was about to pop out of her mouth.

"Yes, honey."

"Can we surprise Uncle Rogan at work today? I've never seen a fire truck real close."

I hadn't expected that. "Well, Rogan has a meeting first. So why don't we do what we had planned and if you still have energy left, then I'll take you to his office. I'll need to check with him first, though. We don't want to turn up and him not be there."

"He might be at a fire?"

"Yes."

"Do you like him being a firefighter?"

"Hmm, well I much prefer the job he has now. He goes into buildings when the fire is out to investigate how they started."

"That sounds cool. I want to do that when I grow up."

"You do, huh? So you don't want to be a cop like your daddy?"

She shook her head so hard her blond curls whipped around her face. "No. I don't like guns. Daddy has to wear one for his job. Mommy said Daddy is good at his job and not to worry. I know Mommy worries."

I was surprised that Julia hadn't been able to hide

her worry from Poppy. Then again, it would be a miracle to hide anything from such an inquisitive child.

"So you want to be a fire investigator, huh? I'm sure Uncle Rogan will absolutely love to tell your daddy." I grinned behind my cup of coffee. Rogan would love that so much. He and his friends still acted like kids when they got together, and I knew Rogan, and there was no way he'd be able to stay quiet.

"Auntie Fallon, will you read me one of your books before we go out." Poppy grinned.

It made my heart full to know she loved my books. It was because of her that I created them. I don't do the illustrations because I have no talent with pencils, but I do write them. The series is called Poppy's Adventures with Peanut and Butter. My goddaughter inspired them, and so did her puppies, which drove Leon up the wall. They loved his shoes.

"Which one should I read you?"

"Um..." She placed her elbows on the kitchen table and rested her chin in her hands while her brows drew together in a thinking frown.

She was so cute and made my heart beat just that bit quicker at my love for her. I had good days when it didn't bother me that I could never have children, then there would be bad days when I craved to hold Rogan's baby in my arms. Rogan understood and did everything to make me believe he was happy with how things were. He was convincing and I believed him. It didn't make things easier on my own heart, though, especially when I watched Poppy.

"I still can't decide." She grinned. "We could read all of them."

I chuckled and sipped my coffee. "I think we should read Poppy's Adventures with Peanut and Butter into the Wilderness."

"I don't remember that one."

I had a surprise for her. "Well, it isn't published yet."

Her eyes widened in surprise and she bounced in her chair. The next moment she ran into my arms and I wrapped her tightly in a hug. "It's sitting on my desk and is wrapped in pretty pink paper with a large bow. Do you want to go and get it?"

She was out of my arms like lightning, and the phone started to ring throughout the apartment.

Growing up, my mother always said, "Things happen for a reason," however, I would never be able to fathom the reasoning behind such a loss of life.

55

ROGAN

I SHOULD HAVE TOLD FALLON ABOUT THIS MORNING. I'd let her believe I had to get to a meeting but the truth was, I'd been ordered to be in the town's charity calendar. I hated it and really hadn't wanted to do it, so my boss had put me on the spot. So here I was in my navy blue pants and T-shirt while the others here had no trouble taking their shirts off. Not me. If they wanted me in it, then they'd have to take me as I was. I'd go ballistic if Fallon did anything like this, which is why I hadn't told her. With a bit of luck she wouldn't find out. She would. I'd end up confessing. I had a problem with keeping my mouth shut were Fallon was concerned.

"Hey, Scott! Get your butt over here." Seddon, also

a fire investigator, tossed his shirt on his way over to me. "You didn't get laid last night, huh?"

"What the fuck?"

"With the look on your face, I'd say maybe a month or two."

"Not that it's any of your business," I said, my voice laced with anger, "I make love to my wife every day! I'm pissed because I have better things I could be doing instead of this."

"Jeez, ease up. I'm sorry, okay? Truth is I'm nervous. I've never done anything like this before. My sister thought it would be a laugh, but then I met my girlfriend and I'm not laughing. Neither will she be when she sees it. Oh, and she will see it because she works out of the main office."

My lips twitched. "If it helps, I haven't told my wife either." I sighed and watched as a big black SUV pulled into the garage. "I haven't decided whether she'd tease the fuck out of me for being chosen, or be pissed." I chuckled. "I think I'm more scared of the teasing than her being pissed."

"How long have you been together?"

"Eight years."

He blinked. "High school sweethearts?"

"Yeah, you could say that."

"She's a looker." He nodded toward the SUV where the calendar crew exited.

I followed his gaze with my arms crossed in front of my chest. The woman looked familiar but I couldn't place her. She looked around and met my gaze, and my heart dropped to my damn feet. *Amber Sinclair*—the girl I took to prom and dumped on poor Chase.

Well shit!

Amber greeted a few of the other firefighters and then slowly made her way over to where I stood with John Seddon.

"You know her?" he asked from the corner of his mouth.

"Unfortunately."

"Well, well, well, if it isn't Rogan Scott." Amber tilted her head and licked her lips. Her eyes trailed over me and made my skin crawl. I hid my grin when she spotted the wedding band on my finger.

"You're married?"

"Three years."

I had to keep my cool because the woman in front of me could blow everything out into the open. She knew Fallon and me, and she'd been angry for a long time after the debacle of prom. Of course she had a different memory of prom than I did. Prom had been the first time I'd truly made love to Fallon. The memory of that special night hadn't left me.

"How do you two know each other?" Seddon asked, looking between us. I also hadn't missed the others watching closely.

Men were worse than women for gossiping.

I winced as I thought about having to explain all of this to Fallon. I could only hope she'd see the humor in it all. She'd probably say it served me right for not telling her about the calendar in the first place.

"High school," Amber said after a moment of silence. "He left me high and dry at prom."

"Fuck, Amber!" I cursed, not expecting her to blurt something like that out. Why would she want people to know she was dumped at prom?

"Now, Rogan, you know it's true." She rolled her eyes and stared at Seddon. "Can you believe he left *me*, with his gay friend while he went off with his sister?" She smirked while I was about to knock her off the pedestal she sat on.

"Um..." Seddon stumbled over his words. "Knowing Scott, there was probably a good reason for him leaving a babe like you."

Amber rolled her eyes and glanced back to my wedding band. "Anyone I know?"

Now was the time to put an end to this discussion with Amber. We all had other places to be, and I had no wish to "catch up" with the woman.

"Don't you have a job to do?" I raised a brow.

"You're not going to get rid of me that easily. We'll get drinks later." She turned her back and I clenched my fists.

"Amber," I growled.

She paused and turned her head.

"No, we won't. I'm married, and if I wasn't, I still wouldn't want to do drinks."

Her blush worked up her neck to her face and I felt bad for being so vocal in front of the others. My only excuse was that I wasn't about to allow her to walk all over me with her requests. I had no wish to see her again.

"Scott?" Captain Reine shouted, he found me amongst the bodies, and lowered his voice, "Your wife is here." He looked behind him and said, "I think there's something wrong."

In the next moment, I caught sight of Fallon behind him and I turned cold. Tears ran down her face and from her ragged look I'd say they'd been falling for some time.

Hearing, "Fallon?" whispered by Amber, "She's not his wife," my feet started moving toward my woman.

Fallon gasped and ran straight into me, her arms went around my neck and she held on sobbing into my shoulder. I tightened my arms around her waist. A burning sensation hit behind my eyes and I fought to hold my tears back. I had no idea why she was so upset, but it had to be bad for her to show up like this.

"You need to tell me what's wrong?" I begged. "Where's Poppy?"

"With Marion." Marion Sutcliffe was our neighbor who looked after her granddaughters during the day. Poppy knew and liked to paint pictures with the twin girls.

So nothing was wrong with Poppy. I wanted to give Fallon time to calm down and talk to me but frustration welled in my belly, and fear.

"She is his wife. I've met her a few times." I clenched my jaw at Seddon arguing with Amber.

"She's his sister, not his wife, you idiot. I've known them forever."

Fucking hell!

Reaching up, I cupped Fallon's face between my palms and held her gaze. "Tell me, please, Fallon. You're killing me."

"Leon and Julia, they're gone." Fallon broke down

into fresh sobs as I heard her words but I couldn't comprehend what she actually said. No way can they be gone. I only spoke to Leon last night.

"No, they're not," I whispered brokenly. "They can't be."

My body went numb as I held Fallon while she clung to me, however the voice behind me wouldn't shut the fuck up.

I snapped, and gently untangled myself from Fallon but kept her against me. "Amber," I hissed, "shut the fuck up! Get over yourself. High school was seven years ago. So what if I dumped you with my *gay* friend at prom. You had nothing I ever wanted. As for Fallon, we are not related. She's my wife!"

"What is going on in my station?" Captain Reine appeared.

Breathing heavily, I tried to control my own pain, but as tears burned in my eye sockets, I knew it was a battle I would lose. "Our best friends are...gone." I couldn't even say the word properly. "I don't know how to tell their four-year-old daughter who is waiting for us back at the apartment with our neighbor."

I turned to Fallon. "We need to get Poppy."

Captain Reine offered, "I'll drive you both. It isn't up for discussion."

He gave orders to the others and then I was huddled in the back of his SUV with a broken Fallon in my arms. I wasn't just hurting on the inside because of Leon's death. I was hurting because I couldn't make it right for Fallon.

"I'll contact your boss and let him know you're taking personal time and why." Captain Reine glanced at Fallon and back to me. "Amber?"

"Amber"—I sighed and rested my head back on the seat—"was a pain in my ass in high school. She was jealous of the time I spent with Fallon." I met his gaze through the rearview mirror. "My father married Fallon's mother. That's the family relationship. We didn't ask to fall in love with each other, but we did. Amber hated coming second."

He nodded. "I understand." He glanced away. "I understand more than you know."

I frowned at his weird comment. He offered me a wry smile. "My wife is twenty-one years my junior. She's only ever looked at me. I love her. Age, family, nothing kept us apart in the end, although I did try to do the right thing. Didn't work. I only hurt us both."

"Yeah, I did that when I was in college. I've hated myself for that."

Silence followed until we got to the apartment.

"Rogan, you do what you have to do to make sure

your wife and your friends' daughter are taken care of. Don't worry about work. I'll make sure your job is still here when you're ready to come back."

Unable to find the words, I nodded.

It wasn't until we entered our apartment that I my legs gave out and I broke down in Fallon's arms.

My best friend was gone.

56

FALLON

IT'S BEEN TWO DAYS SINCE WE RECEIVED THE NEWS about Julia and Leon and it didn't seem real. They'd been our friends for so long that not having them in our lives wouldn't sink into my brain. Unable to sleep, I sat in a chair by the window and gazed out at nothing.

We'd arrived in town last night with Poppy, and although Mom had told us to bring her home to their house, Rogan had booked us a suite in the hotel. It was a beautiful place and if my heart wasn't so broken right now, I'd have enjoyed the elegance. Mom hadn't been happy with our choice, but I hadn't wanted to be separated from Rogan nor him me. As for Poppy, our pixie goddaughter, we tried to explain to her that an accident had happened and her parents were now stars. I wasn't sure she totally believed us, but we'd be there for her no matter what.

Poppy slept in a bed of her own with her puppies on either side of her, and the sight brought tears to my eyes. The puppies knew something was off. Dogs had a good sense about those things.

My eyes drifted toward the man who'd held me together and continued to do so, even when he hurt too. We'd held each other together. He was my world, and now, so was Poppy.

As I tried to force the tears back, I realized Rogan watched me. He held his hand out and I didn't hesitate. I took it and allowed him to cradle me in his arms. He kissed my cheeks before brushing a soft kiss to my lips. His warmth seeped into me and I held on tighter. I cried softly into his neck, not wanting to wake Poppy. I felt wetness on the curve of my neck and realized Rogan cried too.

"I hate that I'm not able to be strong for you," he whispered.

"I don't need you to be strong for me. I need you to be here. I need you to hold me. To love me. To *just* be here. That's all I need, Rogan. You. And Poppy."

He cupped the back of my head and wrapped his fingers in my hair. "I'm not going anywhere."

"I feel guilty," I admitted. "I feel guilty that we now

have Poppy to raise. I've always wanted to have your child. You know that. And fate has done this. I feel so guilty that we have Poppy. We're going to see her grow up, get married, have children of her own, and her mom and dad won't get to see that. I'm eaten away with guilt, and it breaks my heart that eventually our life together will be all the more fulfilling because of Poppy, and yet it's because her parents, our friends, died."

Rogan held me closer still and it felt like he was trying to get me to merge with him. I felt better for getting that out to him, but the guilt was still there. In was a tight ball inside of my belly along with the anguish over losing our friends.

Julia had always been there for me, apart from the time when she found out about Rogan and me. However, once she came out to San Diego, we'd gotten our act together and been there for each other since then. Not a day would go by without me speaking to her and Poppy. Rogan would often talk with Leon while they played *Call of Duty* on the PS4. Kids at heart. Rogan even played a *My Little Pony* game online with Poppy a few times. She of course sat on her dad's lap at the time. Julia used to laugh saying that it was really Leon playing the game.

"Everything you said has flittered through my

mind over the past couple of days. We can't feel guilt because of how we feel about Poppy. About having our goddaughter to raise." Rogan cleared his throat. "A month ago Leon made me promise him something." Rogan tiled my face up to his and held my gaze. "When he accepted the job in the sheriff's office, he wanted me to promise that if anything happened to him that I'd take care of Julia and Poppy. He was insistent, so I promised."

"You never told me."

"He didn't want me to tell anyone." Rogan sighed and kissed my forehead before he rested his against mine. "He told me that Julia worried and he needed to be reassured that she'd have support. I told him that he should know better than to ask. He was worried, Fallon."

"They died in a car wreck along the coast highway. It had nothing to do with Leon's job."

"I know. It's just a coincidence that a month later, they're both dead." He swallowed hard and rolled to his back, taking me with him. "I never thought there would be a day when I had to say a last goodbye to him. I don't know what to do." His body shook as he became overwhelmed with tears.

I crawled up his body and wrapped my arms around his broad shoulders, and held him. I didn't know what else to say because we both felt the loss of Julia and Leon, and I knew it wasn't something we'd get over in a day, like we would an argument. It would take so much longer. The one thing I did know and that was no matter what, we would protect Poppy with every breath we had.

57

ROGAN

UNCLIPPING POPPY FROM HER CAR SEAT, I BROUGHT her close to my chest and had to fight back tears when her little arms wrapped around my neck and her legs tried to wrap around my body, which wouldn't work. I let her cling and placed an arm under her so that she was secure against me. I then turned and my heart cracked a little bit more at the sight of Fallon standing in front of the car with Peanut and Butter on their leashes. I'd never seen her so unsure before, so I held a hand out. Her cold fingers immediately intertwined with mine and I gave them a gentle squeeze.

"We have this, Fallon. No more hiding. We need each other more than ever, and I want the whole

495

world to know that you're my girl." I became even more serious. "I love you with my body and soul."

Fallon moved in closer and reached up to kiss my lips. She whispered, "I love you too, more than I'll ever be able to tell you or show you." Her face nuzzled into my shoulder as we stood in a tight circle with Poppy between us.

Then a small voice said, "I love you, Auntie Fallon." Poppy turned her face to mine and pressed her small hands to my face. "I love you, Uncle Rogan." Her lips pouted and she pressed them to my lips. Her action had me rapidly blinking back tears, which Fallon saw and wiped at them with her thumbs.

"We love you, Poppy. We'll always keep you warm and safe."

"And Peanut and Butter?" She stared at her puppies.

The two Pomeranian puppies were cute when they weren't yapping every two damn minutes. I cast a quick glance at Fallon, who looked amused.

"Them too! They're yours, so of course we'll keep them warm and safe; however, it better be your shoes they chew and not mine." I tickled her in the side, relieved that the moment between us had lightened.

The next few days wouldn't be so good for Poppy. Fallon and I had decided that we wouldn't keep

Poppy away from any of the funeral arrangements. We didn't want or need to have any regrets where she was concerned.

"Mom's seen us."

I straightened my spine and moved up the front path with my family. Our childhood home hadn't changed all that much over the years, and our parents, although older, were still fairly young.

The front door opened and out came Mom. Concern was etched onto her face as she moved to take Poppy from me, but Poppy clung so tight I felt strangled.

"It's okay, Poppy." I tugged her arms away slightly. "I won't let you go."

"Promise."

"I promise."

Mom quickly swiped at her tears and reached for Fallon. I felt the loss the moment she had no choice but to let go of my hand to return Mom's embrace.

"We'll put the dogs out back. They won't be able to get out. Then we'll have refreshments in the kitchen." She stroked Poppy's hair and kissed her cheek. "I've made your favorite."

"Banana muffins?"

Mom smiled. "Yes. How would you like one with a

glass of milk while your puppies get up to trouble in the garden?"

She giggled. "Yes, please."

Mom cupped the back of my head and reached up, giving me a kiss on the cheek.

"Come inside then."

In the kitchen it felt odd to be sitting around the table with Fallon and Poppy while Mom stared at us, and the bands on our fingers. This was the first time we'd been home together in years. We'd wanted to keep our secret back then, and now, I didn't know why I'd felt it was so important to do so. I wasn't ashamed to be with Fallon, but I had been scared while we'd been dependent on our parents. I sounded like a bastard. I loved our parents, but I loved Fallon more. She was my life. I couldn't survive without her.

The silence was suddenly broken when Dad came through the front door with Chase. It had been a little over twelve months since we'd seen Chase, and I wished it were under different circumstances. I held Poppy tightly and moved toward him, wrapping him in a bear hug. We both held on for a good minute before I felt Fallon's hand on my back. I tilted my head and looked at her, my arm moving to let her into our circle, Poppy being the center.

Clearing my throat, I passed Poppy to Chase when

she held her arms out to him. He patted her gently on the back and wandered into the front room. He spread out on the couch and settled her with him. I didn't know what he said, but he'd always been able to settle her down.

"Do you know what's going to happen to Poppy?" Dad asked.

"You know we're her godparents." I took Fallon's hand and tugged her beside me at the kitchen table. Mom and Dad joined us. I didn't miss the heated look on Dad's face at our joined hands. "Julia and Leon left a legal document that gives us the guardianship rights to Poppy in the event anything should happen to them."

"What about Julia's parents?" Mom asked. "I know they were horrible to Julia when she needed them, but they're still Poppy's grandparents."

"No way!" Fallon hissed. "They never once wanted to see Poppy or accepted Leon. When they moved back here they wanted to see Julia, as long as she left Poppy and Leon at home. So there is no way Poppy is going to them. We have legal rights to her and we'll fight anyone who says otherwise."

I switched hands and continued to hold onto to Fallon while I laid my palm against the back of her neck. She leaned into me, and I did the most natural thing and kissed the top of her head. Whenever I kissed her there it had always been with utter affection.

"I was right, wasn't I? Years ago when I suspected there being something between you both. I've known it was true. It stared us in the face. I just didn't want to think that my son had"—Dad swallowed hard—"touched my daughter."

Fallon gasped. "It was never…not once, like that. I've been in love with Rogan for as long as I can remember. Don't you dare accuse him of bad things. I won't have it."

Dad tightened his fists on the table and opened his mouth, except Mom shut him up with a dark glare, her eyes going into the front room. "Now isn't the time for this discussion."

"No it isn't. We have to bury our best friends and take care of their daughter." I pointed out. "There isn't a right or wrong time to discuss Fallon and me. In fact, there isn't anything to discuss. We're together and have been for years. Nothing anyone says will make a difference to our relationship. You either accept it or you don't."

"That's why you never visit together, and why you're now staying in a hotel instead of with us?"

"Yes. We're not going to apologize. I just wish we'd

have been honest with you both from the start." I sighed and held Fallon close. "If you have anything to say about us, please leave it until after the funeral. I don't think either of us can handle anything else right now."

Dad stared and nodded his head. "We'll talk another time, but in the meanwhile, if you need any help with anything, you both have to let us know. Regardless of how I feel or don't feel about you being together, your mom and I are still your family. We help each other out."

Swallowing back emotion, I shook his hand. "Thanks, Dad."

Fallon had been silent after her outburst, but as I focused on her, I realized her tears had finally stopped and she looked as though she could finally handle everything. So knowing Chase was here as well, I whispered for her ears only. "I have something to do. Don't leave here until I come back for you."

She frowned. "Where are you going?"

"You'll tell me not to go." I kissed her cheek. "It's best not talking about it."

It took her a moment and then her eyes widened. "You can't do that alone. Let me come."

I shook my head. "I know you'll be waiting for me.

I don't want you to see them, but I have to. I can't explain it."

"Rogan," she whispered hoarsely, wrapping her arms around my shoulders. "Come straight to me. Promise me."

"I promise."

Going to the funeral home was not what I wanted to do. If I didn't have something pulling me toward the building, I wouldn't be anywhere near it. But there was something I had to do.

Something for Poppy.

58

FALLON

POPPY TIGHTLY CLUNG TO MY HAND AND PARTLY HID IN the skirt of my dress. She wore a favorite dress that her mother had bought her. It was white with bright yellow sunflowers on it. Mom had been surprised when she'd seen what Poppy wore, but I'd shaken my head before she commented. As far as Rogan and I were concerned, Leon and Julia's daughter could wear what she wanted on this day.

The weather was muggy albeit cloudy and I felt sweat on my forehead. Rogan came toward me and I swallowed hard as my emotions threatened to poor out. Immediately, he wrapped an arm around my waist and pulled me against him. "We'll get through this," he whispered and after placing a kiss to my forehead, he bent and kissed Poppy on the cheek. He brushed a gentle finger down her cheek and stood. He glanced around and asked, "Do you want to go inside yet?"

I didn't want to go inside at all and have to see the caskets. I hadn't been able to visit them at the funeral home like Rogan had. He'd come back to collect Poppy and I from our parents' house and he'd looked gray with grief.

Rogan wrapped my hand up in his much larger one and gave me a reassuring squeeze.

The thick doors separating the sanctuary from the entrance loomed ahead. Today they were open as soft music drifted toward us. As soon as we entered, I was assailed with the smell of polished wooden pews, and incense. It was so familiar. Although we hadn't been to church for years, this was the church we'd been brought up in. Every Sunday like clockwork.

Swallowing hard, I couldn't bring myself to look toward the altar. I didn't want to see the caskets.

My eyes took in the Bibles and songbooks stacked neatly on a table. Beautiful white lilies had been placed on the end of each pew leading toward the front of the church. Mom had done this as it had been a request of Julia's. Leon and Julia had left a joint funeral plan, which had shocked us, but Rogan had moved heaven and earth to make sure every last detail had been carried out. It hadn't gone well with Julia's parents, but their lawyer had informed the Quinn's that they couldn't do anything about it. The document had been witnessed and signed by officials.

With reluctance, I felt Rogan let go of my hand. He kissed my cheek and moved beside Poppy. He took her small hand and my heart turned over with love for the man.

Eyes followed us down the aisle to the front where Chase and his husband, Vince, waited. I gripped Chase's hand as tightly as Poppy had gripped mine.

Chase pulled me into a hug and I didn't want to let go. My eyes blurred and I tried to focus on the stained glass window behind Vince.

As we sat down, Rogan lifted Poppy to his lap and moved as close as he could get to me. I wrapped my arm around his tightly and tried to take strength from him while giving him some of mine.

However, as Father Gardner started the funeral, I could no longer avoid looking at the altar.

Tears that I'd kept under control came into my eyes and spilled down my cheeks. Reality finally crashed around me.

My friends were gone.

The oak caskets each had a small bunch of lilies

wrapped in pink ribbon as a final gift from their daughter.

My tears soaked Rogan's sleeve as I clung to him. He dipped his head and rested his mouth against my forehead.

Chase shoved a large tissue into my hand, and whispered, "It's clean." His words broke through my anguish and I smiled at the damp patch on Rogan's dark gray jacket.

I glanced up at Jesus on the large cross hanging above the altar. Father Gardner spoke of how Julia and Leon were in a better place. His words were meant to offer comfort, but they did not. I'm not a religious person, but how can being taken away from their daughter be a better place?

I knew Julia had been a regular at this church over the years since they'd moved back home, so the words would have been a comfort to her had she heard them.

While I'd been arguing in my head, Father Gardner stepped to the side of the pulpit, and Rogan slipped Poppy to the pew.

It was time for him to deliver the eulogy.

Quickly grabbing his hand, I squeezed and gave him a watery smile. It hurt to watch Rogan being so brave when I knew he was falling apart inside.

He nervously cleared his throat and started.

"Trying to sum up Leon and Julia in a few short words, I discovered wasn't possible, but I've tried.

"I met Leon when 'girls' was a gross word before we even started preschool. Not long after we became friends with Chase, and since then our friendship has been strong and unbreakable, until now.

"As children we called ourselves The Three Musketeers because we stuck together no matter what. Like the time Leon got it into his head to comfort his mom when their family dog died. He didn't know anyone who would lend him a dog, so he dared me and Chase into borrowing Mr. Hennessy's baby python, Sid. Apparently it was what brothers had to do to help out another brother. Needless to say, Angela Davies had no voice for a week after shouting and screaming at the three of us. That's one of the many memories Chase and I have of our years spent with Leon."

Rogan paused and glanced at Chase before he swallowed hard a few times and continued.

"Julia became friends with Fallon when they were both thirteen, and drove us three boys crazy. We couldn't turn around without having them following us, and especially spying on us.

"From the moment Julia discovered boys, it had only ever been Leon. I'd never seen my friend so confused over a girl before. Eventually, they both grew up and became inseparable, and their love produced a daughter."

He stared at Poppy.

"Poppy, your mom and dad loved you so much, and one day when you're older, Chase and I will tell you about the stupid antics only boys can get up to. Fallon no doubt will have lots of stories to share about your mom.

"Fallon and I want you to know that we'll always be here for you. Your home is with us now and together we're going to make your parents proud."

Looking around the church, Rogan deeply inhaled and stared at me. I offered him an encouraging smile through my tears.

"Julia and Leon will be missed more than I will ever be able to say.

"Thank you."

Not a dry eye remained in the church by the time Rogan stepped down and came back to us. I quickly passed Poppy to Chase, and then reached for Rogan. I wrapped my arms tightly around his shoulders and just held him while he cried into my neck. Tears poured from my eyes. We both felt broken right now. The mourners stood and started to sing "All Things Bright and Beautiful."

Eventually, I felt like I could breathe when we exited the church into the sunny afternoon. The clouds had disappeared leaving the sky so blue.

Chase carried Poppy, who to our surprise had fallen asleep on his shoulder. He'd always been able to get her to sleep.

Heat from someone's gaze hit me hard and I turned sharply.

"What's wrong?" Rogan asked, forever in tune with me.

"We're being watched." I then caught sight of a couple moving through friends and family toward us.

Julia's parents.

"They don't have any power over us, or Poppy."

Rogan kissed my cheek and slipped his arm around my waist.

Maeve Quinn looked elegant in her black and white dress. Her blond hair had been swept back and minimal makeup was on her face. She was only in her mid-fifties. David Quinn was arrogant and had never bothered with Julia's welfare until she'd gotten pregnant. Then he'd disowned her.

They made me nervous, which Rogan knew, but that stemmed from my fear of losing Poppy. We'd both fight for her if it came to that.

Silence had gone through the mourners and I thought every eye was on us. No wonder when they all knew what had happened between them and Julia.

"We'd like to visit with Poppy," Maeve said. "We're not going to cause trouble, but she's our grand-daughter and we'd like to get to know her."

It was subtle, but I felt Rogan shift beside me. If we hadn't been touching, I wouldn't have noticed.

"You wanted to have nothing to do with Poppy." Rogan paused. "Or Leon. If it hadn't been for Leon and Julia being so organized, you'd have had Julia buried in a different cemetery than Leon."

Maeve's mouth tightened and David looked embarrassed. He was well aware of the attention they had drawn, whereas Maeve didn't.

"Leon did nothing but stand by your daughter. He loved her. Can you say the same?"

David cleared his throat. "I think we need to go somewhere private to discuss things."

"No!" I stamped my foot, annoyed beyond belief. "Everyone here is well aware of how you treated Julia. They're also aware of everything Leon did to make sure Julia and their daughter were looked after. It was Rogan and my parents who helped them out initially. It was the sale of Leon's family home when his mother died that provided a good home for them. You two did nothing, and you deserve nothing."

I glanced at Rogan and felt a load of stress lift from my shoulders. He kissed my cheek and whispered, "I'm so fucking proud of you." He chuckled. The first time in days.

59

ROGAN

OUR PARENTS' HOME WAS FULL TO CAPACITY AS THE funeral reception was being held here. A large decorators table had been shoved to one side of the large hallway. The table was laden with food from neighbors: Casseroles, sandwiches, tarts, veggie platters, crackers, cakes. The small table beside the front door had condolence cards in envelopes. The kitchen bustled with friendly women making tea and coffee and washing dishes.

I figured if one more person offered me condolences, I'd scream. Fallon had taken Poppy out into the back garden to play with her puppies, so I headed out to them.

Fallon had retrieved two seat cushions from the

storage box that doubled as a small table on the back deck. Flower boxes, planters, and hanging baskets provided a burst of color.

Poppy played with Butter while I spotted Peanut meandering around the garden and investigating the corners of the yard. Probably looking for somewhere to dig a hole. The puppy's favorite past time.

The dogs would probably always be known as puppies because they were over two.

Fallon turned and spotted me lingering in the doorway. She held her hand out and I didn't hesitate. I sat and tugged her onto my lap.

I wrapped my arms around her waist and breathed deeply. Her cool hands ran through my hair, which helped settle me. "I needed this."

"I hated leaving you in there alone."

Placing a kiss in the curve of her neck, I rested my chin there and watched Poppy. "I wanted to spare you that, and I knew it would be better for Poppy to be out here."

Fallon raised her gaze and cupped my face. "How are you doing?" She wouldn't let me look away as I struggled with emotion.

"I'm doing okay because I have you. I can survive anything with you here."

"That's how I feel. It hadn't hit me properly until I saw them in church." Tears came swiftly to her eyes. "You always make me so proud, Rogan. Your words also did Julia and Leon proud. I love you."

Unable to find my voice, I buried my face in Fallon's neck. Speaking in church today had been one of the hardest things I'd ever had to do. It drained me, but having Fallon's arms around me after had recharged my energy. The looks of curiosity we'd received during the course of the day hadn't gone unnoticed.

Dad had noticed too. Mom had been distracted with keeping everyone together.

"We'll head back to the hotel soon. I'll get changed and head back here to tidy up. We can take some food back for you and Poppy to eat. Hopefully she'll sleep after eating and a warm bath."

"I want to help you."

"Chase and Vince are going to help." I smiled and kissed her. "Poppy needs you. I need you to relax with her. I'll be able to carry on here knowing you're away from all of the grief. I'll know you're waiting for me." I kissed her again.

Poppy climbed between us and cuddled in Fallon's arms. Her cherub face looked between us both, her eyes drooping.

"Okay. I'll stay at the hotel."

I nodded and caught Dad approaching from the corner of my eye, about the same time as Fallon had.

"How are you both doing?" he asked, his hands in his pockets.

"We're managing." I glanced at Poppy before raising my gaze to Dad.

He nodded toward the tool shed.

I didn't want this talk, but deep inside I knew the sooner we had it the better.

Dad led the way as I quickly glanced at Fallon, who appeared worried. I bent and kissed the top of her head. "Don't worry."

I followed Dad into the shed and coughed when I took a breath. The air was thick with dust. A strong smell of paint permeated the air. It came from the stacked tins along the siding to the right. "Been a while since you were in here, huh?" I banged my shin on the peddles of an old bike.

"It has been a long time since I needed anything from in here."

"Ugh!" I glanced around and decided I wouldn't move a muscle. The workbench I was about to lean against was coated with paint, grease, and potting soil that had tipped over. "Let's get this over with."

Dad sighed. "I don't want this talk, Son. I really don't."

"I can't help loving Fallon. I don't want to anymore. She's the only girl I've ever loved."

"Fallon wears your mother's rings." Dad observed, and heavily sighed. "What happened to Tiffany?"

So we weren't going to discuss the ring and the commitment I'd obviously made to Fallon.

I frowned. "Tiffany? I never dated her. She was crazy."

"Julia said you did."

"Julia saw only what I wanted her to see. Tiffany stalked me, until she got focused on someone else. Last I heard she'd married the poor bastard."

"You're never going to give Fallon up, are you?" he asked wearily.

"No, Dad, I'm not. Asking me to give Fallon up would be like asking me not to breathe. I'm going to be spending the rest of my life with her by my side. She's my wife, Dad. Has been for three years."

Dad stared at me for a long time until he uttered, "Okay," and left me in the dark and dank shed.

Tears burned behind my eyes at his reaction. He was my dad. The only one I had. I loved him and Mom; however, nothing and no one compared to my love for Fallon, and now Poppy was included in that.

After one last glance around the old shed, I spotted Fallon through the cracked and dirty window as worry etched on her face.

I left quickly and reaching Poppy, I took her into my arms, and held Fallon's hand. "We're going home."

PART VI

Epilogue

Rogan, 49 / Fallon, 48 / Poppy, 28

EPILOGUE
POPPY

THE FIRE AT THE WAREHOUSE WAS STILL GOING STRONG four hours later. When I'd arrived my heart had been in my throat because I'd known my boyfriend, Vasily Sokolov, was inside with other members of his ladder company.

A smoky haze covered the sky as dark billowing plumbs of smoke climbed up the walls to the roof. The sound of glass breaking as the flames licked around the windows had my heart thumping in fear. This fire was bad, and I hated that Vasily and others were on the inside trying to put the fire out. The alarm blurred for all fire crews to clear the building and my hand immediately clenched at my chest in fear.

As a fire investigator, our paths crossed often,

after all that was how we'd met. My job wouldn't be fully started on this fire until it was safe to enter, and then the work would really start. I loved my job, even though I'd go home exhausted when the case was a difficult one. The warehouse had been empty for years and the owner hadn't been able to sell it. My nose twitched it was arson, but I'd have to prove it.

Vasily, known to his team as Solo, often teased me about my job. It was the way of things in the department, and I enjoyed the banter between us. He was my love. Vasily had lived in America since he was five years old, coming here with his grandparents. He had no family left, apart from me and mine.

We'd lived together for a year, and he was everything to me. I loved the stubborn twenty-six-year-old Russian-American. He loved to say that he was the younger one in the relationship.

"Scott?" Rogers called.

I swallowed around the lump in my throat, and jogged over to him.

"They're bringing Solo out now." He paused. "He fell through a floor." Rogers grabbed my arm as I turned looking for him. "He's damn lucky. He rolled and managed to break his fall. Concussion maybe. He's strong, Poppy."

"I know," I agreed, hoping Captain Rogers was correct while I fought back tears.

"They're out."

Hearing shouting, I turned and watched the stretcher crew bringing Vasily out toward where the EMT truck waited.

My lips wobbled as I ran to him. His dark blond hair was filthy from the fire. I deeply inhaled and caught a breath when his eye stayed closed. I climbed into the truck with him and took his hand into mine. My eyes focused on the EMT who I knew because we worked out of the same building downtown.

"Poppy, breathe, honey." Simon checked his vitals and hooked him up with a saline drip. "Everything looks has it should, and he's waking up."

My eyes shot up to Vasily and his bright blue eyes were focused on my face. Tears of relief hovered on my lashes as I smiled through them. "You scared me." I bent and kissed his cheek. Hovering close to his lips, I held his gaze, and whispered, "I love you." I pressed a soft kiss to his lips and sat back.

"You two need to stop scaring each other." Simon observed.

"I only needed a bit of oxygen, that one time."

"That's not how I remember it." Simon checked Vasily again and sat back writing on his clipboard.

"I'm going to be okay." Vasily squeezed my hand. "I'll bruise and I'll let you kiss them better."

I rolled my eyes. "Do I want to know where these bruises are?"

He grinned so wide. "God, I love you." His eyes lit with amusement. "I'll show you the bruises when we're alone."

Chuckling, I kept hold of his hand until I was forced to part with him when we arrived at the emergency entrance of the hospital.

Feeling antsy, I grabbed my phone from my jacket pocket and texted my family. I needed them. Vasily needed them. No matter what he said, he'd had a scare tonight at the fire. My parents loved him as though he was theirs, so I knew they'd come.

EPILOGUE

FALLEN

"HONEY, POPPY SAID HE HAD A MILD CONCUSSION. He'll be fine." Rogan kept his arm around my shoulders and walked into the hospital.

The moment I'd received Poppy's text message, I couldn't get out of the house fast enough. Rogan knew I loved Vasily as part of our family. He did too, but wouldn't admit it. The stubborn man. He'd just grin and laugh when I said he loved our daughter's boyfriend.

At one time we were Aunt and Uncle to Poppy, and then our lives had taken a different direction when Poppy lost her parents, our best friends. She'd been celebrating her sixth birthday when she'd asked if she could call us Mom and Dad. I think Rogan had been more emotional than I had. We'd also changed

524

her name at that point, just before she'd started preschool. It saved questions that Poppy didn't need asking.

She'd grown into a beautiful young woman who her parents would be so proud of, as we were. Rogan had been nervous about Poppy actually following in his footsteps, but we'd both fully supported her.

Her grandparents, Maeve and David Quinn, hadn't been happy, but Poppy was as strong-willed as her mother had been. Yes, we'd eventually got over our anger at how they'd treated our friends, and had let them visit with Poppy, but under our supervision. To be honest, they'd been good for her. Rogan had stipulated that if he ever found out they'd said one wrong word about either Julia or Leon, they would never see Poppy again. They'd agreed to his terms. They were still in her life today.

I ended my thoughts by glancing at the clock on the waiting room wall, and sighed. Only five minutes had passed since we'd arrived. "Where is Poppy?"

"She's coming out to us."

I glanced around but couldn't see her. Rogan kissed my cheek. "I sent her a message. She replied." He kissed me again. "They'll both be okay. Don't worry."

Letting out an unladylike snort, I dug my elbow

into his side. "Are you telling me you weren't worried, Rogan Scott? I'm convinced after all our years together that you only tease me to hear my voice."

"You're on to me." He quickly slapped a kiss to my lips and pulled me to my feet.

Poppy appeared through the private doors and was embraced by Rogan first, and then me. I wiped the tears from her cheeks. "He's okay, right?"

She nodded. "Yes." Wiping at her tears, she added, "I'm just relieved. It was scary seeing him on the stretcher and then in the truck." Breathing deeply, she took a step back. "I'll take you to him."

Rogan intertwined our fingers and held tightly while we followed Poppy into a private room. Vasily was propped up with pillows. His complexion was slightly paler than normal but he appeared in good spirits.

Letting go of Rogan's hand, I went straight up to him and gave him a hug, and kiss to his cheek. "I'm so happy you're going to be all right."

"Thank you." Vasily fidgeted with the sheet as his eyes drifted to Rogan and Poppy. He focused on Poppy and I hid my smile. "She made sure I was being taken care of."

"She's just like her mother. Fierce when it comes

to someone she loves," Rogan told him, and moved closer, shaking Vasily's hand. "Glad you're okay, son."

Vasily blushed and loved it when Rogan called him son. He would be officially our son one day. I knew that, I just wished Poppy and Vasily would get on with it. We weren't getting any younger, and although it would be bittersweet to watch her walk down the aisle, I couldn't wait.

"Would it be okay if we drove out to the house tomorrow and stayed for a few days?" Poppy smiled. "I told Vasily it would be nice to have some home-cooked food, plus I know how much Vasily likes you fussing around him, Mom."

Vasily cleared his throat, obviously embarrassed.

"We're staying overnight." Rogan grinned at me. "So, we'll drive you once Vasily is released. We'll drive you back as well."

"What about work?" I asked.

"Vasily has been given a week of sick leave, and I messaged my boss." Poppy smiled. "I'm off for a few days."

"Okay." I squeezed Poppy's hand. "I can't wait to have my two favorite people home."

EPILOGUE
ROGAN

FALLON CUDDLED AGAINST ME ON THE COUCH AND I couldn't be happier. We've spent half a lifetime together and I looked forward to the rest of our years together, however long that would be. Our journey hadn't always been easy or happy, but together we survived and came out better for the lessons life taught us.

Mom and Dad had been gone for a few years and it hurt us both that they never completely accepted us together. They never cut us out of their life and they had always been willing to support us with Poppy, but there had always been an undercurrent.

Sighing, I ran my fingers through Fallon's hair, enjoying the silky strands on my skin. This woman was my world and my love for her had never wavered.

The life we'd built here in Newport, Rhode Island had been amazing. Poppy had loved growing up here and she still called it home after not living with us since she went to college. Her life was in Boston with the fire department, and for over a year with Vasily, while mine was still in Newport with the girl I fell in love with so many years before.

It had been nice having Poppy and Vasily home for the past three days. It hadn't gone unnoticed by Fallon or me that Vasily had been hesitant a few times around me, which made me think he wanted to ask for Poppy's hand in marriage. They'd both been staying in the guest cabin where Chase and Vince usually stayed when they visited. Poppy's choice was a good man, and you only had to see them together to know how much in love they were. Their love reminded me of falling in love with Fallon. How exciting it had felt. Whereas ours had been a forbidden kind of love, theirs wasn't.

Thinking about them, conjured them up. They walked into the house holding hands. Vasily was taller than Poppy by about a foot, which Fallon thought amusing considering I'm a foot taller than she was.

I raised a brow when I met Poppy's eyes. "Any-thing you'd like to tell us?"

Fallon gasped and sat upright. I wasn't having any of it and pulled her back into my arms.

"Um," Vasily stuttered.

I grinned.

"Dad, you're being a jerk," Poppy accused and laughed. "Vasily has something to ask you both."

"I've been waiting since you arrived here for him to ask," I admitted, and got a finger poking me in the stomach for my trouble. "What? You're not telling me you didn't know they wanted to ask us something?"

"I love your daughter and would like her to be my wife," Vasily said, surprising me with the strength of his voice, considering my amusement.

Becoming serious, I held Vasily's gaze and swal-lowed back the tears that suddenly burned behind my eyes. "Yes," I whispered huskily. "Yes, both Fallon and I would love for you to take Poppy off our hands."

Poppy rolled her eyes. "*Dad!*"

Standing, I held my hand out to Vasily. "We would love to have you become an official part of our family. I give you our blessing."

"Thanks, Dad." Poppy flew into my arms. I held her tightly and knew now was the time.

"Give me a minute. I have something for you

both." Running upstairs to the bedroom I shared with Fallon, I walked straight to the tall boy beside the window. Inside, buried under my T-shirts was a brown box that I'd kept safe for twenty-four years. I brought the box out and clenched it tightly in my hand while I thought about how I came to have the contents.

It was the day I'd left Fallon and Poppy at our parents' house. Three days after Julia and Leon had died in a car wreck. There had been an oil spill on the coast highway, and Leon had lost control of the car.

Robert Clifton had been the new director of the funeral home, and I'd gone to school with him. He'd told me that I needed to remember my best friends full of life and not like they were. I'd gone with the intention of visiting with them, but in the end, I hadn't. Because it was the truth. I'd wanted to keep my memory of Leon and Julia as they had been.

It had been difficult just walking into the building, and even harder asking what I had. I'd asked for Leon and Julia's wedding bands to keep for Poppy. Robert had obliged and I was forever grateful.

Swallowing around the lump in my throat, I wiped the tears I hadn't known fell from my eyes and left the bedroom.

Fallon smiled softly when she saw me appear

and held her hand out to me. She knew what I was about to do, and nodded her head, her smile encouraging.

"What's going on?" Poppy asked, glancing between us.

I indicated she needed to sit and I crouched in front of them, and squeezed her knee. "I have something that I've kept for a long time, and it's time I gave them to you."

Poppy looked confused and glanced at Vasily before she looked down at the box in my hands.

Nervous, I opened the lid and let them see what was inside, and Poppy caught her breath. "Mom and Dad's wedding bands?"

I nodded and felt Fallon's hand on my back. "I asked for them so you would have something of your parents."

Openly crying, Poppy leaned forward and wrapped her arms around my neck. "Thank you, Dad," she whispered.

"Vasily, I hope you understand the trust I'm showing you by giving you Leon's wedding band."

"I do. I'll treasure it just like I will Poppy. I love her."

"I know you do, son."

Fallon tugged me up from the floor and we

walked arm in arm out onto the back porch with the view of the ocean I'd taught Poppy to swim in.

The sun was setting on the horizon as I tugged Fallon in front of me and surrounded her with my body, resting my hands on either side of her on the porch railing.

"Do you ever regret moving to Newport?"

Fallon's eyes shot up to mine in alarm. "Why are you asking me that?"

"Guess I'm feeling old, and I've never asked you before."

"Never." She held my face in the palm of her hands. "I'm glad we moved here," she added, sighing softly. "I've never once doubted my love for you. You know that, right?"

I kissed her neck and wrapped my arms around her stomach. "I've never doubted you. Guess I'm feeling old now that we're on the verge of watching Julia and Leon's daughter walk up the aisle."

"They'd be so proud of the beautiful, clever, woman she's become. And please don't ever doubt my happiness."

I dropped a kiss to the top of her head. "They would be proud. Leon would still be complaining about Poppy being a fire investigator instead of following in his footsteps as a cop."

"I want to say that she chose the safer profession, but that isn't the case. The amount of times I've worried about you, and Poppy." Fallon shook her head. "Sometimes, I hate you leaving to go to work. I want to hold on to you and make you stay home with me. I can't survive if I lost you."

Turning Fallon around, I cupped her beautiful face in my hands, and slowly lowered my face and captured her lips. I gave her everything I felt in the way I kissed her.

"My beautiful girl. I love you so much, Fallon Scott."

THE END

Thank you for reading Tears in the Rain by Lexi Buchanan.

DEAR READER

Thank you for reading *Tears in the Rain,* and thank you for your reviews! It's really appreciated.

Subscribe with your email to be alerted about new releases, sales, and events.
http://lexibuchanan.com/

OTHER BOOKS BY AUTHOR

Hawke's Ridge

Maddox (2025)

Den Hollows

One of Six · Two of Six (2025)

Den of Filth (New MC Series 2025)

Reckless Wilder (2026)

Fifth Realm Series (Romantasy)

Quiver of Chaos · Wings & Arrows (2026)

Standalone Romantasy

Persephone Unchained

Tallulah James Mystery

*Dead and a Murder or Two · Dead and the Wedding Crashers ·
Dead and a Deadly Deed · Dead and a Best Friend*

Boston Bay Vikings

*Camden · Bennett · Ethan · Sutton · Carter · Bryson · Ivan · Theo
· Noah · Knox · Jericho · Roman*

Boston Bay Vikings Minor League

Lake · Rhodes · Nikoli · Dario · Madden · Bradford

Single Titles

Butterflies and Darkness · Come Back to Me · Indecent Villain · Lawful · Love Stryker · Tears in the Rain · Whispers of Yesterday

Holiday Season

Holiday Kisses in the Snow · Jingle Bells

Romantic Suspense Series

Twenty Eight Days · The Next Victim (2025)

Blossom Creek

Christmas at Emelia's · A Rake in Blossom Creek · Heatwave in Blossom Creek · Secret Love in Blossom Creek · Mischief in Blossom Creek · Runaway Bride in Blossom Creek · Naughty & Nice in Blossom Creek

Bad Boy Rockers

My Brother's Girl · Past Sins · My Best Friend's Sister · Never Let Go · Saving Jace · Silent Night (Novella)

Kincaid Sisters

Meant to be Mine · You Were Always Mine · Will You be Mine

McKenzie Brothers

Playing with the Boss · A McKenzie Wedding (Novella) · Playing with Fire · Playing with Desire · Playing with Trouble · Playing with their Hearts · A McKenzie Christmas (Novella)

De La Fuente Family (McKenzie Spinoff)

Love in Montana · Love in Purgatory · Love in Bloom · Love in Country · Love in Flame · Love in Game · Love in Education

McKenzie Cousins

(McKenzie Spinoff)

ABOUT THE AUTHOR

While Lexi is the author of the chick lit series, Tallulah James Mystery, and the sexy wild Alaska series, Hawke's Ridge, she also writes romantasy. This author has over seventy published novels. Based in Ireland, this British author has been writing since 2013.

Follow on social media:

Website: http://www.lexibuchanan.com
Email: authorlexibuchanan@gmail.com

facebook.com/lexibuchananauthor
x.com/AuthorLexi
instagram.com/authorlexib
bookbub.com/author/lexi-buchanan
amazon.com/Lexi-Buchanan/e/B009SPA94U